JOSEPH CONRAD, a paradox in the history of English literature, became one of England's greatest novelists and prose stylists although he was born a Pole and did not see England until he was 21. Before his first novel was published, when he was nearly 40, Conrad had spent 20 years as a merchant seaman. In some of his finest stories he evokes the romance of the sea as no other writer has done, providing dramatic and symbolic settings for inner dramas of the human conscience.

Here are two superb stories of the sea, utterly different from each other, but both have the special aura of Conrad's genius.

ALBERT J. GUERARD, who has written the introduction to The Laurel Conrad, is a novelist, a critic and a Professor of English at Harvard University. He is the author of a critical work on Conrad entitled *Conrad the Novelist*.

The Nigger of the Narcissus

and

The End of the Tether

by Joseph Conrad

with a general introduction by

Albert J. Guerard

THE LAUREL CONRAD

Published by
DELL PUBLISHING CO., INC.
750 Third Avenue
New York 17, N.Y.

This is an authorized edition of
The Nigger of the Narcissus and *The End of the Tether*,
reprinted by arrangement with Doubleday & Co., Inc.,
New York, and J. M. Dent & Sons Ltd., London.

Designed and produced by
Western Printing & Lithographing Company

Cover painting by Richard Powers

First printing—February, 1960

Printed in U.S.A.

Introduction

1

There are certain writers who do not improve with acquaintance. But this is not true of Conrad. For the Conrad of the biographers—this austere, aloof, aristocratic, conservative, secretive man with his protective mustache and alert, distrustful eyes—becomes, when we see him through the screen of certain very intimate books, a different and more engaging person. And so too his long novels *Lord Jim* and *Nostromo*—exasperatingly difficult in the first hour we give to them, labyrinthine in structure and dark of allusion—become as familiar to us as anything else of major importance in our lives. The position to take at the outset is that Conrad's best books change upon rereading and were written to be read more than once. And we, as we emerge from these readings and rereadings, discover that we too have changed. The novel has been rightly described as the richest mode of personal communication ever devised: this communication between a man writing at his desk (and often saying things he wouldn't say to his best friends) and another man sitting in a chair. And of great novelists, Conrad is one of the most personal. We enjoy his novels for suspense and adventure and even for exotic glamour. Yet all the while these stories play subtly upon our sensibilities and tamper with our convictions. At the least they demand of us more complex sympathies than we ordinarily need to muster in the everyday business of our lives. This is one reason why they do not leave us as we were.

Joseph Conrad, born Teodor Jozef Konrad Korzeniowski (1857–1924), left his native Poland when he was not quite seventeen, having most improbably decided on a career at sea. He made his decision against the urgings of his guardian and his relatives, who saw it as the action of a man bent on throwing his life away. The departure from occupied Poland could even be regarded by them as unpatriotic. For Conrad was the son of a noted leader in the struggle against Russian oppression, and the deaths of both his parents had been accelerated by exile. It is safe to say that Conrad's feelings toward his father and toward Poland were never satisfactorily resolved. Surely this has something to do with his insistent claims to fidelity in his essays and letters, and with his repeated dramatization (in the novels) of betrayal and desertion. But it would be another twenty years before Conrad began to publish novels. And if it seems unlikely a Pole by birth should become one of England's greatest novelists and prose stylists, it would seem quite as unlikely for such a man to become a master-mariner in the British merchant marine.

The first years after leaving Poland were adventurous enough. There were voyages on French ships to Central and South America, perhaps involving gun-running. (On one such trip Conrad was to acquire in a few days those impressions which would help make *Nostromo* the greatest novel in English about South American politics.) And before he was twenty-one Conrad was, if we are to believe his statements and listen to his hints, co-owner of a small ship smuggling arms and messages to Spain on behalf of the Pretender Don Carlos. Moreover he may have been the lover of one "Doña Rita," mistress of the "king." It was largely for her, Conrad implies, that he made his smuggling voyages on board the *Tremolino,* and for her he fought a duel with an American adventurer named Blunt. But this period of his life is still deeply shrouded in ambiguities. No record of a *Tremolino* has been found, and a recently rediscovered letter suggests Conrad's revolver wound may have come not from a duel but from attempted suicide, after the loss of all his money at Monte Carlo. If this is true, Conrad covered his traces most elaborately. He was to become one of the most subjective of British novelists, but by no means one of the most openly confessional. His very evasiveness of temperament led him to dramatize ambiguities and secrecies of spirit, and to use highly involuted forms. The spidery complexity of his best longer novels is a true reflection of his temperament.

It has been the fashion in recent years to discount Conrad's long experience as a seaman and officer, and to consider only the probing psychological novelist and lover of artistic experiment. But a Conrad who had not been to sea would not be the same writer at all. His career, after those early voyages, involved no further illegal activities, so far as we know. Once committed to England (and still only 21) Conrad became more British than the British, and acquired profound respect for the pitiless maritime ethic and stern tradition of duty. But the man deeply divided between order and anarchy can seldom leave his conflicts wholly behind. Conrad the officer was, according to one of his friends, noted both for his risky maneuvers at sea and for his meticulous care to details of stowage. And it is wholly characteristic that in a series of fictions Conrad should have associated several famous crimes at sea with his own first command of the tiny *Otago*. This long-delayed and then long-becalmed first voyage on the Gulf of Siam with a cholera- and dysentery-ridden crew returned repeatedly to Conrad's imagination as an archetypal experience of self-testing. In "The Secret Sharer" it invites a story of dark introspection and loyalty to an outlaw "double," who must be recognized before full command can be achieved. And in *The Shadow Line* that first voyage becomes a test of rationality clung to in the face of extreme bad luck. This brooding short novel, the last of Conrad's works to possess any real merit, even seems to reflect or symbolize an effort to throw off the blackness of immobilizing depression. Conrad the master-mariner had a solid, real knowledge of ships and seamen. But the sea was even for him "the unstable element," and had its part in the experience of guilt and in the act of self-scrutiny, those two foundations of Conrad's fictional world.

Conrad came to novel-writing abnormally late and was almost forty before he published his first novel. Even then he had not wholly abandoned all thoughts of returning to the sea. Nevertheless, most of his best work was done in one great decade, from *Almayer's Folly* of 1895 to *Nostromo* of 1904. This is the period that primarily concerns us, though *The Secret Agent* (1907) and *Under Western Eyes* (1911) have great merit. (Conrad's period of commercial success, beginning with *Chance* in 1913, corresponds fairly exactly with his period of sharp decline in energy and art.) But the work of the first decade offers the essential Conradian dreams and the three great segments of his fictional world. These are, to group very roughly: the *sea,* where both ships and men are tested; the *jungle,* where men deteriorate in solitude, or are corrupted by native intrigue; and *politics,* where dreams and self-delusions become history. The groupings are indeed rough, since certain human traits and obsessive fears may exist anywhere. But there is something to be gained from this roughness, and from looking at the three areas in turn.

2

The line between fact and fiction is a slender and wavering one in Conrad's writings on the sea. *The Mirror of the Sea* (1906) is the work of a professional seaman who does not like to see nautical terms misused, and who evokes ships, seas, rivers, weather, winds with a loving precision. Still, this book of essays and recollections, which claims to hold back nothing, obviously holds back a great deal; its chapters on the Carlist adventure remain distinctly suspect. This is supposed to be non-fiction. The ship *Narcissus* of the famous short novel actually existed, on the other hand, and I have seen the details of its sturdy shipmaking in a Lloyd's Register of the time—a ship on which, because of her beauty, Conrad chose to sail in 1884. Even earlier he sailed on the ill-fated *Palestine,* which became the *Judea* of the short novel *Youth.* And there are the two famous crimes of the summer of 1880 which became attached to very personal narratives—the killing of a sailor aboard the *Cutty Sark* (which went into both "The Secret Sharer" and *Lord Jim)* and that abandonment of the *Jeddah (Patna)* which became the central incident of *Lord Jim.* To them we may add the crime of cannibalism which, in the story "Falk," also became associated with Conrad's first command.

But all this only means that everything Conrad wrote about the sea had its personal accent and undertone. A more useful distinction, it may be, would separate the stories which present life at sea in its own terms from the stories in which such life becomes generalized, visionary, symbolic—would separate, in a word, *The End of the Tether* from *The Nigger of the "Narcissus,"* with *Typhoon* somewhere between the two.

The End of the Tether derives directly enough from voyages Conrad made as first mate on the *Vidar* in 1887 and early 1888, between Singapore and Borneo, trading "among dark islands on a blue-scarred sea." These were the voyages that would give him his closest view of Malayan life and provide him with the settings for four of his novels. We know from the captain of the *Vidar* that Conrad was worried about his eyesight at that time; we know too that this was for him a period of restlessness and undefined spiritual crisis. Yet *The End of the Tether* seems to be one of Conrad's most impersonal works, carefully controlled in overall structure and style. The technical problem of the story—to work very close to Captain Whalley's consciousness yet withhold from the reader the central preoccupation of that consciousness—was a most difficult one, deliberately and successfully solved. This problem was the more severe, too, because Conrad was never wholly comfortable when using the objective, third-person narrative form in writing about the interior life. Still *The End of the Tether,* overlong and perhaps oversimple of plot, and revealing its specific area of guilt only near the end, contains some of Conrad's most pleasing evocations of the sea. The unobsessed writing has the beauty of exactness.

Typhoon too is a simple, controlled and, on the whole, impersonal reflection of Conrad's experience at sea. Other and greater works may profit by the devil's share of unconscious creation. But the rugged strength of *Typhoon* derives from the author's full conscious control of his fiction—Conrad the retired officer supplying the expert knowledge of ship and storm and psychology of command; Conrad the artist carefully planning his effects and wisely omitting the very worst of the storm; Conrad the moralist shrewdly weighing the merits of the three officers, and very exactly exposing his theme of justice triumphing over sentiment.

"MacWhirr is not an acquaintance of a few hours, or of a few weeks, or a few months. He is the product of twenty years of life. My own life." In these prefatory words Conrad suggested that *Typhoon* was a very personal story. But it was so only in a curiously indirect and compensatory way. For Conrad so distrusted imagination and introspection and intellectual complexity (and all the other qualities that made him a great writer) that he came to overvalue the simple men who did not possess them, and who were free from his own anxieties. He could almost idealize, in certain hours and moods, such a stolid, unimaginative, unintellectual man as MacWhirr, untroubled by the past, for whom the future "was not there yet." The typhoon of the story (and the chaotic situation of the coolies tumbling in the hold) puts this extrovert simplicity to the test. MacWhirr substitutes stubbornness and courage for "storm-strategy," will for intellect. And in his ignorance of what such a storm could do and be, he is momentarily demoralized. Significantly he is saved by order and routine: by finding in the darkness a towel in just the place it is supposed to be. (These are the extremes of Conrad's moral world: the perilous night journey into self, and finding a towel in the right place!)

At least MacWhirr proves himself a good officer of his

kind, against whom Mr. Jukes must stand in calculated and shameful contrast. This imaginative and even sentimental officer—who anticipates catastrophe, and in the midst of crisis hopes to be praised—wanted to alter the course of the ship so the coolies could ride more comfortably. This, to Captain MacWhirr, is nonsense. But it is MacWhirr who does the only fair thing with the coolies, by dividing the scattered dollars among them. His unromantic and stolid fairness becomes a kind of heroism.

These are controlled, balanced and eminently readable short novels. *The Nigger of the "Narcissus,"* however, is one of the summits of the art of fiction. It is tempting to read it as the record of a real voyage and a real ship, though Conrad himself left her at Dunkirk, not London, and though the name "Wait" was taken from a Negro on board another ship. And he would be a desecrator indeed who saw here only a symbolic ship and metaphysical seas. This short novel is a tribute to certain remembered "children of the sea" and a memorial to the era of sail. For one of Conrad's aims, as he says in his eloquent Preface, was to seize "a passing phase of life from the remorseless rush of time." These simple men, tested by the storm and tempted by the foul, mutinous Donkin, tested and tempted even more insidiously by James Wait and his debilitating egoism, turn out all right in the end. And the white female ship, with her known weakness, turns out all right: the human protagonist pitted against a storm of seemingly preternatural malevolence. This is truly a substantial sea. The account of the ship's overthrow by that wave "like a wall of green glass topped with snow" is exceeded, as dramatic writing, only by that of the ship's deliberate, human and heroic rising hours later, and her subsequent wild rush along a towering sea, "spouting thick streams of water through every opening of her wounded sides." The lovely *Narcissus*—binding the parts of the novel—is its central figure, to be desecrated at the end by the grime of London and by the feet of alien landsmen, the soiling touch of commerce. But heroic too is the simple, unsentimental Singleton, who still steered with care after thirty hours of storm at the wheel, and with his white beard deliberately tucked under his coat.

Life itself and such writing about it may well be more important than buried subtleties of symbol and theme. But these other interests exist too, and in fact we would hardly care as much as we do for the sea narrative if it did not speak to us on a more personal level. Some themes and symbols in *The Nigger of the "Narcissus"* are perfectly conscious and overt. We see that Conrad clearly intended this voyage as symbolic of life and this ship as a microcosm of the freighted earth. We see too that he intended to express an ultimate skepticism when he makes his equation of God and the immortal sea, in the first paragraph of chapter four. It is evident that Conrad wanted to express his profound distrust of human qualities many people are accustomed to revere—pity, for instance, or intellectual complexity. And surely it is also evident that Conrad intended to represent, in James Watt, a certain *blackness* within human nature, a blackness which the ship must be rid of before she can end her journey. Hence the occult circumstance of a favorable wind rising at the very moment Wait's body is deposited, like Jonah's, in the sea.

There are, in fact, symbols and meanings more elusive than these, though presumably less conscious. A powerful imagination and waking dream may discover, as it were, inadvertently, certain archetypal patterns of the human spirit and universal myths. Thus we say with some assurance that "The Secret Sharer" and *Heart of Darkness* (beneath the level of explicit theme, and far beneath the level of adventure story) dramatize a deep, introspective descent into the half-conscious and unconscious mind. The rescue of James Wait strikes us as suggesting such a descent. But at the very least we can say that these men absurdly strive to save the force that has almost destroyed them; or again, considering all the imagery of difficult childbirth, that we have attended the rebirth of evil on the ship.

Whatever we may feel about the existence of such buried

meanings, we can make no doubt about the concealed yet solid artistry of the novel's structure—the skill with which Conrad juxtaposes the two tests of the crew, that of the storm and that of the demoralizing Wait; or the skill with which he restores our faith in the crew by making the ship herself heroic in that beat up the channel toward home; or the care with which he modulates his narrative downward from the elevated rhetoric of Singleton at the wheel to the prosaic life of everyday; or, centrally, the tact with which he prepares us by tone and imagery to accept the audacious symbolic coincidence of Wait's burial and the wind's rising.

3

The Malayan voyages of 1887 and the Congo journey of 1890 were closely associated in Conrad's imagination and left much the same dark impact on his work. *Almayer's Folly* (with its sequels *An Outcast of the Islands* and *The Rescue)* has interest as a document on Bornean politics, and on the squalid inertia of native life. And *Heart of Darkness* is an unforgettable report on Belgian exploitation and cruelty. But these works, together with such stories as "An Outpost of Progress," "Karain" and "The Lagoon," form a cluster of brooding, pessimistic visions of deterioration and collapse. The same themes and preoccupations appear in these works, and often the same lush and sinuous prose.

The first of these themes involves the fascination and moral peril of involvement in native affairs. Conrad's imagination was caught by the historical figure of James Brooke, the fabulously successful first white Rajah of Sarawak, but also by an enigmatic, obscure personage named Wyndham, who traded with certain natives, became a benevolent despot over them, and in the end could not tear himself away. Conrad himself encountered the prototype of his Kurtz (of *Heart of Darkness)*, one Georges-Antoine Klein, who died on the *Roi des Belges*. Kurtz goes further than any of Conrad's other meddlers in native intrigue, since he becomes one of the high devils of the land, worshiped in unspeakable ceremonies. Captain Tom Lingard, many years before the opening action of *Almayer's Folly*, rescued a Malayan prince and his sister and worked to help them recover their kingdom. The nameless white man of "The Lagoon" has also been involved in native intrigue, and the skulking Willems of *An Outcast of the Islands* betrays Lingard's secret for the embraces of a native girl. The implication is that only extraordinary strength of will can survive any traffic with natives, or overcome the languor it invites. In the jungle outpost or native village, and freed from the watching eye of policeman or European neighbor, the white man is threatened with moral collapse.

The second theme or preoccupation concerns the character of the intervening "benevolent despot," this vulnerable, romantic idealist. Captain Tom Lingard is such a romantic meddler, with his indiscriminate rescues of the unfortunate and his bland magisterial control of their lives. And even the Kurtz of unspeakable lusts and gratifications had gone to the Congo with idealistic ardor, to bring enlightenment and progress. The burden of the message is to beware of the sentimental humanitarian, bemused by his generous dreams. The Lord Jim of Patusan is thus intoxicated by his power to do good, and his protection of the community at last brings it ruin. The vain dreamer may be possessed at last by what he thought to possess: "He looked with an owner's eye at the peace of the evening, at the river, at the houses, at the everlasting life of the forests, at the life of the old mankind, at the secrets of the land, at the pride of his own heart: but it was they that possessed him and made him their own to the innermost thought, to the slightest stir of blood, to his last breath."

The third recurring preoccupation, intimately related to the first two, can best be described as a dread of *immobilization*. A menace of sexual failure, or of peril attaching to sexual fulfillment, is repeatedly associated with the fecund jungle of *Almayer's Folly* and *An Outcast of the Islands;* some of Conrad's gloomiest jungle descriptions accompany the clandestine meetings of lovers. But beyond the sexual fear, and perhaps related to it, is fear of an inability to act at all. The dream landscape of "The Lagoon" is "bewitched into an immobility perfect and final," and within it the guilty Arsat is immobilized by remorse over his desertion of his brother, an impulsive, unintended betrayal. And the ship moving toward Kurtz and the Inner Station moves through a fog and silence like a "state of trance." Kurtz himself is once referred to as an enchanted princess, and Marlow's task is to "break the spell." But this immobilized devil does not want to be saved.

This concern with immobilization appears in many of Conrad's novels and stories. Men may be immobilized by sexual bondage but also, as in *Victory,* by sexless intellectual detachment. The Decoud of *Nostromo* is immobilized by skepticism; various characters by guilt, remorse and even by the recognition of one's own guilt in another person. And of course men may be immobilized by deep introspection and self-analysis. Thus "The Secret Sharer" (with its Jungian descent into self) and *The Shadow Line* (with its black and utter calm) seem at the very heart of Conrad's meaning. But so too is *Lord Jim.* For Jim is literally immobilized at the critical moments of his life. As a boy on the training-ship he cannot move and loses his chance to join in the rescue. On board the *Patna* the conscious man stands still for twenty-seven minutes, till something less than consciousness makes him jump . . . into an immobilizing guilt, an everlasting black hole. Thereafter he is paralyzed by all chance reminders of the *Patna* incident. His inability to act —his immobilization by his "double" Gentleman Brown— brings on the catastrophe.

We know that Conrad broke off *Lord Jim* to write *Heart of Darkness,* and we know that a man named Marlow serves as narrator in both works. But their roles are very different. The Marlow of *Heart of Darkness* is the true protagonist of his story, and however we interpret that journey up the Congo, it is unmistakably an inward journey. This is the intimate narrative of a man cut off from his familiar surroundings and habits, and compelled to choose between the mean, flabby rapacity of ordinary exploiters and the legendary, already suspect Kurtz. It would be rash to say dogmatically what the meeting and struggle with Kurtz signify in psychological terms. But at least this confrontation, the "culminating point" in Marlow's experience, involves subtler temptations than a crude reversion to savagery, the urge to have a howl and a dance. Perhaps it is best to say that this, like any richly rendered subjective experience, defies single and simple summation.

So this Marlow is protagonist, the very subject of his own tale. But the Marlow of *Lord Jim*, though he too has his inward debates, is first of all narrator and listener, the chief of several witnesses to Jim's state of being and soul. *Lord Jim* is a moral drama, and the reader's ultimate task is to locate this vulnerable idealist and conscientious failure on a moral spectrum. He must decide whether Jim's is a drama of bruised vanity or a tragedy of conscience. This is the chief question that the novel, through Marlow, asks. "I don't mean to say that I regret my action, nor will I pretend that I can't sleep o' nights in consequence; still the idea obtrudes itself that he made so much of his disgrace while it is the guilt alone that matters." And does Jim redeem himself in Patusan? Can we even categorically say that Jim's final act is one of moral self-repudiation, rather than one last gesture of selfish pride?

Such are the questions asked by this long and circumspect novel. The answers cannot be found in what Jim says about himself, nor even wholly in what Marlow and Stein say. Jim himself would have it that intentions are more important than actions, with the pure heart excusing many an ugly deed. But this is not Conrad's view; his view is that our acts especially matter. Thus the acts of various other characters (or "reflectors") modify our attitude toward Jim. We notice that the French Lieutenant stayed on board the *Patna* for thirty-six hours, concerned less because the ship might sink at any moment than because he had no wine with his meals. There is big Brierly, who commits suicide after recognizing that he too might have committed such a crime as Jim's. There is little Bob Stanton, who drowns trying to save one person while Jim deserted eight hundred. And there is even that heroic native helmsman who never thought of leaving the ship. Conrad, as in most of his books, exhibits deep personal sympathy for his victims of romantic illusion and criminal failures of good intention. But also he presents the grounds for moral condemnation. The emotional appeal of *Lord Jim* largely derives from the interplay of incorrigible sympathy and stern, ironic judgment. This duality, and the need for an ebb and flow of sympathy and for an ever-changing distance, partly account for the novel's involuted form, and for its long withholding of certain facts we need to know. The reader is not permitted easy commitment. Instead, struggling for foothold and lost in the scrambled chronology, bewildered by the conflicting evidence, he must face the issues as he would face them in real life. There is no omniscient author consistently present to help him. He must, instead, explore these ambiguities and arrive at his own moral judgments.

4

Conrad's last important full-length novels—*Nostromo* (1904), *The Secret Agent* (1907) and *Under Western Eyes* (1911)—enter the urban world of politics. The dates of the novels are surprising, since all three seem so contemporary: *Nostromo* as up-to-date as the latest Central or South American revolution. All three, though written in the relatively secure Edwardian days, reflect our own age of moral anarchy and latent violence, of espionage and counter-espionage, of deceptive and self-deceptive propaganda, of growing callousness to atrocity. And all three reflect not so much Conrad's political conservatism as a deep skepticism concerning all political motive and intention, be it conservative, radical or liberal.

We may prefer the interior resonance and minute artistry of *Lord Jim* or the disturbing short novels. But *Nostromo,* though radically defective in its second half, remains Conrad's richest creation of life. His few days in South America a quarter of a century before, the reading of a book about Paraguay, a few stories and personal memories—these seem to be all Conrad needed to bring into existence his Republic of Costaguana, as substantial and real a place as any we can hope to visit. The imagined state and city have, certainly, a greater reality than Bangkok and the Bornean villages Conrad actually knew. And there is a far more impressive range of characters than in any of his other novels—from chiefs of state to the florid person of French extraction and mistress of the Finance Minister who sells her influence; from Father Corbelàn, austere head of the Church and the country's first Cardinal-Archbishop, to Father Roman, great snuff-taker and card-player, who had "shriven many simple souls on the battlefields of the Republic"; from General Barrios and the backwoods General Montero to the craven Colonel Sotillo and the craven Señor Hirsch. Various personages seem entirely new to Conrad's fictional world. The loquacious politicians are always convincing. So too are Mrs. Gould and Antonia Avellanos, the first interesting white women in the work of a man who showed much misogynist distrust. Perhaps the major disappointment of the novel, in terms of characterization, is Nostromo himself, the Capataz de Cargadores and idealizer of his own vanity. Charles Gould, who sacrifices everything to the idealization of his silver mine, is a pallid figure. But such he was intended to be.

The very number of vivid characters and incidents, and the impressionistic structure of the first part, make *Nostromo* the most difficult of Conrad's novels to begin. The narrative flows backward and forward in time with the waywardness of casual memory; only about a tenth of Part

One exists in the present. Thus we have the illusion that events occurring over only a few days actually cover years; so too events long past may be dramatized with intense immediacy. Essential information, moreover, may reach us through a digression within a digression, while matters of no real importance may be given sharp visual emphasis. All this can be exasperating, and on a first reading it is perhaps unwise to try to untangle all the threads. For one desired effect is likely to be enjoyed anyway, by all but the most resistant reader—the effect of being immersed in a bewildering actuality. The reader becomes truly a visitor in Sulaco: one who arrives without guidebook or written history, and who must try to make himself at home in a world of revolution and counter-revolution.

The political realities emerge more clearly after those first rich and difficult chapters. We begin to discern political alignments. And presently a certain political vision and authorial attitude also begin to emerge: a profoundly skeptical "philosophy of history." Corruption and cynicism are rife in Costaguana, which has its long history of venality and brutal dictatorship. But even the idealists pursue a fatality of failure and are corrupted by their generous dreams. The slogans and enthusiasms of the liberals are futile and the pages of Don José's exposé of misrule are used as wadding for guns.

The critique of idealization is particularly incisive in its assessment of industry and capitalism, often referred to as "material interest." It is in the nature of material interest to subvert moral principle, as Dr. Monygham perceives. But the sentimental Charles Gould idealizes his silver mine, the chief political force in the country, and insists on the incorruptible metal's power to bring progress and order. He could not "act or exist without idealizing every simple feeling, desire, or achievement. He could not believe his own motives if he did not make them first a part of some fairy tale." Holroyd too, the San Francisco financier, must moralize his sinister game of power. He "would not drop his idea of introducing, not only justice, industry, peace, to the benighted continents, but also that pet dream of his of a purer form of Christianity." Are Costaguana and Sulaco better off in the end, for the mine and its American financing, for the control of government by capital? The case is by no means clear. Holroyd himself predicts, in any event, what would happen in the coming decades, and suggests history may escape man's reason and will. "We shall run the world's business whether the world likes it or not. The world can't help it—and neither can we, I guess." The best intentions of men are subject to brute chance and inhuman process. And their ideals however generous are undermined by the egoism that fostered them. The magnitude of men is destroyed by their "irremediable littleness."

Nostromo is not yet, entirely, an historical novel. The regular torturing of political opponents was almost a thing of the past in the Costaguana of the novel but was reported from Paraguay on the day I wrote these lines. The dependence of a backward Costaguana is reflected in the present plight of Bolivia. And few Latin American countries have escaped the absurd cycles of reform dictatorship and military junta, proclamation and plebiscite. *Nostromo* suggests, however, that the larger political forces at work in Costaguana may be at work anywhere: the vanities and illusions and secret pulls of power, and especially the easily corrupted force of words, especially man's incorrigible gift for deceiving himself with the words by which he intended to deceive others.

5

Such are some of the interests—psychological, moral, political, artistic—of Conrad's fictional world. *The Secret Agent* (1907), dealing with the underside of political life and international intrigue, represents a new departure in form, a controlled, ironic and suspenseful story not unlike certain "entertainments" of Graham Greene. *Under Western Eyes* (1911) returns us to Conrad's central story of marginal crime and betrayal of the outlaw "brother," with betrayer and betrayed now Russians, and in a European setting. His not unsympathetic portrait of Russia and Russians is an act of high imaginative integrity on the part of a novelist who hated and distrusted both; and *Under Western Eyes* is a great novel.

Otherwise, except for scattered pages and except for the brief *Shadow Line,* Conrad's later novels are inferior. Attempting a more charitable ethic and more generous psychology, and a more affirmative attitude toward love, the late novels succeed only in becoming slack, sentimental, tired. In time they will be forgotten. But the works of the first decade, from *Almayer's Folly* through *Nostromo,* constitute an extraordinary personal vision and creation, dark yet glowingly alive. They are more than enough to assure Conrad his austere and very high place.

ALBERT J. GUERARD

The Nigger of the Narcissus

PREFACE

A work that aspires, however humbly, to the condition of art should carry its justification in every line. And art itself may be defined as a single-minded attempt to render the highest kind of justice to the visible universe, by bringing to light the truth, manifold and one, underlying its every aspect. It is an attempt to find in its forms, in its colors, in its light, in its shadows, in the aspects of matter and in the facts of life, what of each is fundamental, what is enduring and essential—their one illuminating and convincing quality—the very truth of their existence. The artist, then, like the thinker or the scientist, seeks the truth and makes his appeal. Impressed by the aspect of the world the thinker plunges into ideas, the scientist into facts—whence, presently, emerging they make their appeal to those qualities of our being that fit us best for the hazardous enterprise of living. They speak authoritatively to our common sense, to our intelligence, to our desire of peace or to our desire of unrest; not seldom to our prejudices, sometimes to our fears, often to our egoism—but always to our credulity. And their words are heard with reverence, for their concern is with weighty matters: with the cultivation of our minds and the proper care of our bodies, with the attainment of our ambitions, with the perfection of the means and the glorification of our precious aims.

It is otherwise with the artist.

Confronted by the same enigmatical spectacle the artist descends within himself, and in that lonely region of stress and strife, if he be deserving and fortunate, he finds the terms of his appeal. His appeal is made to our less obvious capacities: to that part of our nature which, because of the warlike conditions of existence, is necessarily kept out of sight within the more resisting and hard qualities—like the vulnerable body within a steel armor. Hs appeal is less loud, more profound, less distinct, more stirring—and sooner forgotten. Yet its effect endures forever. The changing wisdom of successive generations discards ideas, questions facts, demolishes theories. But the artist appeals to that part of our being which is not dependent on wisdom: to that in us which is a gift and not an acquisition—and, therefore, more permanently enduring. He speaks to our capacity for delight and wonder, to the sense of mystery surrounding our lives; to our sense of pity, and beauty, and pain; to the latent feeling of fellowship with all creation—and to the subtle but invincible conviction of solidarity that knits together the loneliness of innumerable hearts, to the solidarity in dreams, in joy, in sorrow, in aspirations, in illusions, in hope, in fear, which binds men to each other, which binds together all humanity—the dead to the living and the living to the unborn.

It is only some such train of thought, or rather of feeling, that can in a measure explain the aim of the attempt, made in the tale which follows, to present an unrestful episode in the obscure lives of a few individuals out of all the disregarded multitude of the bewildered, the simple and the voiceless. For, if any part of truth dwells in the belief confessed above, it becomes evident that there is not a place of splendor or a dark corner of the earth that does not deserve if only a passing glance of wonder and pity. The motive then, may be held to justify the matter of the work; but this preface, which is simply an avowal of endeavor, cannot end here—for the avowal is not yet complete.

Fiction—if it at all aspires to be art—appeals to temperament. And in truth it must be, like painting, like music, like all art, the appeal of one temperament to all the other innumerable temperaments whose subtle and resistless power endows passing events with their true meaning, and creates the moral, the emotional, atmosphere of the place and time. Such an appeal to be effective must be an impression conveyed through the senses; and, in fact, it cannot be made in any other way, because temperament, whether individual or collective, is not amenable to persuasion. All art, therefore, appeals primarily to the senses, and the artistic aim when expressing itself in written words must also make its appeal through the senses, if its high desire is to reach the secret spring of responsive emotions. It must strenuously aspire to the plasticity of sculpture, to the color of painting, and to the magic suggestiveness of music—which is the art of arts. And it is only through complete, unswerving devotion to the perfect blending of form and substance; it is only through an unremitting never-discouraged care for the shape and ring of sentences that an approach can be made to plasticity, to color, and that the light of magic suggestiveness may be brought to play for an evanescent instant over the commonplace surface of words: of the old, old words, worn thin, defaced by ages of careless usage.

The sincere endeavor to accomplish that creative task, to go as far on that road as his strength will carry him, to go undeterred by faltering, weariness or reproach, is the only valid justification for the worker in prose. And if his conscience is clear, his answer to those who in the fullness of a wisdom which looks for immediate profit, demand specifically to be edified, consoled, amused; who demand to be promptly improved, or encouraged, or frightened, or shocked, or charmed, must run thus: My task which I am trying to achieve is, by the power of the written word to make you hear, to make you feel—it is, before all, to make you see. That—and no more, and it is everything. If I succeed, you shall find there according to your deserts: encouragement, consolation, fear, charm—all you demand—and, perhaps, also that glimpse of truth for which you have forgotten to ask.

To snatch in a moment of courage, from the remorseless rush of time, a passing phase of life, is only the beginning of the task. The task approached in tenderness and faith is to hold up unquestioningly, without choice and without fear, the rescued fragment before all eyes in the light of a sincere mood. It is to show its vibration, its color, its form; and through its movement, its form, and its color, reveal the substance of its truth—disclose its inspiring secret: the stress and passion within the core of each convincing moment. In a singleminded attempt of that kind, if one be deserving and fortunate, one may perchance attain to such clearness of sincerity that at last the presented vision of regret or pity, of terror or mirth, shall awaken in the hearts of the beholders that feeling of unavoidable solidarity; of the solidarity in mysterious origin, in toil, in joy, in hope, in uncertain fate, which binds men to each other and all mankind to the visible world.

It is evident that he who, rightly or wrongly, holds by the convictions expressed above cannot be faithful to any one of the temporary formulas of his craft. The enduring part of them—the truth which each only imperfectly veils—should abide with him as the most precious of his possessions, but they all: Realism, Romanticism, Naturalism, even the unofficial sentimentalism (which like the poor, is exceedingly difficult to get rid of), all these gods must, after a short period of fellowship, abandon him—even on the very threshold of the temple—to the stammerings of his conscience and to the outspoken consciousness of the difficulties of his work. In that uneasy solitude the supreme cry of Art for Art itself loses the exciting ring of its apparent immorality. It sounds far off. It has ceased to be a cry, and is heard only as a whisper, often incomprehensible, but at times and faintly encouraging.

Sometimes, stretched at ease in the shade of a roadside tree, we watch the motions of a laborer in a distant field, and, after a time, begin to wonder languidly as to what the fellow may be at. We watch the movements of his body, the waving of his arms, we see him bend down, stand up, hesitate, begin again. It may add to the charm of an idle hour to be told the purpose of his exertions. If we know he is trying to lift a stone, to dig a ditch, to uproot a stump, we look with a more real interest at his efforts; we are disposed to condone the jar of his agitation upon the restfulness of the landscape; and even, if in a brotherly frame of mind, we may bring ourselves to forgive his failure. We understood his object, and, after all, the fellow has tried, and perhaps he had not the strength—and perhaps he had not the knowledge. We forgive, go on our way—and forget.

And so it is with the workman of art. Art is long and life is short, and success is very far off. And thus, doubtful of strength to travel so far, we talk a little about the aim—the aim of art, which, like life itself, is inspiring, difficult—obscured by mists. It is not in the clear logic of a triumphant conclusion; it is not in the unveiling of one of those heartless secrets which are called the Laws of Nature. It is not less great, but only more difficult.

To arrest, for the space of a breath, the hands busy about the work of the earth, and compel men entranced by the sight of distant goals to glance for a moment at the surrounding vision of form and color, of sunshine and shadows; to make them pause for a look, for a sigh, for a smile—such is the aim, difficult and evanescent, and reserved only for a very few to achieve. But sometimes, by the deserving and the fortunate, even that task is accomplished. And when it is accomplished—behold!—all the truth of life is there: a moment of vision, a sigh, a smile—and the return to an eternal rest.

1897 J. C.

CHAPTER 1

Mr. Baker, chief mate of the ship *Narcissus,* stepped in one stride out of his lighted cabin into the darkness of the quarter-deck. Above his head, on the break of the poop, the night watchman rang a double stroke. It was nine o'clock. Mr. Baker, speaking up to the man above him, asked: "Are all the hands aboard, Knowles?"

The man limped down the ladder, then said reflectively:

"I think so, sir. All our old chaps are there, and a lot of new men has come. . . . They must be all there."

"Tell the boastswain to send all hands aft," went on Mr. Baker, "and tell one of the youngsters to bring a good lamp here. I want to muster our crowd."

The main deck was dark aft, but halfway from forward, through the open doors of the forecastle, two streaks of brilliant light cut the shadow of the quiet night that lay upon the ship. A hum of voices was heard there, while port and starboard, in the illuminated doorways, silhouettes of moving men appeared for a moment, very black, without relief, like figures cut out of sheet tin. The ship was ready for sea. The carpenter had driven in the last wedge of the main-hatch battens, and, throwing down his maul, had wiped his face with great deliberation, just on the stroke of five. The decks had been swept, the windlass oiled and made ready to heave up the anchor; the big tow-rope lay in long bights along one side of the main deck, with one end carried up and hung over the bows in readiness for the tug that would come paddling and hissing noisily, hot and smoky, in the limpid, cool quietness of the early morning. The captain was ashore, where he had been engaging some new hands to make up his full crew; and, the work of the day over, the ship's officers had kept out of the way, glad of a little breathing time. Soon after dark the few liberty men and the new hands began to arrive in shore boats rowed by white-clad Asiatics, who clamored fiercely for payment before coming alongside the gangway ladder. The feverish and shrill babble of Eastern language struggled against the masterful tones of tipsy seamen, who argued against brazen claims and dishonest hopes by profane shouts. The resplendent and bestarred peace of the East was torn into squalid tatters by howls of rage and shrieks of lament raised over sums ranging from five annas to half a rupee; and every soul afloat in Bombay Harbor became aware that the new hands were joining the *Narcissus.*

Gradually the distracting noise had subsided. The boats came no longer in splashing clusters of three or four together, but dropped alongside singly, in a subdued buzz of expostulation cut short by a "Not a pice more! You go to the devil!" from some man staggering up the accommodation ladder—a dark figure, with a long bag poised on the shoulder. In the forecastle the newcomers, upright and swaying amongst corded boxes and bundles of bedding, made friends with the old hands, who sat one above another in the two tiers of bunks, gazing at their future shipmates with glances critical but friendly. The two forecastle lamps were turned up high and shed an intense hard glare; shoregoing round hats were pushed far on the backs of heads, or rolled about on the deck amongst the chain cables; white collars, undone, stuck out on each side of red faces; big arms in white sleeves gesticulated; the growling voices hummed steady amongst bursts of laughter and hoarse calls. "Here, sonny, take that bunk! . . . Don't you do it! . . . What's your last ship? . . . I know her. . . . Three years ago, in Puget Sound. . . . This here berth leaks, I tell you! . . . Come on; give us a chance to swing that chest! . . . Did you bring a bottle, any of you shore toffs? . . . Give us a bit of 'baccy. . . . I know her; her skipper drank himself to death. . . . He was a dandy boy! . . . Liked his lotion inside, he did! . . . No! . . . Hold your row, you chaps! . . . I tell you, you came on board a hooker, where they get their money's worth out of poor Jack by ——! . . ."

A little fellow, called Craik and nicknamed Belfast, abused the ship violently, romancing on principle, just to give the new hands something to think over. Archie, sitting aslant on his sea chest, kept his knees out of the way and pushed the needle steadily through a white patch in a pair of blue trousers. Men in black jackets and stand-up collars, mixed with men barefooted, bare-armed, with colored shirts open on hairy chests, pushed against one another in the middle of the forecastle. The group swayed, reeled, turning upon itself with the motion of a scrimmage, in a haze of tobacco smoke. All were speaking together, swearing at every second word. A Russian Finn, wearing a yellow shirt with pink stripes, stared upwards, dreamy-eyed, from under a mop of tumbled hair. Two young giants with smooth, baby faces—two Scandinavians—helped each other to spread their bedding, silent, and smiling placidly at the tempest of good-humored and meaningless curses. Old Singleton, the oldest able seaman in the ship, sat apart on the deck right under the lamps, stripped to the waist, tattooed like a cannibal chief all over his powerful chest and enormous biceps. Between the blue and red patterns his white skin gleamed like satin; his bare back was propped against the heel of the bowsprit and he held a book at arm's length before his big, sunburnt face. With his spectacles and a venerable white beard, he resembled a learned and savage patriarch, the incarnation of barbarian wisdom serene in the blasphemous turmoil of the world. He was intensely absorbed, and as he turned the pages an expression of grave surprise would pass over his rugged features. He was reading *Pelham*. The popularity of Bulwer-Lytton in the forecastles of southern-going ships is a wonderful and bizarre phenomenon. What ideas do his polished and so curiously insincere sentences awaken in the simple minds of the big children who people those dark and wandering places of the earth? What meaning can their rough, inexperienced souls find in the elegant verbiage of his pages? What excitement?—what forgetfulness?—what appeasement? Mystery! Is it the fascination of the incomprehensible?—is it the charm of the impossible? Or are those beings who exist beyond the pale of life stirred by his tales as by an enigmatical disclosure of a resplendent world that exists within the frontier of infamy and filth, within that border of dirt and hunger, of misery and dissipation, that comes down on all sides to the water's edge of the incorruptible ocean and is the only thing they know of life, the only thing they see of surrounding land—those lifelong prisoners of the sea? Mystery!

Singleton, who had sailed to the southward since the age of twelve, who in the last forty-five years had lived (as we had calculated from his papers) no more than forty months ashore—old Singleton, who boasted, with the mild composure of long years well spent, that generally from the day he was paid off from one ship till the day he shipped in another he seldom was in a condition to distinguish daylight—old Singleton sat unmoved in the clash of voices and cries, spelling through *Pelham* with slow labor, and lost in an absorption profound enough to resemble a trance. He breathed regularly. Every time he turned the book in his enormous and blackened hands the muscles of his big white arms rolled slightly under the smooth skin. Hidden by the white mustache, his lips, stained with tobacco juice that trickled down the long beard, moved in inward whisper. His bleared eyes gazed fixedly from behind the glitter of black-rimmed glasses. Opposite to him, and on a level with his face, the ship's cat sat on the barrel of the windlass in the pose of a crouching chimera, blinking its green eyes at its old friend. It seemed to meditate a leap onto the old man's lap over the bent back of the ordinary seaman who sat at Singleton's feet. Young Charley was lean and long-necked. The ridge of his backbone made a chain of small hills under the old shirt. His face of a streetboy—a face precocious, sagacious, and ironic, with deep downward folds on each side of the thin, wide mouth—hung low over his bony knees. He was learning to make a lanyard knot with a bit of an old rope. Small drops of perspiration stood out on his bulging forehead; he sniffed strongly from time to time, glancing out of the corners of his restless eyes at the old seaman, who took no notice of the puzzled youngster muttering at his work.

The noise increased. Little Belfast seemed, in the heavy heat of the forecastle, to boil with facetious fury. His eyes danced; in the crimson of his face, comical as a mask, the mouth yawned black, with strange grimaces. Facing him, a half-undressed man held his sides, and, throwing his head back, laughed with wet eyelashes. Others stared with amazed eyes. Men sitting doubled up in the upper bunks smoked short pipes, swinging bare brown feet above the heads of those who, sprawling below on sea chests, listened, smiling stupidly or scornfully. Over the white rims of berths stuck out heads with blinking eyes; but the bodies were lost in the gloom of those places, that resembled narrow niches for coffins in a whitewashed and lighted mortuary. Voices buzzed louder. Archie, with compressed lips, drew himself in, seemed to shrink into a smaller space, and sewed steadily, industrious and dumb. Belfast shrieked like an inspired Dervish: ". . . So I seez to him, boys, seez I, 'Beggin' yer pardon, sorr,' seez I to that second mate of that steamer—'beggin' your-r-r pardon, sorr, the Board of Trade must 'ave been drunk when they granted you your certificate!' 'What do you say, you ——!' seez he, comin' at me like a mad bull . . . all in his white clothes; and I up with my tarpot and capsizes it all over his blamed lovely face and his lovely jacket. . . . 'Take that!' seez I. 'I am a sailor, anyhow, you nosing, skipper-licking, useless, sooperfloos bridge stanchion, you! That's the kind of man I am!' shouts I. . . . You should have seed him skip, boys! Drowned, blind with tar, he was! So——"

"Don't 'ee believe him! He never upset no tar; I was there!" shouted somebody. The two Norwegians sat on a chest side by side, alike and placid, resembling a pair of lovebirds on a perch, and with round eyes stared innocently; but the Russian Finn, in the racket of explosive shouts and rolling laughter, remained motionless, limp and dull, like a deaf man without a backbone. Near him Archie smiled at his needle. A broad-chested, slow-eyed newcomer spoke deliberately to Belfast during an exhausted lull in the noise: "I wonder any of the mates here are alive yet with such a chap as you on board! I concloode they ain't that bad now, if you had the taming of them, sonny."

"Not bad! Not bad!" screamed Belfast. "If it wasn't for us sticking together . . . Not bad! They ain't never bad when they ain't got a chawnce, blast their black 'arts. . . ." He foamed, whirling his arms, then suddenly grinned and, taking a tablet of black tobacco out of his pocket, bit a piece off with a funny show of ferocity. Another new hand—a man with shifty eyes and a yellow hatchet face, who had been listening open-mouthed in the shadow of the midship locker—observed in a squeaky voice: "Well, it's a 'omeward trip, anyhow. Bad or good, I can do it on my 'ed—s'long as I get 'ome. And I can look after my rights! I will show 'em!" All the heads turned towards him. Only the ordinary seaman and the cat took no notice. He stood with arms akimbo, a little fellow with white eyelashes. He looked as if he had known all the degradations and all the furies. He looked as if he had been cuffed, kicked, rolled in the mud; he looked as if he had been scratched, spat upon, pelted with unmentionable filth . . . and he smiled with a sense of security at the faces around. His ears were bending down under the weight of his battered felt hat. The torn tails of his black coat flapped in fringes about the calves of his legs. He unbuttoned the only two buttons that remained and every one saw that he had no shirt under it. It was his deserved misfortune that those rags which nobody could possibly be supposed to own looked on him as if they had been stolen. His neck was long and thin; his eyelids were red; rare hairs hung about his jaws; his shoulders were peaked and drooped like the broken wings of a bird; all his left side was caked with mud which showed that he had lately slept in a wet ditch. He had saved his inefficient carcass from violent destruction by running away from an American ship where, in a moment of forgetful folly, he had dared to engage himself; and he had knocked about for a fortnight ashore in the native quarter, cadging for drinks, starving, sleeping on rubbish heaps, wandering in sunshine: a startling visitor from a world of nightmares. He stood repulsive and smiling in the sudden silence. This clean white forecastle was his refuge; the place where he could be lazy; where he could wallow, and lie and eat—and curse the food he ate; where he could display his talents for shirking work, for cheating, for cadging; where he could find surely someone to wheedle and someone to bully—and where he would be paid for doing all this. They all knew him. Is there a spot on earth where such a man is unknown, an ominous survival testifying to the eternal fitness of lies and impudence? A taciturn long-armed shellback, with hooked fingers, who had been lying on his back smoking, turned in his bed to examine him dispassionately, then, over his head, sent a long jet of clear saliva towards the door. They all knew him! He was the man that cannot steer, that cannot splice, that dodges the work on dark nights; that, aloft, holds on frantically with both arms and legs, and swears at the wind, the sleet, the darkness; the man who curses the sea while others work. The man who is the last out and the first in when all hands are called. The man who can't do most things and won't do the rest. The pet of philanthropists and self-seeking landlubbers. The sympathetic and deserving creature that knows all about his rights, but knows nothing of courage, of endurance, and of the unexpressed faith, of the unspoken loyalty that knits together a ship's company. The independent offspring of the ignoble freedom of the slums full of disdain and hate for the austere servitude of the sea.

Someone cried at him: "What's your name?"—"Donkin," he said, looking round with cheerful effrontery.—"What are you?" asked another voice.—"Why, a sailor like you, old man," he replied, in a tone that meant to be hearty but was impudent.—"Blamme if you don't look a blamed sight worse than a broken-down fireman," was the comment in a convinced mutter. Charley lifted his head and piped in a cheeky voice: "He is a man and a sailor"—then wiping his nose with the back of his hand bent down industriously over his bit of rope. A few laughed. Others stared doubtfully. The ragged newcomer was indignant—"That's a fine way to welcome a chap into a fo'c'sle," he snarled. "Are you men or a lot of 'artless cannybals?"—"Don't take your shirt off for a word, shipmate," called out Belfast, jumping up in front, fiery, menacing, and friendly at the same time.—"Is that 'ere bloke blind?" asked the indomitable scarecrow, looking right and left with affected surprise. "Can't 'ee see I 'aven't got no shirt?"

He held both his arms out crosswise and shook the rags that hung over his bones with dramatic effect.

" 'Cos why?" he continued very loud. "The bloody Yankees been tryin' to jump my guts out 'cos I stood up for my rights like a good 'un. I am an Englishman, I am. They set upon me an' I 'ad to run. That's why. A'n't yer never seed a man 'ard up? Yah! What kind of blamed ship is this? I'm dead broke. I 'aven't got nothink. No bag, no bed, no blanket, no shirt—not a bloomin' rag but what I stand in. But I 'ad the 'art to stand up agin' them Yankees. 'As any of you 'art enough to spare a pair of old pants for a chum?"

He knew how to conquer the naïve instincts of that crowd. In a moment they gave him their compassion, jocularly, contemptuously, or surlily; and at first it took the shape of a blanket thrown at him as he stood there with the white skin of his limbs showing his human kinship through the black fantasy of his rags. Then a pair of old shoes fell at his muddy feet. With a cry: "From under," a rolled-up pair of canvas trousers, heavy with tar stains, struck him on the shoulder. The gust of their benevolence sent a wave of sentimental pity through their doubting hearts. They were touched by their own readiness to alleviate a shipmate's misery. Voices cried: "We will fit you out, old man." Murmurs: "Never seed seech a hard case. . . . Poor beggar. . . . I've got an old singlet. . . . Will that be of any use to you? . . . Take it, matey. . . ." Those friendly murmurs filled the forecastle. He pawed around with his naked foot, gathering the things in a heap and looked about for more. Unemotional Archie perfunctorily contributed to the pile an old cloth cap with the peak torn off. Old Singleton, lost in the serene regions of fiction, read on unheeding. Charley, pitiless with the wisdom of youth, squeaked: "If you want brass buttons for your new uny-forms I've got two for you." The filthy object of universal charity shook his fist at the youngster. "I'll make you keep this 'ere fo'c'sle clean, young feller," he snarled viciously. "Never you fear. I will learn you to be civil to an able seaman, you ignerant ass." He glared harmfully, but saw Singleton shut his book, and his little beady eyes began to roam from berth to berth.—"Take that bunk by the door there—it's pretty fair," suggested Belfast. So advised, he gathered the gifts at his feet, pressed them in a bundle against his breast, then looked cautiously at the Russian Finn, who stood on one side with an unconscious gaze, contemplating, perhaps, one of those weird visions that haunt the men of his race.—"Get out of my road, Dutchy," said the victim of Yankee brutality. The Finn did not move—did not hear. "Get out, blast ye," shouted the other, shoving him aside with his elbow. "Get out, you blanked deaf and dumb fool. Get out." The man staggered, recovered himself, and gazed at the speaker in silence.—"Those damned furriners should be kept under," opined the amiable Donkin to the forecastle. "If you don't teach 'em their place they put on you like anythink." He flung all his worldy possessions into the empty bed place, gauged with another shrewd look the risks of the proceeding, then leaped up to the Finn, who stood pensive and dull. "I'll teach you to swell around," he yelled. "I'll plug your eyes for you, you blooming squarehead." Most of the men were now in their bunks and the two had the forecastle clear to themselves. The development of the destitute Donkin aroused interest. He danced all in tatters before the amazed Finn, squaring from a distance at the heavy, unmoved face. One or two men cried encouragingly: "Go it, Whitechapel!" settling themselves luxuriously in their beds to survey the fight. Others shouted: "Shut yer row! . . . Go an' put yer 'ed in a bag! . . ." The hubbub was recommencing. Suddenly many heavy blows struck with a handspike on the deck above boomed like discharges of small cannon through the forecastle. Then the boatswain's voice rose outside the door with an authoritative note in its drawl: "D'ye hear, below there? Lay aft! Lay aft to muster all hands!"

There was a moment of surprised stillness. Then the forecastle floor disappeared under men whose bare feet flopped on the planks as they sprang clear out of their berths. Caps were rooted for amongst tumbled blankets. Some, yawning, buttoned waistbands. Half-smoked pipes were knocked hurriedly against woodwork and stuffed under pillows. Voices growled: "What's up? . . . Is there no rest for us?" Donkin yelped: "If that's the way of this ship, we'll 'ave to change all that. . . . You leave me alone. . . . I will soon . . ." None of the crowd noticed him. They were lurching in twos and threes through the doors, after the manner of merchant Jacks who cannot go out of a door fairly, like mere landsmen. The votary of change followed them. Singleton, struggling into his jacket, came last, tall and fatherly, bearing high his head of a weather-beaten sage on the body of an old athlete. Only Charley remained alone in the white glare of the empty place, sitting between the two rows of iron links that stretched into the narrow gloom forward. He pulled hard at the strands in a hurried endeavor to finish his knot. Suddenly he started up, flung the rope at the cat, and skipped after the black tom, which went off leaping sedately over chain compressors, with its tail carried stiff and upright, like a small flagpole.

Outside the glare of the steaming forecastle the serene purity of the night enveloped the seamen with its soothing breath, with its tepid breath flowing under the stars that hung countless above the mastheads in a thin cloud of luminous dust. On the town side the blackness of the water was streaked with trails of light which undulated gently on slight ripples, similar to filaments that float rooted to the shore. Rows of other lights stood away in straight lines as if drawn up on parade between towering buildings; but on the other side of the harbor somber hills arched high their black spines, on which, here and there, the point of a star resembled a spark fallen from the sky. Far off, Byculla way, the electric lamps at the dock gates shone on the end of lofty standards with a glow blinding and frigid like captive ghosts of some evil moons. Scattered all over the dark polish of the roadstead, the ships at anchor floated in perfect stillness under the feeble gleam of their riding lights, looming up, opaque and bulky, like strange and monumental structures abandoned by men to an everlasting repose.

Before the cabin door Mr. Baker was mustering the crew. As they stumbled and lurched along past the mainmast, they could see aft his round, broad face with a white paper before it, and beside his shoulder the sleepy head, with dropped eyelids, of the boy, who held, suspended at the end of his raised arm, the luminous globe of a lamp. Even before the shuffle of naked soles had ceased along the decks, the mate began to call over the names. He called distinctly in a serious tone befitting this roll call to unquiet loneliness, to inglorious and obscure struggle, or to the more trying endurance of small privations and wearisome duties. As the chief mate read out a name, one of the men would answer: "Yes, sir!" or "Here!" and, detaching himself from the shadowy mob of heads visible above the blackness of starboard bulwarks, would step barefooted into the circle of light and in two noiseless strides pass into the shadows on the port side of the quarter-deck. They answered in divers tones: in thick mutters, in clear, ringing voices; and some, as if the whole thing had been an outrage on their feelings, used an injured intonation: for discipline is not ceremonious in merchant ships, where the sense of hierarchy is weak and where all feel themselves equal before the unconcerned immensity of the sea and the exacting appeal of the work.

Mr. Baker read on steadily: "Hansen—Campbell—Smith—Wamibo. Now then, Wamibo. Why don't you answer? Always got to call your name twice." The Finn emitted at last an uncouth grunt, and, stepping out, passed through the patch of light, weird and gaudy, with the face of a man marching through a dream. The mate went on faster: "Craik—Singleton—Donkin. . . . O Lord!" he involuntarily ejaculated as the incredibly dilapidated figure appeared in the light. It stopped; it uncovered pale gums and long, upper teeth in a malevolent grin.—"Is there anythink wrong with me, Mister Mate?" it asked, with a flavor of insolence in the forced simplicity of its tone. On both sides of the deck subdued titters were heard. "That'll do. Go over," growled Mr. Baker, fixing the new hand with steady blue eyes. And Donkin vanished suddenly out of the light into the dark group of mustered men, to be slapped on the back and to hear flattering whispers: "He ain't afeard, he'll give sport to 'em, see if he don't. . . . Reg'lar Punch and Judy show. . . . Did ye see the mate start at him? . . . Well! Damme, if I ever! . . ."

The last man had gone over and there was a moment of silence while the mate peered at his list. "Sixteen, seventeen," he muttered. "I am one hand short, bo'sun," he said aloud. The big west-countryman at his elbow, swarthy and bearded like a gigantic Spaniard, said in a rumbling bass: "There's no one left forward, sir. I had a look round. He ain't aboard, but he may turn up before daylight."—"Aye. He may or he may not," commented the mate, "can't make out that last name. It's all a smudge. . . . That will do, men. Go below."

The distinct and motionless group stirred, broke up, began to move forward.

"Wait!" cried a deep, ringing voice.

All stood still. Mr. Baker, who had turned away yawning, spun round open-mouthed. At last, furious, he blurted out: "What's this? Who said 'Wait'? What . . ."

But he saw a tall figure standing on the rail. It came down and pushed through the crowd, marching with a heavy tread towards the light on the quarter-deck. Then again the sonorous voice said with insistence: "Wait!" The lamplight lit up the man's body. He was tall. His head was away up in the shadows of lifeboats that stood on skids above the deck. The whites of his eyes and his teeth gleamed distinctly, but the face was indistinguishable. His hands were big and seemed gloved.

Mr. Baker advanced intrepidly. "Who are you? How dare you . . ." he began.

The boy, amazed like the rest, raised the light to the man's face. It was black. A surprised hum—a faint hum that sounded like the suppressed mutter of the word "Nigger"—ran along the deck and escaped out into the night. The nigger seemed not to hear. He balanced himself where he stood in a swagger that marked time. After a moment he said calmly: "My name is Wait—James Wait."

"Oh!" said Mr. Baker. Then, after a few seconds of smoldering silence, his temper blazed out. "Ah! Your name is Wait. What of that? What do you want? What do you mean, coming shouting here?"

The nigger was calm, cool, towering, superb. The men had approached and stood behind him in a body. He overtopped the tallest by half a head. He said: "I belong to the ship." He enunciated distinctly, with soft precision. The deep, rolling tones of his voice filled the deck without effort. He was naturally scornful, unaffectedly condescending, as if from his height of six foot three he had surveyed all the vastness of human folly and had made up his mind not to be too hard on it. He went on: "The captain shipped me this morning. I couldn't get aboard sooner. I saw you all aft as I came up the ladder, and could see directly you were mustering the crew. Naturally I called out my name. I thought you had it on your list, and would understand. You misapprehended." He stopped short. The folly around him was confounded. He was right as ever, and as ever ready to forgive. The disdainful tones had ceased, and, breathing heavily, he stood still, surrounded by all these white men. He held his head up in the glare of the lamp—a head vigorously modeled into deep shadows and shining lights—a head powerful and misshapen with a tormented and flattened face—a face pathetic and brutal: the tragic, the mysterious, the repulsive mask of a nigger's soul.

Mr. Baker, recovering his composure, looked at the paper close. "Oh, yes; that's so. All right, Wait. Take your gear forward," he said.

Suddenly the nigger's eyes rolled wildly, became all whites. He put his hand to his side and coughed twice, a cough metallic, hollow, and tremendously loud; it resounded like two explosions in a vault; the dome of the sky rang to it and the iron plates of the ship's bulwarks seemed to vibrate in unison, then he marched off forward with the others. The officers lingering by the cabin door could hear him say: "Won't some of you chaps lend a hand with my dunnage? I've got a chest and a bag." The words, spoken sonorously, with an even intonation, were heard all over the ship, and the question was put in a manner that made refusal impossible. The short, quick shuffle of men carrying something heavy went away forward, but the tall figure of the nigger lingered by the main hatch in a knot of smaller shapes. Again he was heard asking: "Is your cook a colored gentleman?" Then a disappointed and disapproving "Ah! h'm!" was his comment upon the information that the cook happened to be a mere white man. Yet, as they went all together towards the forecastle, he condescended to put his head through the galley door and boom out inside a magnificent "Good evening, doctor!" that made all the saucepans ring. In the dim light the cook dozed on the coal locker in front of the captain's supper. He jumped up as if he had been cut with a whip and dashed wildly on deck to see the backs of several men going away laughing. Afterwards, when talking about that voyage, he used to say: "The poor fellow had scared me. I thought I had seen the devil." The cook had been seven years in the ship with the same captain. He was a serious-minded man with a wife and three children, whose society he enjoyed on an average one month out of twelve. When on shore he took his family to church twice every Sunday. At sea he went to sleep every evening with his lamp turned up full, a pipe in his mouth, and an open Bible in his hand. Someone had always to go during the night to put out the light, take the book from his hand and the pipe from between his teeth. "For"—Belfast used to say, irritated and complaining—"some night, you stupid cookie, you'll swallow your ould clay, and we will have no cook."—"Ah! sonny, I am ready for my Maker's call . . . wish you all were," the other would answer with a benign serenity that was altogether imbecile and touching. Belfast outside the gallery door danced with vexation. "You holy fool! I don't want you to die," he howled, looking up with furious, quivering face and tender eyes. "What's the hurry? You blessed wooden-headed ould heretic, the divvle will have you soon enough. Think of Us . . . of Us . . . of Us!" And he would go away, stamping, spitting aside, disgusted and worried; while the other, stepping out, saucepan in hand, hot, begrimed and placid, watched with a superior, cocksure smile the back of his "queer little man" reeling in a rage. They were great friends.

Mr. Baker, lounging over the afterhatch, sniffed the humid night in the company of the second mate. "Those West India niggers run fine and large—some of them. . . . Ough! . . . Don't they? A fine, big man that, Mr. Creighton. Feel him on a rope. Hey? Ough! I will take him into my watch, I think." The second mate, a fair, gentlemanly young fellow, with a resolute face and a splendid physique, observed quietly that it was just about what he expected. There could be felt in his tone some slight bitterness which Mr. Baker very kindly set himself to argue away. "Come, come, young man," he said, grunting between the words.

"Come! Don't be too greedy. You had that big Finn in your watch all the voyage. I will do what's fair. You may have those two young Scandinavians and I . . . Ough! . . . I get the nigger, and will take that . . . Ough! that cheeky costermonger chap in a black frock coat. I'll make him . . . Ough . . . make him toe the mark, or my . . . Ough! . . . name isn't Baker. Ough! Ough! Ough!"

He grunted thrice—ferociously. He had that trick of grunting so between his words and at the end of sentences. It was a fine, effective grunt that went well with his menacing utterance, with his heavy, bullnecked frame, his jerky, rolling gait; with his big, seamed face, his steady eyes, and sardonic mouth. But its effect had been long ago discounted by the men. They liked him; Belfast—who was a favorite, and knew it—mimicked him, not quite behind his back. Charley—but with greater caution—imitated his rolling gait. Some of his sayings became established, daily quotations in the forecastle. Popularity can go no farther! Besides, all hands were ready to admit that on a fitting occasion the mate could "jump down a fellow's throat in a reg'lar Western Ocean style."

Now he was giving his last orders. "Ough! . . . You, Knowles! Call all hands at four. I want . . . Ough! . . . to heave short before the tug comes. Look out for the captain. I am going to lie down in my clothes. . . . Ough! . . . Call me when you see the boat coming. Ough! Ough! . . . The old man is sure to have something to say when he gets aboard," he remarked to Creighton. "Well, good night. . . . Ough! A long day before us tomorrow. . . . Ough! . . . Better turn in now. Ough! Ough!"

Upon the dark deck a band of light flashed, then a door slammed, and Mr. Baker was gone into his neat cabin. Young Creighton stood leaning over the rail, and looked dreamily into the night of the East. And he saw in it a long country lane, a lane of waving leaves and dancing sunshine. He saw stirring boughs of old trees outspread, and framing in their arch the tender, the caressing blueness of an English sky. And through the arch a girl in a light dress, smiling under a sunshade, seemed to be stepping out of the tender sky.

At the other end of the ship the forecastle, with only one lamp burning now, was going to sleep in a dim emptiness traversed by loud breathings, by sudden short sighs. The double row of berths yawned black, like graves tenanted by uneasy corpses. Here and there a curtain of gaudy chintz, half drawn, marked the resting place of a sybarite. A leg hung over the edge very white and lifeless. An arm stuck straight out with a dark palm turned up, and thick fingers half closed. Two light snores, that did not synchronize, quarreled in funny dialogue. Singleton, stripped again—the old man suffered much from prickly heat—stood cooling his back in the doorway, with his arms crossed on his bare and adorned chest. His head touched the beam of the deck above. The nigger, half-undressed, was busy casting adrift the lashing of his box and spreading his bedding in an upper berth. He moved about in his socks, tall and noiseless, with a pair of braces beating about his calves. Amongst the shadows of stanchions and bowsprit, Donkin munched a piece of hard ship's bread, sitting on the deck with upturned feet and restless eyes; he held the biscuit up before his mouth in the whole fist and snapped his jaws at it with a raging face. Crumbs fell between his outspread legs. Then he got up.

"Where's our water cask?" he asked in a contained voice.

Singleton, without a word, pointed with a big hand that held a short smoldering pipe. Donkin bent over the cask, drank out of the tin, splashing the water, turned round and noticed the nigger looking at him over the shoulder with calm loftiness. He moved up sideways.

"There's a blooming supper for a man," he whispered bitterly. "My dorg at 'ome wouldn't 'ave it. It's fit enouf for you an' me. 'Ere's a big ship's fo'c'sle! . . . Not a blooming scrap of meat in the kids. I've looked in all the lockers. . . ."

The nigger stared like a man addressed unexpectedly in

a foreign language. Donkin changed his tone: "Give us a bit of 'baccy, mate," he breathed out confidentially, "I 'aven't 'ad smoke or chew for the last month. I am rampin' mad for it. Come on, old man!"

"Don't be familiar," said the nigger. Donkin started and sat down on a chest near by, out of sheer surprise. "We haven't kept pigs together," continued James Wait in a deep undertone. "Here's your tobacco." Then, after a pause, he inquired: "What ship?"—"*Golden State,*" muttered Donkin indistinctly, biting the tobacco. The nigger whistled low. "Ran?" he said curtly. Donkin nodded: one of his cheeks bulged out. "In course I ran," he mumbled. "They booted the life hout of one Dago chap on the passage 'ere, then started on me. I cleared hout 'ere."—"Left your dunnage behind?"—"Yes, dunnage and money," answered Donkin, raising his voice a little; "I got nothink. No clothes, no bed. A bandy-legged little Hirish chap 'ere 'as give me a blanket. . . . Think I'll go an' sleep in the fore-topmast staysail tonight."

He went on deck trailing behind his back a corner of the blanket. Singleton, without a glance, moved slightly aside to let him pass. The nigger put away his shore togs and sat in clean working clothes on his box, one arm stretched over his knees. After staring at Singleton for some time he asked without emphasis: "What kind of ship is this? Pretty fair? Eh?"

Singleton didn't stir. A long while after he said, with unmoved face: "Ship! . . . Ships are all right. It is the men in them!"

He went on smoking in the profound silence. The wisdom of half a century spent in listening to the thunder of the waves had spoken unconsciously through his old lips. The cat purred on the windlass. Then James Wait had a fit of roaring, rattling cough that shook him, tossed him like a hurricane, and flung him panting with staring eyes headlong on his sea chest. Several men woke up. One said sleepily out of his bunk: " 'Struth! what a blamed row!"—"I have a cold on my chest," gasped Wait.—"Cold! you call it," grumbled the man; "should think 'twas something more. . . ."—"Oh! you think so," said the nigger upright and loftily scornful again. He climbed into his berth and began coughing persistently while he put his head out to glare all round the forecastle. There was no further protest. He fell back on the pillow, and could be heard there wheezing regularly like a man oppressed in his sleep.

Singleton stood at the door with his face to the light and his back to the darkness. And alone in the dim emptiness of the sleeping forecastle he appeared bigger, colossal, very old; old as Father Time himself, who should have come there into this place as quiet as a sepulcher to contemplate with patient eyes the short victory of sleep, the consoler. Yet he was only a child of time, a lonely relic of a devoured and forgotten generation. He stood, still strong, as ever unthinking; a ready man with a vast empty past and with no future, with his childlike impulses and his man's passions already dead within his tattooed breast. The men who could understand his silence were gone—those men who knew how to exist beyond the pale of life and within sight of eternity. They had been strong, as those are strong who know neither doubts or hopes. They had been impatient and enduring, turbulent and devoted, unruly and faithful. Well-meaning people had tried to represent those men as whining over every mouthful of their food; as going about their work in fear of their lives. But in truth they had been men who knew toil, privation, violence, debauchery—but knew not fear, and had no desire of spite in their hearts. Men hard to manage, but easy to inspire; voiceless men—but men enough to scorn in their hearts the sentimental voices that bewailed the hardness of their fate. It was a fate unique and their own; the capacity to bear it appeared to them the privilege of the chosen! Their generation lived inarticulate and indispensable, without knowing the sweetness of affections or the refuge of a home—and died free from the dark menace of a narrow grave. They were the everlasting children of the mysterious sea. Their successors are the grown-up children of a discontented earth. They are less naughty, but less innocent; less profane, but perhaps also less believing; and if they have learned how to speak they have also learned how to whine. But the others were strong and mute; they were effaced, bowed and enduring, like stone caryatides that hold up in the night the lighted halls of a resplendent and glorious edifice. They are gone now—and it does not matter. The sea and the earth are unfaithful to their children: a truth, a faith, a generation of men goes—and is forgotten, and it does not matter! Except, perhaps, to the few of those who believed the truth, confessed the faith—or loved the men.

A breeze was coming. The ship that had been lying tide-rode swung to a heavier puff; and suddenly the slack of the chain cable between the windlass and the hawsepipe clinked, slipped forward an inch, and rose gently off the deck with a startling suggestion as of unsuspected life that had been lurking stealthily in the iron. In the hawsepipe the grinding links sent through the ship a sound like a low groan of a man sighing under a burden. The strain came on the windlass, the chain tautened like a string, vibrated —and the handle of the screw brake moved in slight jerks. Singleton stepped forward.

Till then he had been standing meditative and unthinking, reposeful and hopeless, with a face grim and blank— a sixty-year-old child of the mysterious sea. The thoughts of all his lifetime could have been expressed in six words, but the stir of those things that were as much part of his existence as his beating heart called up a gleam of alert understanding upon the sternness of his aged face. The flame of the lamp swayed, and the old man, with knitted and bushy eyebrows, stood over the brake, watchful and motionless in the wild saraband of dancing shadows. Then the ship, obedient to the call of her anchor, forged ahead slightly and eased the strain. The cable, relieved, hung down, and after swaying imperceptibly to and fro dropped with a loud tap on the hardwood planks. Singleton seized the high lever, and, by a violent throw forward of his body, wrung out another half-turn from the brake. He recovered himself, breathed largely, and remained for a while glaring down at the powerful and compact engine that squatted on the deck at his feet like some quiet monster—a creature amazing and tame.

"You . . . hold!" he growled at it masterfully, in the incult tangle of his white beard.

CHAPTER 2

Next morning, at daylight, the *Narcissus* went to sea. A slight haze blurred the horizon. Outside the harbor the measureless expanse of smooth water lay sparkling like a floor of jewels and as empty as the sky. The short black tug gave a pluck to windward, in the usual way, then let go the rope and hovered for a moment on the quarter with her engines stopped, while the slim, long hull of the ship moved ahead slowly under lower topsails. The loose upper canvas blew out in the breeze with soft round contours, resembling small white clouds snared in the maze of ropes. Then the sheets were hauled home, the yards hoisted, and the ship became a high and lonely pyramid, gliding, all shining and white, through the sunlit mist. The tug turned short round and went away towards the land. Twenty-six pairs of eyes watched her low broad stern crawling languidly over the smooth swell between the two paddle wheels that turned fast, beating the water with fierce hurry. She resembled an enormous and aquatic black beetle, surprised by the light, overwhelmed by the sunshine, trying to escape with ineffectual effort into the distant gloom of the land. She left a lingering smudge of smoke on the sky, and two vanishing trails of foam on the water. On the place where she had stopped a round black patch of soot remained, undulating on the swell—an unclean mark of the creature's rest.

The *Narcissus,* left alone, heading south, seemed to stand resplendent and still upon the restless sea, under the moving sun. Flakes of foam swept past her sides; the water struck her with flashing blows; the land glided away slowly fading; a few birds screamed on motionless wings over the swaying mastheads. But soon the land disappeared, the birds went away; and to the west the pointed sail of an Arab dhow running for Bombay, rose triangular and upright above the sharp edge of the horizon, lingered and vanished like an illusion. Then the ship's wake, long and straight, stretched itself out through a day of immense solitude. The setting sun, burning on the level of the water, flamed crimson below the blackness of heavy rain clouds. The sunset squall, coming up from behind, dissolved itself into the short deluge of a hissing shower. It left the ship glistening from trucks to waterline, and with darkened sails. She ran easily before a fair monsoon, with her decks cleared for the night; and, moving along with her, was heard the sustained and monotonous swishing of the waves, mingled with the low whispers of men mustered aft for the setting of watches; the short plaint of some block aloft; or, now and then, a loud sigh of wind.

Mr. Baker, coming out of his cabin, called out the first name sharply before closing the door behind him. He was going to take charge of the deck. On the homeward trip, according to an old custom of the sea, the chief officer takes the first night watch—from eight till midnight. So Mr. Baker, after he had heard the last "Yes, sir!" said moodily, "Relieve the wheel and lookout"; and climbed with heavy feet the poop ladder to windward. Soon after, Mr. Creighton came down, whistling softly, and went into the cabin. On the doorstep the steward lounged, in slippers, meditative, and with his shirt sleeves rolled up to the armpits. On the main deck the cook, locking up the galley doors, had an altercation with young Charley about a pair of socks. He could be heard saying impressively, in the darkness amidships: "You don't deserve a kindness. I've been drying them for you, and now you complain about the holes—and you swear, too! Right in front of me! If I hadn't been a Christian—which you ain't, you young ruffian—I would give you a clout on the head. . . . Go away!" Men in couples or threes stood pensive or moved silently along the bulwarks in the waist. The first busy day of a homeward passage was sinking into the dull peace of resumed routine. Aft, on the high poop, Mr. Baker walked shuffling and grunted to himself in the pauses of his thoughts. Forward, the lookout man, erect between the flukes of the two anchors, hummed an endless tune, keeping his eyes fixed dutifully ahead in a vacant stare. A multitude of stars coming out into the clear night peopled the emptiness of the sky. They glittered as if alive above the sea; they surrounded the running ship on all sides, more intense than the eyes of a staring crowd, and as inscrutable as the souls of men.

The passage had begun and the ship, a fragment detached from the earth, went on lonely and swift like a small planet. Round her the abysses of sky and sea met in an unattainable frontier. A great circular solitude moved with her, ever changing and ever the same, always monotonous and always imposing. Now and then another wandering white speck, burdened with life, appeared far off—disappeared; intent on its own destiny. The sun looked upon her all day and every morning rose with a burning, round stare of undying curiosity. She had her own future; she was alive with the lives of those beings who trod her decks; like that earth which had given her up to the sea, she had an intolerable load of regrets and hopes. On her lived timid truth and audacious lies; and, like the earth, she was unconscious, fair to see—and condemned by men to an ignoble fate. The august loneliness of her path lent dignity to the sordid inspiration of her pilgrimage. She drove foaming to the southward, as if guided by the courage of a high endeavor. The smiling greatness of the sea dwarfed the extent of time. The days raced after one another, brilliant and quick like the flashes of a lighthouse, and the nights, eventful and short, resembled fleeting dreams.

The men had shaken into their places and the half-hourly voice of the bells ruled their life of unceasing care. Night and day the head and shoulders of a seaman could be seen aft by the wheel, outlined high against sunshine or starlight, very steady above the stir of revolving spokes. The faces changed, passing in rotation. Youthful faces, bearded faces, dark faces: faces serene, or faces moody, but all akin with the brotherhood of the sea; all with the same attentive expression of eyes, carefully watching the compass or the sails. Captain Allistoun, serious, and with an old red muffler round his throat, all day long pervaded the poop. At night, many times he rose out of the darkness of the companion, such as a phantom above a grave, and stood watchful and mute under the stars, his nightshirt fluttering like a flag—then, without a sound, sank down again. He was born on the shores of the Pentland Firth. In his youth he attained the rank of harpooner in Peterhead whalers. When he spoke of that time his restless gray eyes became still and cold, like the loom of ice. Afterwards he went into the East Indian trade for the sake of change. He had commanded the *Narcissus* since she was built. He loved his ship, and drove her unmercifully; for his secret ambition was to make her accomplish some day a brilliantly quick passage which would be mentioned in nautical papers. He pronounced his owner's name with a sardonic smile, spoke but seldom to his officers, and reproved errors in a gentle voice, with words that cut to the quick. His hair was iron-gray, his face hard and of the color of pump leather. He shaved every morning of his life—at six—but once (being caught in a fierce hurricane eighty miles southwest of Mauritius) he had missed three consecutive days. He feared naught but an unforgiving God, and wished to end his days in a little house, with a plot of ground attached—far in the country—out of sight of the sea.

He, the ruler of that minute world, seldom descended from the Olympian heights of his poop. Below him—at his feet, so to speak—common mortals led their busy and insignificant lives. Along the main deck, Mr. Baker grunted in a manner bloodthirsty and innocuous; and kept all our noses to the grindstone, being—as he once remarked—paid for doing that very thing. The men working about the deck were healthy and contented—as most seamen are, when once well out to sea. The true peace of God begins at any spot a thousand miles from the nearest land; and when He sends there the messengers of His might it is not in terrible wrath against crime, presumption, and folly, but paternally, to chasten simple hearts—ignorant hearts that know nothing of life, and beat undisturbed by envy or greed.

In the evening the cleared decks had a reposeful aspect, resembling the autumn of the earth. The sun was sinking to rest, wrapped in a mantle of warm clouds. Forward, on the end of the spare spars, the boatswain and the carpenter sat together with crossed arms; two men friendly, powerful, and deep-chested. Beside them the short, dumpy sailmaker—who had been in the Navy—related, between the whiffs of his pipe, impossible stories about admirals. Couples tramped backwards and forwards, keeping step and balance without effort, in a confined space. Pigs grunted in the big pigsty. Belfast, leaning thoughtfully on his elbow, above the bars, communed with them through the silence of his meditation. Fellows with shirts open wide on sunburnt breasts sat upon the mooring bitts, and all up the steps of the forecastle ladders. By the foremast a few discussed in a circle the characteristics of a gentleman. One said: "It's money as does it." Another maintained: "No, it's the way they speak." Lame Knowles stumped up with an unwashed face (he had the distinction of being the dirty man of the forecastle), and, showing a few yellow fangs in a shrewd smile, explained craftily that he "had seen some of their pants." The backsides of them—he had observed—were thinner than paper from constant sitting down in offices, yet otherwise they looked first-rate and would last for years. It was all appearance. "It was," he said, "bloomin' easy to be a gentleman when you had a clean job for life." They disputed endlessly, obstinate and childish; they repeated in shouts and with inflamed faces their amazing arguments; while the soft breeze, eddying down the enormous cavity of the foresail, distended above their bare heads, stirred the tumbled hair with a touch passing and light like an indulgent caress.

They were forgetting their toil, they were forgetting themselves. The cook approached to hear, and stood by, beaming with the inward consciousness of his faith, like a conceited saint unable to forget his glorious reward; Donkin, solitary and brooding over his wrongs on the forecastlehead, moved closer to catch the drift of the discussion below him; he turned his sallow face to the sea, and his thin nostrils moved, sniffing the breeze, as he lounged negligently by the rail. In the glow of sunset faces shone with interest, teeth flashed, eyes sparkled. The walking couples stood still suddenly, with broad grins; a man bending over a washtub sat up, entranced, with the soapsuds flecking his wet arms. Even the three petty officers listened leaning back, comfortably propped, and with superior smiles. Belfast left off scratching the ear of his favorite pig, and, open-mouthed, tried with eager eyes to have his say. He lifted his arms, grimacing and baffled. From a distance Charley screamed at the ring: "I know about gentlemen more'n any of you. I've been intermit with 'em. . . . I've blacked their boots." The cook, craning his neck to hear better, was scandalized. "Keep your mouth shut when your elders speak, you impudent young heathen—you."—"All right, old Hallelujah, I'm done," answered Charley, soothingly. At some opinion of dirty Knowles, delivered with an air of supernatural cunning, a ripple of laughter ran along, rose like a wave, burst with a startling roar. They stamped with both feet; they turned their shouting faces to the sky; many, spluttering, slapped their thighs; while one or two, bent double, gasped, hugging themselves with both arms like men in pain. The carpenter and the boatswain, without changing their attitude, shook with laughter where they sat; the sailmaker, charged with an anecdote about a commodore, looked sulky; the cook was wiping his eyes with a greasy rag; and lame Knowles, astonished at his own success, stood in their midst showing a slow smile.

Suddenly the face of Donkin leaning high-shouldered over the afterrail became grave. Something like a weak rattle was heard through the forecastle door. It became a murmur; it ended in a sighing groan. The washerman plunged both his arms into the tub abruptly; the cook became more crestfallen than an exposed backslider; the boatswain moved his shoulders uneasily; the carpenter got up with a spring and walked away—while the sailmaker seemed mentally to give his story up and began to puff at his pipe with somber determination. In the blackness of the doorway a pair of eyes glimmered white, and big, and staring. Then James Wait's head protruding became visible, as if suspended between the two hands that grasped a doorpost on each side of the face. The tassel of his blue woolen nightcap, cocked forward, danced gaily over his left eyelid. He stepped out in a tottering stride. He looked powerful as ever, but showed a strange and affected unsteadiness in his gait; his face was perhaps a trifle thinner, and his eyes appeared rather startlingly prominent. He seemed to hasten the retreat of departing light by his very presence; the setting sun dipped sharply, as though fleeing before our nigger; a black mist emanated from him, a subtle and dismal influence, a something cold and gloomy that floated out and settled on all the faces like a mourning veil. The circle broke up. The joy of laughter died on stiffened lips. There was not a smile left among all the ship's company. Not a word was spoken. Many turned their backs, trying to look unconcerned; others, with averted heads, sent half-reluctant glances out of the corners of their eyes. They resembled criminals conscious of misdeeds more than honest men distracted by doubt; only two or three stared frankly, but stupidly, with lips slightly open.

All expected James Wait to say something, and, at the same time, had the air of knowing beforehand what he would say. He leaned his back against the doorpost, and with heavy eyes swept over them a glance domineering and pained, like a sick tyrant overawing a crowd of abject but untrustworthy slaves.

No one went away. They waited in fascinated dread. He said ironically, with gasps between the words:

"Thank you . . . chaps. You . . . are nice . . . and . . . quiet . . . you are! Yelling so . . . before . . . the door. . . ."

He made a longer pause, during which he worked his ribs in an exaggerated labor of breathing. It was intolerable. Feet were shuffled. Belfast let out a groan; but Donkin above blinked his red eyelids with invisible eyelashes, and smiled bitterly over the nigger's head.

The nigger went on again with surprising ease. He gasped no more, and his voice rang, hollow and loud, as though he had been talking in an empty cavern. He was contemptuously angry.

"I tried to get a wink of sleep. You know I can't sleep o' nights. And you come jabbering near the door here like a blooming lot of old women. . . . You think yourselves good shipmates. Do you? . . . Much you care for a dying man!"

Belfast spun away from the pigsty. "Jimmy," he cried tremulously, "if you hadn't been sick I would——"

He stopped. The nigger waited awhile, then said, in a gloomy tone: "You would. . . . What? Go an' fight another such one as yourself. Leave me alone. It won't be for long. I'll soon die. . . . It's coming right enough!"

Men stood around very still and with exasperated eyes. It was just what they had expected, and hated to hear, that idea of a stalking death, thrust at them many times a day like a boast and like a menace by this obnoxious nigger. He seemed to take a pride in that death which, so far, had attended only upon the ease of his life; he was overbearing about it, as if no one else in the world had ever been intimate with such a companion; he paraded it unceasingly before us with an affectionate persistence that made its presence indubitable, and at the same time incredible. No man could be suspected of such monstrous friendship! Was he a reality—or was he a sham—this ever-expected visitor of Jimmy's? We hesitated between pity and mistrust, while, on the slightest provocation, he shook before our eyes the bones of his bothersome and infamous skeleton. He was forever trotting him out. He would talk of that coming death as though it had been already there, as if it had been walking the deck outside, as if it would presently come in to sleep in the only empty bunk; as if it had sat by his side at every meal. It interfered daily with our occupations, with our leisure, with our amusements. We had no songs and no music in the evening, because Jimmy (we all lovingly called him Jimmy, to conceal our hate of his accomplice) had managed, with that prospective decease of his, to disturb even Archie's mental balance. Archie was the owner of the concertina; but after a couple of stinging lectures from Jimmy he refused to play any more. He said: "Yon's an uncanny joker. I dinna ken what's wrang wi' him, but there's something verra wrang, verra wrang. It's nae manner of use asking me. I won't play." Our singers became mute because Jimmy was a dying man. For the same reason no chap—as Knowles remarked—could "drive in a nail to hang his few poor rags upon," without being made aware of the enormity he committed in disturbing Jimmy's interminable last moments. At night, instead of the cheerful yell, "One bell! Turn out! Do you hear there? Hey! hey! hey! Show leg!" the watches were called man by man, in whispers, so as not to interfere with Jimmy's, possibly, last slumber on earth. True, he was always awake, and managed, as we sneaked out on deck, to plant in our backs some cutting remark that, for the moment, made us feel as if we had been brutes, and afterwards made us suspect ourselves of being fools. We spoke in low tones within that fo'c'sle as though it had been a church. We ate our meals in silence and dread, for Jimmy was capricious with his food, and railed bitterly at the salt meat, at the biscuits, at the tea, as at articles unfit for human consumption—"let alone for a dying man!" He would say: "Can't you find a better slice of meat for a sick man who's trying to get home to be cured—or buried? But there! If I had a chance, you fellows would do away with it. You would poison me. Look at what you have given me!" We served him in his bed with rage and humility, as though we had been the base courtiers of a hated prince; and he rewarded us by his unconciliating criticism. He had found the secret of keeping forever on the run the fundamental imbecility of mankind; he had the secret of life, that confounded dying man, and he made himself master of every moment of our existence. We grew desperate, and remained submissive. Emotional little Belfast was forever on the verge of assault or on the verge of tears. One evening he confided to Archie: "For a ha'penny I would knock his ugly black head off—the skulking dodger!" And the straightforward Archie pretended to be shocked! Such was the infernal spell which that casual St. Kitts nigger had cast upon our guileless manhood! But the same night Belfast stole from the galley the officers' Sunday fruit pie, to tempt the fastidious appetite of Jimmy. He endangered not only his long friendship with the cook but also—as it appeared—his eternal welfare. The cook was overwhelmed with grief; he did not know the culprit but he knew that wickedness flourished; he knew that Satan was abroad amongst those men, whom he looked upon as in some way under his spiritual care. Whenever he saw three or four of us standing together he would leave his stove, to run out and preach. We fled from him; and only Charley (who knew the thief) affronted the cook with a candid gaze which irritated the good man. "It's you, I believe," he groaned, sorrowful and with a patch of soot on his chin. "It's you. You are a brand for the burning! No more of YOUR socks in my galley." Soon, unofficially, the information was spread about that, should there be another case of stealing, our marmalade (an extra allowance: half a pound per man) would be stopped. Mr. Baker ceased to heap jocular abuse upon his favorites, and grunted suspiciously at all. The captain's cold eyes, high up on the poop, glittered mistrustful, as he surveyed us trooping in a small mob from halyards to braces for the usual evening pull at all the ropes. Such stealing in a merchant ship is difficult to check, and may be taken as a declaration by men of their dislike for their officers. It is a bad symptom. It may end in God knows what trouble. The *Narcissus* was still a peaceful ship, but mutual confidence was shaken. Donkin did not conceal his delight. We were dismayed.

Then illogical Belfast reproached our nigger with great fury. James Wait, with his elbow on the pillow, choked, gasped out: "Did I ask you to bone the dratted thing? Blow your blamed pie. It has made me worse—you little Irish lunatic, you!" Belfast, with scarlet face and trembling lips, made a dash at him. Every man in the forecastle rose with a shout. There was a moment of wild tumult. Some one shrieked piercingly: "Easy, Belfast! Easy! . . ." We expected Belfast to strangle Wait without more ado. Dust flew. We heard through it the nigger's cough, metallic and explosive like a gong. Next moment we saw Belfast hanging over him. He was saying plaintively: "Don't! Don't, Jimmy! Don't be like that. An angel couldn't put up with ye—sick as ye are." He looked round at us from Jimmy's bedside, his comical mouth twitching, and through tearful eyes; then he tried to put straight the disarranged blankets. The unceasing whisper of the sea filled the forecastle. Was James Wait frightened, or touched, or repentant? He lay on his back with a hand to his side, and as motionless as if his expected visitor had come at last. Belfast fumbled about his feet, repeating with emotion: "Yes. We know. Ye are bad, but . . . Just say what ye want done, and . . . We all know ye are bad—very bad. . . ." No! Decidedly James Wait was not touched or repentant. Truth to say, he seemed rather startled. He sat up with incredible suddenness and ease. "Ah! You think I am bad, do you?" he said gloomily, in his clearest baritone voice (to hear him speak sometimes you would never think there was anything wrong with that man). "Do you? . . . Well, act according! Some of you haven't sense enough to put a blanket ship-shape over a sick man. There! Leave it alone! I can die anyhow!" Belfast turned away limply with a gesture of discouragement. In the silence of the forecastle, full of interested men, Donkin pronounced distinctly: "Well, I'm blowed!" and sniggered. Wait looked at him. He looked at him in a quite friendly manner. Nobody could tell what would please our incomprehensible invalid: but for us the scorn of that snigger was hard to bear.

Donkin's position in the forecastle was distinguished but unsafe. He stood on the bad eminence of a general dislike. He was left alone; and in his isolation he could do nothing but think of the gales of the Cape of Good Hope and envy us the possession of warm clothing and waterproofs. Our sea boots, our oilskin coats, our well-filled sea chests, were to him so many causes for bitter meditation: he had none of those things, and he felt instinctively that no man, when the need arose, would offer to share them with him. He was impudently cringing to us and systematically insolent to the officers. He anticipated the best results, for himself, from such a line of conduct—and was mistaken. Such natures forget that under extreme provocation men will be just—whether they want to be so or not. Donkin's insolence to long-suffering Mr. Baker became at last intolerable to us, and we rejoiced when the mate, one dark night, tamed him for good. It was done neatly, with great decency and decorum, and with little noise. We had been called—just before midnight—to trim the yards, and Donkin—as usual—made insulting remarks. We stood sleepily in a row with the forebrace in our hands waiting for the next order, and heard in the darkness a scuffly trampling of feet, an exclamation of surprise, sounds of cuffs and slaps, suppressed, hissing whispers: "Ah! Will you!" . . . "Don't! . . . Don't!" . . . "Then behave." . . . "Oh! Oh! . . ." Afterwards there were soft thuds mixed with the rattle of iron things as if a man's body had been tumbling helplessly amongst the main-pump rods. Before we could realize the situation, Mr. Baker's voice was heard very near and a little impatient: "Haul away, men! Lay back on that rope!" And we did lay back on the rope with great alacrity. As if nothing had happened, the chief mate went on trimming the yards with his usual and exasperating fastidiousness. We didn't at the time see anything of Donkin, and did not care. Had the chief officer thrown him overboard, no man would have said as much as "Hallo! he's gone!" But, in truth, no great harm was done—even if Donkin did lose one of his front teeth. We perceived this in the morning, and preserved a ceremonious silence: the etiquette of the forecastle commanded us to be blind and dumb in such a case, and we cherished the decencies of our life more than ordinary landsmen respect theirs. Charley, with unpardonable want of *savoir vivre,* yelled out: "'Ave you been to your dentyst? . . . Hurt ye, didn't it?" He got a box on the ear from one of his best friends. The boy was surprised, and remained plunged in grief for at least three hours. We were sorry for him, but youth requires even more discipline than age. Donkin grinned venomously. From that day he became pitiless; told Jimmy that he was a "black fraud"; hinted to us that we were an imbecile lot, daily taken in by a vulgar nigger. And Jimmy seemed to like the fellow!

Singleton lived untouched by human emotions. Taciturn and unsmiling, he breathed amongst us—in that alone resembling the rest of the crowd. We were trying to be decent chaps, and found it jolly difficult; we oscillated between the desire of virtue and the fear of ridicule; we wished to save ourselves from the pain of remorse, but did not want to be made the contemptible dupes of our sentiment. Jimmy's hateful accomplice seemed to have blown with his impure breath undreamt-of subtleties into our hearts. We were disturbed and cowardly. That we knew. Singleton seemed to know nothing, understand nothing. We had thought him till then as wise as he looked, but now we dared, at times, suspect him of being stupid—from old age. One day, however, at dinner, as we sat on our boxes round a tin dish that stood on the deck within the circle of our feet, Jimmy expressed his general disgust with men and things in words that were particularly disgusting. Singleton lifted his head. We became mute. The old man, addressing Jimmy, asked: "Are you dying?" Thus interrogated, James Wait appeared horribly startled and confused. We all were startled. Mouths remained open; hearts thumped, eyes blinked; a dropped tin fork rattled in the dish; a man rose as if to go out, and stood still. In less than a minute Jimmy pulled himself together: "Why? Can't you see I am?" he answered shakily. Singleton lifted a piece of soaked biscuit ("his teeth"—he declared—"had no edge on them now") to his lips. "Well, get on with your dying," he said with venerable mildness; "don't raise a blamed fuss with us over that job. We can't help you." Jimmy fell back in his bunk, and for a long time lay very still wiping the perspiration off his chin. The dinner tins were put away quickly. On deck we discussed the incident in whispers. Some showed a chuckling exultation. Many looked grave. Wamibo, after long periods of staring dreaminess, attempted abortive smiles; and one of the young Scandinavians, much tormented by doubt, ventured in the second dog-watch to approach Singleton (the old man did not encourage us much to speak to him) and ask sheepishly: "You think he will die?" Singleton looked up. "Why, of course he will die," he said deliberately. This seemed decisive. It was promptly imparted to everyone by him who had consulted the oracle. Shy and eager, he would step up and with averted gaze recite his formula: "Old Singleton says he will die." It was a relief! At last we knew that our compassion would not be misplaced, and we could again smile without misgivings—but we reckoned without Donkin. Donkin "didn't want to 'ave no truck with 'em dirty furriners." When Nilsen came to him with the news: "Singleton says he will die," he answered him by a spiteful "And so will you—you fat-headed Dutchman. Wish you Dutchmen were all dead—'stead comin' takin' our money inter your starvin' country." We were appalled. We perceived that after all Singleton's answer meant nothing. We began to hate him for making fun of us. All our certitudes were going; we were on doubtful terms with our officers; the cook had given us up for lost; we had overheard the boatswain's opinion that "we were a crowd of softies." We suspected Jimmy, one another, and even our very selves. We did not know what to do. At every insignificant turn of our humble life we met Jimmy overbearing and blocking the way, arm-in-arm with his awful and veiled familiar. It was a weird servitude.

It began a week after leaving Bombay and came on us stealthily like any other great misfortune. Everyone had remarked that Jimmy from the first was very slack at his work; but we thought it simply the outcome of his philosophy of life. Donkin said: "You put no more weight on a rope than a bloody sparrer." He disdained him. Belfast, ready for a fight, exclaimed provokingly: "You don't kill yourself, old man!"—"Would YOU?" he retorted with extreme scorn—and Belfast retired. One morning, as we were washing decks, Mr. Baker called to him: "Bring your broom over here, Wait." He strolled languidly. "Move yourself! Ough!" grunted Mr. Baker; "what's the matter with your hind legs?" He stopped dead short. He gazed slowly with eyes that bulged out with an expression audacious and sad. "It isn't my legs," he said, "it's my lungs." Everybody listened. "What's . . . Ough! . . . What's wrong with them?" inquired Mr. Baker. All the watch stood around on the wet deck, grinning, and with brooms or buckets in their hands. He said mournfully: "Going—or gone. Can't you see I'm a dying man? I know it!" Mr. Baker was disgusted. "Then why the devil did you ship aboard here?"—"I must live till I die—mustn't I?" he replied. The grins became audible. "Go off the deck—get out of my sight," said Mr. Baker. He was nonplused. It was a unique experience. James Wait, obedient, dropped his broom, and walked slowly forward. A burst of laughter followed him. It was too funny. All hands laughed. . . . They laughed! . . . Alas!

He became the tormentor of all our moments; he was worse than a nightmare. You couldn't see that there was anything wrong with him: a nigger does not show. He was not very fat—certainly—but then he was no leaner than other niggers we had known. He coughed often, but the most prejudiced person could perceive that, mostly, he coughed when it suited his purpose. He wouldn't, or couldn't, do his work—and he wouldn't lie up. One day he would skip aloft with the best of them, and next time we would be obliged to risk our lives to get his limp body down. He was reported, he was examined; he was remonstrated with, threatened, cajoled, lectured. He was called into the cabin to interview the captain. There were wild rumors. It was said he had cheeked the old man; it was said he had frightened him. Charley maintained that [illegible] "skipper, weepin', 'as giv' 'im 'is blessin' an' a pot of jam." Knowles had it from the steward that the unspeakable Jimmy had been reeling against the cabin furniture; that he had groaned; that he had complained of general brutality and disbelief; and had ended by coughing all over the old man's meteorological journals which were then spread on the table. At any rate, Wait returned forward supported by the steward, who, in a pained and shocked voice, entreated us: "Here! Catch hold of him, one of you. He is to lie up." Jimmy drank a tin mugful of coffee, and, after bullying first one and then another, went to bed. He remained there most of the time, but when it suited him would come on deck and appear amongst us. He was scornful and brooding; he looked ahead upon the sea, and no one could tell what was the meaning of that black man sitting apart in a meditative attitude and as motionless as a carving.

He refused steadily all medicine; he threw sago and corn flour overboard till the steward got tired of bringing it to him. He asked for paregoric. They [illegible] [illegible] to poison a wilderness of babies. He kept it between his mattress and the deal lining of the ship's side, and nobody ever saw him take a dose. Donkin abused him to his face, jeered at him while he gasped; and the same day Wait would lend him a warm jersey. Once Donkin reviled him for half an hour; reproached him with the extra work his malingering gave to the watch; and ended by calling him "a black-faced swine." Under the spell of our accursed perversity we were horror-struck. But Jimmy positively seemed to revel in that abuse. It made him look cheerful—and Donkin had a pair of old sea boots thrown at him. "Here, you East-end trash," boomed Wait, "you may have that."

At last Mr. Baker had to tell the captain that James Wait was disturbing the peace of the ship. "Knock discipline on the head—he will, Ough," grunted Mr. Baker. As a matter of fact, the starboard watch came as near as possible to refusing duty, when ordered one morning by the boatswain to wash out their forecastle. It appears Jimmy objected to a wet floor—and that morning we were in a compassionate mood. We thought the boatswain a brute, and practically told him so. Only Mr. Baker's delicate tact prevented an all-fired row: he refused to take us seriously. He came bustling forward, and called us many unpolite names but in such a hearty and seamanlike manner that we began to feel ashamed of ourselves. In truth, we thought him much too good a sailor to annoy him willingly: and after all Jimmy might have been a fraud—probably was! The forecastle got a cleanup that morning; but in the afternoon a sick bay was fitted up in the deckhouse. It was a nice little cabin opening on deck, and with two berths. Jimmy's belongings were transported there, and then—notwithstanding his protests—Jimmy himself. He said he couldn't walk. Four men carried him on a blanket. He complained that he would have to die there alone, like a dog. We grieved for him, and were delighted to have him removed from the forecastle. We attended him as before. The galley was next door, and the cook looked in many times a day. Wait became a little more cheerful. Knowles affirmed having heard him laugh to himself in peals one day. Others had seen him walking about on deck at night. His little place, with the door ajar on a long hook, was always full of tobacco smoke. We spoke through the crack cheerfully, sometimes abusively, as we passed by, intent on our work. He fascinated us. He would never let doubt die. He overshadowed the ship. Invulnerable in his promise of speedy corruption he trampled on our self-respect, he demonstrated to us daily our want of moral courage; he tainted our lives. Had we been a miserable gang of wretched immortals, unhallowed alike by hope and fear, he could not have lorded it over us with a more pitiless assertion of his sublime privilege.

CHAPTER 3

Meantime the *Narcissus*, with square yards, ran out of the fair monsoon. She drifted slowly, swinging round and round the compass, through a few days of baffling light airs. Under the patter of short warm showers, grumbling men whirled the heavy yards from side to side; they caught hold of the soaked ropes with groans and sighs, while their officers, sulky and dripping with rain water, unceasingly ordered them about in wearied voices. During the short respites they looked with disgust into the smarting palms of their stiff hands, and asked one another bitterly: "Who would be a sailor if he could be a farmer?" All the tempers were spoilt, and no man cared what he said. One black night, when the watch, panting in the heat and half-drowned with the rain, had been through four mortal hours hunted from brace to brace, Belfast declared that he would "chuck the sea forever and go in a steamer." This was excessive, no doubt. Captain Allistoun, with great self-control, would mutter sadly to Mr. Baker: "It is not so bad—not so bad," when he had managed to shove, and dodge, and maneuver his smart ship through sixty miles in twenty-four hours. From the doorstep of the little cabin, Jimmy, chin in hand, watched our distasteful labors with insolent and melancholy eyes. We spoke to him gently—and out of his sight exchanged sour smiles.

Then again, with a fair wind and under a clear sky, the ship went on piling up the South Latitude. She passed outside Madagascar and Mauritius without a glimpse of the land. Extra lashings were put on the spare spars. Hatches were looked to. The steward in his leisure moments and with a worried air tried to fit washboards to the cabin doors. Stout canvas was bent with care. Anxious eyes looked to the westward, towards the cape of storms. The ship began to dip into a southwest swell, and the softly luminous sky of low latitudes took on a harder sheen from day to day above our heads: it arched high above the ship vibrating and pale, like an immense dome of steel, resonant with the deep voice of freshening gales. The sunshine gleamed cold on the white curls of black waves. Before the strong breath of westerly squalls the ship, with reduced sail, lay slowly over, obstinate and yielding. She drove to and fro in the unceasing endeavor to fight her way through the invisible violence of the winds: she pitched headlong into dark smooth hollows; she struggled upwards over the snowy ridges of great running seas; she rolled, restless, from side to side, like a thing in pain. Enduring and valiant, she answered to the call of men; and her slim spars, waving forever in abrupt semicircles, seemed to beckon in vain for help towards the stormy sky.

It was a bad winter off the Cape that year. The relieved helmsmen came off flapping their arms, or ran stamping hard and blowing into swollen, red fingers. The watch on deck dodged the sting of cold sprays or, crouching in sheltered corners, watched dismally the high and merciless seas boarding the ship time after time in unappeasable fury. Water tumbled in cataracts over the forecastle doors. You had to dash through a waterfall to get into your damp bed. The men turned in wet and turned out stiff to face the redeeming and ruthless exactions of their glorious and obscure fate. Far aft, and peering watchfully to windward, the officers could be seen through the mist of squalls. They stood by the weather rail, holding on grimly, straight and glistening in their long coats; and in the disordered plunges of the hard-driven ship they appeared high up, attentive, tossing violently above the gray line of a clouded horizon in motionless attitudes.

They watched the weather and the ship as men on shore watch the momentous chances of fortune. Captain Allistoun never left the deck, as though he had been part of the ship's fittings. Now and then the steward, shivering, but always in shirt sleeves, would struggle towards him with some hot coffee, half of which the gale blew out of the cup before it reached the master's lips. He drank what was left gravely in one long gulp, while heavy sprays pattered loudly on his oilskin coat, the seas swishing broke about his high boots; and he never took his eyes off the ship. He kept his gaze riveted upon her as a loving man watches the unselfish toil of a delicate woman upon the slender thread of whose existence is hung the whole meaning and joy of the world. We all watched her. She was beautiful and had a weakness. We loved her no less for that. We admired her qualities aloud, we boasted of them to one another, as though they had been our own, and the consciousness of her only fault we kept buried in the silence of our profound affection. She was born in the thundering peal of hammers beating upon iron, in black eddies of smoke, under a gray sky, on the banks of the Clyde. The clamorous and somber stream gives birth to things of beauty that float away into the sunshine of the world to be loved by men. The *Narcissus* was one of that perfect brood. Less perfect than many perhaps, but she was ours, and, consequently, incomparable. We were proud of her. In Bombay, ignorant landlubbers alluded to her as that "pretty gray ship." Pretty! A scurvy meed of commendation! We knew she was the most magnificent sea boat ever launched. We tried to forget that, like many good sea boats, she was at times rather crank. She was exacting. She wanted care in loading and handling, and no one knew exactly how much care would be enough. Such are the imperfections of mere men! The ship knew, and sometimes would correct the presumptuous human ignorance by the wholesome discipline of fear. We had heard ominous stories about past voyages. The cook (technically a seaman, but in reality no sailor)—the cook, when unstrung by some misfortune, such as the rolling over of a saucepan, would mutter gloomily while he wiped the floor: "There! Look at what she has done! Some voy'ge she will drown all hands! You'll see if she won't." To which the steward, snatching in the galley a moment to draw breath in the hurry of his worried life, would remark philosophically: "Those that see won't tell, anyhow. I don't want to see it." We derided those fears. Our hearts went out to the old man when he pressed her hard so as to make her hold her own, hold to every inch gained to windward; when he made her, under reefed sails, leap obliquely at enormous waves. The men, knitted together aft into a ready group by the first sharp order of an officer coming to take charge of the deck in bad weather: "Keep handy the watch," stood admiring her valiance. Their eyes blinked in the wind; their dark faces were wet with drops of water more salt and bitter than human tears; beards and mustaches, soaked, hung straight and dripping like fine seaweed. They were fantastically misshapen; in high boots, in hats like helmets, and swaying clumsily, stiff and bulky in glistening oilskins, they resembled men strangely equipped for some fabulous adventure. Whenever she rose easily to a towering green sea, elbows dug ribs, faces brightened, lips murmured: "Didn't she do it cleverly," and all the heads turning like one watched with sardonic grins the foiled wave go roaring to leeward, white with the foam of a monstrous rage. But when she had not been quick enough and, struck heavily, lay over trembling under the blow, we clutched at ropes, and, looking up at the narrow bands of drenched and strained sails waving desperately aloft, we thought in our hearts: "No wonder. Poor thing!"

The thirty-second day out of Bombay began inauspiciously. In the morning a sea smashed one of the galley doors. We dashed in through lots of steam and found the cook very wet and indignant with the ship: "She's getting worse every day. She's trying to drown me in front of my own stove!" He was very angry. We pacified him, and the carpenter, though washed away twice from there, managed to repair the door. Through that accident our dinner was not ready till late, but it didn't matter in the end because Knowles, who went to fetch it, got knocked down by a sea and the dinner went over the side. Captain Allistoun, looking more hard and thin-lipped than ever, hung on to full topsails and foresail, and would not notice that the ship, asked to do too much, appeared to lose heart altogether for the first time since we knew her. She refused to rise, and bored her way sullenly through the seas. Twice running, as though she had been blind or weary of life, she put her nose deliberately into a big wave and swept the decks from end to end. As the boatswain observed with marked annoyance, while we were splashing about in a body to try and save a worthless washtub: "Every blooming thing in the ship is going overboard this afternoon." Venerable Singleton broke his habitual silence and said with a glance aloft: "The old man's in a temper with the weather, but it's no good bein' angry with the winds of heaven." Jimmy had shut his door, of course. We knew he was dry and comfortable within his little cabin, and in our absurd way were pleased one moment, exasperated the next, by that certitude. Donkin skulked shamelessly, uneasy and miserable. He grumbled: "I'm perishin' with cold outside in bloomin' wet rags, an' that 'ere black sojer sits dry on a blamed chest full of bloomin' clothes; blank his black soul!" We took no notice of him; we hardly gave a thought to Jimmy and his bosom friend. There was no leisure for idle probing of hearts. Sails blew adrift. Things broke loose. Cold and wet, we were washed about the deck while trying to repair damages. The ship tossed about, shaken furiously, like a toy in the hand of a lunatic. Just at sunset there was a rush to shorten sail before the menace of a somber hail cloud. The hard gust of wind came brutal like the blow of a fist. The ship, relieved of her canvas in time, received it pluckily: she yielded reluctantly to the violent onset; then, coming up with a stately and irresistible motion, brought her spars to windward in the teeth of the screeching squall. Out of the abysmal darkness of the black cloud overhead white hail streamed on her, rattled on the rigging, leaped in handfuls off the yards, rebounded on the deck—round and gleaming in the murky turmoil like a shower of pearls. It passed away. For a moment a livid sun shot horizontally the last rays of sinister light between the hills of steep, rolling waves. Then a wild night rushed in—stamped out in a great howl that dismal remnant of a stormy day.

There was no sleep on board that night. Most seamen remember in their life one or two such nights of a culminating gale. Nothing seems left of the whole universe but darkness, clamor, fury—and the ship. And like the last vestige of a shattered creation she drifts, bearing an anguished remnant of sinful mankind, through the distress, tumult, and pain of an avenging terror. No one slept in the forecastle. The tin oil lamp suspended on a long string, smoking, described wide circles; wet clothing made dark heaps on the glistening floor; a thin layer of water rushed to and fro. In the best places men lay booted, resting on elbows and with open eyes. Hung-up suits of oilskin swung out and in, lively and disquieting like reckless ghosts of decapitated seamen dancing in a tempest. No one spoke and all listened. Outside the night moaned and sobbed to the accompaniment of a continuous loud tremor as of innumerable drums beating far off. Shrieks passed through the air. Tremendous dull blows made the ship tremble while she rolled under the weight of the seas toppling on her deck. At times she soared up swiftly as if to leave this earth forever, then during interminable moments fell through a void with all the hearts on board of her standing still, till a frightful shock, expected and sudden, started them off again with a big thump. After every dislocating jerk of the ship, Wamibo, stretched full length, his face on the pillow, groaned slightly with the pain of his tormented universe. Now and then, for the fraction of an intolerable second, the ship, in the fiercer burst of a terrible uproar, remained on her side, vibrating and still, with a stillness more appalling than the wildest motion. Then upon all those prone bodies a stir would pass, a shiver of suspense. A man would protrude his anxious head and a pair of eyes glistened in the sway of light glaring wildly. Some moved their legs a little as if making ready to jump out. But several, motionless on their backs and with one hand gripping hard the edge of the bunk, smoked nervously with quick puffs, staring upwards; immobilized in a great craving for peace.

At midnight, orders were given to furl the fore and mizzen topsails. With immense efforts men crawled aloft through a merciless buffeting, saved the canvas and crawled down almost exhausted, to bear in panting silence the cruel battering of the seas. Perhaps for the first time in the history of the merchant service the watch, told to go below, did not leave the deck, as if compelled to remain there by the fascination of a venomous violence. At every heavy gust men, huddled together, whispered to one another: "It can blow no harder"—and presently the gale would give them the lie with a piercing shriek, and drive their breath back into their throats. A fierce squall seemed to burst asunder the thick mass of sooty vapors, and above the wrack of torn clouds glimpses could be caught of the high moon rushing backwards with frightful speed over the sky, right into the wind's eye. Many hung their heads, muttering that it "turned their inwards out" to look at it. Soon the clouds closed up and the world again became a raging, blind darkness that howled, flinging at the lonely ship salt sprays and sleet.

About half-past seven the pitchy obscurity round us turned a ghastly gray, and we knew that the sun had risen. This unnatural and threatening daylight, in which we could see one another's wild eyes and drawn faces, was only an added tax on our endurance. The horizon seemed to have come on all sides within arm's length of the ship. Into that narrowed circle furious seas leaped in, struck, and leaped out. A rain of salt, heavy drops flew aslant like mist. The main-topsail had to be goosewinged, and with stolid resignation everyone prepared to go aloft once more; but the officers yelled, pushed back, and at last we understood that no more men would be allowed to go on the yard than were absolutely necessary for the work. As at any moment the masts were likely to be jumped out or blown overboard, we concluded that the captain didn't want to see all his crowd go over the side at once. That was reasonable. The watch then on duty, led by Mr. Creighton, began to struggle up the rigging. The wind flattened them against the ratlines; then, easing a little, would let them ascend a couple of steps; and again, with a sudden gust, pin all up the shrouds the whole crawling line in attitudes of crucifixion. The other watch plunged down on the main deck to haul up the sail. Men's heads bobbed up as the water flung them irresistibly from side to side. Mr. Baker grunted encouragingly in our midst, spluttering and blowing amongst the tangled ropes like an energetic porpoise. Favored by an ominous and untrustworthy lull, the work was done without anyone being lost either off the deck or from the yard. For the moment the gale seemed to take off, and the ship, as if grateful for our efforts, plucked up heart and made better weather of it.

At eight the men off duty, watching their chance, ran forward over the flooded deck to get some rest. The other half of the crew remained aft for their turn of "seeing her through her trouble," as they expressed it. The two mates urged the master to go below. Mr. Baker grunted in his ear: "Ough! surely now . . . Ough! . . . confidence in us . . . nothing more to do . . . she must lay it out or go. Ough! Ough!" Tall young Mr. Creighton smiled down at him cheerfully: ". . . She's as right as a trivet! Take a spell, sir." He looked at them stonily with bloodshot, sleepless eyes. The rims of his eyelids were scarlet, and he moved his jaws unceasingly with a slow effort, as though he had been masticating a lump of India rubber. He shook his head. He repeated: "Never mind me. I must see it out—I must see it out," but he consented to sit down for a moment on the skylight, with his hard face turned unflinchingly to windward. The sea spat at it—and, stoical, it streamed with water as though he had been weeping. On the weather side of the poop the watch, hanging on to the mizzen rigging and to one another, tried to exchange encouraging words. Singleton, at the wheel, yelled out: "Look out for yourselves!" His voice reached them in a warning whisper. They were startled.

A big, foaming sea came out of the mist; it made for the ship, roaring wildly, and in its rush it looked as mischievous and discomposing as a madman with an ax. One or two, shouting, scrambled up the rigging; most, with a convulsive catch of the breath, held on where they stood. Singleton dug his knees under the wheelbox, and carefully eased the helm to the headlong pitch of the ship, but without taking his eyes off the coming wave. It towered close-to and high, like a wall of green glass topped with snow. The ship rose to it as though she had soared on wings, and for a moment rested poised upon the foaming crest as if she had been a great sea bird. Before we could draw breath a heavy gust struck her, another roller took her unfairly under the weather bow, she gave a toppling lurch, and filled her decks. Captain Allistoun leaped up, and fell; Archie rolled over him, screaming: "She will rise!" She gave another lurch to leeward; the lower deadeyes dipped heavily; the men's feet flew from under them, and they hung kicking above the slanting poop. They could see the ship putting her side in the water, and shouted all together: "She's going!" Forward the forecastle doors flew open, and the watch below were seen leaping out one after another, throwing their arms up; and, falling on hands and knees, scrambled aft on all fours along the high side of the deck, sloping more than the roof of a house. From leeward the seas rose, pursuing them; they looked wretched in a hopeless struggle, like vermin fleeing before a flood; they fought up the weather ladder of the poop one after another, half naked and staring wildly; and as soon as they got up they shot to leeward in clusters, with closed eyes, till they brought up heavily with their ribs against the iron stanchions of the rail; then, groaning, they rolled in a confused mass. The immense volume of water thrown forward by the last scend of the ship had burst the lee door of the forecastle. They could see their chests, pillows, blankets, clothing, come out floating upon the sea. While they struggled back to windward they looked in dismay. The straw beds swam high, the blankets, spread out, undulated; while the chests, waterlogged and with a heavy list, pitched heavily like dismasted hulks, before they sank; Archie's big coat passed with outspread arms, resembling a drowned seaman floating with his head under water. Men were slipping down while trying to dig their fingers into the planks; others, jammed in corners, rolled enormous eyes. They all yelled unceasingly: "The masts! Cut! Cut! . . ." A black squall howled low over the ship, that lay on her side with the weather yardarms pointing to the clouds; while the tall masts, inclined nearly to the horizon, seemed to be of an immeasurable length. The carpenter let go his hold, rolled against the skylight, and began to crawl to the cabin entrance, where a big ax was kept ready for just such an emergency. At that moment the topsail sheet parted, the end of the heavy chain racketed aloft, and sparks of red fire streamed down through the flying sprays. The sail flapped once with a jerk that seemed to tear our hearts out through our teeth, and instantly changed into a bunch of fluttering narrow ribbons that tied themselves into knots and became quiet along the yard. Captain Allistoun struggled, managed to stand up with his face near the deck, upon which men swung on the ends of ropes, like nest robbers upon a cliff. One of his feet was on somebody's chest, his face was purple; his lips moved. He yelled also; he yelled, bending down: "No! No!" Mr. Baker, one leg over the binnacle stand, roared out: "Did you say no? Not cut?" He shook his head madly. "No! No!" Between his legs the crawling carpenter heard, collapsed at once, and lay full length in the angle of the skylight. Voices took up the shout—"No! No!" Then all became still. They waited for the ship to turn over altogether, and shake them out into the sea; and upon the terrific noise of wind and sea not a murmur of remonstrance came out from those men, who each would have given ever so many years of life to see "them damned sticks go overboard!" They all believed it their only chance; but a little hard-faced man shook his gray head and shouted "No!" without giving them as much as a glance. They were silent, and gasped. They gripped rails, they had wound rope's ends under their arms; they clutched ringbolts, they crawled in heaps where there was foothold; they held on with both arms, hooked themselves to anything to windward with elbows, with chins, almost with their teeth: and some, unable to crawl away from where they had been flung, felt the sea leap up, striking against their backs as they struggled upwards. Singleton had stuck to the wheel. His hair flew out in the wind; the gale seemed to take its lifelong adversary by the beard and shake his old head. He wouldn't let go, and, with his knees forced between the spokes, flew up and down like a man on a bough. As Death appeared unready, they began to look about. Donkin, caught by one foot in a loop of some rope, hung, head down, below us, and yelled, with his face to the deck: "Cut! Cut!" Two men lowered themselves cautiously to him; others hauled on the rope. They caught him up, shoved him into a safer place, held him. He shouted curses at the master, shook his fist at him with horrible blasphemies, called upon us in filthy words to "Cut! Don't mind that murdering fool! Cut, some of you!" One of his rescuers struck him a backhanded blow over the mouth; his head banged on the deck, and he became suddenly very quiet, with a white face, breathing hard, and with a few drops of blood trickling from his cut lip. On the lee side another man could be seen stretched out as if stunned; only the washboard prevented him from going over the side. It was the steward. We had to sling him up like a bale, for he was paralyzed with fright. He had rushed up out of the pantry when he felt the ship go over, and had rolled down helplessly, clutching a china mug. It was not broken. With difficulty we tore it away from him, and when he saw it in our hands he was amazed. "Where did you get that thing?" he kept on asking us in a trembling voice. His shirt was blown to shreds; the ripped sleeves flapped like wings. Two men made him fast, and, doubled over the rope that held him, he resembled a bundle of wet rags. Mr. Baker crawled along the line of men, asking: "Are you all there?" and looking them over. Some blinked vacantly, others shook convulsively; Wamibo's head hung over his breast; and in painful attitudes, cut by lashings, exhausted with clutching, screwed up in corners, they breathed heavily. Their lips twitched, and at every sickening heave of the overturned ship they opened them wide as if to shout. The cook, embracing a wooden stanchion, unconsciously repeated a prayer. In every short interval of the fiendish noises around he could be heard there, without cap or slippers, imploring in that storm the Master of our lives not to lead him into temptation. Soon he also became silent. In all that crowd of cold and hungry men, waiting wearily for a violent death, not a voice was heard; they were mute, and in somber thoughtfulness listened to the horrible imprecations of the gale.

Hours passed. They were sheltered by the heavy inclination of the ship from the wind that rushed in one long unbroken moan above their heads, but cold rain showers fell at times into the uneasy calm of their refuge. Under the torment of that new infliction a pair of shoulders would writhe a little. Teeth chattered. The sky was clearing, and bright sunshine gleamed over the ship. After every burst of battering seas, vivid and fleeting rainbows arched over the drifting hull in the flick of sprays. The gale was ending in a clear blow, which gleamed and cut like a knife. Between two bearded shellbacks Charley, fastened with somebody's long muffler to a deck ringbolt, wept quietly, with rare tears wrung out by bewilderment, cold, hunger, and general misery. One of his neighbors punched him in the ribs asking roughly: "What's the matter with your cheek? In fine weather there's no holding you, youngster." Turning about with prudence he worked himself out of his coat and threw it over the boy. The other man closed up, muttering: "'Twill make a bloomin' man of you, sonny." They flung their arms over and pressed against him. Charley drew his feet up and his eyelids dropped. Sighs were heard, as men, perceiving that they were not to be "drowned in a hurry," tried easier positions. Mr. Creighton, who had hurt his leg, lay amongst us with compressed lips. Some fellows belonging to his watch set about securing him better. Without a word or a glance he lifted his arms one after another to facilitate the operation, and not a muscle moved in his stern, young face. They asked him with solicitude: "Easier now, sir?" He answered with a curt: "That'll do." He was a hard young officer, but many of his watch used to say they liked him well enough because he had "such a gentlemanly way of damning us up and down the deck." Others, unable to discern such fine shades of refinement, respected him for his smartness. For the first time since the ship had gone down on her beam-ends Captain Allistoun gave a short glance down at his men. He was almost upright—one foot against the side of the skylight, one knee on the deck; and with the end of the vang round his waist swung back and forth with his gaze fixed ahead, watchful, like a man looking out for a sign. Before his eyes the ship, with half her deck below water, rose and fell on heavy seas that rushed from under her flashing in the cold sunshine. We began to think she was wonderfully buoyant—considering. Confident voices were heard shouting: "She'll do, boys!" Belfast exclaimed with fervor: "I would give a month's pay for a draw at a pipe!" One or two, passing dry tongues on their salt lips, muttered something about a "drink of water." The cook, as if inspired, scrambled up with his breast against the poop water cask and looked in. There was a little at the bottom. He yelled, waving his arms, and two men began to crawl backwards and forwards with the mug. We had a good mouthful all round. The master shook his head impatiently, refusing. When it came to Charley one of his neighbors shouted: "That bloomin' boy's asleep." He slept as though he had been dosed with narcotics. They let him be. Singleton held to the wheel with one hand while he drank, bending down to shelter his lips from the wind. Wamibo had to be poked and yelled at before he saw the mug held before his eyes. Knowles said sagaciously: "It's better'n a tot o' rum." Mr. Baker grunted: "Thank ye." Mr. Creighton drank and nodded. Donkin gulped greedily, glaring over the rim. Belfast made us laugh when with grimacing mouth he shouted: "Pass it this way. We're all taytottlers here." The master, presented with the mug again by a crouching man, who screamed up at him: "We all had a drink, captain," groped for it without ceasing to look ahead, and handed it back stiffly as though he could not spare half a glance away from the ship. Faces brightened. We shouted to the cook: "Well done, doctor!" He sat to leeward, propped by the water cask and yelled back abundantly, but the seas were breaking in thunder just then, and we only caught snatches that sounded like: "Providence" and "born again." He was at his old game of preaching. We made friendly but derisive gestures at him, and from below he lifted one arm, holding on with the other, moved his lips; he beamed up to us, straining his voice—earnest, and ducking his head before the sprays.

Suddenly someone cried: "Where's Jimmy?" and we were appalled once more. On the end of the row the boatswain shouted hoarsely: "Has any one seed him come out?" Voices exclaimed dismally: "Drowned—is he? . . . No! In his cabin! . . . Good Lord! . . . Caught like a bloomin' rat in a trap. . . . Couldn't open his door. . . . Aye! She went over too quick and the water jammed it. . . . Poor beggar! . . . No help for 'im. . . . Let's go and see. . . ." "Damn him, who could go?" screamed Donkin.—"Nobody expects you to," growled the man next to him: "you're only a thing."—"Is there half a chance to get at 'im?" inquired two or three men together. Belfast untied himself with blind impetuosity, and all at once shot down to leeward quicker than a flash of lightning. We shouted all together with dismay; but with his legs overboard he held and yelled for a rope. In our extremity nothing could be terrible; so we judged him funny kicking there, and with his scared face. Someone began to laugh, and, as if hysterically infected with the screaming merriment, all those haggard men went off laughing, wild-eyed, like a lot of maniacs tied up on a wall. Mr. Baker swung off the binnacle stand and tendered him one leg. He scrambled up rather scared, and consigning us with abominable words to the "divvle." "You are. . . . Ough! You're a foul-mouthed beggar, Craik," grunted Mr. Baker. He answered, stuttering with indignation: "Look at 'em, sorr. The bloomin' dirty images! laughing at a chum going overboard. Call themselves men, too." But from the break of the poop the boatswain called out: "Come along," and Belfast crawled away in a hurry to join him. The five men, poised and gazing over the edge of the poop, looked for the best way to get forward. They seemed to hesitate. The others, twisting in their lashings, turned painfully, stared with open lips. Captain Allistoun saw nothing; he seemed with his eyes to hold the ship up in a superhuman concentration of effort. The wind screamed loud in sunshine; columns of spray rose straight up; and in the glitter of rainbows bursting over the trembling hull the men went over cautiously, disappearing from sight with deliberate movements.

They went swinging from belaying pin to cleat above the seas that beat the half-submerged deck. Their toes scraped the planks. Lumps of green cold water toppled over the bulwark and on their heads. They hung for a moment on strained arms, with the breath knocked out of them, and with closed eyes—then, letting go with one hand, balanced with lolling heads, trying to grab some rope or stanchion further forward. The long-armed and athletic boatswain swung quickly, gripping things with a fist hard as iron, and remembering suddenly snatches of the last letter from his "old woman." Little Belfast scrambled in a rage spluttering "cursed nigger." Wamibo's tongue hung out with excitement; and Archie, intrepid and calm, watched his chance to move with intelligent coolness.

When above the side of the house, they let go one after another, and, falling heavily, sprawled, pressing their palms to the smooth teakwood. Round them the backwash of waves seethed white and hissing. All the doors had become trap doors, of course. The first was the galley door. The galley extended from side to side, and they could hear the sea splashing with hollow noises in there. The next door was that of the carpenter's shop. They lifted it, and looked down. The room seemed to have been devastated by an earthquake. Everything in it had tumbled on the bulkhead facing the door, and on the other side of that bulkhead there was Jimmy dead or alive. The bench, a half-finished meat safe, saws, chisels, wire rods, axes, crowbars, lay in a heap besprinkled with loose nails. A sharp adz stuck up with a shining edge that gleamed dangerously down there like a wicked smile. The men clung to one another, peering. A sickening, sly lurch of the ship nearly sent them overboard in a body. Belfast howled "Here goes!" and leaped down. Archie followed cannily, catching at shelves that gave way with him, and eased himself in a great crash of ripped wood. There was hardly room for three men to move. And in the sunshiny blue square of the door, the boatswain's face bearded and dark, Wamibo's face, wild and pale, hung over —watching.

Together they shouted: "Jimmy! Jim!" From above the boatswain contributed a deep growl: "You . . . Wait!" In a pause, Belfast entreated: "Jimmy, darlin', are ye aloive?" The boatswain said: "Again! All together, boys!" All yelled excitedly. Wamibo made noises resembling loud barks. Belfast drummed on the side of the bulkhead with a piece of iron. All ceased suddenly. The sound of screaming and hammering went on thin and distinct—like a solo after a chorus. He was alive. He was screaming and knocking below us with the hurry of a man prematurely shut up in a coffin. We went to work. We attacked with desperation the abominable heap of things heavy, of things sharp, of things clumsy to handle. The boatswain crawled away to find somewhere a flying end of a rope; and Wamibo, held back by shouts: "Don't jump! . . . Don't come in here, muddle-head!"—remained glaring above us—all shining eyes, gleaming fangs, tumbled hair; resembling an amazed and half-witted fiend gloating over the extraordinary agitation of the damned. The boatswain adjured us to "bear a hand," and a rope descended. We made things fast to it and they went up spinning, never to be seen by man again. A rage to fling things overboard possessed us. We worked fiercely, cutting our hands and speaking brutally to one another. Jimmy kept up a distracting row; he screamed piercingly, without drawing breath, like a tortured woman; he banged with hands and feet. The agony of his fear wrung our hearts so terribly that we longed to abandon him, to get out of that place deep as a well and swaying like a tree, to get out of his hearing, back on the poop where we could wait passively for death in incomparable repose. We shouted to him to "shut up, for God's sake." He redoubled his cries. He must have fancied we could not hear him. Probably he heard his own clamor but faintly. We could picture him crouching on the edge of the upper berth, letting out with both fists at the wood, in the dark, and with his mouth wide open for that unceasing cry. Those were loathsome moments. A cloud driving across the sun would darken the doorway menacingly. Every movement of the ship was pain. We scrambled about with no room to breathe, and felt frightfully sick. The boatswain yelled down at us: "Bear a hand! Bear a hand! We two will be washed away from here directly if you ain't quick!" Three times a sea leaped over the high side and flung bucketfuls of water on our heads. Then Jimmy, startled by the shock, would stop his noise for a moment—waiting for the ship to sink, perhaps—and began again, distressingly loud, as if invigorated by the gust of fear. At the bottom the nails lay in a layer several inches thick. It was ghastly. Every nail in the world, not driven in firmly somewhere, seemed to have found its way into that carpenter's shop. There they were, of all kinds, the remnants of stores from seven voyages. Tin tacks, copper tacks (sharp as needles); pump nails with big heads, like tiny iron mushrooms; nails without any heads (horrible); French nails polished and slim. They lay in a solid mass more inabordable than a hedgehog. We hesitated, yearning for a shovel, while Jimmy below us yelled as though he had been flayed. Groaning, we dug our fingers in, and, very much hurt, shook our hands, scattering nails and drops of blood. We passed up our hats full of assorted nails to the boatswain, who, as if performing a mysterious and appeasing rite, cast them wide upon a raging sea.

We got to the bulkhead at last. Those were stout planks. She was a ship well-finished in every detail—the *Narcissus* was. They were the stoutest planks ever put into a ship's bulkhead—we thought—and then we perceived that, in our hurry, we had sent all the tools overboard. Absurd little Belfast wanted to break it down with his own weight, and with both feet leaped straight up like a springbok, cursing the Clyde shipwrights for not scamping their work. Incidentally he reviled all North Britain, the rest of the earth, the sea—and all his companions. He swore, as he alighted heavily on his heels, that he would never, never any more associate with any fool that "hadn't savvy enough to know his knee from his elbow." He managed by his thumping to scare the last remnant of wits out of Jimmy. We could hear the object of our exasperated solicitude darting to and fro under the planks. He had cracked his voice at last, and could only squeak miserably. His back or else his head rubbed the planks, now here, now there, in a puzzling manner. He squeaked as he dodged the invisible blows. It was more heartrending even than his yells. Suddenly Archie produced a crowbar. He had kept it back; also a small hatchet. We howled with satisfaction. He struck a mighty blow and small chips flew at our eyes. The boatswain above shouted: "Look out! Look out there. Don't kill the man. Easy does it!" Wamibo, maddened with excitement, hung head down and insanely urged us: "Hoo! Strook 'im! Hoo! Hoo!" We were afraid he would fall in and kill one of us and, hurriedly, we entreated the boatswain to "shove the blamed Finn overboard." Then, all together, we yelled down at the planks: "Stand from under! Get forward," and listened. We only heard the deep hum and moan of the wind above us, the mingled roar and hiss of the seas. The ship, as if overcome with despair, wallowed lifelessly, and our heads swam with that unnatural motion. Belfast clamored: "For the love of God, Jimmy, where are ye? . . . Knock! Jimmy darlint! . . . Knock! You bloody black beast! Knock!" He was as quiet as a dead man inside a grave; and, like men standing above a grave, we were on the verge of tears—but with vexation, the strain, the fatigue; with the great longing to be done with it, to get away, and lie down to rest somewhere where we could see our danger and breathe. Archie shouted: "Gi'e me room!" We crouched behind him, guarding our heads, and he struck time after time in the joint of planks. They cracked. Suddenly the crowbar went halfway in through a splintered oblong hole. It must have missed Jimmy's head by less than an inch. Archie withdrew it quickly, and that infamous nigger rushed at the hole, put his lips to it, and whispered "Help" in an almost extinct voice; he pressed his head to it, trying madly to get out through that opening one inch wide and three inches long. In our disturbed state we were absolutely paralyzed by his incredible action. It seemed impossible to drive him away. Even Archie at last lost his composure. "If ye don't clear oot I'll drive the crowbar thro' your head," he shouted in a determined voice. He meant what he said, and his earnestness seemed to make an impression on Jimmy. He disappeared suddenly, and we set to prising and tearing at the planks with the eagerness of men trying to get at a mortal enemy, and spurred by the desire to tear him limb from limb. The wood split, cracked, gave way. Belfast plunged in head and shoulders and groped viciously. "I've got 'im! Got 'im," he shouted. "Oh! There! . . . He's gone; I've got 'im! . . . Pull at my legs! . . . Pull!" Wamibo hooted unceasingly. The boatswain shouted directions: "Catch hold of his hair, Belfast; pull straight up, you two! . . . Pull fair!" We pulled fair. We pulled Belfast out with a jerk, and dropped him with disgust. In a sitting posture, purple-faced, he sobbed despairingly: "How can I hold on to 'is blooming short wool?" Suddenly Jimmy's head and shoulders appeared. He stuck halfway, and with rolling eyes foamed at our feet. We flew at him with brutal impatience, we tore the shirt off his back, we tugged at his ears, we panted over him; and all at once he came away in our hands as though somebody had let go his legs. With the same movement, without a pause, we swung him up. His breath whistled, he kicked our upturned faces, he grasped two pairs of arms above his head, and he squirmed up with such precipitation that he seemed positively to escape from our hands like a bladder full of gas. Streaming with perspiration, we swarmed up the rope, and, coming into the blast of cold wind, gasped like men plunged into icy water. With burning faces we shivered to the very marrow of our bones. Never before had the gale seemed to us more furious, the sea more mad, the sunshine more merciless and mocking, and the position of the ship more hopeless and appalling. Every movement of her was ominous of the end of her agony and of the beginning of ours. We staggered away from the door, and, alarmed by a sudden roll, fell down in a bunch. It appeared to us that the side of the house was more smooth than glass and more slippery than ice. There was nothing to hang on to but a long brass hook used sometimes to keep back an open door. Wamibo held on to it and we held on to Wamibo, clutching our Jimmy. He had completely collapsed now. He did not seem to have the strength to close his hand. We stuck to him blindly in our fear. We were not afraid of Wamibo letting go (we remembered that the brute was stronger than any three men in the ship), but we were afraid of the hook giving way, and we also believed that the ship had made up her mind to turn over at last. But she didn't. A sea swept over us. The boatswain spluttered: "Up and away. There's a lull. Away aft with you, or we will all go to the devil here." We stood up surrounding Jimmy. We begged him to hold up, to hold on, at least. He glared with his bulging eyes, mute as a fish, and with all the stiffening knocked out of him. He wouldn't stand; he wouldn't even as much as clutch at our necks; he was only a cold black skin loosely stuffed with soft cotton wool; his arms and legs swung jointless and pliable; his head rolled about; the lower lip hung down, enormous and heavy. We pressed round him, bothered and dismayed; sheltering him we swung here and there in a body; and on the very brink of eternity we tottered all together with concealing and absurd gestures, like a lot of drunken men embarrassed with a stolen corpse.

Something had to be done. We had to get him aft. A rope was tied slack under his armpits, and, reaching up at the risk of our lives, we hung him on the foresheet cleat. He emitted no sound; he looked as ridiculously lamentable as a doll that had lost half its sawdust, and we started on our perilous journey over the main deck, dragging along with care that pitiful, that limp, that hateful burden. He was not very heavy, but had he weighed a ton he could not have been more awkward to handle. We literally passed him from hand to hand. Now and then we had to hang him up on a handy belaying pin, to draw a breath and re-form the line. Had the pin broken he would have irretrievably gone into the Southern Ocean, but he had to take his chance of that; and after a little while, becoming apparently aware of it, he groaned slightly, and with a great effort whispered a few words. We listened eagerly. He was reproaching us with our carelessness in letting him run such risks: "Now, after I got myself out from there," he breathed out weakly. "There" was his cabin. And he got himself out. We had nothing to do with it apparently! . . . No matter. . . . We went on and let him take his chances, simply because we could not help it; for though at that time we hated him more than ever—more than anything under heaven—we did not want to lose him. We had so far saved him; and it had become a personal matter between us and the sea. We meant to stick to him. Had we (by an incredible hypothesis) undergone similar toil and trouble for an empty cask, that cask would have become as precious to us as Jimmy was. More precious, in fact, because we would have had no reason to hate the cask. And we hated James Wait. We could not get rid of the monstrous suspicion that this astounding black man was shamming sick, had been malingering heartlessly in the face of our toil, of our scorn, of our patience—and now was malingering in the face of our devotion—in the face of death. Our vague and imperfect morality rose with disgust at his unmanly lie. But he stuck to it manfully—amazingly. No! It couldn't be. He was at all extremity. His cantankerous temper was only the result of the provoking invincibleness of that death he felt by his side. Any man may be angry with such a masterful chum. But, then, what kind of men were we—with our thoughts! Indignation and doubt grappled within us in a scuffle that trampled upon the finest of our feelings. And we hated him because of the suspicion; we detested him because of the doubt. We could not scorn him safely—neither could we pity him without risk to our dignity. So we hated him, and passed him carefully from hand to hand. We cried, "Got him?"—"Yes. All right. Let go." And he swung from one enemy to another, showing about as much life as an old bolster would do. His eyes made two narrow white slits in the black face. The air escaped through his lips with a noise like the sound of bellows. We reached the poop ladder at last, and, it being a comparatively safe place, we lay for a moment in an exhausted heap to rest a little. He began to mutter. We were always incurably anxious to hear what he had to say. This time he mumbled peevishly, "It took you some time to come. I began to think the whole smart lot of you had been washed overboard. What kept you back? Hey? Funk?" We said nothing. With sighs we started again to drag him up. The secret and ardent desire of our hearts was the desire to beat him viciously with our fists about the head; and we handled him as tenderly as though he had been made of glass. . . .

The return on the poop was like the return of wanderers after many years amongst people marked by the desolation of time. Eyes were turned slowly in their sockets, glancing at us. Faint murmurs were heard, "Have you got 'im after all?" The well-known faces looked strange and familiar; they seemed faded and grimy; they had a mingled expression of fatigue and eagerness. They seemed to have become much thinner during our absence, as if all these men had been starving for a long time in their abandoned attitudes. The captain, with a round turn of a rope on his wrist, and kneeling on one knee, swung with a face cold and stiff; but with living eyes he was still holding the ship up, heeding no one, as if lost in the unearthly effort of that endeavor. We fastened up James Wait in a safe place. Mr. Baker scrambled along to lend a hand. Mr. Creighton, on his back, and very pale, muttered, "Well done," and gave us, Jimmy and the sky, a scornful glance, then closed his eyes slowly. Here and there a man stirred a little, but most of them remained apathetic, in cramped positions, muttering between shivers. The sun was setting. A sun enormous, unclouded and red, declining low as if bending down to look into their faces. The wind whistled across long sunbeams that, resplendent and cold, struck full on the dilated pupils of staring eyes without making them wink. The wisps of hair and the tangled beards were gray with the salt of the sea. The faces were earthy, and the dark patches under the eyes extended to the ears, smudged into the hollows of sunken cheeks. The lips were livid and thin, and when they moved it was with difficulty, as though they had been glued to the teeth. Some grinned sadly in the sunlight, shaking with cold. Others were sad and still. Charley, subdued by the sudden disclosure of the insignificance of his youth, darted fearful glances. The two smooth-faced Norwegians resembled decrepit children, staring stupidly. To leeward, on the edge of the horizon, black seas leaped up towards the glowing sun. It sank slowly, round and blazing, and the crests of waves splashed on the edge of the luminous circle. One of the Norwegians appeared to catch sight of it, and, after giving a violent start, began to speak. His voice, startling the others, made them stir. They moved their heads stiffly, or turning with difficulty, looked at him with surprise, with fear, or in grave silence. He chattered at the setting sun, nodding his head, while the big seas began to roll across the crimson disk; and over miles of turbulent waters the shadows of high waves swept with a running darkness the faces of men. A crested roller broke with a loud hissing roar, and the sun, as if put out, disappeared. The chattering voice faltered, went out together with the light. There were sighs. In the sudden lull that follows the crash of a broken sea a man said wearily, "Here's that blooming Dutchman gone off his chump." A seaman, lashed by the middle, tapped the deck with his open hand with unceasing quick flaps. In the gathering grayness of twilight a bulky form was seen rising aft, and began marching on all fours with the movements of some big cautious beast. It was Mr. Baker passing along the line of men. He grunted encouragingly over every one, felt their fastenings. Some, with half-open eyes, puffed like men oppressed by heat; others mechanically and in dreamy voices answered him, "Aye! aye! sir!" He went from one to another grunting, "Ough! . . . See her through it yet," and unexpectedly, with loud angry outbursts, blew up Knowles for cutting off a long piece from the fall of the relieving tackle. "Ough! . . . Ashamed of yourself . . . Relieving tackle . . . Don't you know better . . . Ough! . . . Able seaman! Ough!" The lame man was crushed. He muttered, "Get som'think for a lashing for myself, sir."—"Ough! Lashing . . . yourself. Are you a tinker or a sailor . . . What? Ough! . . . May want that tackle directly . . . Ough! . . . More use to the ship than your lame carcass. Ough! . . . Keep it! . . . Keep it, now you've done it." He crawled away slowly, muttering to himself about some men being "worse than children." It had been a comforting row. Low exclamations were heard: "Hallo . . . Hallo." . . . Those who had been painfully dozing asked with convulsive starts: "What's up? . . . What is it?" The answers came with unexpected cheerfulness: "The mate is going bald-headed for lame Jack about something or other."—"No!" . . . "What 'as he done?" Someone even chuckled. It was like a whiff of hope, like a reminder of safe days. Donkin, who had been stupefied with fear, revived suddenly and began to shout:

" 'Ear 'im; that's the way they tawlk to us. Vy donch 'ee 'it 'im—one ov yer? 'It 'im. 'It 'im! Comin' the mate over us. We are as good men as 'ee! We're all goin' to 'ell now. We 'ave been starved in this rotten ship, an now we're goin' to be drowned for them black-'earted bullies! 'It 'im!" He shrieked in the deepening gloom, he blubbered and sobbed, screaming: " 'It im! 'It 'im!" The rage and fear of his disregarded right to live tried the steadfastness of hearts more than the menacing shadows of the night that advanced through the unceasing clamor of the gale. From aft Mr. Baker was heard: "Is one of you men going to stop him—must I come along?" "Shut up!" . . . "Keep quiet!" cried various voices, exasperated, trembling with cold. "You'll get one across the mug from me directly," said an invisible seaman, in a weary tone. "I won't let the mate have the trouble." He ceased and lay still with the silence of despair. On the black sky the stars, coming out, gleamed over an inky sea that, speckled with foam, flashed back at them the evanescent and pale light of a dazzling whiteness born from the black turmoil of the waves. Remote in the eternal calm they glittered hard and cold above the uproar of the earth; they surrounded the vanquished and tormented ship on all sides: more pitiless than the eyes of a triumphant mob, and as unapproachable as the hearts of men.

The icy south wind howled exultingly under the somber splendor of the sky. The cold shook the men with a resistless violence as though it had tried to shake them to pieces. Short moans were swept unheard off the stiff lips. Some complained in mutters of "not feeling themselves below the waist," while those who had closed their eyes imagined they had a block of ice on their chests. Others, alarmed at not feeling any pain in their fingers, beat the deck feebly with their hands—obstinate and exhausted. Wamibo stared vacant and dreamy. The Scandinavians kept on a meaningless mutter through chattering teeth. The spare Scotchmen, with determined efforts, kept their lower jaws still. The west-countrymen lay big and stolid in an invulnerable surliness. A man yawned and swore in turns. Another breathed with a rattle in his throat. Two elderly hard-weather shellbacks, fast side by side, whispered dismally to one another about the landlady of a boardinghouse in Sunderland, whom they both knew. They extolled her motherliness and her liberality; they tried to talk about the joint of beef and the big fire in the downstairs kitchen. The words, dying faintly on their lips, ended in light sighs. A sudden voice cried into the cold night, "O Lord!" No one changed his position or took any notice of the cry. One or two passed, with a repeated and vague gesture, their hand over their faces, but most of them kept very still. In the benumbed immobility of their bodies they were excessively wearied by their thoughts, which rushed with the rapidity and vividness of dreams. Now and then, by an abrupt and startling exclamation, they answered the weird hail of some illusion; then, again, in silence contemplated the vision of known faces and familiar things. They recalled the aspect of forgotten shipmates and heard the voice of dead and gone skippers. They remembered the noise of gaslit streets, the steamy heat of taprooms or the scorching sunshine of calm days at sea.

Mr. Baker left his insecure place and crawled, with stoppages, along the poop. In the dark and on all fours he resembled some carnivorous animal prowling amongst corpses. At the break, propped to windward of a stanchion, he looked down on the main deck. It seemed to him that the ship had a tendency to stand up a little more. The wind had eased a little, he thought, but the sea ran as high as ever. The waves foamed viciously, and the lee side of the deck disappeared under a hissing whiteness as of boiling milk, while the rigging sang steadily with a deep vibrating note, and, at every upward swing of the ship, the wind rushed with a long-drawn clamor amongst the spars. Mr. Baker watched very still. A man near him began to make a blabbing noise with his lips, all at once and very loud, as though the cold had broken brutally through him. He went on: "Ba—ba—ba—brrr—brr—ba—ba."—"Stop that!" cried Mr. Baker, groping in the dark. "Stop it!" He went on shaking the leg he found under his hand. "What is it, sir?" called out Belfast, in the tone of a man awakened suddenly; "we are looking after that 'ere Jimmy."—"Are you? Ough! Don't make that row then. Who's that near you?"—"It's me —the boatswain, sir," growled the west-countryman; "we are trying to keep life in that poor devil."—"Aye, aye!" said Mr. Baker. "Do it quietly, can't you?"—"He wants us to hold him up above the rail," went on the boatswain, with irritation, "says he can't breathe here under our jackets."— "If we lift 'im, we drop 'im overboard," said another voice, "we can't feel our hands with cold."—"I don't care. I am choking!" exclaimed James Wait in a clear tone.—"Oh, no, my son," said the boatswain, desperately, "you don't go till we all go on this fine night."—"You will see yet many a worse," said Mr. Baker, cheerfully.—"It's no child's play, sir!" answered the boatswain. "Some of us further aft, here, are in a pretty bad way."—"If the blamed sticks had been cut out of her she would be running along on her bottom now like any decent ship, an' giv' us all a chance," said someone, with a sigh.—"The old man wouldn't have it . . . much he cares for us," whispered another.—"Care for you!" exclaimed Mr. Baker, angrily. "Why should he care for you? Are you a lot of women passengers to be taken care of? We are here to take care of the ship—and some of you ain't up to that. Ough! . . . What have you done so very smart to be taken care of? Ough! . . . Some of you can't stand a bit of a breeze without crying over it."— "Come, sorr. We ain't so bad," protested Belfast, in a voice shaken by shivers; "we ain't . . . brr . . ."—"Again," shouted the mate, grabbing at the shadowy form; "again! . . . Why, you're in your shirt! What have you done?"— "I've put my oilskin and jacket over that half-dead naygurr —and he says he chokes," said Belfast, complainingly.— "You wouldn't call me nigger if I wasn't half dead, you Irish beggar!" boomed James Wait, vigorously.—"You . . . brrr . . . You wouldn't be white if you were ever so well . . . I will fight you . . . brrr . . . in fine weather . . . brrr

. . . with one hand tied behind my back . . . brrrrr . . ."—"I don't want your rags—I want air," gasped out the other faintly, as if suddenly exhausted.

The sprays swept over whistling and pattering. Men disturbed in their peaceful torpor by the pain of quarrelsome shouts, moaned, muttering curses. Mr. Baker crawled off a little way to leeward where a water cask loomed up big, with something white against it. "Is it you, Podmore?" asked Mr. Baker. He had to repeat the question twice before the cook turned, coughing feebly. "Yes, sir. I've been praying in my mind for a quick deliverance; for I am prepared for any call. . . . I——"—"Look here, cook," interrupted Mr. Baker, "the men are perishing with cold."—"Cold!" said the cook, mournfully; "they will be warm enough before long."—"What?" asked Mr. Baker, looking along the deck into the faint sheen of frothing water.—"They are a wicked lot," continued the cook solemnly, but in an unsteady voice, "about as wicked as any ship's company in this sinful world! Now, I"—he trembled so that he could hardly speak; his was an exposed place, and, in a cotton shirt, a thin pair of trousers, and with his knees under his nose, he received, quaking, the flicks of stinging, salt drops; his voice sounded exhausted—"now, I—any time . . . My eldest youngster, Mr. Baker . . . a clever boy . . . last Sunday on shore before this voyage he wouldn't go to church, sir. Says I, 'You go and clean yourself, or I'll know the reason why!' What does he do? . . . Pond, Mr. Baker—fell into the pond in his best rig, sir! . . . Accident? . . . 'Nothing will save you, fine scholar though you are!' says I. . . . Accident! . . . I whopped him, sir, till I couldn't lift my arm. . . ." His voice faltered. "I whopped 'im!" he repeated, rattling his teeth; then, after a while, let out a mournful sound that was half a groan, half a snore. Mr. Baker shook him by the shoulders. "Hey! Cook! Hold up, Podmore! Tell me—is there any fresh water in the galley tank? The ship is lying along less, I think; I would try to get forward. A little water would do them good. Hallo! Look out! Look out!" The cook struggled. "Not you, sir—not you!" He began to scramble to windward. "Galley! . . . my business!" he shouted.—"Cook's going crazy now," said several voices. He yelled: "Crazy, am I? I am more ready to die than any of you, officers incloosive—there! As long as she swims I will cook! I will get you coffee."—"Cook, ye are a gentleman!" cried Belfast. But the cook was already going over the weather ladder. He stopped for a moment to shout back on the poop: "As long as she swims I will cook!" and disappeared as though he had gone overboard. The men who had heard sent after him a cheer that sounded like a wail of sick children. An hour or more afterwards some one said distinctly: "He's gone for good."—"Very likely," assented the boatswain; "even in fine weather he was as smart about the deck as a milch cow on her first voyage. We ought to go and see." Nobody moved. As the hours dragged slowly through the darkness Mr. Baker crawled back and forth along the poop several times. Some men fancied they had heard him exchange murmurs with the master, but at that time the memories were incomparably more vivid than anything actual, and they were not certain whether the murmurs were heard now or many years ago. They did not try to find out. A mutter more or less did not matter. It was too cold for curiosity, and almost for hope. They could not spare a moment or a thought from the great mental occupation of wishing to live. And the desire of life kept them alive, apathetic and enduring, under the cruel persistence of wind and cold; while the bestarred black dome of the sky revolved slowly above the ship, that drifted, bearing their patience and their suffering, through the stormy solitude of the sea.

Huddled close to one another, they fancied themselves utterly alone. They heard sustained loud noises, and again bore the pain of existence through long hours of profound silence. In the night they saw sunshine, felt warmth, and suddenly, with a start, thought that the sun would never rise upon a freezing world. Some heard laughter, listened to songs; others, near the end of the poop, could hear loud human shrieks, and, opening their eyes, were surprised to hear them still, though very faint, and far away. The boatswain said: "Why, it's the cook, hailing from forward, I think." He hardly believed his own words or recognized his own voice. It was a long time before the man next to him gave a sign of life. He punched hard his other neighbor and said: "The cook's shouting!" Many did not understand, others did not care; the majority further aft did not believe. But the boatswain and another man had the pluck to crawl away forward to see. They seemed to have been gone for hours, and were very soon forgotten. Then suddenly men who had been plunged in a hopeless resignation became as if possessed with a desire to hurt. They belabored one another with fists. In the darkness they struck persistently anything soft they could feel near, and, with a greater effort than for a shout, whispered excitedly: "They've got some hot coffee. . . . Boss'en got it. . . ." "No! . . . Where?" . . . "It's coming! Cook made it." James Wait moaned. Donkin scrambled viciously, caring not where he kicked, and anxious that the officers should have none of it. It came in a pot, and they drank in turns. It was hot, and while it blistered the greedy palates, it seemed incredible. The men sighed out, parting with the mug: "How 'as he done it?" Some cried weakly: "Bully for you, doctor!"

He had done it somehow. Afterwards Archie declared that the thing was "meeraculous." For many days we wondered and it was the one ever-interesting subject of conversation to the end of the voyage. We asked the cook, in fine weather, how he felt when he saw his stove "reared up on end." We inquired, in the northeast trade and on serene evenings, whether he had to stand on his head to put things right somewhat. We suggested he had used his breadboard for a raft, and from there comfortably had stoked his grate; and we did our best to conceal our admiration under the wit of fine irony. He affirmed not to know anything about it, rebuked our levity, declared himself, with solemn animation, to have been the object of a special mercy for the saving of our unholy lives. Fundamentally he was right, no doubt; but he need not have been so offensively positive about it—

he need not have hinted so often that it would have gone hard with us had he not been there, meritorious and pure, to receive the inspiration and the strength for the work of grace. Had we been saved by his recklessness or his agility, we could have at length become reconciled to the fact; but to admit our obligation to anybody's virtue and holiness alone was as difficult for us as for any other handful of mankind. Like many benefactors of humanity, the cook took himself too seriously, and reaped the reward of irreverence. We were not ungrateful, however. He remained heroic. His saying—*the* saying of his life—becamc proverbial in the mouth of men as are the sayings of conquerors or sages. Later, whenever one of us was puzzled by a task and advised to relinquish it, he would express his determination to persevere and to succeed by the words: "As long as she swims I will cook!"

The hot drink helped us through the bleak hours that precede the dawn. The sky low by the horizon took on the delicate tints of pink and yellow like the inside of a rare shell. And higher, where it glowed with a pearly sheen, a small black cloud appeared, like a forgotten fragment of the night set in a border of dazzling gold. The beams of light skipped on the crests of waves. The eyes of men turned to the eastward. The sunlight flooded their weary faces. They were giving themselves up to fatigue as though they had done forever with their work. On Singleton's black oilskin coat the dried salt glistened like hoarfrost. He hung on by the wheel, with open and lifeless eyes. Captain Allistoun, unblinking, faced the rising sun. His lips stirred, opened for the first time in twenty-four hours, and with a fresh firm voice he cried, "Wear ship!"

The commanding sharp tones made all these torpid men start like a sudden flick of a whip. Then again, motionless where they lay, the force of habit made some of them repeat the order in hardly audible murmurs. Captain Allistoun glanced down at his crew, and several, with fumbling fingers and hopeless movements, tried to cast themselves adrift. He repeated impatiently, "Wear ship. Now then, Mr. Baker, get the men along. What's the matter with them?"—"Wear ship. Do you hear there?—Wear ship!" thundered out the boatswain suddenly. His voice seemed to break through a deadly spell. Men began to stir and crawl. "I want the foretopmast staysail run up smartly," said the master, very loudly; "if you can't manage it standing up you must do it lying down—that's all. Bear a hand!"—"Come along! Let's give the old girl a chance," urged the boatswain.—"Aye, aye! Wear ship!" exclaimed quavering voices. The forecastle men, with reluctant faces, prepared to go forward. Mr. Baker pushed ahead, grunting, on all fours to show the way, and they followed him over the break. The others lay still with a vile hope in their hearts of not being required to move till they got saved or drowned in peace.

After some time they could be seen forward appearing on the forecastle head, one by one in unsafe attitudes; hanging on to the rails, clambering over the anchors; embracing the crosshead of the windlass or hugging the forecapstan. They were restless with strange exertions, waved their arms, knelt, lay flat down, staggered up, seemed to strive their hardest to go overboard. Suddenly a small white piece of canvas fluttered amongst them, grew larger, beating. Its narrow head rose in jerks—and at last it stood distended and triangular in the sunshine. "They have done it!" cried the voices aft. Captain Allistoun let go the rope he had round his wrist and rolled to leeward headlong. He could be seen casting the lee main braces off the pins while the backwash of waves splashed over him. "Square the main yard!" he shouted up to us—who stared at him in wonder. We hesitated to stir. "The main brace, men. Haul! haul anyhow! Lay on your backs and haul!" he screeched, half-drowned down there. We did not believe we could move the main yard, but the strongest and the less discouraged tried to execute the order. Others assisted half-heartedly. Singleton's eyes blazed suddenly as he took a fresh grip of the spokes. Captain Allistoun fought his way up to windward. "Haul, men! Try to move it! Haul, and help the ship." His hard face worked suffused and furious. "Is she going off,

Singleton?" he cried.—"Not a move yet, sir," croaked the old seaman in a horribly hoarse voice.—"Watch the helm, Singleton," spluttered the master. "Haul, men! Have you no more strength than rats? Haul, and earn your salt." Mr. Creighton, on his back, with a swollen leg and a face as white as a piece of paper, blinked his eyes; his bluish lips twitched. In the wild scramble men grabbed at him, crawled over his hurt leg, knelt on his chest. He kept perfectly still, setting his teeth without a moan, without a sigh. The master's ardor, the cries of that silent man, inspired us. We hauled and hung in bunches on the rope. We heard him say with violence to Donkin, who sprawled abjectly on his stomach, "I will brain you with this belaying pin if you don't catch hold of the brace," and that victim of men's injustice, cowardly and cheeky, whimpered: "Are you goin' to murder us now?" while with sudden desperation he gripped the rope. Men sighed, shouted, hissed meaningless words, groaned. The yards moved, came slowly square against the wind, that hummed loudly on the yardarms.—"Going off, sir," shouted Singleton, "she's just started."—"Catch a turn with that brace. Catch a turn!" clamored the master. Mr. Creighton, nearly suffocated and unable to move, made a mighty effort, and with his left hand managed to nip the rope. "All fast!" cried someone. He closed his eyes as if going off into a swoon, while huddled together about the brace we watched with scared looks what the ship would do now.

She went off slowly as though she had been weary and disheartened like the men she carried. She paid off very gradually, making us hold our breath till we choked, and as soon as she had brought the wind abaft the beam she started to move, and fluttered our hearts. It was awful to see her, nearly overturned, begin to gather way and drag her submerged side through the water. The deadeyes of the rigging churned the breaking seas. The lower half of the deck was full of mad whirlpools and eddies; and the long line of the lee rail could be seen showing black now and then in the swirls of a field of foam as dazzling and white as a field of snow. The wind sang shrilly amongst the spars; and at every slight lurch we expected her to slip to the bottom sideways from under our backs. When dead before it she made the first distinct attempt to stand up, and we encouraged her with a feeble and discordant howl. A great sea came running up aft and hung for a moment over us with a curling top; then crashed down under the counter and spread out on both sides into a great sheet of bursting froth. Above its fierce hiss we heard Singleton's croak: "She is steering!" He had both his feet now planted firmly on the grating, and the wheel spun fast as he eased the helm. "Bring the wind on the port quarter and steady her!" called out the master, staggering to his feet, the first man up from amongst our prostrate heap. One or two screamed with excitement: "She rises!" Far away forward, Mr. Baker and three others were seen erect and black on the clear sky, lifting their arms, and with open mouths as though they had been shouting all together. The ship trembled, trying to lift her side, lurched back, seemed to give up with a nerveless dip, and suddenly with an unexpected jerk swung violently to windward, as though she had torn herself out from a deadly grasp. The whole immense volume of water, lifted by her deck, was thrown bodily across to starboard. Loud cracks were heard. Iron ports breaking open thundered with ringing blows. The water topped over the starboard rail with the rush of a river falling over a dam. The sea on deck, and the seas on every side of her, mingled together in a deafening roar. She rolled violently. We got up and were helplessly run or flung about from side to side. Men, rolling over and over, yelled, "The house will go!"—"She clears herself!" Lifted by a towering sea she ran along with it for a moment, spouting thick streams of water through every opening of her wounded sides. The lee braces having been carried away or washed off the pins, all the ponderous yards on the fore swung from side to side and with appalling rapidity at every roll. The men forward were seen crouching here and there with fearful glances upwards at the enormous spars that whirled about over their heads. The torn canvas and the end of broken gear streamed in the wind like wisps of hair. Through the clear sunshine, over the flashing turmoil and uproar of the seas, the ship ran blindly, disheveled and headlong, as if fleeing for her life; and on the poop we spun, we tottered about, distracted and noisy. We all spoke at once in a thin babble; we had the aspect of invalids and the gestures of maniacs. Eyes shone, large and haggard, in smiling, meager faces that seemed to have been dusted over with powdered chalk. We stamped, clapped our hands, feeling ready to jump and do anything; but in reality hardly able to keep on our feet. Captain Allistoun, hard and slim, gesticulated madly from the poop at Mr. Baker: "Steady these foreyards! Steady them the best you can!" On the main deck, men excited by his cries splashed, dashing aimlessly here and there with the foam swirling up to their waists. Apart, far aft, and alone by the helm, old Singleton had deliberately tucked his white beard under the top button of his glistening coat. Swaying upon the din and tumult of the seas, with the whole battered length of the ship launched forward in a rolling rush before his steady old eyes, he stood rigidly still, forgotten by all, and with an attentive face. In front of his erect figure only the two arms moved crosswise with a swift and sudden readiness, to check or urge again the rapid stir of circling spokes. He steered with care.

CHAPTER 4

On men reprieved by its disdainful mercy, the immortal sea confers in its justice the full privilege of desired unrest. Through the perfect wisdom of its grace they are not permitted to meditate at ease upon the complicated and acrid savor of existence. They must without pause justify their life to the eternal pity that commands toil to be hard and unceasing, from sunrise to sunset, from sunset to sunrise; till the weary succession of nights and days tainted by the obstinate clamor of sages, demanding bliss and an empty heaven, is redeemed at last by the vast silence of pain and labor, by the dumb fear and the dumb courage of men obscure, forgetful, and enduring.

The master and Mr. Baker coming face to face stared for a moment, with the intense and amazed looks of men meeting unexpectedly after years of trouble. Their voices were gone, and they whispered desperately at one another. "Any one missing?" asked Captain Allistoun.—"No. All there." —"Anybody hurt?"—"Only the second mate."—"I will look after him directly. We're lucky."—"Very," articulated Mr. Baker, faintly. He gripped the rail and rolled bloodshot eyes. The little gray man made an effort to raise his voice above a dull mutter, and fixed his chief mate with a cold gaze, piercing like a dart. "Get sail on the ship," he said, speaking authoritatively and with an inflexible snap of his thin lips. "Get sail on her as soon as you can. This is a fair wind. At once, sir—don't give the men time to feel themselves. They will get done up and stiff, and we will never . . . We must get her along now"—he reeled to a long heavy roll; the rail dipped into the glancing, hissing water. He caught a shroud, swung helplessly against the mate—"now we have a fair wind at last. . . . Make . . . sail." His head rolled from shoulder to shoulder. His eyelids began to beat rapidly. "And the pumps . . . pumps, Mr. Baker." He peered as though the face within a foot of his eyes had been half a mile off. "Keep the men on the move to . . . to get her along," he mumbled in a drowsy tone, like a man going off into a doze. He pulled himself together suddenly. "Mustn't stand. Won't do," he said with a painful attempt at a smile. He let go his hold, and, propelled by the dip of the ship, ran aft unwillingly, with small steps, till he brought up against the binnacle stand. Hanging on there he looked up in an aimless manner at Singleton, who, unheeding him, watched anxiously the end of the jib boom. "Steering gear works all right?" he asked. There was a noise in the old seaman's throat, as though the words had been rattling together before they could come out. "Steers . . . like a little boat," he said, at last, with hoarse tenderness, without giving the master as much as half a glance—then, watchfully, spun the wheel down, steadied, flung it back again. Captain Allistoun tore himself away from the delight of leaning against the binnacle, and began to walk the poop, swaying and reeling to preserve his balance. . . .

The pump rods, clanking, stamped in short jumps while the flywheels turned smoothly, with great speed, at the foot of the mainmast, flinging back and forth with a regular impetuosity two limp clusters of men clinging to the handles. They abandoned themselves, swaying from the hip with twitching faces and stony eyes. The carpenter, sounding from time to time, exclaimed mechanically: "Shake her up! Keep her going!" Mr. Baker could not speak, but found his voice to shout; and, under the goad of his objurgations, men looked to the lashings, dragged out new sails; and, thinking themselves unable to move, carried heavy blocks aloft—overhauled the gear. They went up the rigging with faltering and desperate efforts. Their heads swam as they shifted their hold, stepped blindly on the yards like men in the dark; or trusted themselves to the first rope at hand with the negligence of exhausted strength. The narrow escapes from falls did not disturb the languid beat of their hearts; the roar of the seas seething far below them sounded continuous and faint like an indistinct noise from another world: the wind filled their eyes with tears, and with heavy gusts tried to push them off from where they swayed in insecure positions. With streaming faces and blowing hair they flew up and down between sky and water, bestriding the ends of yardarms, crouching on footropes, embracing lifts to have their hands free, or standing up against chain ties. Their thoughts floated vaguely between the desire of rest and the desire of life, while their stiffened fingers cast off head earings, fumbled for knives, or held with tenacious grip against the violent shocks of beating canvas. They glared savagely at one another, made frantic signs with one hand while they held their life in the other, looked down on the narrow strip of flooded deck, shouted along to leeward: "Light-to!" . . . "Haul out!" . . . "Make fast!" Their lips moved, their eyes started, furious and eager with the desire to be understood, but the wind tossed their words unheard upon the disturbed sea. In an unendurable and unending strain they worked like men driven by a merciless dream to toil in an atmosphere of ice or flame. They burnt and shivered in turns. Their eyeballs smarted as if in the smoke of a conflagration; their heads were ready to burst with every shout. Hard fingers seemed to grip their throats. At every roll they thought: Now I must let go. It will shake us all off—and thrown about aloft they cried wildly: "Look out there—catch the end." . . . "Reeve clear." . . . "Turn this block. . . ." They nodded desperately; shook infuriated faces, "No! No! From down up." They seemed to hate one another with a deadly hate. The longing to be done with it all gnawed their breasts, and the wish to do things well was a burning pain. They cursed their fate, contemned their life, and wasted their breath in deadly imprecations upon one another. The sailmaker, with his bald head bared, worked feverishly, forgetting his intimacy with so many admirals. The boatswain, climbing up with marlinspikes and bunches of spun-yarn rovings, or kneeling on the yard and ready to take a turn with the midship stop, had acute and fleeting visions of his old woman and the youngsters in a moorland village. Mr. Baker, feeling very weak, tottered here and there, grunting and inflexible, like a man of iron. He waylaid those who, coming from aloft, stood gasping for breath. He ordered, encouraged, scolded. "Now then—to the main topsail now! Tally on to that gantline. Don't stand about there!"—"Is there no rest for us?" muttered voices. He spun round fiercely, with a sinking heart. "No! No rest till the work is done. Work till you drop. That's what you're here for." A bowed seaman at his elbow gave a short laugh. "Do or die," he croaked bitterly, then spat into his broad palms, swung up his long arms, and grasping the rope high above his head sent out a mournful, wailing cry for a pull all together. A sea boarded the quarter-deck and sent the whole lot sprawling to leeward. Caps, handspikes floated. Clenched hands, kicking legs, with here and there a spluttering face, stuck out of the white hiss of foaming water. Mr. Baker, knocked down with the rest, screamed: "Don't let go that rope! Hold on to it! Hold!" And sorely bruised by the brutal fling, they held on to it as though it had been the fortune of their life. The ship ran, rolling heavily, and the topping crests glanced past port and starboard flashing their white heads. Pumps were freed. Braces were rove. The three topsails and foresail were set. She spurted faster over the water, outpacing the swift rush of waves. The menacing thunder of distanced seas rose behind her—filled the air with the tremendous vibrations of its voice. And devastated, battered, and wounded she drove foaming to the northward, as though inspired by the courage of a high endeavor. . . .

The forecastle was a place of damp desolation. They looked at their dwelling with dismay. It was slimy, dripping; it hummed hollow with the wind, and was strewn with shapeless wreckage like a half-tide cavern in a rocky and exposed coast. Many had lost all they had in the world, but most of the starboard watch had preserved their chests; thin streams of water trickled out of them, however. The beds were soaked; the blankets spread out and saved by some nail squashed under foot. They dragged wet rags from evil-smelling corners, and, wringing the water out, recognized their property. Some smiled stiffly. Others looked round blank and mute. There were cries of joy over old waistcoats, and groans of sorrow over shapeless things found among the splinters of smashed bed boards. One lamp was discovered jammed under the bowsprit. Charley whimpered a little. Knowles stumped here and there, sniffing, examining dark places for salvage. He poured dirty water out of a boot, and was concerned to find the owner. Those who, overwhelmed by their losses, sat on the forepeak hatch, remained elbows on knees, and, with a fist against each cheek, disdained to look up. He pushed it under their noses. "Here's a good boot. Yours?" They snarled, "No—get out." One snapped at him, "Take it to hell out of this." He seemed surprised. "Why? It's a good boot," but remembering suddenly that he had lost every stitch of his clothing, he dropped his find and began to swear. In the dim light cursing voices clashed. A man came in and, dropping his arms, stood still, repeating from the doorstep, "Here's a bloomin' old go! Here's a bloomin' old go!" A few rooted anxiously in flooded chests for tobacco. They breathed hard, clamored with heads down. "Look at that Jack!" . . . "Here! Sam! Here's my shoregoing rig spoilt forever." One blasphemed tearfully, holding up a pair of dripping trousers. No one looked at him. The cat came out from somewhere. He had an ovation. They snatched him from hand to hand, caressed him in a murmur of pet names. They wondered where he had "weathered it out," disputed about it. A squabbling argument began. Two men brought in a bucket of fresh water and all crowded round it; but Tom, lean and mewing, came up with every hair astir and had the first drink. A couple of hands went aft for oil and biscuits.

Then in the yellow light and in the intervals of mopping the deck they crunched hard bread, arranging to "worry through somehow." Men chummed as to beds. Turns were settled for wearing boots and having the use of oilskin coats. They called one another "old man" and "sonny" in cheery voices. Friendly slaps resounded. Jokes were shouted. One or two stretched on the wet deck, slept with heads pillowed on their bent arms, and several, sitting on the hatch, smoked. Their weary faces appeared through a thin blue haze, pacified and with sparkling eyes. The boatswain put his head through the door. "Relieve the wheel, one of you"—he shouted inside—"it's six. Blamme if that old Singleton hasn't been there more'n thirty hours. You are a fine lot." He slammed the door again. "Mate's watch on deck," said someone. "Hey, Donkin, it's your relief!" shouted three or four together. He had crawled into an empty bunk and on wet planks lay still. "Donkin, your wheel." He made no sound. "Donkin's dead," guffawed someone. "Sell 'is bloomin' clothes," shouted another. "Donkin, if ye don't go to the bloomin' wheel they will sell your clothes—d'ye hear?" jeered a third. He groaned from his dark hole. He complained about pains in all his bones, he whimpered pitifully. "He won't go," exclaimed a contemptuous voice, "your turn, Davis." The young seaman rose painfully, squaring his shoulders. Donkin stuck his head out, and it appeared in the yellow light, fragile and ghastly. "I will give yer a pound of terbaccer," he whined in a conciliating voice, "so soon as I draw it from aft. I will —s'elp me . . ." Davis swung his arm backhanded and the head vanished. "I'll go," he said, "but you will pay for it." He walked unsteady but resolute to the door. "So I will," yelped Donkin, popping out behind him. "So I will—s'elp me . . . a pound . . . three bob they chawrge." Davis flung the door open. "You will pay my price . . . in fine weather," he shouted over his shoulder. One of the men unbuttoned his wet coat rapidly, threw it at his head. "Here, Taffy—take that, you thief!" "Thank you!" he cried from the darkness above the swish of rolling water. He could be heard splashing; a sea came on board with a thump. "He's got his bath already," remarked a grim shellback. "Aye, aye!" grunted others. Then, after a long silence, Wamibo made strange noises. "Hallo, what's up with you?" said someone grumpily. "He says he would have gone for Davy," explained Archie, who was the Finn's interpreter generally. "I believe him!" cried voices. . . . "Never mind, Dutchy. . . . You'll do, muddlehead. . . . Your turn will come soon enough. . . . You don't know when ye're well off." They ceased, and all together turned their faces to the door. Singleton stepped in, advanced two paces, and stood swaying slightly. The sea hissed, flowed roaring past the bows, and the forecastle trembled, full of deep murmurs; the lamp flared, swinging like a pendulum. He looked with a dreamy and puzzled stare, as though he could not distinguish the still men from their restless shadows. There were awestruck exclamations: "Hallo, hallo." . . . "How does it look outside now, Singleton?" Those who sat on the hatch lifted their eyes in silence, and the next oldest seaman in the ship (those two understood one another, though they hardly exchanged three words in a day) gazed up at his friend attentively for a moment, then taking a short clay pipe out of his mouth offered it without a word. Singleton put out his arm towards it, missed, staggered, and suddenly fell forward, crashing down, stiff and headlong like an uprooted tree. There was a swift rush. Men pushed, crying: "He's done!" . . . "Turn him over!" . . . "Stand clear there!" Under a crowd of startled faces bending over him he lay on his back, staring upwards in a continuous and intolerable manner. In the breathless silence of a general consternation, he said in a grating murmur: "I am all right," and clutched with his hands. They helped him up. He mumbled despondently: "I am getting old . . . old."—"Not you," cried Belfast, with ready tact. Supported on all sides, he hung his head.—"Are you better?" they asked. He glared at them from under his eyebrows with large black eyes, spreading over his chest the bushy whiteness of a beard long and thick. "Old! old!" he repeated sternly. Helped along, he reached his bunk. There was in it a slimy soft heap of something that smelt, as does at dead low water a muddy foreshore. It was his soaked straw bed. With a convulsive effort he pitched himself on it, and in the darkness of the narrow place could be heard growling angrily, like an irritated and savage animal uneasy in its den: "Bit of breeze . . . small thing . . . can't stand up . . . old!" He slept at last, high-booted, sou'wester on head, and his oilskin clothes rustled when with a deep sighing groan he turned over. Men conversed about him in quiet, concerned whispers. "This will break 'im up" . . . "Strong as a horse" . . . "Aye. But he ain't what he used to be." . . . In sad murmurs they gave him up. Yet at midnight he turned out to duty as if nothing had been the matter, and answered to his name with a mournful "Here!" He brooded alone more than ever, in an impenetrable silence and with a saddened face. For many years he had heard himself called "Old Singleton," and had serenely accepted the qualification, taking it as a tribute of respect due to a man who through half a century had measured his strength against the favors and the rages of the sea. He had never given a thought to his mortal self. He lived unscathed, as though he had been indestructible, surrendering to all the temptations, weathering many gales. He had panted in sunshine, shivered in the cold; suffered hunger, thirst, debauch; passed through many trials—known all the furies. Old! It seemed to him he was broken at last. And like a man bound treacherously while he sleeps, he woke up fettered by the long chain of disregarded years. He had to take up at once the burden of all his existence, and found it almost too heavy for his strength. Old! He moved his arms, shook his head, felt his limbs. Getting old . . . and then? He looked upon the immortal sea with the awakened and groping perception of its heartless might; he saw it unchanged, black and foaming under the eternal scrutiny of the stars; he heard its impatient voice calling for him out of a pitiless vastness full of unrest, of turmoil, and of terror. He looked afar upon it, and he saw an immensity tormented and blind, moaning and furious, that claimed all the days of his tenacious life, and, when life was over, would claim the worn-out body of its slave. . . .

This was the last of the breeze. It veered quickly, changed to a black southeaster, and blew itself out, giving the ship a famous shove to the northward into the joyous sunshine of the trade. Rapid and white she ran homewards in a straight path, under a blue sky and upon the plain of a blue sea. She carried Singleton's completed wisdom, Donkin's delicate susceptibilities, and the conceited folly of us all. The hours of ineffective turmoil were forgotten; the fear and anguish of these dark moments were never mentioned in the glowing peace of fine days. Yet from that time our life seemed to start afresh as though we had died and had been resuscitated. All the first part of the voyage, the Indian Ocean on the other side of the Cape, all that was lost in a haze, like an ineradicable suspicion of some previous existence. It had ended—then there were blank hours: a livid blur—and again we lived! Singleton was possessed of sinister truth; Mr. Creighton of a damaged leg; the cook of fame—and shamefully abused the opportunities of his distinction. Donkin had an added grievance. He went about repeating with insistence: " 'E said 'e would brain me—did yer 'ear? They are goin' to murder us now for the least little thing." We began at last to think it was rather awful. And we were conceited! We boasted of our pluck, of our capacity for work, of our energy. We remembered honorable episodes: our devotion, our indomitable perseverance—and were proud of them as though they had been the outcome of our unaided impulses. We remembered our danger, our toil—and conveniently forgot our horrible scare. We decried our officers—who had done nothing—and listened to the fascinating Donkin. His care for our rights, his disinterested concern for our dignity, were not discouraged by the invariable contumely of our words, by the disdain of our looks. Our contempt for him was unbounded—and we could not but listen with interest to that consummate artist. He told us we were good men—a "bloomin' condemned lot of good men." Who thanked us? Who took any notice of our wrongs? Didn't we lead a "dorg's loife for two pun' ten a month?" Did we think that miserable pay enough to compensate us for the risk to our lives and for the loss of our clothes? "We've lost every rag!" he cried. He made us forget that he, at any rate, had lost nothing of his own. The younger men listened, thinking: this 'ere Donkin's a long-headed chap, though no kind of man, anyhow. The Scandinavians were frightened at his audacities; Wamibo did not understand; and the older seamen thoughtfully nodded their heads, making the thin gold earrings glitter in the fleshy lobes of hairy ears. Severe, sunburnt faces were propped meditatively on tattooed forearms. Veined, brown fists held in their knotted grip the dirty white clay of smoldering pipes. They listened, impenetrable, broad-backed, with bent shoulders, and in grim silence. He talked with ardor, despised and irrefutable. His picturesque and filthy loquacity flowed like a troubled stream from a poisoned source. His beady little eyes danced, glancing right and left, ever on the watch for the approach of an officer. Sometimes Mr. Baker going forward to take a look at the head sheets would roll with his uncouth gait through the sudden stillness of the men; or Mr. Creighton limped along, smooth-faced, youthful, and more stern than ever, piercing our short silence with a keen glance of his clear eyes. Behind his back Donkin would begin again darting stealthy, sidelong looks. " 'Ere's one of 'em. Some of yer 'as made 'im fast that day. Much thanks yer got for it. Ain't 'ee a-drivin' yer wusse'n ever? . . . Let 'im slip overboard. . . . Vy not? It would 'ave been less trouble. Vy not?" He advanced confidentially, backed away with great effect; he whispered, he screamed, waved his miserable arms no thicker than pipestems—stretched his lean neck—spluttered—squinted. In the pauses of his impassioned orations the wind sighed quietly aloft, the calm sea unheeded murmured in a warning whisper along the ship's side. We abominated the creature and could not deny the luminous truth of his contentions. It was all so obvious. We were indubitably good men; our deserts were great and our pay small. Through our exertions we had saved the ship and the skipper would get the credit of it. What had he done? we wanted to know. Donkin asked: "What 'ee could do without hus?" and we could not answer. We were oppressed by the injustice of the world, surprised to perceive how long we had lived under its burden without realizing our unfortunate state, annoyed by the uneasy suspicion of our undiscerning stupidity. Donkin assured us it was all our "good-'eartedness," but we would not be consoled by such shallow sophistry. We were men enough to courageously admit to ourselves our intellectual shortcomings; though from that time we refrained from kicking him, tweaking his nose, or from accidentally knocking him about, which last, after we had weathered the Cape, had been rather a popular amusement. Davis ceased to talk at him provokingly about black eyes and flattened noses. Charley, much subdued since the gale, did not jeer at him. Knowles deferentially and with a crafty air propounded questions such as: "Could we all have the same grub as the mates? Could we all stop ashore till we got it? What would be the next thing to try for if we got that?" He answered readily with contemptuous certitude; he strutted with assurance in clothes that were much too big for him as though he had tried to disguise himself. These were Jimmy's clothes mostly—though he would accept anything from anybody; but nobody, except Jimmy, had anything to spare. His devotion to Jimmy was unbounded. He was forever dodging in the little cabin, ministering to Jimmy's wants, humoring his whims, submitting to his exacting peevishness, often laughing with him. Nothing could keep him away from the pious work of visiting the sick, especially when there was some heavy hauling to be done on deck. Mr. Baker had on two occasions jerked him out from there by the scruff of the neck to our inexpressible scandal. Was a sick chap to be left without attendance? Were we to be ill-used for attending a shipmate? "What?" growled Mr. Baker, turning menacingly at the mutter, and the whole half-circle like one man stepped back a pace. "Set the topmast stunsail. Away aloft, Donkin, overhaul the gear," ordered the mate inflexibly. "Fetch the sail along; bend the downhaul clear. Bear a hand." Then, the sail set, he would go slowly aft and stand looking at the compass for a long time, careworn, pensive, and breathing hard as if stifled by the taint of unaccountable ill-will that pervaded the ship. "What's up amongst them?" he thought. "Can't make out this hanging back and growling. A good crowd, too, as they go nowadays." On deck the men exchanged bitter words, suggested by a silly exasperation against something unjust and irremediable that would not be denied, and would whisper into their ears long after Donkin had ceased speaking. Our little world went on its curved and unswerving path carrying a discontented and aspiring population. They found comfort of a gloomy kind in an interminable and conscientious analysis of their unappreciated worth; and inspired by Donkin's hopeful doctrines they dreamed enthusiastically of the time when every lonely ship would travel over a serene sea, manned by a wealthy and well-fed crew of satisfied skippers.

It looked as if it would be a long passage. The southeast trades, light and unsteady, were left behind; and then, on the equator and under a low gray sky, the ship, in close heat, floated upon a smooth sea that resembled a sheet of ground glass. Thunder squalls hung on the horizon, circled round the ship, far off and growling angrily, like a troop of wild beasts afraid to charge home. The invisible sun, sweeping above the upright masts, made on the clouds a blurred stain of rayless light, and a similar patch of faded radiance kept pace with it from east to west over the unglittering level of the waters. At night, through the impenetrable darkness of earth and heaven, broad sheets of flame waved noiselessly; and for half a second the becalmed craft stood out with its masts and rigging, with every sail and every rope distinct and black in the center of a fiery outburst, like a charred ship enclosed in a globe of fire. And, again, for long hours she remained lost in a vast universe of night and silence where gentle sighs, wandering here and there like forlorn souls, made the still sails flutter as in sudden fear, and the ripple of a beshrouded ocean whisper its compassion afar—in a voice mournful, immense, and faint. . . .

When the lamp was put out, and, through the door thrown wide open, Jimmy, turning on his pillow, could see vanishing beyond the straight line of topgallant rail, the quick, repeated visions of a fabulous world made up of leaping fire and sleeping water, the lightning gleamed in his big sad eyes that seemed in a red flicker to burn themselves out in his black face, and then he would lie blinded and invisible in the midst of an intense darkness. He could hear on the quiet deck soft footfalls, the breathing of some man lounging on the doorstep; the low creak of swaying masts; or the calm voice of the watch officer reverberating aloft, hard and loud, amongst the unstirring sails. He listened with avidity, taking a rest in the attentive perception of the slightest sound from the fatiguing wanderings of his sleeplessness. He was cheered by the rattling of blocks, reassured by the stir and murmur of the watch, soothed by the slow yawn of some sleepy and weary seaman settling himself deliberately for a snooze on the planks. Life seemed an indestructible thing. It went on in darkness, in sunshine, in sleep; tireless, it hovered affectionately round the imposture of his ready death. It was bright, like the twisted flare of lightning, and more full of surprises than the dark night. It made him safe, and the calm of its overpowering darkness was as precious as its restless and dangerous light.

But in the evening, in the dogwatches, and even far into the first night watch, a knot of men could always be seen congregated before Jimmy's cabin. They leaned on each side of the door peacefully interested and with crossed legs; they stood astride the doorstep discoursing, or sat in silent couples on his sea chest; while against the bulwark, along the spare topmast, three or four in a row stared meditatively, with their simple faces lit up by the projected glare of Jimmy's lamp. The little place, repainted white, had, in the night, the brilliance of a silver shrine where a black idol, reclining stiffly under a blanket, blinked its weary eyes and received our homage. Donkin officiated. He had the air of a demonstrator showing a phenomenon, a manifestation bizarre, simple, and meritorious that, to the beholders, should be a profound and an everlasting lesson. "Just look at 'im, 'ee knows what's what—never fear!" he exclaimed now and then, flourishing a hand hard and fleshless like the claw of a snipe. Jimmy, on his back, smiled with reserve and without moving a limb. He affected the languor of extreme weakness, so as to make it manifest to us that our delay in hauling him out from his horrible confinement, and then that night spent on the poop among our selfish neglect of his needs, had "done for him." He rather liked to talk about it, and of course we were always interested. He spoke spasmodically, in fast rushes with long pauses between, as a tipsy man walks. . . . "Cook had just given me a pannikin of hot coffee. . . . Slapped it down there, on my chest—banged the door to. . . . I felt a heavy roll coming; tried to save my coffee, burnt my fingers . . . and fell out of my bunk. . . . She went over so quick . . . Water came in through the ventilator. . . . I couldn't move the door . . . dark as a grave . . . tried to scramble up into the upper berth. . . . Rats . . . a rat bit my finger as I got up. . . . I could hear him swimming below me. . . . I thought you would never come. . . . I thought you were all gone overboard . . . of course. . . . Could hear nothing but the wind. . . . Then you came . . . to look for the corpse, I suppose. A little more and . . ."

"Man! But ye made a rare lot of noise in here," observed Archie, thoughtfully.

"You chaps kicked up such a confounded row above. . . . Enough to scare anyone. . . . I didn't know what you were up to. . . . Bash in the blamed planks . . . my head. . . . Just what a silly, scary gang of fools would do. . . . Not much good to me anyhow. . . . Just as well . . . drown. . . . Pah."

He groaned, snapped his big white teeth, and gazed with scorn. Belfast lifted a pair of dolorous eyes, with a broken-hearted smile, clenched his fists stealthily; blue-eyed Archie caressed his red whiskers with a hesitating hand; the boatswain at the door stared a moment and brusquely went away with a loud guffaw. Wamibo dreamed. . . . Donkin felt all over his sterile chin for the few rare hairs and said, triumphantly, with a sidelong glance at Jimmy: "Look at 'im! Wish I was 'arf has 'ealthy as 'ee is—I do." He jerked a short thumb over his shoulder towards the after end of the ship. "That's the blooming way to do 'em!" he yelped, with forced heartiness. Jimmy said: "Don't be a dam' fool," in a pleasant voice. Knowles, rubbing his shoulder against the doorpost, remarked shrewdly: "We can't all go an' be took sick—it would be mutiny." "Mutiny—gawn!" jeered Donkin, "there's no bloomin' law against bein' sick." "There's six weeks' hard for refoosing dooty," argued

Knowles. "I mind I once seed in Cardiff the crew of an overloaded ship—leastways she weren't overloaded, only a fatherly old gentleman with a white beard and an umbreller came along the quay and talked to the hands. Said as how it was crool hard to be drownded in winter just for the sake of a few pounds more for the owner—he said. Nearly cried over them—he did; and he had a square mainsail coat, and a gaff-topsail hat too—all proper. So they chaps they said they wouldn't go to be drownded in winter—depending upon that 'ere Plimsoll man to see 'em through the court. They thought to have a bloomin' lark and two or three days' spree. And the beak give 'em six weeks—coss the ship warn't overloaded. Anyways they made it out in court that she wasn't. There wasn't one overloaded ship in Penarth Dock at all. 'Pears that old coon he was only on pay and allowance from some kind people, under orders to look for overloaded ships, and he couldn't see no further than the length of his umbreller. Some of us in the boardinghouse where I live when I'm looking for a ship in Cardiff stood by to duck that old weeping spunger in the dock. We kept a good lookout, too—but he topped his boom directly he was outside the court. , . . Yes. They got six weeks' hard. . . ."

They listened, full of curiosity, nodding in the pauses their rough pensive faces. Donkin opened his mouth once or twice, but restrained himself. Jimmy lay still with open eyes and not at all interested. A seaman emitted the opinion that after a verdict of atrocious partiality "the bloomin' beaks go an' drink at the skipper's expense." Others assented. It was clear, of course. Donkin said: "Well, six weeks ain't much trouble. You sleep all night in, reg'lar, in chokey. Do it on my 'ead." "You are used to it ainch'ee, Donkin?" asked somebody. Jimmy condescended to laugh. It cheered up everyone wonderfully. Knowles, with surprising mental agility, shifted his ground. "If we all went sick what would become of the ship? eh?" He posed the problem and grinned all round. "Let 'er go to 'ell;" sneered Donkin. "Damn 'er. She ain't yourn." "What? Just let her drift?" insisted Knowles in a tone of unbelief. "Aye! Drift, an' be blowed," affirmed Donkin with fine recklessness. The other did not see it—meditated. "The stores would run out," he muttered, "and . . . never get anywhere . . . and what about payday?" he added with greater assurance. "Jack likes a good payday," exclaimed a listener on the doorstep. "Aye, because then the girls put one arm round his neck an' t'other in his pocket, and call him ducky. Don't they, Jack?"—"Jack, you're a terror with the gals."—"He takes three of 'em in tow to once, like one of 'em Watkinses two-funnel tugs waddling away with three schooners behind."—"Jack, you're a lame scamp."—"Jack, tell us about that one with a blue eye and a black eye. Do."—"There's plenty of girls with one black eye along the Highway by——" —"No, that's a speshul one—come, Jack." Donkin looked severe and disgusted; Jimmy very bored; a gray-haired sea dog shook his head slightly, smiling at the bowl of his pipe, discreetly amused. Knowles turned about bewildered; stammered first at one, then at another. "No! . . . I never! . . . can't talk sensible sense midst you. . . . Always on the kid." He retired bashfully—muttering and pleased. They laughed, hooting in the crude light, around Jimmy's bed, where on a white pillow his hollowed black face moved to and fro restlessly. A puff of wind came, made the flame of the lamp leap, and outside, high up, the sails fluttered, while near by the block of the foresheet struck a ringing blow on the iron bulwark. A voice far off cried, "Helm up!" another, more faint, answered, "Hard-up, sir!" They became silent—waited expectantly. The gray-haired seaman knocked his pipe on the doorstep and stood up. The ship leaned over gently and the sea seemed to wake up, murmuring drowsily. "Here's a little wind comin'," said someone very low. Jimmy turned over slowly to face the breeze. The voice in the night cried loud and commanding: "Haul the spanker out." The group before the door vanished out of the light. They could be heard tramping aft while they repeated with varied intonations: "Spanker out!" . . . "Out spanker, sir!" Donkin remained alone with Jimmy. There was a silence. Jimmy opened and shut his lips several times as if swallowing draughts of fresher air; Donkin moved the toes of his bare feet and looked at them thoughtfully.

"Ain't you going to give them a hand with the sail?" asked Jimmy.

"No. If six ov 'em ain't 'nough beef to set that blamed, rotten spanker, they ain't fit to live," answered Donkin in a bored, faraway voice, as though he had been talking from the bottom of a hole. Jimmy considered the conical, fowllike profile with a queer kind of interest; he was leaning out of his bunk with the calculating, uncertain expression of a man who reflects how best to lay hold of some strange creature that looks as though it could sting or bite. But he said only: "The mate will miss you—and there will be ructions."

Donkin got up to go. "I will do for 'im some dark night; see if I don't," he said over his shoulder.

Jimmy went on quickly: "You're like a poll parrot, like a screechin' poll parrot." Donkin stopped and cocked his head attentively on one side. His big ears stood out, transparent and veined, resembling the thin wings of a bat.

"Yuss?" he said, with his back towards Jimmy.

"Yes! Chatter out all you know—like . . . like a dirty white cockatoo."

Donkin waited. He could hear the other's breathing, long and slow; the breathing of a man with a hundredweight or so on the breastbone. Then he asked calmly: "What do I know?"

"What? . . . What I tell you . . . not much. What do you want . . . to talk about my health so——"

"It's a blooming imposyshun. A bloomin', stinkin', first-class imposyshun—but it don't tyke me in. Not it."

Jimmy kept still. Donkin put his hands in his pockets, and in one slouching stride came up to the bunk.

"I talk—what's the odds. They ain't men 'ere—sheep they are. A driven lot of sheep. I 'old you up. . . . Vy not? You're well orf."

"I am . . . I don't say anything about that. . . ."

"Well. Let 'em see it. Let 'em larn what a man can do. I am a man, I know all about yer. . . ." Jimmy threw himself further away on the pillow; the other stretched out his skinny neck, jerked his bird face down at him as though pecking at the eyes. "I am a man. I've seen the inside of every chokey in the Colonies rather'n give up my rights. . . ."

"You are a jail-prop," said Jimmy, weakly.

"I am . . . an' proud of it, too. You! You 'aven't the bloomin' nerve—so you inventyd this 'ere dodge. . . ." He paused; then with marked afterthought accentuated slowly: "Yer ain't sick—are yer?"

"No," said Jimmy, firmly. "Been out of sorts now and again this year," he mumbled with a sudden drop in his voice.

Donkin closed one eye, amicable and confidential. He whispered: "Ye 'ave done this afore 'aven'tchee?" Jimmy smiled—then as if unable to hold back he let himself go: "Last ship—yes. I was out of sorts on the passage. See? It was easy. They paid me off in Calcutta, and the skipper made no bones about it either. . . . I got my money all right. Laid up fifty-eight days! The fools! O Lord! The fools! Paid right off." He laughed spasmodically. Donkin chimed in giggling. Then Jimmy coughed violently. "I am as well as ever," he said, as soon as he could draw breath.

Donkin made a derisive gesture. "In course," he said, profoundly, "anyone can see that." "They don't," said Jimmy, gasping like a fish. "They would swallow any yarn," affirmed Donkin. "Don't you let on too much," admonished Jimmy in an exhausted voice. "Your little gyme? Eh?" commented Donkin, jovially. Then with sudden disgust: "Yer all for yerself, s'long as ye're right. . . ."

So charged with egoism James Wait pulled the blanket up to his chin and lay still for a while. His heavy lips protruded in an everlasting black pout. "Why are you so hot on making trouble?" he asked without much interest.

" 'Cos it's a bloomin' shayme. We are put upon . . . bad

food, bad pay . . . I want us to kick up a bloomin' row; a blamed 'owling row that would make 'em remember! Knocking people about . . . brain us . . . indeed! Ain't we men?" His altruistic indignation blazed. Then he said calmly: "I've been airing yer clothes." "All right," said Jimmy, languidly, "bring them in." "Giv' us the key of your chest, I'll put 'em away for yer," said Donkin with friendly eagerness. "Bring 'em in, I will put them away myself," answered James Wait with severity. Donkin looked down, muttering. . . . "What d'you say? What d'you say?" inquired Wait anxiously. "Nothink. The night's dry, let 'em 'ang out till the morning," said Donkin, in a strangely trembling voice, as though restraining laughter or rage. Jimmy seemed satisfied. "Give me a little water for the night in my mug—there," he said. Donkin took a stride over the doorstep. "Git it yerself," he replied in a surly tone. "You can do it, unless you are sick." "Of course I can do it," said Wait, "only . . ." "Well, then, do it," said Donkin, viciously, "if yer can look after yer clothes, yer can look after yerself." He went on deck without a look back.

Jimmy reached out for the mug. Not a drop. He put it back gently with a faint sigh—and closed his eyes. He thought: That lunatic Belfast will bring me some water if I ask. Fool. I am very thirsty. . . . It was very hot in the cabin, and it seemed to turn slowly round, detach itself from the ship, and swing out smoothly into a luminous, arid space where a black sun shone, spinning very fast. A place without any water! No water! A policeman with the face of Donkin drank a glass of beer by the side of an empty well, and flew away flapping vigorously. A ship whose mastheads protruded through the sky and could not be seen, was discharging grain, and the wind whirled the dry husks in spirals along the quay of a dock with no water in it. He whirled along with the husks—very tired and light. All his inside was gone. He felt lighter than the husks—and more dry. He expanded his hollow chest. The air streamed in, carrying away in its rush a lot of strange things that resembled houses, trees, people, lampposts. . . .

No more! There was no more air—and he had not finished drawing his long breath. But he was in jail! They were locking him up. A door slammed. They turned the key twice, flung a bucket of water over him—Phoo! What for?

He opened his eyes, thinking the fall had been very heavy for an empty man—empty—empty. He was in his cabin. Ah! All right! His face was streaming with perspiration, his arms heavier than lead. He saw the cook standing in the doorway, a brass key in one hand and a bright tin hook pot in the other.

"I have locked up the galley for the night," said the cook, beaming benevolently. "Eight bells just gone. I brought you a pot of cold tea for your night's drinking, Jimmy. I sweetened it with some white cabin sugar, too. Well—it won't break the ship."

He came in, hung the pot on the edge of the bunk, asked perfunctorily, "How goes it?" and sat down on the box. "H'm," grunted Wait, inhospitably. The cook wiped his face with a dirty cotton rag, which, afterwards, he tied round his neck. "That's how them firemen do in steamboats," he said, serenely, and much pleased with himself. "My work is as heavy as theirs—I'm thinking—and longer hours. Did you ever see them down the stokehold? Like fiends they look—firing—firing—firing—down there."

He pointed his forefinger at the deck. Some gloomy thought darkened his shining face, fleeting, like the shadow of a traveling cloud over the light of a peaceful sea. The relieved watch tramped noisily forward, passing in a body across the sheen of the doorway. Someone cried, "Good night!" Belfast stopped for a moment and looked at Jimmy, quivering and speechless with repressed emotion. He gave the cook a glance charged with dismal foreboding, and vanished. The cook cleared his throat. Jimmy stared upwards and kept as still as a man in hiding.

The night was clear, with a gentle breeze. Above the mastheads the resplendent curve of the Milky Way spanned the sky like a triumphal arch of eternal light thrown over the dark pathway of the earth. On the forecastle head a man whistled with loud precision a lively jig, while another could be heard faintly, shuffling and stamping in time. There came from forward a confused murmur of voices, laughter—snatches of song. The cook shook his head, glanced obliquely at Jimmy, and began to mutter. "Aye. Dance and sing. That's all they think of. I am surprised that Providence don't get tired. . . . They forget the day that's sure to come . . . but you . . ."

Jimmy drank a gulp of tea, hurriedly, as though he had stolen it, and shrank under his blanket, edging away towards the bulkhead. The cook got up, closed the door, then sat down again and said distinctly:

"Whenever I poke my galley fire I think of you chaps—swearing, stealing, lying, and worse—as if there was no such thing as another world. . . . Not bad fellows, either, in a way," he conceded, slowly; then, after a pause of regretful musing, he went on in a resigned tone: "Well, well. They will have a hot time of it. Hot! Did I say? The furnaces of one of them White Star boats ain't nothing to it."

He kept very quiet for a while. There was a great stir in his brain; an addled vision of bright outlines; an exciting row of rousing songs and groans of pain. He suffered, enjoyed, admired, approved. He was delighted, frightened, exalted—as on that evening (the only time in his life—twenty-seven years ago; he loved to recall the number of years) when as a young man he had—through keeping bad company—become intoxicated in an East-end music hall. A tide of sudden feeling swept him clean out of his body. He soared. He contemplated the secret of the hereafter. It commended itself to him. It was excellent; he loved it, himself, all hands, and Jimmy. His heart overflowed with tenderness, with comprehension, with the desire to meddle, with anxiety for the soul of that black man, with the pride of possessed eternity, with the feeling of might. Snatch him up in his arms and pitch him right into the middle of salvation. . . . The black soul—blacker body—rot—Devil. No! Talk—strength—Samson. . . . There was a great din as of cymbals in his ears; he flashed through an ecstatic jumble of shining faces, lilies, prayer books, unearthly joy, white skirts, gold harps, black coats, wings. He saw flowing garments, clean shaved faces, a sea of light—a lake of pitch. There were sweet scents, a smell of sulphur—red tongues of flame licking a white mist. An awesome voice thundered! . . . It lasted three seconds.

"Jimmy!" he cried in an inspired tone. Then he hesitated. A spark of human pity glimmered yet through the infernal fog of his supreme conceit.

"What?" said James Wait, unwillingly. There was a silence. He turned his head just the least bit, and stole a cautious glance. The cook's lips moved without a sound; his face was rapt, his eyes turned up. He seemed to be mentally imploring deck beams, the brass hook of the lamp, two cockroaches.

"Look here," said Wait, "I want to go to sleep. I think I could."

"This is no time for sleep!" exclaimed the cook, very loud. He had prayerfully divested himself of the last vestige of his humanity. He was a voice—a fleshless and sublime thing, as on that memorable night—the night when he went walking over the sea to make coffee for perishing sinners. "This is no time for sleeping," he repeated with exaltation. "*I* can't sleep."

"Don't care damn," said Wait, with factitious energy. "I can. Go an' turn in."

"Swear . . . in the very jaws! . . . In the very jaws! Don't you see the everlasting fire . . . don't you feel it? Blind, chock-full of sin! Repent, repent! I can't bear to think of you. I hear the call to save you. Night and day. Jimmy, let me save you!" The words of entreaty and menace broke out of him in a roaring torrent. The cockroaches ran away. Jimmy perspired, wriggling stealthily under his blanket. The cook yelled. . . . "Your days are numbered! . . ." "Get out of this," boomed Wait, courageously. "Pray with me! . . ." "I won't! . . ." The little cabin was as hot as an oven. It contained an immensity of fear and pain; an atmosphere of shrieks and moans; prayers vociferated like blasphemies and whispered curses. Outside, the men, called by Charley, who informed them in tones of delight that there was a holy row going on in Jimmy's place, crowded before the closed door, too startled to open it. All hands were there. The watch below had jumped out on deck in their shirts, as after a collision. Men running up asked: "What is it?" Others said: "Listen!" The muffled screaming went on: "On your knees! On your knees!"—"Shut up!"—"Never! You are delivered into my hands. . . . Your life has been saved. . . . Purpose . . . Mercy . . . Repent"—"You are a crazy fool!"—"Account of you . . . you . . . Never sleep in this world, if I ——"—"Leave off."—"No! . . . stokehold . . . only think! . . ." Then an impassioned screeching babble where words pattered like hail. "No!" shouted Wait.—"Yes. You are! . . . No help . . . Everybody says so."—"You lie!" —"I see you dying this minnyt . . . before my eyes . . . as good as dead already."—"Help!" shouted Jimmy, piercingly. "Not in this valley. . . . look upwards," howled the other. "Go away! Murder! Help!" clamored Jimmy. His voice broke. There were moanings, low mutters, a few sobs.

"What's the matter now?" said a seldom-heard voice. "Fall back, men! Fall back, there!" repeated Mr. Creighton, sternly, pushing through. "Here's the old man," whispered some. "The cook's in there, sir," exclaimed several, backing away. The door clattered open; a broad stream of light darted out on wondering faces: a warm whiff of vitiated air passed. The two mates towered head and shoulders above the spare, gray-haired man who stood revealed between them, in shabby clothes, stiff and angular, like a small carved figure, and with a thin, composed face. The cook got up from his knees. Jimmy sat high in the bunk, clasping his drawn-up legs. The tassel of the blue nightcap almost imperceptibly trembled over his knees. They gazed astonished at his long, curved back, while the white corner of one eye gleamed blindly at them. He was afraid to turn his head, he shrank within himself; and there was an aspect astounding and animallike in the perfection of his expectant immobility. A thing of instinct—the unthinking stillness of a scared brute.

"What are you doing here?" asked Mr. Baker, sharply. "My duty," said the cook, with ardor. "Your . . . what?" began the mate. Captain Allistoun touched his arm lightly. "I know his caper," he said, in a low voice. "Come out of that, Podmore," he ordered, aloud.

The cook wrung his hands, shook his fists above his head, and his arms dropped as if too heavy. For a moment he stood distracted and speechless. "Never," he stammered, "I . . . he . . . I . . ." "What—do—you—say?" pronounced Captain Allistoun. "Come out at once—or——" "I am going," said the cook, with a hasty and somber resignation. He strode over the doorstep firmly—hesitated—made a few steps. They looked at him in silence. "I make you responsible!" he cried, desperately, turning half round. "That man is dying. I make you——" "You there yet?" called the master in a threatening tone. "No, sir," he exclaimed, hurriedly, in a startled voice. The boatswain led him away by the arm; someone laughed; Jimmy lifted his head for a stealthy glance and in one unexpected leap sprang out of his bunk; Mr. Baker made a clever catch and felt him very limp in his arms; the group at the door grunted with surprise. "He lies," gasped Wait, "he talked about black devils—he is a devil—a white devil—I am all right." He stiffened himself, and Mr. Baker, experimentally, let him go. He staggered a pace or two; Captain Allistoun watched him with a quiet and penetrating gaze; Belfast ran to his support. He did not appear to be aware of anyone near him; he stood silent for a moment, battling singlehanded with a legion of nameless terrors, amidst the eager looks of excited men who watched him far off, utterly alone in the impenetrable solitude of his fear. The sea gurgled through the scuppers as the ship heeled over to a short puff of wind.

"Keep him away from me," said James Wait at last in his fine baritone voice, and leaning with all his weight on

Belfast's neck. "I've been better this last week . . . I am well . . . I was going back to duty . . . tomorrow—now if you like—Captain." Belfast hitched his shoulders to keep him upright.

"No," said the master, looking at him, fixedly.

Under Jimmy's armpit Belfast's red face moved uneasily. A row of eyes gleaming stared on the edge of light. They pushed one another with elbows, turned their heads, whispered. Wait let his chin fall on his breast and, with lowered eyelids, looked round in a suspicious manner.

"Why not?" cried a voice from the shadows, "the man's all right, sir."

"I am all right," said Wait, with eagerness. "Been sick . . . better . . . turn-to now." He sighed. "Howly Mother!" exclaimed Belfast with a heave of the shoulders, "stand up, Jimmy." "Keep away from me then," said Wait, giving Belfast a petulant push, and reeling fetched against the doorpost. His cheekbones glistened as though they had been varnished. He snatched off his nightcap, wiped his perspiring face with it, flung it on the deck. "I am coming out," he declared without stirring.

"No. You don't," said the master, curtly. Bare feet shuffled, disapproving voices murmured all round; he went on as if he had not heard: "You have been skulking nearly all the passage and now you want to come out. You think you are near enough to the pay table now. Smell the shore, hey?"

"I've been sick . . . now—better," mumbled Wait, glaring in the light. "You have been shamming sick," retorted Captain Allistoun with severity; "Why . . ." he hesitated for less than half a second. "Why, anybody can see that. There's nothing the matter with you, but you choose to lie-up to please yourself—and now you shall lie-up to please me. Mr. Baker, my orders are that this man is not to be allowed on deck to the end of the passage."

There were exclamations of surprise, triumph, indignation. The dark group of men swung across the light. "What for?"—"Told you so . . ."—"Bloomin' shame . . ." "We've got to say somethink about that," screeched Donkin from the rear. "Never mind, Jim—we will see you righted," cried several together. An elderly seaman stepped to the front. "D'ye mean to say, sir," he asked, ominously, "that a sick chap ain't allowed to get well in this 'ere hooker?" Behind him Donkin whispered excitedly amongst a staring crowd where no one spared him a glance, but Captain Allistoun shook a forefinger at the angry bronzed face of the speaker. "You—you hold your tongue," he said, warningly. "This isn't the way," clamored two or three younger men. "Are we bloomin' masheens?" inquired Donkin in a piercing tone, and dived under the elbows of the front rank.—"Soon show 'im we ain't boys . . ."—"The man's a man if he is black."—"We ain't goin' to work this bloomin' ship shorthanded if Snowball's all right . . ."—"He says he is."—"Well then, strike, boys, strike!"—"That's the bloomin' ticket." Captain Allistoun said sharply to the second mate: "Keep quiet, Mr. Creighton," and stood composed in the tumult, listening with profound attention to mixed growls and screeches, to every exclamation and every curse of the sudden outbreak. Somebody slammed the cabin door to with a kick; the darkness full of menacing mutters leaped with a short clatter over the streak of light, and the men became gesticulating shadows that growled, hissed, laughed excitedly. Mr. Baker whispered: "Get away from them, sir." The big shape of Mr. Creighton hovered silently about the slight figure of the master. "We have been hymposed upon all this voyage," said a gruff voice. "but this 'ere fancy takes the cake."—"That man is a shipmate."—"Are we bloomin' kids?"—"The port watch will refuse duty." Charley, carried away by his feeling, whistled shrilly, then yelped: "Give us our Jimmy!" This seemed to cause a variation in the disturbance. There was a fresh burst of squabbling uproar. A lot of quarrels were set going at once. "Yes."—"No."—"Never been sick."—"Go for them to once."—"Shut yer mouth, youngster—this is men's work." "Is it?" muttered Captain Allistoun, bitterly. Mr. Baker grunted: "Ough! They're gone silly. They've been simmering for the last month." "I did notice," said the master. "They have started a row amongst themselves now," said Mr. Creighton with disdain, "better get aft, sir. We will soothe them." "Keep your temper, Creighton," said the master. And the three men began to move slowly towards the cabin door.

In the shadows of the forerigging a dark mass stamped, eddied, advanced, retreated. There were words of reproach, encouragement, unbelief, execration. The elder seamen, bewildered and angry, growled their determination to go through with something or other; but the younger school of advanced thought exposed their and Jimmy's wrongs with confused shouts, arguing amongst themselves. They clustered round that moribund carcass, the fit emblem of their aspirations, and encouraging one another they swayed, they tramped on one spot, shouting that they would not be "put upon." Inside the cabin, Belfast, helping Jimmy into his bunk, twitched all over in his desire not to miss all the row, and with difficulty restrained the tears of his facile emotion. James Wait, flat on his back under the blanket, gasped complaints. "We will back you up, never fear," assured Belfast, busy about his feet. "I'll come out tomorrow morning . . . take my chance . . . you fellows must . . ." mumbled Wait, "I come out tomorrow—skipper or no skipper." He lifted one arm with great difficulty, passed the hand over his face. "Don't you let that cook . . ." he breathed out. "No, no," said Belfast, turning his back on the bunk, "I will put a head on him if he comes near you." "I will smash his mug!" exclaimed faintly Wait, enraged and weak. "I don't want to kill a man, but . . ." He panted fast like a dog after a run in sunshine. Someone just outside the door shouted, "He's as fit as any ov us!" Belfast put his hand on the door handle. "Here!" called James Wait, hurriedly, and in such a clear voice that the other spun round with a start. James Wait, stretched out black and deathlike in the dazzling light, turned his head on the pillow. His eyes stared at Belfast, appealing and impudent. "I am rather weak from lying-up so long," he said, distinctly. Belfast nodded. "Getting quite well now," insisted Wait. "Yes. I noticed you getting better this . . . last month," said Belfast, looking down. "Hallo! What's this?" he shouted and ran out.

He was flattened directly against the side of the house by two men who lurched against him. A lot of disputes seemed to be going on all round. He got clear and saw three indistinct figures standing along in the fainter darkness under the arched foot of the mainsail, that rose above their heads like a convex wall of a high edifice. Donkin hissed: "Go for them . . . it's dark!" The crowd took a short run aft in a body—then there was a check. Donkin, agile and thin, flitted past with his right arm going like a windmill—and then stood still suddenly with his arm pointing rigidly above his head. The hurtling flight of some heavy object was heard; it passed between the heads of the two mates, bounded heavily along the deck, struck the after hatch with a ponderous and deadened blow. The bulky shape of Mr. Baker grew distinct. "Come to your senses, men!" he cried, advancing at the arrested crowd. "Come back, Mr. Baker!" called the master's quiet voice. He obeyed unwillingly. There was a minute of silence, then a deafening hubbub arose. Above it Archie was heard energetically: "If ye do oot ageen I wull tell!" There were shouts. "Don't!"—"Drop it!"—"We ain't that kind!" The black cluster of human forms reeled against the bulwark, back again towards the house. Ringbolts rang under stumbling feet.—"Drop it!"—"Let me!"—"No!"—"Curse you . . . hah!" Then sounds as of someone's face being slapped; a piece of iron fell on the deck; a short scuffle, and someone's shadowy body scuttled rapidly across the main hatch before the shadow of a kick. A raging voice sobbed out a torrent of filthy language . . . —"Throwing things—good God!" grunted Mr. Baker in dismay. "That was meant for me," said the master, quietly; "I felt the wind of that thing; what was it—an iron belaying pin?" "By Jove!" muttered Mr. Creighton. The confused voices of men talking amidships mingled with the wash of the sea, ascended between the silent and distended sails—seemed to flow away into the night, further than the horizon, higher than the sky. The stars burned steadily over the inclined mastheads. Trails of light lay on the water, broke before the advancing hull, and, after she had passed, trembled for a long time as if in awe of the murmuring sea.

Meantime the helmsman, anxious to know what the row was about, had let go the wheel, and, bent double, ran with long, stealthy footsteps to the break of the poop. The *Narcissus,* left to herself, came up gently to the wind without any one being aware of it. She gave a slight roll, and the sleeping sails woke suddenly, coming all together with a mighty flap against the masts, then filled again one after another in a quick succession of loud reports that ran down the lofty spars, till the collapsed mainsail flew out last with a violent jerk. The ship trembled from trucks to keel; the sails kept on rattling like a discharge of musketry; the chain sheets and loose shackles jingled aloft in a thin peal; the gin blocks groaned. It was as if an invisible hand had given the ship an angry shake to recall the men that peopled her decks to the sense of reality, vigilance, and duty. "Helm up!" cried the master, sharply. "Run aft, Mr. Creighton, and see what that fool there is up to." "Flatten in the head sheets. Stand by the weather forebraces," growled Mr. Baker. Startled men ran swiftly repeating the orders. The watch below, abandoned all at once by the watch on deck, drifted toward the forecastle in twos and threes, arguing noisily as they went. "We shall see tomorrow!" cried a loud voice, as if to cover with a menacing hint an inglorious retreat. And then only orders were heard, the falling of heavy coils of rope, the rattling of blocks. Singleton's white head flitted here and there in the night, high above the deck, like the ghost of a bird. "Going off, sir!" shouted Mr. Creighton from aft.—"Full again."—"All right . . ."—"Ease off the head sheets. That will do the braces. Coil the ropes up," grunted Mr. Baker, bustling about.

Gradually the tramping noises, the confused sound of

voices, died out, and the officers, coming together on the poop, discussed the events. Mr. Baker was bewildered and grunted; Mr. Creighton was calmly furious; but Captain Allistoun was composed and thoughtful. He listened to Mr. Baker's growling argumentation, to Creighton's interjected and severe remarks; while looking down on the deck he weighed in his hand the iron belaying pin—that a moment ago had just missed his head—as if it had been the only tangible fact of the whole transaction. He was one of those commanders who speak little, seem to hear nothing, look at no one—and know everything, hear every whisper, see every fleeting shadow of their ship's life. His two big officers towered above his lean, short figure; they talked over his head; they were dismayed, surprised, and angry, while between them the little quiet man seemed to have found his taciturn serenity in the profound depths of a larger experience. Lights were burning in the forecastle; now and then a loud gust of babbling chatter came from forward, swept over the decks, and became faint, as if the unconscious ship, gliding gently through the great peace of the sea, had left behind and forever the foolish noise of turbulent mankind. But it was renewed again and again. Gesticulating arms, profiles of heads with open mouths, appeared for a moment in the illuminated squares of doorways; black fists darted—withdrew . . . "Yes. It was most damnable to have such an unprovoked row sprung on one," assented the master. . . . A tumult of yells rose in the light, abruptly ceased. . . . He didn't think there would be any further trouble just then. . . . A bell was struck aft; another, forward, answered in a deeper tone, and the clamor of ringing metal spread round the ship in a circle of wide vibrations that ebbed away into the immeasurable night of an empty sea. . . . Didn't he know them! Didn't he! In past years. Better men, too. Real men to stand by one in a tight place. Worse than devils too sometimes—downright, horned devils. Pah! This—nothing. A miss as good as a mile. . . . The wheel was being relieved in the usual way.—"Full and by," said, very loud, the man going off.—"Full and by," repeated the other, catching hold of the spokes. "This head wind is my trouble," exclaimed the master, stamping his foot in sudden anger; "head wind! all the rest is nothing." He was calm again in a moment. "Keep them on the move tonight, gentlemen; just to let them feel we've got hold all the time—quietly, you know. Mind you keep your hands off them, Creighton. Tomorrow I will talk to them like a Dutch uncle. A crazy crowd of tinkers! Yes, tinkers! I could count the real sailors amongst them on the fingers of one hand. Nothing will do but a row—if—you—please." He paused. "Did you think I had gone wrong there, Mr. Baker?" He tapped his forehead, laughed short. "When I saw him standing there, three parts dead and so scared—black amongst that gaping lot—no grit to face what's coming to us all—the notion came to me all at once, before I could think. Sorry for him—like you would be for a sick brute. If ever creature was in a mortal funk to die! . . . I thought I would let him go out in his own way. Kind of impulse. It never came into my head, those fools . . . h'm! Stand to it now—of course." He stuck the belaying pin in his pocket, seemed ashamed of himself, then sharply: "If you see Podmore at his tricks again tell him I will have him put under the pump. Had to do it once before. The fellow breaks out like that now and then. Good cook though." He walked away quickly, came back to the companion. The two mates followed him through the starlight with amazed eyes. He went down three steps, and, changing his tone, spoke with his head near the deck: "I shan't turn in tonight, in case of anything; just call out if . . . Did you see the eyes of that sick nigger, Mr. Baker? I fancied he begged me for something. What? Past all help. One lone black beggar amongst the lot of us, and he seemed to look through me into the very hell. Fancy, this wretched Podmore! Well, let him die in peace. I am master here after all. Let him be. He might have been half a man once. . . . Keep a good lookout." He disappeared down below, leaving his mates facing one another, and more impressed than if they had seen a stone image shed a miraculous tear of compassion over the incertitudes of life and death. . . .

In the blue mist spreading from twisted threads that stood upright in the bowls of pipes, the forecastle appeared as vast as a hall. Between the beams a heavy cloud stagnated; and the lamps surrounded by halos burned each at the core of a purple glow in two lifeless flames without rays. Wreaths drifted in denser wisps. Men sprawled about on the deck, sat in negligent poses, or, bending a knee drooped with one shoulder against a bulkhead. Lips moved, eyes flashed, waving arms made sudden eddies in the smoke. The murmur of voices seemed to pile itself higher and higher as if unable to run out quick enough through the narrow doors. The watch below, in their shirts and striding on long white legs, resembled raving somnambulists; while now and then one of the watch on deck would rush in, looking strangely overdressed, listen a moment, fling a rapid sentence into the noise and run out again; but a few remained near the door, fascinated, and with one ear turned to the deck. "Stick together, boys," roared Davis. Belfast tried to make himself heard. Knowles grinned in a slow, dazed way. A short fellow with a thick clipped beard kept on yelling periodically: "Who's afeard? Who's afeard?" Another one jumped up, excited, with blazing eyes, sent out a string of unattached curses and sat down quietly. Two men discussed familiarly, striking one another's breast in turn, to clinch arguments. Three others, with their heads in a bunch, spoke all together with a confidential air, and at the top of their voices. It was a stormy chaos of speech where intelligible fragments, tossing, struck the ear. One could hear: "In the last ship"—"Who cares? Try it on any one of us if——" "Knock under"—"Not a hand's turn"—"He says he is all right"—"I always thought"—"Never mind. . . ." Donkin, crouching all in a heap against the bowsprit, hunched his shoulder blades as high as his ears, and, hanging a peaked nose, resembled a sick vulture with ruffled plumes. Belfast, straddling his legs, had a face red with yelling, and, with arms thrown up, figured a Maltese cross. The two Scandinavians, in a corner, had the dumfounded and distracted aspect of men gazing at a cataclysm. And, beyond the light, Singleton stood in the smoke, monumental, indistinct, with his head touching the beam; like a statue of heroic size in the gloom of a crypt.

He stepped forward, impassive and big. The noise subsided like a broken wave: but Belfast cried once more with uplifted arms: "The man is dying I tell ye!" then sat down suddenly on the hatch and took his head between his hands. All looked at Singleton, gazing upwards from the deck, staring out of dark corners, or turning their heads with curious glances. They were expectant and appeased as if that old man, who looked at no one, had possessed the secret of their uneasy indignations and desires, a sharper vision, a clearer knowledge. And indeed, standing there amongst them, he had the uninterested appearance of one who had seen multitudes of ships, had listened many times to voices such as theirs, had already seen all that could happen on the wide seas. They heard his voice rumble in his broad chest as though the word had been rolling towards them out of a rugged past. "What do you want to do?" he asked. No one answered. Only Knowles muttered—"Aye, aye," and somebody said low: "It's a bloomin' shame." He waited, made a contemptuous gesture. "I have seen rows aboard ship before some of you were born," he said, slowly, "for something or nothing; but never for such a thing." "The man is dying, I tell ye," repeated Belfast, woefully, sitting at Singleton's feet. "And a black fellow, too," went on the old seaman, "I have seen them die like flies." He stopped, thoughtful, as if trying to recollect gruesome things, details of horrors, hecatombs of niggers. They looked at him fascinated. He was old enough to remember slavers, bloody mutinies, pirates perhaps; who could tell through what violences and terrors he had lived! What would he say? He said: "You can't help him; die he must." He made another pause. His mustache and beard stirred. He chewed words, mumbled behind tangled white hairs; incomprehensible and exciting, like an oracle behind a veil. . . .—"Stop ashore . . .

sick. . . . Instead . . . bringing all this head wind. Afraid. The sea will have her own. . . . Die in sight of land. Always so. They know it . . . long passage . . . more days, more dollars. . . . You keep quiet. . . . What do you want? Can't help him." He seemed to wake up from a dream. "You can't help yourselves," he said, austerely. "Skipper's no fool. He has something in his mind. Look out—I say! I know 'em!" With eyes fixed in front he turned his head from right to left, from left to right, as if inspecting a long row of astute skippers. " 'Ee said 'ee would brain me!" cried Donkin in a heartrending tone. Singleton peered downwards with puzzled attention, as though he couldn't find him. "Damn you!" he said, vaguely, giving it up. He radiated unspeakable wisdom, hard unconcern, the chilling air of resignation. Round him all the listeners felt themselves somehow completely enlightened by their disappointment, and, mute, they lolled about with the careless ease of men who can discern perfectly the irremediable aspect of their existence. He, profound and unconscious, waved his arm once and strode out on deck without another word.

Belfast was lost in a round-eyed meditation. One or two vaulted heavily into upper berths, and, once there, sighed; others dived head first inside lower bunks—swift, and turning round instantly upon themselves, like animals going into lairs. The grating of a knife scraping burnt clay was heard. Knowles grinned no more. Davis said, in a tone of ardent conviction: "Then our skipper's loony." Archie muttered: "My faith! we haven't heard the last of it yet!" Four bells were struck. "Half our watch below gone!" cried Knowles in alarm, then reflected. "Well, two hours' sleep is something towards a rest," he observed, consolingly. Some already pretended to slumber; and Charley, sound asleep, suddenly said a few slurred words in an arbitrary, blank voice. "This blamed boy has worrums!" commented Knowles from under a blanket, in a learned manner. Belfast got up and approached Archie's berth. "We pulled him out," he whispered, sadly. "What?" said the other, with sleepy discontent. "And now we will have to chuck him overboard," went on Belfast, whose lower lip trembled. "Chuck what?" asked Archie. "Poor Jimmy," breathed out Belfast. "He be blowed!" said Archie with untruthful brutality, and sat up in his bunk. "It's all through him. If it hadn't been for me, there would have been murder on board this ship!" " 'Tain't his fault, is it?" argued Belfast in a murmur. "I've put him to bed . . . an' he ain't no heavier than an empty beef cask," he added, with tears in his eyes. Archie looked at him steadily, then turned his nose to the ship's side with determination. Belfast wandered about as though he had lost his way in the dim forecastle, and nearly fell over Donkin. He contemplated him from on high for a while. "Ain't ye going to turn in?" he asked. Donkin looked up hopelessly. "That black-'earted Scotch son of a thief kicked me!" he whispered from the floor, in a tone of utter desolation. "And a good job, too!" said Belfast, still very depressed. "You were as near hanging as damn-it tonight, sonny. Don't you play any of your murthering games around my Jimmy! You haven't pulled him out. You just mind! 'Cos if I start to kick you"—he brightened up a bit—"if I start to kick you, it will be Yankee fashion—to break something!" He tapped lightly with his knuckles the top of the bowed head. "You moind that, my bhoy!" he concluded, cheerily. Donkin let it pass. "Will they split on me?" he asked, with pained anxiety. "Who—split?" hissed Belfast, coming back a step. "I would split your nose this minyt if I hadn't Jimmy to look after! Who d'ye think we are?" Donkin rose and watched Belfast's back lurch through the doorway. On all sides invisible men slept, breathing calmly. He seemed to draw courage and fury from the peace around him. Venomous and thin-faced, he glared from the ample misfit of borrowed clothes as if looking for something he could smash. His heart leaped wildly in his narrow chest. They slept! He wanted to wring necks, gouge eyes, spit on faces. He shook a dirty pair of meager fists at the smoking lights. "Ye're no men!" he cried, in a deadened tone. No one moved. "Yer 'aven't the pluck of a mouse!" His voice rose to a husky screech. Wamibo darted out a disheveled head, and looked at him wildly. "Ye're sweepings ov ships! I 'ope you will all rot before you die!" Wamibo blinked, uncomprehending but interested. Donkin sat down heavily; he blew with force through quivering nostrils, he ground and snapped his teeth, and, with the chin pressed hard against the breast, he seemed busy gnawing his way through it, as if to get at the heart within. . . .

In the morning the ship, beginning another day of her wandering life, had an aspect of sumptuous freshness, like the springtime of the earth. The washed decks glistened in a long clear stretch; the oblique sunlight struck the yellow brasses in dazzling splashes, darted over the polished rods in lines of gold, and the single drops of salt water forgotten here and there along the rail were as limpid as drops of dew, and sparkled more than scattered diamonds. The sails slept, hushed by a gentle breeze. The sun, rising lonely and splendid in the blue sky, saw a solitary ship gliding close-hauled on the blue sea.

The men pressed three deep abreast of the mainmast and opposite the cabin door. They shuffled, pushed, had an irresolute mien and stolid faces. At every slight movement Knowles lurched heavily on his short leg. Donkin glided behind backs, restless and anxious, like a man looking for an ambush. Captain Allistoun came out on the quarter-deck suddenly. He walked to and fro before the front. He was gray, slight, alert, shabby in the sunshine, and as hard as adamant. He had his right hand in the side pocket of his jacket, and also something heavy in there that made folds all down that side. One of the seamen cleared his throat ominously. "I haven't till now found fault with you men," said the master, stopping short. He faced them with his worn, steely gaze, that by a universal illusion looked straight into every individual pair of the twenty pairs of eyes before his face. At his back Mr. Baker, gloomy and bullnecked, grunted low; Mr. Creighton, fresh as paint, had rosy cheeks and a ready, resolute bearing. "And I don't now," continued the master; "but I am here to drive this ship and keep every man jack aboard of her up to the mark. If you knew your work as well as I do mine, there would be no trouble. You've been braying in the dark about 'See tomorrow morning!' Well, you see me now. What do you want?" He waited, stepping quickly to and fro, giving them searching glances. What did they want? They shifted from foot to foot, they balanced their bodies; some, pushing back their caps, scratched their heads. What did they want? Jimmy was forgotten; no one thought of him, alone forward in his cabin, fighting great shadows, clinging to brazen lies, chuckling painfully over his transparent deceptions. No, not Jimmy; he was more forgotten than if he had been dead. They wanted great things. And suddenly all the simple words they knew seemed to be lost forever in the immensity of their vague and burning desire. They knew what they wanted, but they could not find anything worth saying. They stirred on one spot, swinging, at the end of muscular arms, big tarry hands with crooked fingers. A murmur died out. "What is it—food?" asked the master; "you know the stores have been spoiled off the Cape." "We know that, sir," said a bearded shellback in the front rank. "Work too hard—eh? Too much for your strength?" he asked again. There was an offended silence. "We don't want to go shorthanded, sir," began at last Davis in a wavering voice, "and this 'ere black——" "Enough!" cried the master. He stood scanning them for a moment, then walking a few steps this way and that began to storm at them coldly, in gusts violent and cutting like the gales of those icy seas that had known his youth. "Tell you what's the matter? Too big for your boots. Think yourselves damn good men. Know half your work. Do half your duty. Think it too much. If you did ten times as much it wouldn't be enough."—"We did our best by her, sir," cried someone with shaky exasperation. "Your best," stormed on the master. "You hear a lot on shore, don't you? They don't tell you there your best isn't much to boast of. I tell you—your best is no better than bad. You can do no more? No, I know, and say nothing.

But you stop your caper or I will stop it for you. I am ready for you! Stop it!" He shook a finger at the crowd. "As to that man," he raised his voice very much, "as to that man, if he puts his nose out on deck without my leave I will clap him in irons. There!" The cook heard him forward, ran out of the galley lifting his arms, horrified, unbelieving, amazed, and ran in again. There was a moment of profound silence during which a bowlegged seaman, stepping aside, expectorated decorously into the scupper. "There is another thing," said the master, calmly. He made a quick stride and with a swing took an iron belaying pin out of his pocket. "This!" His movement was so unexpected and sudden that the crowd stepped back. He gazed fixedly at their faces, and some at once put on a surprised air as though they had never seen a belaying pin before. He held it up. "This is my affair. I don't ask you any questions, but you all know it; it has got to go where it came from." His eyes became angry. The crowd stirred uneasily. They looked away from the piece of iron, they appeared shy, they were embarrassed and shocked as though it had been something horrid, scandalous, or indelicate, that in common decency should not have been flourished like this in broad daylight. The master watched them attentively. "Donkin," he called out in a short, sharp tone.

Donkin dodged behind one, then behind another, but they looked over their shoulders and moved aside. The ranks kept on opening before him, closing behind, till at last he appeared alone before the master as though he had come up through the deck. Captain Allistoun moved close to him. They were much of a size, and at short range the master exchanged a deadly glance with the beady eyes. They wavered. "You know this?" asked the master. "No, I don't," answered the other, with cheeky trepidation. "You are a cur. Take it," ordered the master. Donkin's arms seemed glued to his thighs; he stood, eyes front, as if drawn on parade. "Take it," repeated the master, and stepped closer; they breathed on one another. "Take it," said Captain Allistoun again, making a menacing gesture. Donkin tore away one arm from his side. "Vy are yer down on me?" he mumbled with effort and as if his mouth had been full of dough. "If you don't . . ." began the master. Donkin snatched at the pin as though his intention had been to run away with it, and remained stock-still holding it like a candle. "Put it back where you took it from," said Captain Allistoun, looking at him fiercely. Donkin stepped back opening wide eyes. "Go, you blackguard, or I will make you," cried the master, driving him slowly backwards by a menacing advance. He dodged, and with the dangerous iron tried to guard his head from a threatening fist. Mr. Baker ceased grunting for a moment. "Good! By Jove," murmured appreciatively Mr. Creighton in the tone of a connoisseur. "Don't tech me," snarled Donkin, backing away. "Then go. Go faster." "Don't yer 'it me. . . . I will pull yer up afore the magistryt. . . . I'll show yer up." Captain Allistoun made a long stride, and Donkin, turning his back fairly, ran off a little, then stopped and over his shoulder showed yellow teeth. "Further on, forerigging," urged the master, pointing with his arm. "Are yer goin' to stand by and see me bullied?" screamed Donkin at the silent crowd that watched him. Captain Allistoun walked at him smartly. He started off again with a leap, dashed at the forerigging, rammed the pin into its hole violently. "I'll be even with yer yet," he screamed at the ship at large and vanished beyond the foremast. Captain Allistoun spun round and walked back aft with a composed face, as though he had already forgotten the scene. Men moved out of his way. He looked at no one. "That will do, Mr. Baker. Send the watch below," he said, quietly. "And you men try to walk straight for the future," he added in a calm voice. He looked pensively for a while at the backs of the impressed and retreating crowd. "Breakfast, steward," he called in a tone of relief through the cabin door. "I didn't like to see you—Ough!—give that pin to that chap, sir," observed Mr. Baker; "he could have bust—Ough!—bust your head like an eggshell with it." "Oh! he!" muttered the master, absently. "Queer lot," he went on in a low voice. "I suppose it's all right now. Can never tell though, nowadays, with such a . . . Years ago—I was a young master then—one China voyage I had a mutiny; real mutiny, Baker. Different men though. I knew what they wanted: they wanted to broach the cargo and get at the liquor. Very simple. . . . We knocked them about for two days, and when they had enough—gentle as lambs. Good crew. And a smart trip I made." He glanced aloft at the yards braced sharp up. "Head wind day after day," he exclaimed, bitterly. "Shall we never get a decent slant this passage?" "Ready, sir," said the steward, appearing before them as if by magic and with a stained napkin in his hand. "Ah! All right. Come along, Mr. Baker—it's late—with all this nonsense."

CHAPTER 5

A heavy atmosphere of oppressive quietude pervaded the ship. In the afternoon men went about washing clothes and hanging them out to dry in the unprosperous breeze with the meditative languor of disenchanted philosophers. Very little was said. The problem of life seemed too voluminous for the narrow limits of human speech, and by common consent it was abandoned to the great sea that had from the beginning enfolded it in its immense grip; to the sea that knew all, and would in time infallibly unveil to each the wisdom hidden in all the errors, the certitude that lurks in doubts, the realm of safety and peace beyond the frontiers of sorrow and fear. And in the confused current of impotent thoughts that set unceasingly this way and that through bodies of men, Jimmy bobbed up upon the surface, compelling attention, like a black buoy chained to the bottom of a muddy stream. Falsehood triumphed. It triumphed through doubt, through stupidity, through pity, through sentimentalism. We set ourselves to bolster it up, from compassion, from recklessness, from a sense of fun. Jimmy's steadfastness to his untruthful attitude in the face of the inevitable truth had the proportions of a colossal enigma—of a manifestation grand and incomprehensible that at times inspired a wondering awe; and there was also, to many, something exquisitely droll in fooling him thus to the top of his bent. The latent egoism of tenderness to suffering appeared in the developing anxiety not to see him die. His obstinate nonrecognition of the only certitude whose approach we could watch from day to day was as disquieting as the failure of some law of nature. He was so utterly wrong about himself that one could not but suspect him of having access to some source of supernatural knowledge. He was absurd to the point of inspiration. He was unique, and as fascinating as only something inhuman could be; he seemed to shout his denials already from beyond the awful border. He was becoming immaterial like an apparition; his cheekbones rose, the forehead slanted more; the face was all hollows, patches of shade; and the fleshless head resembled a disinterred black skull, fitted with two restless globes of silver in the sockets of eyes. He was demoralizing. Through him we were becoming highly humanized, tender, complex, excessively decadent: we understood the subtlety of his fear, sympathized with all his repulsions, shrinkings, evasions, delusions—as though we had been overcivilized, and rotten, and without any knowledge of the meaning of life. We had the air of being initiated in some infamous mysteries; we had the profound grimaces of conspirators, exchanged meaning glances, significant short words. We were inexpressibly vile and very much pleased with ourselves. We lied to him with gravity, with emotion, with unction, as if performing some moral trick with a view to an eternal reward. We made a chorus of affirmation to his wildest assertions, as though he had been a millionaire, a politician, or a reformer—and we a crowd of ambitious lubbers. When we ventured to question his statements we did it after the manner of obsequious sycophants, to the end that his glory should be augmented by the flattery of our dissent. He influenced the moral tone of our world as though he had it in his power to distribute honors, treasures, or pain; and he could give us nothing but his contempt. It was immense; it seemed to grow gradually larger, as his body day by day shrank a little more, while we looked. It was the only thing about him—of him—that gave the impression of durability and vigor. It lived within him with an unquenchable life. It spoke through the eternal pout of his black lips; it looked at us through the impertinent mournfulness of his languid and enormous stare. We watched him intently. He seemed unwilling to move, as if distrustful of his own solidity. The slightest gesture must have disclosed to him (it could not surely be otherwise) his bodily weakness, and caused a pang of mental suffering. He was chary of movements. He lay stretched out, chin on blanket, in a kind of sly, cautious immobility. Only his eyes roamed over faces: his eyes disdainful, penetrating and sad.

It was at that time that Belfast's devotion—and also his pugnacity—secured universal respect. He spent every moment of his spare time in Jimmy's cabin. He tended him, talked to him; was as gentle as a woman, as tenderly gay as an old philanthropist, as sentimentally careful of his nigger as a model slaveowner. But outside he was irritable, explosive as gun-powder, somber, suspicious, and never more brutal than when most sorrowful. With him it was a tear and a blow; a tear for Jimmy, a blow for anyone who did not seem to take a scrupulously orthodox view of Jimmy's case. We talked about nothing else. The two Scandinavians, even, discussed the situation—but it was impossible to know in what spirit, because they quarreled in their own language. Belfast suspected one of them of irreverence, and in this incertitude thought that there was no option but to fight them both. They became very much terrified by his truculence, and henceforth lived amongst us, dejected, like a pair of mutes. Wamibo never spoke intelligibly, but he was as smileless as an animal—seemed to know much less about it all than the cat—and consequently was safe. Moreover, he had belonged to the chosen band of Jimmy's rescuers, and was above suspicion. Archie was silent generally, but often spent an hour or so talking to Jimmy quietly with an air of proprietorship. At any time of the day and often through the night some man could be seen sitting on Jimmy's box. In the evening, between six and eight, the cabin was crowded, and there was an interested group at the door. Everyone stared at the nigger.

He basked in the warmth of our interest. His eyes gleamed ironically, and in a weak voice he reproached us with our cowardice. He would say, "If you fellows had stuck out for me I would be now on deck." We hung our heads. "Yes, but if you think I am going to let them put me in irons just to show you sport . . . Well, no. . . . It ruins my health, this lying-up, it does. You don't care." We were as abashed as if it had been true. His superb impudence carried all before it. We would not have dared to revolt. We didn't want to, really. We wanted to keep him alive till home—to the end of the voyage.

Singleton as usual held aloof, appearing to scorn the insignificant events of an ended life. Once only he came along, and unexpectedly stopped in the doorway. He peered at Jimmy in profound silence, as if desirous to add that black image to the crowd of Shades that peopled his old memory. We kept very quiet, and for a long time Singleton stood there as though he had come by appointment to call for someone, or to see some important event. James Wait lay perfectly still, and apparently not aware of the gaze scrutinizing him with a steadiness full of expectation. There was a sense of a contest in the air. We felt the inward strain of men watching a wrestling bout. At last Jimmy with perceptible apprehension turned his head on the pillow. "Good evening," he said in a conciliating tone.—"H'm," answered the old seaman, grumpily. For a moment longer he looked at Jimmy with severe fixity, then suddenly went away. It was a long time before anyone spoke in the little cabin, though we all breathed more freely as men do after an escape from some dangerous situation. We all knew the old man's ideas about Jimmy, and nobody dared to combat them. They were unsettling, they caused pain; and, what was worse, they might have been true for all we knew. Only once did he condescend to explain them fully, but the impression was lasting. He said that Jimmy was the cause of head winds. Mortally sick men—he maintained—linger till the first sight of land, and then die; and Jimmy knew that the very first land would draw his life from him. It is so in every ship. Didn't we know it? He asked us with austere contempt: what did we know? What would we doubt next? Jimmy's desire encouraged by us and aided by Wamibo's (he was a Finn—wasn't he? Very well!) by Wamibo's spells delayed the ship in the open sea. Only lubberly fools couldn't see it. Whoever heard of such a run of calms and head winds? It wasn't natural. . . . We could not deny that it was strange. We felt uneasy. The common saying, "More days, more dollars," did not give the usual comfort because the stores were running short. Much had been spoiled off the Cape, and we were on half allowance of biscuit. Peas, sugar and tea had been finished long ago. Salt meat was giving out. We had plenty of coffee but very little water to make it with. We took up another hole in our belts and went on scraping, polishing, painting the ship from morning to night. And soon she looked as though she had come out of a bandbox; but hunger lived on board of her. Not dead starvation, but steady living hunger that stalked about the decks, slept in the forecastle; the tormentor of waking moments, the disturber of dreams. We looked to windward for signs of change. Every few hours of night and day we put her round with the hope that she would come up on that tack at last! She didn't. She seemed to have forgotten the way home; she rushed to and fro, heading northwest, heading east; she ran backwards and forwards, distracted, like a timid creature at the foot of a wall. Sometimes, as if tired to death, she would wallow languidly for a day in the smooth swell of an unruffled sea. All up the swinging masts the sails thrashed furiously through the hot stillness of the calm. We were weary, hungry, thirsty; we commenced to believe Singleton, but with unshaken fidelity dissembled to Jimmy. We spoke to him with jocose allusiveness, like cheerful accomplices in a clever plot; but we looked to the westward over the rail with longing eyes for a sign of hope, for a sign of fair wind; even if its first breath should bring death to our reluctant Jimmy. In vain! The universe conspired with James Wait. Light airs from the northward sprang up again; the sky remained clear; and round our weariness the glittering sea, touched by the breeze, basked voluptuously in the great sunshine, as though it had forgotten our life and trouble.

Donkin looked out for a fair wind along with the rest. No one knew the venom of his thoughts now. He was silent, and appeared thinner, as if consumed slowly by an inward rage at the injustice of men and of fate. He was ignored by all and spoke to no one, but his hate for every man dwelt in his furtive eyes. He talked with the cook only, having somehow persuaded the good man that he—Donkin—was a much calumniated and persecuted person. Together they bewailed the immorality of the ship's company. There could be no greater criminals than we, who by our lies conspired to send the unprepared soul of a poor ignorant black man to everlasting perdition. Podmore cooked what there was to cook, remorsefully, and felt all the time that by preparing the food of such sinners he imperiled his own salvation. As to the Captain—he had sailed with him for seven years, now, he said, and would not have believed it possible that such a man . . . "Well. Well . . . There it was . . . Can't get out of it. Judgment capsized all in a minute . . . Struck in all his pride . . . More like a sudden visitation than anything else." Donkin, perched sullenly on the coal locker, swung his legs and concurred. He paid in the coin of spurious assent for the privilege to sit in the galley; he was disheartened and scandalized; he agreed with the cook;

could find no word severe enough to criticize our conduct; and when in the heat of reprobation he swore at us, Podmore, who would have liked to swear also if it hadn't been for his principles, pretended not to hear. So Donkin, unrebuked, cursed enough for two, cadged for matches, borrowed tobacco, and loafed for hours, very much at home, before the stove. From there he could hear us on the other side of the bulkhead, talking to Jimmy. The cook knocked the saucepans about, slammed the oven door, muttered prophesies of damnation for all the ship's company; and Donkin, who did not admit of any hereafter (except for purposes of blasphemy) listened, concentrated and angry, gloating fiercely over a called-up image of infinite torment—as men gloat over the accursed images of cruelty and revenge, of greed, and of power. . . .

On clear evenings the silent ship, under the cold sheen of the dead moon, took on a false aspect of passionless repose resembling the winter of the earth. Under her a long band of gold barred the black disk of the sea. Footsteps echoed on her quiet decks. The moonlight clung to her like a frosted mist, and the white sails stood out in dazzling cones as of stainless snow. In the magnificence of the phantom rays the ship appeared pure like a vision of ideal beauty, illusive like a tender dream of serene peace. And nothing in her was real, nothing was distinct and solid but the heavy shadows that filled her decks with their unceasing and noiseless stir: the shadows darker than the night and more restless than the thoughts of men.

Donkin prowled spiteful and alone amongst the shadows, thinking that Jimmy too long delayed to die. That evening land had been reported from aloft, and the master, while adjusting the tubes of the log glass, had observed with quiet bitterness to Mr. Baker that, after fighting our way inch by inch to the Western Islands, there was nothing to expect now but a spell of calm. The sky was clear and the barometer high. The light breeze dropped with the sun, and an enormous stillness, forerunner of a night without wind, descended upon the heated waters of the ocean. As long as daylight lasted, the hands collected on the forecastle head watched on the eastern sky the island of Flores, that rose above the level expanse of the sea with irregular and broken outlines like a somber ruin upon a vast and deserted plain. It was the first land seen for nearly four months. Charley was excited, and in the midst of general indulgence took liberties with his betters. Men strangely elated without knowing why, talked in groups, and pointed with bared arms. For the first time that voyage Jimmy's sham existence seemed for a moment forgotten in the face of a solid reality. We had got so far anyhow. Belfast discoursed, quoting imaginary examples of short homeward runs from the Islands. "Them smart fruit schooners do it in five days," he affirmed. "What do you want?—only a good little breeze." Archie maintained that seven days was the record passage, and they disputed amicably with insulting words. Knowles declared he could already smell home from there, and with a heavy list on his short leg laughed fit to split his sides. A group of grizzled sea dogs looked out for a time in silence and with grim absorbed faces. One said suddenly: " 'Tain't far to London now." "My first night ashore, blamme if I haven't steak and onions for supper . . . and a pint of bitter," said another.—"A barrel ye mean," shouted someone.—"Ham an' eggs three times a day. That's the way I live!" cried an excited voice. There was a stir, appreciative murmurs; eyes began to shine; jaws champed; short, nervous laughs were heard. Archie smiled with reserve all to himself. Singleton came up, gave a careless glance, and went down again without saying a word, indifferent, like a man who had seen Flores an incalculable number of times. The night traveling from the East blotted out of the limpid sky the purple stain of the high land. "Dead calm," said somebody quietly. The murmur of lively talk suddenly wavered, died out; the clusters broke up; men began to drift away one by one, descending the ladders slowly and with serious faces as if sobered by that reminder of their dependence upon the invisible. And when the big yellow moon ascended gently above the sharp rim of the clear horizon it found the ship wrapped up in a breathless silence; a fearless ship that seemed to sleep profoundly, dreamlessly, on the bosom of the sleeping and terrible sea.

Donkin chafed at the peace—at the ship—at the sea that, stretching away on all sides, merged into the illimitable silence of all creation. He felt himself pulled up sharp by unrecognized grievances. He had been physically cowed, but his injured dignity remained indomitable, and nothing could heal his lacerated feelings. Here was land already—home very soon—a bad payday—no clothes—more hard work. How offensive all this was. Land. The land that draws away life from sick sailors. That nigger there had money—clothes—easy times; and would not die. Land draws life away. . . . He felt tempted to go and see whether it did. Perhaps already . . . It would be a bit of luck. There was money in the beggar's chest. He stepped briskly out of the shadows into the moonlight, and, instantly, his craving, hungry face from sallow became livid. He opened the door of the cabin and had a shock. Sure enough, Jimmy was dead! He moved no more than a recumbent figure with clasped hands, carved on the lid of a stone coffin. Donkin glared with avidity. Then Jimmy, without stirring, blinked his eyelids, and Donkin had another shock. Those eyes were rather startling. He shut the door behind his back with gentle care, looking intently the while at James Wait as though he had come in there at a great risk to tell some secret of startling importance. Jimmy did not move but glanced languidly out of the corners of his eyes. "Calm?" he asked. "Yuss," said Donkin, very disappointed, and sat down on the box.

Jimmy was used to such visits at all times of night or day. Men succeeded one another. They spoke in clear voices, pronounced cheerful words, repeated old jokes, listened to him; and each, going out, seemed to leave behind a little of his own vitality, surrender some of his own strength, renew the assurance of life—the indestructible thing! He did not like to be alone in his cabin, because, when he was alone, it seemed to him as if he hadn't been there at all. There was nothing. No pain. Not now. Perfectly right—but he couldn't enjoy his healthful repose unless someone was by to see it. This man would do as well as anybody. Donkin watched him stealthily: "Soon home now," observed Wait. "Vy d'yer whisper?" asked Donkin with interest, "can't yer speak up?" Jimmy looked annoyed and said nothing for a while; then in a lifeless, unringing voice: "Why should I shout? You ain't deaf that I know." "Oh! I can 'ear right enough," answered Donkin in a low tone, and looked down. He was thinking sadly of going out when Jimmy spoke again. "Time we did get home . . . to get something decent to eat . . . I am always hungry." Donkin felt angry all of a sudden. "What about me," he hissed, "I am 'ungry too an' got ter work. You, 'ungry!" "Your work won't kill you," commented Wait, feebly; "there's a couple of biscuits in the lower bunk there—you may have one. I can't eat them." Donkin dived in, groped in the corner and when he came up again his mouth was full. He munched with ardor. Jimmy seemed to doze with open eyes. Donkin finished his hard bread and got up. "You're not going?" asked Jimmy, staring at the ceiling. "No," said Donkin, impulsively, and instead of going out leaned his back against the closed door. He looked at James Wait, and saw him long, lean, dried up, as though all his flesh had shriveled on his bones in the heat of a white furnace; the meager fingers of one hand moved lightly upon the edge of the bunk playing an endless tune. To look at him was irritating and fatiguing; he could last like this for days; he was outrageous—belonging wholly neither to death nor life, and perfectly invulnerable in his apparent ignorance of both. Donkin felt tempted to enlighten him. "What are yer thinkin' of?" he asked, surlily. James Wait had a grimacing smile that passed over the deathlike impassiveness of his bony face, incredible and frightful as would, in a dream, have been the sudden smile of a corpse.

"There is a girl," whispered Wait. . . . "Canton Street

girl. . . . She chucked a third engineer of a Rennie boat . . . for me. Cooks oysters just as I like . . . She says . . . she would chuck . . . any toff . . . for a colored gentleman. . . . That's me. I am kind to wimmen," he added, a shade louder.

Donkin could hardly believe his ears. He was scandalized. "Would she? Yer wouldn't be any good to 'er," he said with unrestrained disgust. Wait was not there to hear him. He was swaggering up the East India Dock Road; saying kindly, "Come along for a treat," pushing glass swing-doors, posing with superb assurance in the gaslight above a mahogany counter. "D'yer think yer will ever get ashore?" asked Donkin, angrily. Wait came back with a start. "Ten days," he said, promptly, and returned at once to the regions of memory that know nothing of time. He felt untired, calm, and safely withdrawn within himself beyond the reach of every grave incertitude. There was something of the immutable quality of eternity in the slow movements of his complete restfulness. He was very quiet and easy amongst his vivid reminiscences, which he mistook joyfully for images of an undoubted future. He cared for no one. Donkin felt this vaguely like a blind man feeling in his darkness the fatal antagonism of all the surrounding existences, that to him shall for ever remain irrealizable, unseen and enviable. He had a desire to assert his importance, to break, to crush; to be even with everybody for everything; to tear the veil, unmask, expose, leave no refuge—a perfidious desire of truthfulness! He laughed in a mocking splutter and said:

"Ten days. Strike me blind if I ever! . . . You will be dead by this time tomorrow p'r'aps. Ten days!" He waited for a while. "D'ye 'ear me? Blamme if yer don't look dead already."

Wait must have been collecting his strength, for he said almost aloud: "You're a stinking, cadging liar. Everyone knows you." And sitting up, against all probability, startled his visitor horribly. But very soon Donkin recovered himself. He blustered.

"What? What? Who's a liar? You are—the crowd are—the skipper—everybody. I ain't! Putting on airs! Who's yer?" He nearly choked himself with indignation. "Who's yer to put on airs," he repeated, trembling. " 'Ave one—'ave one, says 'ee—an' cawn't eat 'em 'isself. Now I'll 'ave both. By Gawd—I will! Yer nobody!"

He plunged into the lower bunk, rooted in there and brought to light another dusty biscuit. He held it up before Jimmy—then took a bite defiantly.

"What now?" he asked with feverish impudence. "Yer may take one—says yer. Why not give me both? No. I'm a mangy dorg. One fur a mangy dorg. I'll tyke both. Can yer stop me? Try. Come on. Try."

Jimmy was clasping his legs and hiding his face on the knees. His shirt clung to him. Every rib was visible. His emaciated back was shaken in repeated jerks by the panting catches of his breath.

"Yer won't? Yer can't! What did I say?" went on Donkin, fiercely. He swallowed another dry mouthful with a hasty effort. The other's silent helplessness, his weakness, his shrinking attitude, exasperated him. "Ye're done!" he cried. "Who's yer to be lied to; to be waited on 'and an' foot like a bloomin' ymperor? Yer nobody. Yer no one at all!" he spluttered with such a strength of unerring conviction that it shook him from head to foot in coming out, and left him vibrating like a released string.

James Wait rallied again. He lifted his head and turned bravely at Donkin, who saw a strange face, an unknown face, a fantastic and grimacing mask of despair and fury. Its lips moved rapidly; and hollow, moaning, whistling sounds filled the cabin with a vague mutter full of menace, complaint and desolation, like the far-off murmur of a rising wind. Wait shook his head; rolled his eyes; he denied, cursed, threatened—and not a word had the strength to pass beyond the sorrowful pout of those black lips. It was incomprehensible and disturbing; a gibberish of emotions, a frantic dumb show of speech pleading for impossible things, promising a shadowy vengeance. It sobered Donkin into a scrutinizing watchfulness.

"Yer can't 'oller. See? What did I tell yer?" he said, slowly, after a moment of attentive examination. The other kept on headlong and unheard, nodding passionately, grinning with grotesque and appalling flashes of big white teeth. Donkin, as if fascinated by the dumb eloquence and anger of that black phantom, approached, stretching his neck out with distrustful curiosity; and it seemed to him suddenly that he was looking only at the shadow of a man crouching high in the bunk on the level with his eyes. "What? What?" he said. He seemed to catch the shape of some words in the continuous panting hiss. "Yer will tell Belfast! Will yer? Are yer a bloomin' kid?" He trembled with alarm and rage: "Tell yer gran'mother! Yer afeard! Who's yer to be afeard more'n anyone?" His passionate sense of his own importance ran away with a last remnant of caution. "Tell an' be damned! Tell, if yer can!" he cried. "I've been treated worse'n a dorg by your blooming backlickers. They 'as set me on, only to turn aginst me. I am the only man 'ere. They clouted me, kicked me—an' yer laffed—yer black, rotten incumbrance, you! You will pay fur it. They giv' yer their grub, their water—yer will pay fur it to me, by Gawd! Who axed me ter 'ave a drink of water? They put their bloomin' rags on yer that night, an' what did they giv' ter me—a clout on the bloomin' mouth—blast their . . . S'elp me! . . . Yer will pay fur it with yer money. I'm goin' ter 'ave it in a minyte; as soon has ye're dead, yer bloomin' useless fraud. That's the man I am. An' ye're a thing—a bloody thing. Yah—you corpse!"

He flung at Jimmy's head the biscuit he had been all the time clutching hard, but it only grazed, and striking with a loud crack the bulkhead beyond burst like a hand grenade into flying pieces. James Wait, as if wounded mortally, fell back on the pillow. His lips ceased to move and the rolling eyes became quiet and stared upwards with an intense and steady persistence. Donkin was surprised; he sat suddenly on the chest, and looked down, exhausted and gloomy.

After a moment, he began to mutter to himself, "Die, you beggar—die. Somebody'll come in . . . I wish I was drunk. . . . Ten days . . . oysters . . ." He looked up and spoke louder. "No. . . . No more fer yer . . . no more bloomin' gals that cook oysters. . . . Who's yer? It's my turn now. . . . I wish I was drunk; I would soon give you a leg up. That's where yer bound to go. Feet fust, through a port . . . Splash! Never see yer any more. Overboard! Good 'nuff fur yer."

Jimmy's head moved slightly and he turned his eyes to Donkin's face; a gaze unbelieving, desolated and appealing, of a child frightened by the menace of being shut up alone in the dark. Donkin observed him from the chest with hopeful eyes; then, without rising, tried the lid. Locked. "I wish I was drunk," he muttered and getting up listened anxiously to the distant sound of footsteps on the deck. They approached—ceased. Someone yawned interminably just outside the door, and the footsteps went away shuffling lazily. Donkin's fluttering heart eased its pace, and when he looked towards the bunk again Jimmy was staring as before at the white beam. " 'Ow d'yer feel now?" he asked. "Bad," breathed out Jimmy.

Donkin sat down patient and purposeful. Every half-hour the bells spoke to one another ringing along the whole length of the ship. Jimmy's respiration was so rapid that it couldn't be counted, so faint that it couldn't be heard. His eyes were terrified as though he had been looking at unspeakable horrors; and by his face one could see that he was thinking of abominable things. Suddenly with an incredibly strong and heartbreaking voice he sobbed out:

"Overboard! . . . I! . . . My God!"

Donkin writhed a little on the box. He looked unwillingly. James Wait was mute. His two long bony hands smoothed the blanket upwards, as though he had wished to gather it all up under his chin. A tear, a big solitary tear, escaped from the corner of his eye and, without touching the hollow cheek, fell on the pillow. His throat rattled faintly.

And Donkin, watching the end of that hateful nigger, felt the anguishing grasp of a great sorrow on his heart at the thought that he himself, someday, would have to go through it all—just like this—perhaps! His eyes became moist. "Poor beggar," he murmured. The night seemed to go by in a flash; it seemed to him he could hear the irremediable rush of precious minutes. How long would this blooming affair last? Too long surely. No luck. He could not restrain himself. He got up and approached the bunk. Wait did not stir. Only his eyes appeared alive and his hands continued their smoothing movement with a horrible and tireless industry. Donkin bent over.

"Jimmy," he called low. There was no answer, but the rattle stopped. "D'yer see me?" he asked, trembling. Jimmy's chest heaved. Donkin, looking away, bent his ear to Jimmy's lips, and heard a sound like the rustle of a single dry leaf driven along the smooth sand of a beach. It shaped itself.

"Light . . . the lamp . . . and . . . go," breathed out Wait.

Donkin, instinctively, glanced over his shoulder at the brilliant flame; then, still looking away, felt under the pillow for a key. He got it at once and for the next few minutes remained on his knees shakily but swiftly busy inside the box. When he got up, his face—for the first time in his life—had a pink flush—perhaps of triumph.

He slipped the key under the pillow again, avoiding to glance at Jimmy, who had not moved. He turned his back squarely from the bunk and started to the door as though he were going to walk a mile. At his second stride he had his nose against it. He clutched the handle cautiously, but at that moment he received the irresistible impression of something happening behind his back. He spun round as though he had been tapped on the shoulder. He was just in time to see Wait's eyes blaze up and go out at once, like two lamps overturned together by a sweeping blow. Something resembling a scarlet thread hung down his chin out of the corner of his lips—and he had ceased to breathe.

Donkin closed the door behind him gently but firmly.

Sleeping men, huddled under jackets, made on the lighted deck shapeless dark mounds that had the appearance of neglected graves. Nothing had been done all through the night and he hadn't been missed. He stood motionless and perfectly astounded to find the world outside as he had left it; there was the sea, the ship—sleeping men; and he wondered absurdly at it, as though he had expected to find the men dead, familiar things gone forever: as though, like a wanderer returning after many years, he had expected to see bewildering changes. He shuddered a little in the penetrating freshness of the air, and hugged himself forlornly. The declining moon drooped sadly in the western board as if withered by the cold touch of a pale dawn. The ship slept. And the immortal sea stretched away, immense and hazy, like the image of life, with a glittering surface and lightless depths. Donkin gave it a defiant glance and slunk off noiselessly as if judged and cast out by the august silence of its might.

Jimmy's death, after all, came as a tremendous surprise. We did not know till then how much faith we had put in his delusions. We had taken his chances of life so much at his own valuation that his death, like the death of an old belief, shook the foundations of our society. A common bond was gone; the strong, effective and respectable bond of a sentimental lie. All that day we mooned at our work, with suspicious looks and a disabused air. In our hearts we thought that in the matter of his departure Jimmy had acted in a perverse and unfriendly manner. He didn't back us up, as a shipmate should. In going he took away with himself the gloomy and solemn shadow in which our folly had posed, with humane satisfaction, as a tender arbiter of fate. And now we saw it was no such thing. It was just common foolishness; a silly and ineffectual meddling with issues of majestic import—that is, if Podmore was right. Perhaps he was? Doubt survived Jimmy; and, like a community of banded criminals disintegrated by a touch of grace, we were profoundly scandalized with each other. Men spoke unkindly to their best chums. Others refused to speak at all. Singleton only was not surprised. "Dead—is he? Of course," he said, pointing at the island right abeam: for the calm still held the ship spellbound within sight of Flores. Dead—of course. *He* wasn't surprised. Here was the land, and there, on the forehatch and waiting for the sailmaker—there was that corpse. Cause and effect. And, for the first time that voyage, the old seaman became quite cheery and garrulous, explaining and illustrating from the stores of experience how, in sickness, the sight of an island (even a very small one) is generally more fatal than the view of a continent. But he couldn't explain why.

Jimmy was to be buried at five, and it was a long day till then—a day of mental disquiet and even of physical disturbance. We took no interest in our work and, very properly, were rebuked for it. This, in our constant state of hungry irritation, was exasperating. Donkin worked with his brow bound in a dirty rag, and looked so ghastly that Mr. Baker was touched with compassion at the sight of this plucky suffering. "Ough! You, Donkin! Put down your work and go lay-up this watch. You look ill." "I am bad, sir—in my 'ead," he said in a subdued voice, and vanished speedily. This annoyed many, and they thought the mate "bloomin' soft today." Captain Allistoun could be seen on the poop watching the sky to the southwest, and it soon got to be known about the decks that the barometer had begun to fall in the night, and that a breeze might be expected before long. This, by a subtle association of ideas, led to violent quarreling as to the exact moment of Jimmy's death. Was it before or after "that 'ere glass started down?" It was impossible to know, and it caused much contemptuous growling at one another. All of a sudden there was a great tumult forward. Pacific Knowles and good-tempered Davis had come to blows over it. The watch below interfered with spirit, and for ten minutes there was a noisy scrimmage round the hatch, where, in the balancing shade of the sails, Jimmy's body, wrapped up in a white blanket, was watched over by the sorrowful Belfast, who, in his desolation, disdained the fray. When the noise had ceased, and the passions had calmed into surly silence, he stood up at the head of the swathed body, lifting both arms on high, cried with pained indignation: "You ought to be ashamed of yourselves! . . ." We were.

Belfast took his bereavement very hard. He gave proofs of unextinguishable devotion, It was he, and no other man, who would help the sailmaker to prepare what was left of Jimmy for a solemn surrender to the insatiable sea. He arranged the weights carefully at the feet: two holystones, an old anchor shackle without its pin, some broken links of a worn-out stream cable. He arranged them this way, then that. "Bless my soul! you aren't afraid he will chafe his heel?" said the sailmaker, who hated the job. He pushed the needle, puffing furiously, with his head in a cloud of tobacco smoke; he turned the flaps over, pulled at the stitches, stretched at the canvas. "Lift his shoulders. . . . Pull to you a bit. . . . So—o—o. Steady." Belfast obeyed, pulled, lifted, overcome with sorrow, dropping tears on the tarred twine. "Don't you drag the canvas too taut over his poor face, Sails," he entreated, tearfully. "What are you fashing yourself for? He will be comfortable enough," assured the sailmaker, cutting the thread after the last stitch, which came about the middle of Jimmy's forehead. He rolled up the remaining canvas, put away the needles. "What makes you take on so?" he asked. Belfast looked down at the long package of gray sailcloth. "I pulled him out," he whispered, "and he did not want to go. If I had sat up with him last night he would have kept alive for me . . . but something made me tired." The sailmaker took vigorous draws at his pipe and mumbled: "When I . . . West India Station . . . In the *Blanche* frigate . . . Yellow Jack . . . sewed in twenty men a week . . . Portsmouth-Devonport men—townies—knew their fathers, mothers, sisters—the whole boiling of 'em. Thought nothing of it. And these niggers like this one —you don't know where it comes from. Got nobody. No use to nobody. Who will miss him?" "I do—I pulled him out," mourned Belfast dismally.

On two planks nailed together and apparently resigned and still under the folds of the Union Jack with a white border, James Wait, carried aft by four men, was deposited slowly, with his feet pointing at an open port. A swell had set in from the westward, and, following on the roll of the ship, the red ensign, at half-mast, darted out and collapsed again on the gray sky, like a tongue of flickering fire; Charley tolled the bell; and at every swing to starboard the whole vast semicircle of steely waters visible on that side seemed to come up with a rush to the edge of the port, as if impatient to get at our Jimmy. Everyone was there but Donkin, who was too ill to come; the Captain and Mr. Creighton stood bareheaded on the break of the poop; Mr. Baker, directed by the master, who had said to him gravely: "You know more about the prayer book than I do," came out of the cabin door quickly and a little embarrassed. All the caps went off. He began to read in a low tone, and with his usual harmlessly menacing utterance, as though he had been for the last time reproving confidentially that dead seaman at his feet. The men listened in scattered groups; they leaned on the fife rail, gazing on the deck; they held their chins in their hands thoughtfully, or, with crossed arms and one knee slightly bent, hung their heads in an attitude of upright meditation. Wamibo dreamed. Mr. Baker read on, grunting reverently at the turn of every page. The words, missing the unsteady hearts of men, rolled out to wander without a home upon the heartless sea; and James Wait, silenced forever, lay uncritical and passive under the hoarse murmur of despair and hopes.

Two men made ready and waited for those words that send so many of our brothers to their last plunge. Mr. Baker began the passage. "Stand by," muttered the boatswain. Mr. Baker read out: "To the deep," and paused. The men lifted the inboard end of the planks, the boatswain snatched off the Union Jack, and James Wait did not move. —"Higher," muttered the boatswain angrily. All the heads were raised; every man stirred uneasily, but James Wait gave no sign of going. In death and swathed up for all eternity, he yet seemed to cling to the ship with the grip of an undying fear. "Higher! Lift!" whispered the boatswain, fiercely. "He won't go," stammered one of the men, shakily, and both appeared ready to drop everything. Mr. Baker waited, burying his face in the book, and shuffling his feet nervously. All the men looked profoundly disturbed; from their midst a faint humming noise spread out—growing louder. . . . "Jimmy!" cried Belfast in a wailing tone, and there was a second of shuddering dismay.

"Jimmy, be a man!" he shrieked, passionately. Every mouth was wide open, not an eyelid winked. He stared wildly, twitching all over; he bent his body forward like a man peering at an horror. "Go!" he shouted, and sprang out of the crowd with his arm extended. "Go, Jimmy!—Jimmy, go! Go!" His fingers touched the head of the body, and the gray package started reluctantly to whizz off the lifted planks all at once, with the suddenness of a flash of lightning. The crowd stepped forward like one man; a deep Ah—h—h! came out vibrating from the broad chests. The ship rolled as if relieved of an unfair burden; the sails flapped. Belfast, supported by Archie, gasped hysterically; and Charley, who, anxious to see Jimmy's last dive, leaped headlong on the rail, was too late to see anything but the faint circle of a vanishing ripple.

Mr. Baker, perspiring abundantly, read out the last prayer in a deep rumor of excited men and fluttering sail. "Amen!" he said in an unsteady growl, and closed the book.

"Square the yards!" thundered a voice above his head. All hands gave a jump; one or two dropped their caps; Mr. Baker looked up surprised. The master, standing on the break of the poop, pointed to the westward. "Breeze coming," he said. "Man the weather braces." Mr. Baker crammed the book hurriedly into his pocket. "Forward, there—let go the foretack!" he hailed joyfully, bareheaded and brisk. "Square the foreyard, you port watch!" "Fair wind—fair wind," muttered the men going to the braces. "What did I tell you?" mumbled old Singleton, flinging down coil after coil with hasty energy; "I knowed it—he's gone, and here it comes."

It came with the sound of a lofty and powerful sigh. The sails filled, the ship gathered way, and the waking sea began to murmur sleepily of home to the ears of men.

That night, while the ship rushed foaming to the northward before a freshening gale, the boatswain unbosomed himself to the petty officers' berth: "The chap was nothing but trouble," he said, "from the moment he came aboard—d'ye remember—that night in Bombay? Been bullying all that softy crowd—cheeked the old man—we had to go fooling all over a half-drowned ship to save him. Dam' nigh a mutiny all for him—and now the mate abused me like a pickpocket for forgetting to dab a lump of grease on them planks. So I did, but you ought to have known better, too, than to leave a nail sticking up—hey, Chips?"

"And you ought to have known better than to chuck all my tools overboard for 'im, like a skeary greenhorn," retorted the morose carpenter. "Well—he's gone after 'em now," he added in an unforgiving tone. "On the China Station, I remember once, the Admiral he says to me . . ." began the sailmaker.

A week afterwards the *Narcissus* entered the chops of the Channel.

Under white wings she skimmed low over the blue sea like a great tired bird speeding to its nest. The clouds raced with her mastheads; they rose astern enormous and white, soared to the zenith, flew past, and, falling down the wide curve of the sky, seemed to dash headlong into the sea—the clouds swifter than the ship, more free, but without a home. The coast, to welcome her, stepped out of space into the sunshine. The lofty headlands trod masterfully into the sea; the wide bays smiled in the light; the shadows of homeless clouds ran along the sunny plains, leaped over valleys, without a check darted up the hills, rolled down the slopes; and the sunshine pursued them with patches of running brightness. On the brows of dark cliffs white lighthouses shone in pillars of light. The Channel glittered like a blue mantle shot with gold and starred by the silver of the capping seas. The *Narcissus* rushed past the headlands and the bays. Outward-bound vessels crossed her track, lying over, and with their masts stripped for a slogging fight with the hard sou'wester. And, inshore, a string of smoking steamboats waddled, hugging the coast, like migrating and amphibious monsters, distrustful of the restless waves.

At night the headlands retreated, the bays advanced into one unbroken line of gloom. The lights of the earth mingled with the lights of heaven; and above the tossing lanterns of a trawling fleet a great lighthouse shone steadily, like an enormous riding light burning above a vessel of fabulous dimensions. Below its steady glow, the coast, stretching away straight and black, resembled the high side of an indestructible craft riding motionless upon the immortal and unresting sea. The dark land lay alone in the midst of waters, like a mighty ship bestarred with vigilant lights—a ship carrying the burden of millions of lives—a ship freighted with dross and with jewels, with gold and with steel. She towered up immense and strong, guarding priceless traditions and untold suffering, sheltering glorious memories and base forgetfulness, ignoble virtues and splendid transgressions. A great ship! For ages had the ocean battered in vain her enduring sides; she was there when the world was vaster and darker, when the sea was great and mysterious, and ready to surrender the prize of fame to audacious men. A ship mother of fleets and nations! The great flagship of the race; stronger than the storms! and anchored in the open sea.

The *Narcissus,* heeling over to offshore gusts, rounded the South Foreland, passed through the Downs, and, in tow, entered the river. Shorn of the glory of her white wings, she wound obediently after the tug through the maze of invisible channels. As she passed them the red-painted light-vessels, swung at their moorings, seemed for an instant to sail with great speed in the rush of tide, and the next moment were left helplessly behind. The big buoys on the tails of banks slipped past her sides very low, and, dropping in her wake, tugged at their chains like fierce watchdogs. The reach narrowed; from both sides the land approached the ship. She went steadily up the river. On the riverside slopes the houses appeared in groups—seemed to stream down the declivities at a run to see her pass, and, checked by the mud of the foreshore, crowded on the banks. Further on, the tall factory chimneys appeared in insolent bands and watched her go by, like a straggling crowd of slim giants, swaggering and upright under the black plumets of smoke, cavalierly aslant. She swept round the bends; an impure breeze shrieked a welcome between her stripped spars; and the land, closing in, stepped between the ship and the sea.

A low cloud hung before her—a great opalescent and tremulous cloud, that seemed to rise from the steaming brows of millions of men. Long drifts of smoky vapors soiled it with livid trails; it throbbed to the beat of millions of hearts, and from it came an immense and lamentable murmur—the murmur of millions of lips praying, cursing, sighing, jeering—the undying murmur of folly, regret, and hope exhaled by the crowds of the anxious earth. The *Narcissus* entered the cloud; the shadows deepened; on all sides there was the clang of iron, the sound of mighty blows, shrieks, yells. Black barges drifted stealthily on the murky stream. A mad jumble of begrimed walls loomed up vaguely in the smoke, bewildering and mournful, like a vision of disaster. The tugs backed and filled in the stream to hold the ship steady at the dock gates; from her bows two lines went through the air whistling and struck at the land viciously, like a pair of snakes. A bridge broke in two before her, as if by enchantment; big hydraulic capstans began to turn all by themselves, as though animated by a mysterious and unholy spell. She moved through a narrow lane of water between two low walls of granite, and men with checkropes in their hands kept pace with her, walking on the broad flagstones. A group waited impatiently on each side of the vanished bridge: rough heavy men in caps; sallow-faced men in high hats; two bareheaded women; ragged children, fascinated, and with wide eyes. A cart coming at a jerking trot pulled up sharply. One of the women screamed at the silent ship—"Hallo, Jack!" without looking at anyone in particular, and all hands looked at her from the forecastle head. "Stand clear! Stand clear of that rope!" cried the dockmen, bending over stone posts. The crowd murmured, stamped where they stood. "Let go your quarter-checks! Let go!" sang out a ruddy-faced old man on the quay. The ropes splashed heavily falling in the water, and the *Narcissus* entered the dock.

The stony shores ran away right and left in straight lines, enclosing a somber and rectangular pool. Brick walls rose high above the water—soulless walls, staring through hundreds of windows as troubled and dull as the eyes of overfed brutes. At their base monstrous iron cranes crouched, with chains hanging from their long necks, balancing cruel-looking hooks over the decks of lifeless ships. A noise of wheels rolling over stones, the thump of heavy things falling, the racket of feverish winches, the grinding of strained chains, floated on the air. Between high buildings the dust of all the continents soared in short flights; and a penetrating smell of perfumes and dirt, of spices and hides, of things costly and of things filthy, pervaded the space, made for it an atmosphere precious and disgusting. The *Narcissus* came gently into her berth; the shadows of soulless walls fell upon her, the dust of all the continents leaped upon her deck, and a swarm of strange men, clambering up her sides, took possession of her in the name of the sordid earth. She had ceased to live.

A toff in a black coat and high hat scrambled with agility, came up to the second mate, shook hands, and said: "Hallo, Herbert." It was his brother. A lady appeared suddenly. A real lady, in a black dress and with a parasol. She looked extremely elegant in the midst of us, and as strange as if she had fallen there from the sky. Mr. Baker touched his cap to her. It was the master's wife. And very soon the Captain, dressed very smartly and in a white shirt, went with her over the side. We didn't recognize him at all till, turning on the quay, he called to Mr. Baker: "Don't forget to wind up the chronometers tomorrow morning." An underhand lot of seedy-looking chaps with shifty eyes wandered in and out of the forecastle looking for a job—they said. "More likely for something to steal," commented Knowles, cheerfully. Poor beggars. Who cared? Weren't we home! But Mr. Baker went for one of them who had given him some cheek, and we were delighted. Everything was delightful. "I've finished aft, sir," called out Mr. Creighton. "No water in the well, sir," reported for the last time the carpenter, sounding rod in hand. Mr. Baker glanced along the decks at the expectant group of sailors, glanced aloft at the yards. "Ough! That will do, men," he grunted. The group broke up. The voyage was ended.

Rolled-up beds went flying over the rail; lashed chests went sliding down the gangway—mighty few of both at that. "The rest is having a cruise off the Cape," explained Knowles enigmatically to a dock loafer with whom he had struck a sudden friendship. Men ran, calling to one another, hailing utter strangers to "lend a hand with the dunnage," then with sudden decorum approached the mate to shake hands before going ashore. "Good-bye, sir," they repeated in various tones. Mr. Baker grasped hard palms, grunted in a friendly manner at everyone, his eyes twinkled. —"Take care of your money, Knowles. Ough! Soon get a nice wife if you do." The lame man was delighted. "Good-bye, sir," said Belfast, with emotion, wringing the mate's hand, and looked up with swimming eyes. "I thought I would take 'im ashore with me," he went on, plaintively. Mr. Baker did not understand, but said kindly: "Take care of yourself, Craik," and the bereaved Belfast went over the rail mourning and alone.

Mr. Baker, in the sudden peace of the ship, moved about solitary and grunting, trying door handles, peering into dark places, never done—a model chief mate! No one waited for him ashore. Mother dead; father and two brothers, Yarmouth fishermen, drowned together on the Dogger

Bank; sister married and unfriendly. Quite a lady. Married to the leading tailor of a little town, and its leading politician, who did not think his sailor brother-in-law quite respectable enough for him. Quite a lady, quite a lady, he thought, sitting down for a moment's rest on the quarter-hatch. Time enough to go ashore and get a bite and sup, and a bed somewhere. He didn't like to part with a ship. No one to think about then. The darkness of a misty evening fell, cold and damp, upon the deserted deck; and Mr. Baker sat smoking, thinking of all the successive ships to whom through many long years he had given the best of a seaman's care. And never a command in sight. Not once! "I haven't somehow the cut of a skipper about me," he meditated, placidly, while the shipkeeper (who had taken possession of the galley), a wizened old man with bleared eyes, cursed him in whispers for "hanging about so." "Now Creighton," he pursued the unenvious train of thought, "quite a gentleman . . . swell friends . . . will get on. Fine young fellow . . . a little more experience." He got up and shook himself. "I'll be back first thing tomorrow morning for the hatches. Don't you let them touch anything before I come, shipkeeper," he called out. Then, at last, he also went ashore—a model chief mate!

The men scattered by the dissolving contact of the land came together once more in the shipping office. "The *Narcissus* pays off," shouted outside a glazed door a brass-bound old fellow with a crown and the capitals B. T. on his cap. A lot trooped in at once but many were late. The room was large, whitewashed, and bare; a counter surmounted by a brass-wire grating fenced off a third of the dusty space, and behind the grating a pasty-faced clerk, with his hair parted in the middle, had the quick, glittering eyes and the vivacious jerky movements of a caged bird. Poor Captain Allistoun also in there, and sitting before a little table with piles of gold and notes on it, appeared subdued by his captivity. Another Board of Trade bird was perching on a high stool near the door: an old bird that did not mind the chaff of elated sailors. The crew of the *Narcissus,* broken up into knots, pushed in the corners. They had new shore togs, smart jackets that looked as if they had been shaped with an ax, glossy trousers that seemed made of crumpled sheet iron, collarless flannel shirts, shiny new boots. They tapped on shoulders, buttonholed one another, asked: "Where did you sleep last night?" whispered gaily, slapped their thighs with bursts of subdued laughter. Most had clean, radiant faces; only one or two turned up disheveled and sad; the two young Norwegians looked tidy, meek, and altogether of a promising material for the kind ladies who patronize the Scandinavian Home. Wamibo, still in his working clothes, dreamed, upright and burly in the middle of the room, and, when Archie came in, woke up for a smile. But the wide-awake clerk called out a name, and the paying-off business began.

One by one they came up to the pay table to get the wages of their glorious and obscure toil. They swept the money with care into broad palms, rammed it trustfully into trousers' pockets, or, turning their backs on the table, reckoned with difficulty in the hollow of their stiff hands. "Money right? Sign the release. There—there," repeated the clerk, impatiently. "How stupid those sailors are!" he thought. Singleton came up, venerable—and uncertain as to daylight; brown drops of tobacco juice hung in his white beard; his hands, that never hesitated in the great light of the open sea, could hardly find the small pile of gold in the profound darkness of the shore. "Can't write?" said the clerk, shocked. "Make a mark, then." Singleton painfully sketched in a heavy cross, blotted the page. "What a disgusting old brute," muttered the clerk. Somebody opened the door for him, and the patriarchal seaman passed through unsteadily, without as much as a glance at any of us.

Archie displayed a pocketbook. He was chaffed. Belfast, who looked wild, as though he had already luffed up through a public house or two, gave signs of emotion and wanted to speak to the Captain privately. The master was surprised. They spoke through the wires, and we could hear the Captain saying: "I've given it up to the Board of Trade." "I should've liked to get something of his," mumbled Belfast. "But you can't, my man. It's given up, locked and sealed, to the Marine Office," expostulated the master; and Belfast stood back, with drooping mouth and troubled eyes. In a pause of the business we heard the master and the clerk talking. We caught: "James Wait—deceased—found no papers of any kind—no relations—no trace—the Office must hold his wages then." Donkin entered. He seemed out of breath, was grave, full of business. He went straight to the desk, talked with animation to the clerk, who thought him an intelligent man. They discussed the account, dropping h's against one another as if for a wager—very friendly. Captain Allistoun paid. "I give you a bad discharge," he said, quietly. Donkin raised his voice: "I don't want your bloomin' discharge—keep it. I'm goin' ter 'ave a job ashore." He turned to us. "No more bloomin' sea fur me," he said, aloud. All looked at him. He had better clothes, had an easy air, appeared more at home than any of us; he stared with assurance, enjoying the effect of his declaration. "Yuss. I 'ave friends well off. That's more'n you got. But I am a man. Yer shipmates for all that. Who's comin' fur a drink?"

No one moved. There was a silence; a silence of blank faces and stony looks. He waited a moment, smiled bitterly, and went to the door. There he faced round once more. "You won't? You bloomin' lot of 'yrpocrits. No? What 'ave I done to yer? Did I bully yer? Did I 'urt yer? Did I? . . . You won't drink? . . . No! . . . Then may ye die of thirst, every mother's son of yer! Not one of yer 'as the sperit of a bug. Ye're the scum of the world. Work and starve!"

He went out, and slammed the door with such violence that the old Board of Trade bird nearly fell off his perch.

"He's mad," declared Archie. "No! No! He's drunk," insisted Belfast, lurching about, and in a maudlin tone. Captain Allistoun sat smiling thoughtfully at the cleared pay table.

Outside, on Tower Hill, they blinked, hesitated clumsily, as if blinded by the strange quality of the hazy light, as if discomposed by the view of so many men; and they who could hear one another in the howl of gales seemed deafened and distracted by the dull roar of the busy earth. "To the Black Horse! To the Black Horse!" cried some. "Let us have a drink together before we part." They crossed the road, clinging to one another. Only Charley and Belfast wandered off alone. As I came up I saw a red-faced, blowsy woman, in a gray shawl and with dusty, fluffy hair, fall on Charley's neck. It was his mother. She slobbered over him: "O, my boy! My boy!"—"Leggo of me," said Charley. "Leggo, mother!" I was passing him at the time, and over the untidy head of the blubbering woman he gave me a humorous smile and a glance ironic, courageous, and profound, that seemed to put all my knowledge of life to shame. I nodded and passed on, but heard him say again, good-naturedly: "If you leggo of me this minyt—ye shall 'ave a bob for a drink out of my pay." In the next few steps I came upon Belfast. He caught my arm with tremulous enthusiasm. "I couldn't go wi' 'em," he stammered, indicating by a nod our noisy crowd, that drifted slowly along the other sidewalk. "When I think of Jimmy . . . Poor Jim! When I think of him I have no heart for drink. You were his chum, too . . . but I pulled him out . . . didn't I? Short wool he had. . . . Yes. And I stole the blooming pie. . . . He wouldn't go. . . . He wouldn't go for nobody." He burst into tears. "I never touched him—never—never!" he sobbed. "He went for me like . . . like . . . a lamb."

I disengaged myself gently. Belfast's crying fits generally ended in a fight with someone, and I wasn't anxious to stand the brunt of his inconsolable sorrow. Moreover, two bulky policemen stood near by, looking at us with a disapproving and incorruptible gaze. "So long!" I said, and went on my way.

But at the corner I stopped to take my last look at the crew of the *Narcissus*. They were swaying irresolute and noisy on the broad flagstones before the Mint. They were bound for the Black Horse, where men, in fur caps with brutal faces and in shirt sleeves, dispense out of varnished barrels the illusions of strength, mirth, happiness; the illusion of splendor and poetry of life, to the paid-off crews of southern-going ships. From afar I saw them discoursing, with jovial eyes and clumsy gestures, while the sea of life thundered into their ears ceaseless and unheeded. And swaying about there on the white stones, surrounded by the hurry and clamor of men, they appeared to be creatures of another kind—lost, alone, forgetful, and doomed; they were like castaways, like reckless and joyous castaways, like mad castaways making merry in the storm and upon an insecure ledge of a treacherous rock. The roar of the town resembled the roar of topping breakers, merciless and strong, with a loud voice and cruel purpose; but overhead the clouds broke; a flood of sunshine streamed down the walls of grimy houses. The dark knot of seamen drifted in sunshine. To the left of them the trees in Tower Gardens sighed, the stones of the Tower, gleaming, seemed to stir in the play of light, as if remembering suddenly all the great joys and sorrows of the past, the fighting prototypes of these men: press gangs; mutinous cries; the wailing of women by the riverside, and the shouts of men welcoming victories. The sunshine of heaven fell like a gift of grace on the mud of the earth, on the remembering and mute stones, on greed, selfishness; on the anxious faces of forgetful men. And to the right of the dark group the stained front of the Mint, cleansed by the flood of light, stood out for a moment dazzling and white like a marble palace in a fairy tale. The crew of the *Narcissus* drifted out of sight.

I never saw them again. The sea took some, the steamers took others, the graveyards of the earth will account for the rest. Singleton has no doubt taken with him the long record of his faithful work into the peaceful depths of an hospitable sea. And Donkin, who never did a decent day's work in his life, no doubt earns his living by discoursing with filthy eloquence upon the right of labor to live. So be it! Let the earth and the sea each have its own.

A gone shipmate, like any other man, is gone forever; and I never met one of them again. But at times the spring flood of memory sets with force up the dark River of the Nine Bends. Then on the waters of the forlorn stream drifts a ship—a shadowy ship manned by a crew of Shades. They pass and make a sign, in a shadowy hail. Haven't we, together and upon the immortal sea, wrung out a meaning from our sinful lives? Good-bye, brothers! You were a good crowd. As good a crowd as ever fisted with wild cries the beating canvas of a heavy foresail; or, tossing aloft, invisible in the night, gave back yell for yell to a westerly gale.

The End of the Tether

CHAPTER 1

For a long time after the course of the steamer *Sofala* had been altered for the land, the low swampy coast had retained its appearance of a mere smudge of darkness beyond a belt of glitter. The sunrays fell violently upon the calm sea—seemed to shatter themselves upon an adamantine surface into sparkling dust, into a dazzling vapour of light that blinded the eye and wearied the brain with its unsteady brightness.

Captain Whalley did not look at it. When his Serang, approaching the roomy cane arm-chair which he filled capably, had informed him in a low voice that the course was to be altered, he had risen at once and had remained on his feet, face forward, while the head of his ship swung through a quarter of a circle. He had not uttered a single word, not even the word to steady the helm. It was the Serang, an elderly, alert, little Malay, with a very dark skin, who murmured the order to the helmsman. And then slowly Captain Whalley sat down again in the arm-chair on the bridge and fixed his eyes on the deck between his feet.

He could not hope to see anything new upon this lane of the sea. He had been on these coasts for the last three years. From Low Cape to Malantan the distance was fifty miles, six hours' steaming for the old ship with the tide, or seven against. Then you steered straight for the land, and by and by three palms would appear on the sky, tall and slim, and with their dishevelled head in a bunch, as if in confidential criticism of the dark mangroves. The *Sofala* would be headed towards the sombre strip of the coast, which at a given moment, as the ship closed with it obliquely, would show several clean shining fractures—the brimful estuary of a river. Then on through a brown liquid, three parts water and one part black earth, on and on between the low shores, three parts black earth and one part brackish water, the *Sofala* would plough her way upstream, as she had done once every month for these seven years or more, long before he was aware of her existence, long before he had ever thought of having anything to do with her and her invariable voyages. The old ship ought to have known the road better than her men, who had not been kept so long at it without a change; better than the faithful Serang, whom he had brought over from his last ship to keep the captain's watch; better than he himself, who had been her captain for the last three years only. She could always be depended upon to make her courses. Her compasses were never out. She was no trouble at all to take about, as if her great age had given her knowledge, wisdom, and steadiness. She made her landfalls to a degree of the bearing, and almost to a minute of her allowed time. At any moment, as he sat on the bridge without looking up, or lay sleepless in his bed, simply by reckoning the days and the hours he could tell where he was—the precise spot of the beat. He knew it well, too, this monotonous huckster's round, up and down the Straits; he knew its order and its sights and its people. Malacca to begin with, in at daylight and out at dusk, to cross over with a rigid phosphorescent wake this highway of the Far East. Darkness and gleams on the water, clear stars on a black sky, perhaps the lights of a home steamer keeping her unswerving course in the middle, or maybe the elusive shadow of a native craft with her mat sails flitting by silently—and low land on the other side in sight at daylight. At noon the three palms of the next place of call, up a sluggish river. The only white man residing there was a retired young sailor, with whom he had become friendly in the course of many voyages. Sixty miles farther on there was another place of call, a deep bay with only a couple of houses on the beach. And so on, in and out, picking up coastwise cargo here and there, and finishing with a hundred miles' steady steaming through the maze of an archipelago of small islands up to a large native town at the end of the beat. There was a three days' rest for the old ship before he started her again in inverse order, seeing the same shores from another bearing, hearing the same voices in the same places, back again to the *Sofala's* port of registry on the great highway to the East, where he would take up a berth nearly opposite the big stone pile of the harbour office till it was time to start again on the old round of 1,600 miles and thirty days. Not a very enterprising life, this, for Captain Whalley, Henry Whalley, otherwise Dare-devil Harry Whalley, of the *Condor,* a famous clipper in her day. No. Not a very enterprising life for a man who had served famous firms, who had sailed famous ships (more than one or two of them his own); who had made famous passages, had been the pioneer of new routes and new trades; who had steered across the unsurveyed tracts of the South Seas, and had seen the sun rise on uncharted islands. Fifty years at sea, and forty out in the East ("a pretty thorough apprenticeship," he used to remark smilingly), had made him honourably known to a generation of shipowners and merchants in all the ports from Bombay clear over to where the East merges into the West upon the coast of the two Americas. His fame remained writ, not very large but plain enough, on the Admiralty charts. Was there not somewhere between Australia and China a Whalley Island and a Condor Reef? On that dangerous coral formation the celebrated clipper had hung stranded for three days, her captain and crew throwing her cargo overboard with one hand and with the other, as it were, keeping off her a flotilla of savage war-canoes. At that time neither the island nor the reef had any official existence. Later the officers of her Majesty's steam-vessel *Fusilier,* despatched to make a survey of the route, recognized in the adoption of these two names the enterprise of the man and the solidity of the ship. Besides, as any one who cares may see, the *General Directory* vol. ii. p. 410, begins the description of the "Malotu or Whalley Passage" with the words: "This advantageous route, first discovered in 1850 by Captain Whalley in the ship *Condor,*" etc., and ends by recommending it warmly to sailing vessels leaving the China ports for the south in the months from December to April inclusive.

This was the clearest gain he had out of life. Nothing could rob him of this kind of fame. The piercing of the Isthmus of Suez, like the breaking of a dam, had let in upon the East a flood of new ships, new men, new methods of trade. It had changed the face of the Eastern seas and the very spirit of their life; so that his early experiences meant nothing whatever to the new generation of seamen.

In those bygone days he had handled many thousands of pounds of his employers' money and of his own; he had attended faithfully, as by law a shipmaster is expected to do, to the conflicting interests of owners, charterers, and underwriters. He had never lost a ship or consented to a shady transaction; and he had lasted well, outlasting in the end the conditions that had gone to the making of his name. He had buried his wife (in the Gulf of Petchili), had married off his daughter to the man of her unlucky choice, and had lost more than an ample competence in the crash of the notorious Travancore and Deccan Banking Corporation, whose downfall had shaken the East like an earthquake. And he was sixty-seven years old.

CHAPTER 2

His age sat lightly enough on him; and of his ruin he was not ashamed. He had not been alone in believing in the stability of the Banking Corporation. Men whose judgment in matters of finance was as expert as his seamanship had commended the prudence of his investments, and had themselves lost much money in the great failure. The only difference between him and them was that he had lost his all. And yet not his all. There had remained to him from his lost fortune a very pretty little barque, *Fair Maid*, which he had bought to occupy his leisure of a retired sailor—"to play with," as he expressed it himself.

He had formally declared himself tired of the sea the year preceding his daughter's marriage. But after the young couple had gone to settle in Melbourne he found out that he could not make himself happy on shore. He was too much of a merchant sea-captain for mere yachting to satisfy him. He wanted the illusion of affairs; and his acquisition of the *Fair Maid* preserved the continuity of his life. He introduced her to his acquaintances in various ports as "my last command." When he grew too old to be trusted with a ship, he would lay her up and go ashore to be buried, leaving directions in his will to have the barque towed out and scuttled decently in deep water on the day of the funeral. His daughter would not grudge him the satisfaction of knowing that no stranger would handle his last command after him. With the fortune he was able to leave her, the value of a 500-ton barque was neither here nor there. All this would be said with a jocular twinkle in his eye: the vigorous old man had too much vitality for the sentimentalism of regret; and a little wistfully withal, because he was at home in life, taking a genuine pleasure in its feelings and its possessions; in the dignity of his reputation and his wealth, in his love for his daughter, and in his satisfaction with the ship—the plaything of his lonely leisure.

He had the cabin arranged in accordance with his simple ideal of comfort at sea. A big bookcase (he was a great reader) occupied one side of his stateroom; the portrait of his late wife, a flat bituminous oil-painting representing the profile and one long black ringlet of a young woman, faced his bedplace. Three chronometers ticked him to sleep and greeted him on waking with the tiny competition of their beats. He rose at five every day. The officer of the morning watch, drinking his early cup of coffee aft by the wheel, would hear through the wide orifice of the copper ventilators all the splashings, blowings, and splutterings of his captain's toilet. These noises would be followed by a sustained deep murmur of the Lord's Prayer recited in a loud earnest voice. Five minutes afterwards the head and shoulders of Captain Whalley emerged out of the companion-hatchway. Invariably he paused for a while on the stairs, looking all round at the horizon; upwards at the trim of the sails; inhaling deep draughts of the fresh air. Only then he would step out on the poop, acknowledging the hand raised to the peak of the cap with a majestic and benign "Good morning to you." He walked the deck till eight scrupulously. Sometimes, not above twice a year, he had to use a thick cudgel-like stick on account of a stiffness in the hip—a slight touch of rheumatism, he supposed. Otherwise he knew nothing of the ills of the flesh. At the ringing of the breakfast bell he went below to feed his canaries, wind up the chronometers, and take the head of the table. From there he had before his eyes the big carbon photographs of his daughter, her husband, and two fat-legged babies—his grandchildren—set in black frames into the maple-wood bulkheads of the cuddy. After breakfast he dusted the glass over these portraits himself with a cloth, and brushed the oil painting of his wife with a plummet kept suspended from a small brass hook by the side of the heavy gold frame. Then with the door of his state-room shut, he would sit down on the couch under the portrait to read a chapter out of a thick pocket Bible—her Bible. But on some days he only sat there for half an hour with his finger between the leaves and the closed book resting on his knees. Perhaps he had remembered suddenly how fond of boat-sailing she used to be.

She had been a real shipmate and a true woman, too. It was like an article of faith with him that there never had been, and never could be, a brighter, cheerier home anywhere afloat or ashore than his home under the poop-deck of the *Condor*, with the big main cabin all white and gold, garlanded as if for a perpetual festival with an unfading wreath. She had decorated the centre of every panel with a cluster of home flowers. It took her a twelvemonth to go round the cuddy with this labour of love. To him it had remained a marvel of painting, the highest achievement of taste and skill; and as to old Swinburne, his mate, every time he came down to his meals he stood transfixed with admiration before the progress of the work. You could almost smell these roses, he declared, sniffing the faint flavour of turpentine which at that time pervaded the saloon, and (as he confessed afterwards) made him somewhat less hearty than usual in tackling his food. But there was nothing of the sort to interfere with his enjoyment of her singing. "Mrs. Whalley is a regular out-and-out nightingale, sir," he would pronounce with a judicial air after listening profoundly over the skylight to the very end of the piece. In fine weather, in the second dog-watch, the two men could hear her trills and roulades going on to the accompaniment of the piano in the cabin. On the very day they got engaged he had written to London for the instrument; but they had been married for over a year before it reached them, coming out round the Cape. The big case made part of the first direct general cargo landed in Hongkong harbour—an event that to the men who walked the busy quays of to-day seemed as hazily remote as the dark ages of history. But Captain Whalley could in a half-hour of solitude live again all his life, with its romance, its idyl, and its sorrow. He had to close her eyes himself. She went away from under the ensign like a sailor's wife, a sailor herself at heart. He had read the service over her, out of her own prayer-book, without a break in his voice. When he raised his eyes he could see old Swinburne facing him with his cap pressed to his breast, and his rugged, weather-beaten, impassive face streaming with drops of water like a lump of chipped red granite in a shower. It was all very well for that old sea-dog to cry. He had to read on to the end; but after the splash he did not remember much of what happened for the next few days. An elderly sailor of the crew, deft at needlework, put together a mourning frock for the child out of one of her black skirts.

He was not likely to forget; but you cannot dam up life like a sluggish stream. It will break out and flow over a man's troubles, it will close upon a sorrow like the sea upon a dead body, no matter how much love has gone to the bottom. And the world is not bad. People had been very kind to him; especially Mrs. Gardner, the wife of the senior partner in Gardner, Patteson & Co., the owners of the *Condor*. It was she who volunteered to look after the little one, and in due course took her to England (something of a journey in those days, even by the overland mail route) with her own girls to finish her education. It was ten years before he saw her again.

As a little child she had never been frightened of bad weather; she would beg to be taken up on deck in the bosom of his oilskin coat to watch the big seas hurling themselves upon the *Condor*. The swirl and crash of the waves seemed to fill her small soul with a breathless delight. "A good boy spoiled," he used to say of her in joke. He had named her Ivy because of the sound of the word, and obscurely fascinated by a vague association of ideas. She had twined herself tightly round his heart, and he intended her to cling close to her father as to a tower of strength; forgetting while she was little, that in the nature of things she would probably elect to cling to someone else. But he loved life well enough for even that event to give him a certain satisfaction, apart from his more intimate feeling of loss.

After he had purchased the *Fair Maid* to occupy his loneliness, he hastened to accept a rather unprofitable freight to Australia simply for the opportunity of seeing his daughter in her own home. What made him dissatisfied there was not to see that she clung now to somebody else, but that the prop she had selected seemed on closer examination "a rather poor stick"—even in the matter of health. He disliked his son-in-law's studied civility perhaps more than his method of handling the sum of money he had given Ivy at her marriage. But of his apprehensions he said nothing. Only on the day of his departure, with the hall-door open all ready, holding her hands and looking steadily into her eyes, he had said, "You know, my dear, all I have is for you and the chicks. Mind you write to me openly." She had answered him by an almost imperceptible movement of her head. She resembled her mother in the colour of her eyes, and in character—and also in this, that she understood him without many words.

Sure enough she had to write; and some of these letters made Captain Whalley lift his white eye-brows. For the rest he considered he was reaping the true reward of his life by being thus able to produce on demand whatever was needed. He had not enjoyed himself so much in a way since his wife had died. Characteristically enough his son-in-law's punctuality in failure caused him at a distance to feel a sort of kindness towards the man. The fellow was so perpetually being jammed on a lee shore that to charge it all to his reckless navigation would be manifestly unfair. No, no! He knew well what that meant. It was bad luck. His own had been simply marvellous, but he had seen in his life too many good men—seamen and others—go under with the sheer weight of bad luck not to recognize the fatal signs. For all that, he was cogitating on the best way of tying up very strictly every penny he had to leave, when with a preliminary rumble of rumours (whose first sound reached him in Shanghai as it happened), the shock of the big failure came; and, after passing through the phases of stupor, of incredulity, of indignation, he had to accept the fact that he had nothing to speak of to leave.

Upon that, as if he had only waited for this catastrophe, the unlucky man, away there in Melbourne, gave up his unprofitable game, and sat down—in an invalid's bath-chair at that, too. "He will never walk again," wrote the wife. For the first time in his life Captain Whalley was a bit staggered.

The *Fair Maid* had to go to work in bitter earnest now. It was no longer a matter of preserving alive the memory of Dare-devil Harry Whalley in the Eastern Seas, or of keeping an old man in pocket-money and clothes, with, perhaps, a bill for a few hundred first-class cigars thrown in at the end of the year. He would have to buckle-to, and keep her going hard on a scant allowance of gilt for the ginger-bread scrolls at her stem and stern.

This necessity opened his eyes to the fundamental changes of the world. Of his past only the familiar names remained, here and there, but the things and the men, as he had known them, were gone. The name of Gardner, Patteson & Co. was still displayed on the walls of warehouses by the waterside, on the brass plates and window-panes in the business quarters of more than one Eastern port, but there was no longer a Gardner or a Patteson in the firm. There was no longer for Captain Whalley an arm-chair and a welcome in the private office, with a bit of business ready to be put in the way of an old friend, for the sake of bygone services. The husbands of the Gardner girls sat behind the desks in that room where, long after he had left the employ, he had kept his right of entrance in the old man's time. Their ships now had yellow funnels with black tops, and a time-table of appointed routes like a confounded service of tramways. The winds of December and June were all one to them; their captains (excellent young men he doubted not) were, to be sure, familiar with Whalley Island, because of late years the Government had established a white fixed light on the north end (with a red danger sector over the Condor Reef), but most of them would have been extremely surprised to hear that a flesh-and-blood Whalley still existed—an old man going about the world trying to pick up a cargo here and there for his little barque.

And everywhere it was the same. Departed the men who would have nodded appreciatively at the mention of his name, and would have thought themselves bound in honour to do something for Dare-devil Harry Whalley. Departed the opportunities which he would have known how to seize; and gone with them the white-winged flock of clippers that lived in the boisterous uncertain life of the winds, skimming big fortunes out of the foam of the sea. In a world that pared down the profits to an irreducible minimum, in a world that was able to count its disengaged tonnage twice over every day and in which lean charters were snapped up by cable three months in advance, there were no chances of fortune for an individual wandering haphazard with a little barque—hardly indeed any room to exist.

He found it more difficult from year to year. He suffered greatly from the smallness of remittances he was able to send his daughter. Meantime he had given up good cigars, and even in the matter of inferior cheroots limited himself to six a day. He never told her of his difficulties, and she never enlarged upon her struggle to live. Their confidence in each other needed no explanations, and their perfect understanding endured without protestations of gratitude or regret. He would have been shocked if she had taken it into her head to thank him in so many words, but he found it perfectly natural that she should tell him she needed two hundred pounds.

He had come in with the *Fair Maid* in ballast to look for a freight in the *Sofala's* port of registry, and her letter met him there. Its tenor was that it was no use mincing matters. Her only resource was in opening a boarding-house, for which the prospects, she judged, were good. Good enough, at any rate, to make her tell him frankly that with two hundred pounds she could make a start. He had torn the envelope open, hastily, on deck, where it was handed to him by the ship-chandler's runner, who had brought his mail at the moment of anchoring. For the second time in his life he was appalled, and remained stock-still at the cabin door with the paper trembling between his fingers. Open a boarding-house! Two hundred pounds for a start! The only resource! And he did not know where to lay his hands on two hundred pence.

All that night Captain Whalley walked the poop of his anchored ship, as though he had been about to close with the land in thick weather, and uncertain of his position after a run of many gray days without a sight of sun, moon, or stars. The black night twinkled with the guiding lights of seamen and the steady straight lines of lights on shore; and all around the *Fair Maid* the riding lights of ships cast trembling trails upon the water of the roadstead. Captain Whalley saw not a gleam anywhere till the dawn broke and he found out that his clothing was soaked through with the heavy dew.

His ship was awake. He stopped short, stroked his wet beard, and descended the poop ladder backwards, with tired feet. At the sight of him the chief officer, lounging about sleepily on the quarterdeck, remained open-mouthed in the middle of a great early-morning yawn.

"Good morning to you," pronounced Captain Whalley, solemnly, passing into the cabin. But he checked himself in the doorway, and without looking back, "By the bye," he said, "there should be an empty wooden case put away in the lazarette. It has not been broken up—has it?"

The mate shut his mouth, and then asked as if dazed, "What empty case, sir?"

"A big flat packing-case belonging to that painting in my room. Let it be taken up on deck and tell the carpenter to look it over. I may want to use it before long."

The chief officer did not stir a limb till he had heard the door of the captain's stateroom slam within the cuddy. Then he beckoned aft the second mate with his forefinger to tell him that there was something "in the wind."

When the bell rang Captain Whalley's authoritative voice boomed out through a closed door, "Sit down and don't wait for me." And his impressed officers took their places, exchanging looks and whispers across the table. What! No breakfast? And after apparently knocking about all night on deck, too! Clearly, there was something in the wind. In the skylight above their heads, bowed earnestly over the plates, three wire cages rocked and rattled to the restless jumping of the hungry canaries; and they could detect the sounds of their "old man's" deliberate movements within his stateroom. Captain Whalley was methodically winding up the chronometers, dusting the portrait of his late wife, getting a clean white shirt out of the drawers, making himself ready in his punctilious, unhurried manner to go ashore. He could not have swallowed a single mouthful of food that morning. He had made up his mind to sell the *Fair Maid*.

CHAPTER 3

Just at that time the Japanese were casting far and wide for ships of European build, and he had no difficulty in finding a purchaser, a speculator who drove a hard bargain, but paid cash down for the *Fair Maid*, with a view to a profitable resale. Thus it came about that Captain Whalley found himself on a certain afternoon descending the steps of one of the most important post offices of the East with a slip of bluish paper in his hand. This was the receipt of a registered letter enclosing a draft for two hundred pounds, and addressed to Melbourne. Captain Whalley pushed the paper into his waistcoat-pocket, took his stick from under his arm, and walked down the street.

It was a recently opened and untidy thoroughfare with rudimentary side-walks and a soft layer of dust cushioning the whole width of the road. One end touched the slummy street of Chinese shops near the harbour, the other drove straight on, without houses, for a couple of miles, through patches of jungle-like vegetation, to the yard gates of the new Consolidated Docks Company. The crude frontages of the new Government buildings alternated with the blank fencing of vacant plots, and the view of the sky seemed to give an added spaciousness to the broad vista. It was empty and shunned by natives after business hours, as though they had expected to see one of the tigers from the neighbourhood of the New Waterworks on the hill coming at a loping canter down the middle to get a Chinese shopkeeper for supper. Captain Whalley was not dwarfed by the solitude of the grandly planned street. He had too fine a presence for that. He was only a lonely figure walking purposefully, with a great white beard like a pilgrim, and with a thick stick that resembled a weapon. On one side the new Courts of Justice had a low and unadorned portico of squat columns half concealed by a few old trees left in the approach. On the other the pavilion wings of the new Colonial Treasury came out to the line of the street. But Captain Whalley, who had now no ship and no home, remembered in passing that on that very site when he first came out from England there had stood a fishing village, a few mat huts erected on piles between a muddy tidal creek and a miry pathway that went writhing into a tangled wilderness without any docks or waterworks.

No ship—no home. And his poor Ivy away there had no home either. A boarding-house is no sort of home though it may get you a living. His feelings were horribly rasped by the idea of the boarding-house. In his rank of life he had that truly aristocratic temperament characterized by a scorn of vulgar gentility and by prejudiced views as to the derogatory nature of certain occupations. For his own part he had always preferred sailing merchant ships (which is a straight-forward occupation) to buying and selling merchandise of which the essence is to get the better of somebody in a bargain—an undignified trial of wits at best. His father had been Colonel Whalley (retired) of the H.E.I. Company's service, with very slender means besides his pension, but with distinguished connections. He could remember as a boy how frequently waiters at the inns, country tradesmen and small people of that sort, used to "My lord" the old warrior on the strength of his appearance.

Captain Whalley himself (he would have entered the Navy if his father had not died before he was fourteen) had something of a grand air which would have suited an old and glorious admiral; but he became lost like a straw in the eddy of a brook amongst the swarm of brown and yellow humanity filling a thoroughfare, that by contrast with the vast and empty avenue he had left seemed as narrow as a lane and absolutely riotous with life. The walls of the houses were blue; the shops of the Chinamen yawned like cavernous lairs; heaps of nondescript merchandise overflowed the gloom of the long range of arcades, and the fiery serenity of sunset took the middle of the street from end to end with a glow like the reflection of a fire. It fell on the bright colours and the dark faces of the bare-footed crowd, on the pallid yellow backs of the half-naked jostling coolies, on the accoutrements of a tall Sikh trooper with a parted beard and fierce moustaches on sentry before the gate of the police compound. Looming very big above the heads in a red haze of dust, the tightly packed car of the cable tramway navigated cautiously up the human stream, with the incessant blare of its horn, in the manner of a steamer groping in a fog.

Captain Whalley emerged like a diver on the other side, and in the desert shade between the walls of closed warehouses removed his hat to cool his brow. A certain disrepute attached to the calling of a landlady of a boarding-house. These women were said to be rapacious, unscrupulous, untruthful; and though he condemned no class of his fellow-creatures—God forbid!—these were suspicions to which it was unseemly that a Whalley should lay herself open. He had not expostulated with her, however. He was confident she shared his feelings; he was sorry for her; he trusted her judgment; he considered it a merciful dispensation that he could help her once more—but in his aristocratic heart of hearts he would have found it more easy to reconcile himself to the idea of her turning seamstress. Vaguely he remembered reading years ago a touching piece called the "Song of the Shirt." It was all very well making songs about poor women. The granddaughter of Colonel Whalley, the landlady of a boarding-house! Pooh! He replaced his hat, dived into two pockets, and stopping a moment to apply a flaring match to the end of a cheap cheroot, blew an embittered cloud of smoke at a world that could hold such surprises.

Of one thing he was certain—that she was the own child of a clever mother. Now he had got over the wrench of parting with his ship, he perceived clearly that such a step had been unavoidable. Perhaps he had been growing aware of it all along with an unconfessed knowledge. But she, far away there, must have had an intuitive perception of it, with the pluck to face that truth and the courage to speak out—all the qualities which had made her mother a woman of such excellent counsel.

It would have had to come to that in the end! It was fortunate that she had forced his hand. In another year or two it would have been an utterly barren sale. To keep the ship going he had been involving himself deeper every year. He was defenceless before the insidious work of adversity, to whose more open assaults he could present a firm front; like a cliff that stands unmoved the open battering of the sea, with a lofty ignorance of the treacherous backwash undermining its base. As it was, every liability satisfied, her request answered, and owing no man a penny, there remained to him from the proceeds a sum of five hundred pounds put away safely. In addition he had upon his person some forty odd dollars—enough to pay his hotel bill, providing he did not linger too long in the modest bedroom where he had taken refuge.

Scantily furnished, and with a waxed floor, it opened into one of the side-verandahs. The straggling building of bricks, as airy as a bird-cage, resounded with the incessant flapping of rattan screens worried by the wind between the whitewashed square pillars of the sea-front. The rooms were lofty, a ripple of sunshine flowed over the ceilings; and the periodical invasions of tourists from some passenger steamer in the harbour flitted through the wind-swept dusk of the apartments with the tumult of their unfamiliar voices and impermanent presences, like relays of migratory shades condemned to speed headlong round the earth without leaving a trace. The babble of their irruptions ebbed out as suddenly as it had arisen; the draughty corridors and the long chairs of the verandahs knew their sight-seeing hurry or their prostrate repose no more; and Captain Whalley, substantial and dignified, left well nigh alone in the vast hotel by each light-hearted skurry, felt more and more like a stranded tourist with no aim in view, like a forlorn traveller without a home. In the solitude of his room he smoked thoughtfully, gazing at the two sea-chests which held all that he could call his own in this world. A thick roll of charts in a sheath of sailcloth leaned in a corner; the flat packing-case containing the portrait in oils and the three carbon photographs had been pushed under the bed. He was tired of discussing terms, of assisting at surveys, of all the routine of the business. What to the other parties was merely the sale of a ship was to him a momentous event involving a radically new view of existence. He knew that after this ship there would be no other; and the hopes of his youth, the exercise of his abilities, every feeling and achievement of his manhood, had been indissolubly connected with ships. He had served ships; he had owned ships; and even the years of his actual retirement from the sea had been made bearable by the idea that he had only to stretch out his hand full of money to get a ship. He had been at liberty to feel as though he were the owner of all the ships in the world. The selling of this one was weary work; but when she passed from him at last, when he signed the last receipt, it was as though all the ships had gone out of the world together, leaving him on the shore of inaccessible oceans with seven hundred pounds in his hands.

Striding firmly, without haste, along the quay, Captain Whalley averted his glances from the familiar roadstead. Two generations of seamen born since his first day at sea stood between him and all these ships at the anchorage. His own was sold, and he had been asking himself, What next?

From the feeling of loneliness, of inward emptiness—and of loss, too, as if his very soul had been taken out of him forcibly—there had sprung at first a desire to start right off and join his daughter. "Here are the last pence," he would say to her; "take them, my dear. And here's your old father: you must take him, too."

His soul recoiled, as if afraid of what lay hidden at the bottom of this impulse. Give up! Never! When one is thoroughly weary all sorts of nonsense come into one's head. A pretty gift it would have been for a poor woman—this seven hundred pounds with the incumbrance of a hale old fellow more than likely to last for years and years to come. Was he not as fit to die in harness as any of the youngsters in charge of these anchored ships out yonder? He was as solid now as ever he had been. But as to who would give him work to do, that was another matter. Were he, with his appearance and antecedents, to go about looking for a junior's berth, people, he was afraid, would not take him seriously; or else if he succeeded in impressing them, he would maybe obtain their pity, which would be like stripping yourself naked to be kicked. He was not anxious to give himself away for less than nothing. He had no use for anybody's pity. On the other hand, a command—the only thing he could try for with due regard for common decency—was not likely to be lying in wait for him at the corner of the next street. Commands don't go a-begging nowadays. Ever since he had come ashore to carry out the business of the sale he had kept his ears open, but had heard no hint of one being vacant in the port. And even if there had been one, his successful past itself stood in his way. He had been his own employer too long. The only credential he could produce was the testimony of his whole life. What better recommendation could any one require? But vaguely he felt that the unique document would be looked upon as an archaic curiosity of the Eastern waters, a screed traced in obsolete words—in a half-forgotten language.

CHAPTER 4

Revolving these thoughts, he strolled on near the railings of the quay, broad-chested, without a stoop, as though his big shoulders had never felt the burden of the loads that must be carried between the cradle and the grave. No single betraying fold or line of care disfigured the reposeful modelling of his face. It was full and untanned; and the upper part emerged, massively quiet, out of the downward flow of silvery hair, with the striking delicacy of its clear complexion and the powerful width of the forehead. The first cast of his glance fell on you candid and swift, like a boy's; but because of the ragged snowy thatch of the eyebrows the affability of his attention acquired the character of a keen and searching scrutiny. With age he had put on flesh a little, had increased his girth like an old tree presenting no symptoms of decay; and even the opulent, lustrous ripple of white hairs upon his chest seemed an attribute of unquenchable vitality and vigour.

Once rather proud of his great bodily strength, and even of his personal appearance, conscious of his worth, and firm in his rectitude, there had remained to him, like the heritage of departed prosperity, the tranquil bearing of a man who had proved himself fit in every sort of way for the life of his choice. He strode on squarely under the projecting brim of an ancient Panama hat. It had a low crown, a crease through its whole diameter, a narrow black ribbon. Imperishable and a little discoloured, this headgear made it easy to pick him out from afar on thronged wharves and in the busy streets. He had never adopted the comparatively modern fashion of pipeclayed cork helmets. He disliked the form; and he hoped he could manage to keep a cool head to the end of his life without all these contrivances for hygienic ventilation. His hair was cropped close, his linen always of immaculate whiteness; a suit of thin gray flannel, worn threadbare but scrupulously brushed, floated about his burly limbs, adding to his bulk by the looseness of its cut. The years had mellowed the good-humoured, imperturbable audacity of his prime into a temper carelessly serene; and the leisurely tapping of his iron-shod stick accompanied his footfalls with a self-confident sound on the flag-stones. It was impossible to connect such a fine presence and this unruffled aspect with the belittling troubles of poverty; the man's whole existence appeared to pass before you, facile and large, in the freedom of means as ample as the clothing of his body.

The irrational dread of having to break into his five hundred pounds for personal expenses in the hotel disturbed the steady poise of his mind. There was no time to lose. The bill was running up. He nourished the hope that this five hundred would perhaps be the means, if everything else failed, of obtaining some work which, keeping his body and soul together (not a matter of great outlay), would enable him to be of use to his daughter. To his mind it was her own money which he employed, as it were, in backing her father and solely for her benefit. Once at work, he would help her with the greater part of his earnings; he was good for many years yet, and this boarding-house business, he argued to himself, whatever the prospects, could not be much of a gold-mine from the first start. But what work? He was ready to lay hold of anything in an honest way so that it came quickly to his hand; because the five hundred pounds must be preserved intact for eventual use. That was the great point. With the entire five hundred one felt a substance at one's back; but it seemed to him that should he let it dwindle to four-fifty or even four-eighty, all the efficiency would be gone out of the money, as though there were some magic power in the round figure. But what sort of work?

Confronted by that haunting question as by an uneasy

ghost, for whom he had no exorcising formula, Captain Whalley stopped short on the apex of a small bridge spanning steeply the bed of a canalized creek with granite shores. Moored between the square blocks a sea-going Malay prau floated half hidden under the arch of masonry, with her spars lowered down, without a sound of life on board, and covered from stem to stern with a ridge of palm-leaf mats. He had left behind him the overheated pavements bordered by the stone frontages that, like the sheer face of cliffs, followed the sweep of the quays; and an unconfined spaciousness of orderly and sylvan aspect opened before him its wide plots of rolled grass, like pieces of green carpet smoothly pegged out, its long ranges of trees lined up in colossal porticos of dark shafts roofed with a vault of branches.

Some of these avenues ended at the sea. It was a terraced shore; and beyond, upon the level expanse, profound and glistening like the gaze of a dark-blue eye, an oblique band of stippled purple lengthened itself indefinitely through the gap between a couple of verdant twin islets. The masts and spars of a few ships far away, hull down in the outer roads, sprang straight from the water in a fine maze of rosy lines pencilled on the clear shadow of the eastern board. Captain Whalley gave them a long glance. The ship, once his own, was anchored out there. It was staggering to think that it was open to him no longer to take a boat at the jetty and get himself pulled off to her when the evening came. To no ship. Perhaps never more. Before the sale was concluded, and till the purchase-money had been paid, he had spent daily some time on board the *Fair Maid*. The money had been paid this very morning, and now, all at once, there was positively no ship that he could go on board of when he liked; no ship that would need his presence in order to do her work—to live. It seemed an incredible state of affairs, something too bizarre to last. And the sea was full of craft of all sorts. There was that prau lying so still swathed in her shroud of sewn palm-leaves—she, too, had her indispensable man. They lived through each other, this Malay he had never seen, and this high-sterned thing of no size that seemed to be resting after a long journey. And of all the ships in sight, near and far, each was provided with a man, the man without whom the finest ship is a dead thing, a floating and purposeless log.

After his one glance at the roadstead he went on since there was nothing to turn back for, and the time must be got through somehow. The avenues of big trees ran straight over the Esplanade, cutting each other at diverse angles, columnar below and luxuriant above. The interlaced boughs high up there seemed to slumber; not a leaf stirred overhead: and the reedy cast-iron lamp-posts in the middle of the road, gilt like sceptres diminished in a long perspective, with their globes of white porcelain atop, resembling a barbarous decoration of ostriches' eggs displayed in a row. The flaming sky kindled a tiny crimson spark upon the glistening surface of each glassy shell.

With his chin sunk a little, his hands behind his back, and the end of his stick marking the gravel with a faint wavering line at his heels, Captain Whalley reflected that if a ship without a man was like a body without a soul, a sailor without a ship was of not much more account in this world than an aimless log adrift upon the sea. The log might be sound enough by itself, tough of fibre, and hard to destroy—but what of that! And a sudden sense of irremediable idleness weighted his feet like a great fatigue.

A succession of open carriages came bowling along the newly opened sea-road. You could see across the wide grass-plots the discs of vibration made by the spokes. The bright domes of the parasols swayed lightly outwards like full-blown blossoms on the rim of a vase; and the quiet sheet of dark-blue water, crossed by a bar of purple, made a background for the spinning wheels and the high action of the horses, whilst the turbaned heads of the Indian servants elevated above the line of the sea horizon glided rapidly on the paler blue of the sky. In an open space near the little bridge each turn-out trotted smartly in a wide curve away from the sunset; then pulling up sharp, entered the main alley in a long slow-moving file with the great red stillness of the sky at the back. The trunks of mighty trees stood all touched with red on the same side, the air seemed aflame under the high foliage, the very ground under the hoofs of the horses was red. The wheels turned solemnly; one after another the sunshades drooped, folding their colours like gorgeous flowers shutting their petals at the end of the day. In the whole half-mile of human beings no voice uttered a distinct word, only a faint thudding noise went on mingled with slight jingling sounds, and the motionless heads and shoulders of men and women sitting in couples emerged stolidly above the lowered hoods—as if wooden. But one carriage and pair coming late did not join the line.

It fled along in a noiseless roll; but on entering the avenue one of the dark bays snorted, arching his neck and shying against the steel-tipped pole; a flake of foam fell from the bit upon the point of a satiny shoulder, and the dusky face of the coachman leaned forward at once over the hands taking a fresh grip of the reins. It was a long dark-green landau, having a dignified and buoyant motion between the sharply curved C-springs, and a sort of strictly official majesty in its supreme elegance. It seemed more roomy than is usual, its horses seemed slightly bigger, the appointments a shade more perfect, the servants perched somewhat higher on the box. The dresses of three women—two young and pretty, and one, handsome, large, of mature age—seemed to fill completely the shallow body of the carriage. The fourth face was that of a man, heavy lidded, distinguished and sallow, with a sombre, thick, iron-gray imperial and moustaches, which somehow had the air of solid appendages. His Excellency——

The rapid motion of that one equipage made all the others appear utterly inferior, blighted, and reduced to crawl painfully at a snail's pace. The landau distanced the whole file in a sort of sustained rush; the features of the occupants whirling out of sight left behind an impression of fixed stares and impassive vacancy; and after it had vanished in full flight as it were, notwithstanding the long line of vehicles hugging the curb at a walk, the whole lofty vista of the avenue seemed to lie open and emptied of life in the enlarged impression of an august solitude.

Captain Whalley had lifted his head to look, and his mind, disturbed in its meditation, turned with wonder (as men's minds will do) to matters of no importance. It struck him that it was to this port, where he had just sold his last ship, that he had come with the very first he had ever owned, and with his head full of a plan for opening a new trade with a distant part of the Archipelago. The then governor had given him no end of encouragement. No Excellency he—this Mr. Denham—this governor with his jacket off; a man who tended night and day, so to speak, the growing prosperity of the settlement with the self-forgetful devotion of a nurse for a child she loves; a lone bachelor who lived as in a camp with the few servants and his three dogs in what was called then the Government Bungalow: a low-roofed structure on the half-cleared slope of a hill, with a new flagstaff in front and a police orderly on the verandah. He remembered toiling up that hill under a heavy sun for his audience; the unfurnished aspect of the cool shaded room; the long table covered at one end with piles of papers, and with two guns, a brass telescope, a small bottle of oil with a feather stuck in the neck at the other—and the flattering attention given to him by the man in power. It was an undertaking full of risk he had come to expound, but a twenty minutes' talk in the Government Bungalow on the hill had made it go smoothly from the start. And as he was retiring Mr. Denham, already seated before the papers, called out after him, "Next month the *Dido* starts for a cruise that way, and I shall request her captain officially to give you a look-in and see how you get on." The *Dido* was one of the smart frigates on the China station—and five-and-thirty years make a big slice of time. Five-and-thirty years ago an enterprise like his had for the colony enough importance to be looked after by a Queen's ship. A big slice of time. Individuals were of some account then. Men like himself; men, too, like poor Evans, for instance, with his red face, his coal-black whiskers, and his restless eyes, who had set up the first patent slip for repairing small ships, on the edge of the forest, in a lonely bay three miles up the coast. Mr. Denham had encouraged that enterprise, too, and yet somehow poor Evans had ended by dying at home deucedly hard up. His son, they said, was squeezing oil out of cocoa-nuts for a living on some God-forsaken islet of the Indian Ocean; but it was from that patent slip in a lonely wooded bay that had sprung the workshops of the Consolidated Docks Company, with its three graving basins carved out of solid rock, its wharves, its jetties, its electric-light plant, its steam-power houses—with its gigantic sheer-legs, fit to lift the heaviest weight ever carried afloat, and whose head could be seen like the top of a queer white monument peeping over bushy points of land and sandy promontories, as you approached the New Harbour from the west.

There had been a time when men counted: there were not so many carriages in the colony then, though Mr. Denham, he fancied, had a buggy. And Captain Whalley seemed to be swept out of the great avenue by the swirl of a mental backwash. He remembered muddy shores, a harbour without quays, the one solitary wooden pier (but that was a public work) jutting out crookedly, the first coal-sheds erected on Monkey Point, that caught fire mysteriously and smouldered for days, so that amazed ships came into a roadstead full of sulphurous fog, and the sun hung blood-red at midday. He remembered the things, the faces, and something more besides—like the faint flavour of a cup quaffed to the bottom, like a subtle sparkle of the air that was not to be found in the atmosphere of to-day.

In this evocation, swift and full of detail like a flash of magnesium light into the niches of a dark memorial hall, Captain Whalley contemplated things once important, the efforts of small men, the growth of a great place, but now robbed of all consequence by the greatness of accomplished facts, by hopes greater still; and they gave him for a moment such an almost physical grip upon time, such a comprehension of our unchangeable feelings, that he stopped short, struck the ground with his stick, and ejaculated mentally, "What the devil am I doing here!" He seemed lost in a sort of surprise; but he heard his name called out in wheezy tones once, twice—and turned on his heels slowly.

He beheld then, waddling towards him autocratically, a man of an old-fashioned and gouty aspect, with hair as white as his own, but with shaved, florid cheeks, wearing a necktie—almost a neckcloth—whose stiff ends projected far beyond his chin; with round legs, round arms, a round body, a round face—generally producing the effect of his short figure having been distended by means of an air-pump as much as the seams of his clothing would stand. This was the Master-Attendant of the port. A master-attendant is a superior sort of harbour-master; a person, out in the East, of some consequence in his sphere; a Government official, a magistrate for the waters of the port, and possessed of vast but ill-defined disciplinary authority over seamen of all classes. This particular Master-Attendant was reported to consider it miserably inadequate, on the ground that it did not include the power of life and death. This was a jocular exaggeration. Captain Eliott was fairly satisfied with his position, and nursed no inconsiderable sense of such power as he had. His conceited and tyrannical disposition did not allow him to let it dwindle in his hands for want of use. The uproarious, choleric frankness of his comments on people's character and conduct caused him to be feared at bottom. Though in conversation many pretended not to mind him in the least, others would only smile sourly at the mention of his name, and there were even some who dared to pronounce him "a meddlesome old ruffian." But for almost all of them one of Captain Eliott's outbreaks was nearly as distasteful to face as a chance of annihilation.

CHAPTER 5

As soon as he had come up quite close he said, mouthing in a growl—

"What's this I hear, Whalley? Is it true you're selling the *Fair Maid?*"

Captain Whalley, looking away, said the thing was done —money had been paid that morning; and the other expressed at once his approbation of such an extremely sensible proceeding. He had got out of his trap to stretch his legs, he explained, on his way home to dinner. Sir Frederick looked well at the end of his time. Didn't he?

Captain Whalley could not say; had only noticed the carriage going past.

The Master-Attendant, plunging his hands into the pockets of an alpaca jacket inappropriately short and tight for a man of his age and appearance, strutted with a slight limp, and with his head reaching only to the shoulder of Captain Whalley, who walked easily, staring straight before him. They had been good comrades years ago, almost intimates. At the time when Whalley commanded the renowned *Condor*, Eliott had charge of the nearly as famous *Ringdove* for the same owners; and when the appointment of Master-Attendant was created, Whalley would have been the only other serious candidate. But Captain Whalley, then in the prime of life, was resolved to serve no one but his own auspicious Fortune. Far away, tending his hot irons, he was glad to hear the other had been successful. There was a wordly suppleness in bluff Ned Eliott that would serve him well in that sort of official appointment. And they were so dissimilar at bottom that as they came slowly to the end of the avenue before the Cathedral, it had never come into Whalley's head that he might have been in that man's place—provided for to the end of his days.

The sacred edifice, standing in solemn isolation amongst the converging avenues of enormous trees, as if to put grave thoughts of heaven into the hours of ease, presented a closed Gothic portal to the light and glory of the west. The glass of the rosace above the ogive glowed like fiery coal in the deep carvings of a wheel of stone. The two men faced about.

"I'll tell you what they ought to do next, Whalley," growled Captain Eliott suddenly.

"Well?"

"They ought to send a real live lord out here when Sir Frederick's time is up. Eh?"

Captain Whalley perfunctorily did not see why a lord of the right sort should not do as well as any one else. But this was not the other's point of view.

"No, no. Place runs itself. Nothing can stop it now. Good enough for a lord," he growled in short sentences. "Look at the changes in our own time. We need a lord here now. They have got a lord in Bombay."

He dined once or twice every year at the Government House—a many-windowed, arcaded palace upon a hill laid out in roads and gardens. And lately he had been taking about a duke in his Master-Attendant's steam-launch to visit the harbour improvements. Before that he had "most obligingly" gone out in person to pick out a good berth for the ducal yacht. Afterwards he had an invitation to lunch on board. The duchess herself lunched with them. A big woman with a red face. Complexion quite sunburnt. He should think ruined. Very gracious manners. They were going on to Japan. . . .

He ejaculated these details for Captain Whalley's edification, pausing to blow out his cheeks as if with a pent-up sense of importance, and repeatedly protruding his thick lips till the blunt crimson end of his nose seemed to dip into the milk of his moustache. The place ran itself; it was fit for any lord; it gave no trouble except in its Marine department—in its Marine department, he repeated twice, and after a heavy snort began to relate how the other day her Majesty's Consul-General in French Cochin-China had cabled to him—in his official capacity—asking for a qualified man to be sent over to take charge of a Glasgow ship whose master had died in Saigon.

"I sent word of it to the officers' quarters in the Sailors' Home," he continued, while the limp in his gait seemed to grow more accentuated with the increasing irritation of his voice. "Place's full of them. Twice as many men as there are berths going in the local trade. All hungry for an easy job. Twice as many—and—What d'you think, Whalley? . . ."

He stopped short; his hands, clenched and thrust deeply downwards, seemed ready to burst the pockets of his jacket. A slight sigh escaped Captain Whalley.

"Hey? You would think they would be falling over each other. Not a bit of it. Frightened to go home. Nice and warm out here to lie about a verandah waiting for a job. I sit and wait in my office. Nobody. What did they suppose? That I was going to sit there like a dummy with the Consul-General's cable before me? Not likely. So I looked up a list of them I keep by me and sent word for Hamilton—the worst loafer of them all—and just made him go. Threatened to instruct the steward of the Sailors' Home to have him turned out neck and crop. He did not think the berth was good enough—if you—please. 'I've your little record by me,' said I. 'You came ashore here eighteen months ago, and you haven't done six months' work since. You are in debt for your board now at the Home, and I suppose you reckon the Marine Office will pay in the end. Eh? So it shall; but if you don't take this chance, away you go to England, assisted passage, by the first homeward steamer that comes along. You are no better than a pauper. We don't want any white paupers here.' I scared him. But look at the trouble all this gave me."

"You would not have had any trouble," Captain Whalley said almost involuntarily, "if you had sent for me."

Captain Eliott was immensely amused; he shook with laughter as he walked. But suddenly he stopped laughing. A vague recollection had crossed his mind. Hadn't he heard it said at the time of the Travancore and Deccan smash that poor Whalley had been cleaned out completely? "Fellow's hard up, by heavens!" he thought; and at once he cast a sidelong upwards glance at his companion. But Captain Whalley was smiling austerely straight before him, with a carriage of the head inconceivable in a penniless man—and he became reassured. Impossible. Could not have lost everything. That ship had been only a hobby of his. And the reflection that a man who had confessed to receiving that very morning a presumably large sum of money was not likely to spring upon him a demand for a small loan put him entirely at his ease again. There had come a long pause in their talk, however, and not knowing how to begin again, he growled out soberly, "We old fellows ought to take a rest now."

"The best thing for some of us would be to die at the oar," Captain Whalley said, negligently.

"Come, now. Aren't you a bit tired by this time of the whole show?" muttered the other, sullenly.

"Are you?"

Captain Eliott was. Infernally tired. He only hung on to his berth so long in order to get his pension on the highest scale before he went home. It would be no better than poverty, anyhow; still, it was the only thing between him and the workhouse. And he had a family. Three girls, as Whalley knew. He gave "Harry, old boy," to understand that these three girls were a source of the greatest anxiety and worry to him. Enough to drive a man distracted.

"Why? What have they been doing now?" asked Captain Whalley with a sort of amused absent-mindedness.

"Doing! Doing nothing. That's just it. Lawn-tennis and silly novels from morning to night. . . ."

If one of them at least had been a boy! But all three! And, as ill-luck would have it, there did not seem to be any decent young fellows left in the world. When he looked around in the club he saw only a lot of conceited popinjays too selfish to think of making a good woman happy. Extreme indigence stared him in the face with all that crowd to keep at home. He had cherished the idea of building himself a little house in the country—in Surrey—to end his days in, but he was afraid it was out of the question . . . and his staring eyes rolled upwards with such a pathetic anxiety that Captain Whalley charitably nodded down at him, restraining a sort of sickening desire to laugh.

"You must know what it is yourself, Harry. Girls are the very devil for worry and anxiety."

"Ay! But mine is doing well," Captain Whalley pronounced slowly, staring to the end of the avenue.

The Master-Attendant was glad to hear this. Uncommonly glad. He remembered her well. A pretty girl she was.

Captain Whalley, stepping out carelessly, assented as if in a dream:

"She was pretty."

The procession of carriages was breaking up.

One after another they left the file to go off at a trot, animating the vast avenue with their scattered life and movement; but soon the aspect of dignified solitude returned and took possession of the straight wide road. A syce in white stood at the head of a Burmah pony harnessed to a varnished two-wheel cart; and the whole thing waiting by the curb seemed no bigger than a child's toy forgotten under the soaring trees. Captain Eliott waddled up to it and made as if to clamber in, but refrained; and keeping one hand resting easily on the shaft, he changed the conversation from his pension, his daughters, and his poverty back again to the only other topic in the world—the Marine Office, the men and the ships of the port.

He proceeded to give instances of what was expected of him; and his thick voice drowsed in the still air like the obstinate droning of an enormous bumble-bee. Captain Whalley did not know what was the force or the weakness that prevented him from saying goodnight and walking away. It was as though he had been too tired to make the effort. How queer. More queer than any of Ned's instances. Or was it that overpowering sense of idleness alone that made him stand there and listen to these stories? Nothing very real had ever troubled Ned Eliott; and gradually he seemed to detect deep in, as if wrapped up in the gross wheezy rumble, something of the clear hearty voice of the young captain of the *Ringdove*. He wondered if he, too, had changed to the same extent; and it seemed to him that the voice of his old chum had not changed so very much—that the man was the same. Not a bad fellow the pleasant, jolly Ned Eliott, friendly, well up to his business—and always a bit of a humbug. He remembered how he used to amuse his poor wife. She could read him like an open book. When the *Condor* and the *Ringdove* happened to be in port together, she would frequently ask him to bring Captain Eliott to dinner. They had not met often since those old days. Not once in five years, perhaps. He regarded from under his white eyebrows this man he could not bring himself to take into his confidence at this juncture; and the other went on with his intimate outpourings, and as remote from his hearer as though he had been talking on a hill-top a mile away.

He was in a bit of a quandary now as to the steamer *Sofala*. Ultimately every hitch in the port came into his hands to undo. They would miss him when he was gone in another eighteen months, and most likely some retired naval officer had been pitchforked into the appointment—a man that would understand nothing and care less. That steamer was a coasting craft having a steady trade connection as far north as Tenasserim; but the trouble was she could get no captain to take her on her regular trip. Nobody would go in her. He really had no power, of course, to order a man to take a job. It was all very well to stretch a point on the demand of a consul-general, but. . . .

"What's the matter with the ship?" Captain Whalley interrupted in measured tones.

"Nothing's the matter. Sound old steamer. Her owner has been in my office this afternoon tearing his hair."

"Is he a white man?" asked Whalley in an interested voice.

"He calls himself a white man," answered the Master-Attendant scornfully; "but if so, it's just skin-deep and no more. I told him that to his face, too."

"But who is he, then?"

"He's the chief engineer of her. See *that,* Harry?"

"I see," Captain Whalley said, thoughtfully. "The engineer. I see."

How the fellow came to be a shipowner at the same time was quite a tale. He came out third in a home ship nearly fifteen years ago, Captain Eliott remembered, and got paid off after a bad sort of row both with his skipper and his chief. Anyway, they seemed jolly glad to get rid of him at all costs. Clearly a mutinous sort of chap. Well, he remained out here, a perfect nuisance, everlastingly shipped and unshipped, unable to keep a berth very long; pretty nigh went through every engine-room afloat belonging to the colony. Then suddenly, "What do you think happened, Harry?"

Captain Whalley, who seemed lost in a mental effort as of doing a sum in his head, gave a slight start. He really couldn't imagine. The Master-Attendant's voice vibrated dully with hoarse emphasis. The man actually had the luck to win the second great prize in the Manila lottery. All these engineers and officers of ships took tickets in that gamble. It seemed to be a perfect mania with them all.

Everybody expected now that he would take himself off home with his money, and go to the devil in his own way. Not at all. The *Sofala,* judged too small and not quite modern enough for the sort of trade she was in, could be got for a moderate price from her owners, who had ordered a new steamer from Europe. He rushed in and bought her. This man had never given any signs of that sort of mental intoxication the mere fact of getting hold of a large sum of money may produce—not till he got a ship of his own; but then he went off his balance all at once: came bouncing into the Marine Office on some transfer business, with his hat hanging over his left eye and switching a little cane in his hand, and told each one of the clerks separately that "Nobody could put him out now. It was his turn. There was no one over him on earth, and there never would be either." He swaggered and strutted between the desks, talking at the top of his voice, and trembling like a leaf all the while, so that the current business of the office was suspended for the time he was in there, and everybody in the big room stood open-mouthed looking at his antics. Afterwards he could be seen during the hottest hours of the day with his face as red as fire rushing along up and down the quays to look at his ship from different points of view: he seemed inclined to stop every stranger he came across just to let them know "that there would be no longer any one over him; he had bought a ship; nobody on earth could put him out of his engine-room now."

Good bargain as she was, the price of the *Sofala* took up pretty near all the lottery-money. He had left himself no capital to work with. That did not matter so much, for these were the halcyon days of steam coasting trade, before some of the home shipping firms had thought of establishing local fleets to feed their main lines. These, when once organized, took the biggest slices out of that cake, of course; and by and by a squad of confounded German tramps turned up east of Suez Canal and swept up all the crumbs. They prowled on the cheap to and fro along the coast and between the islands, like a lot of sharks in the water ready to snap up anything you let drop. And then the high old times were over for good; for years the *Sofala* had made no more, he judged, than a fair living. Captain Eliott looked upon it as his duty in every way to assist an English ship to hold her own; and it stood to reason that if for want of a captain the *Sofala* began to miss her trips she would very soon lose her trade. There was the quandary. The man was too impracticable. "Too much of a begger on horseback from the first," he explained. "Seemed to grow worse as the time went on. In the last three years he's run through eleven skippers; he had tried every single man here, outside of the regular lines. I had warned him before that this would not do. And now, of course, no one will look at the *Sofala*. I had one or two men up at my office and talked to them; but, as they said to me, what was the good of taking the berth to lead a regular dog's life for a month and then get the sack at the end of the first trip? The fellow, of course, told me it was all nonsense; there has been a plot hatching for years against him. And now it had come. All the horrid sailors in the port had conspired to bring him to his knees, because he was an engineer." Captain Eliott emitted a throaty chuckle.

"And the fact is, that if he misses a couple more trips he need never trouble himself to start again. He won't find any cargo in his old trade. There's too much competition nowadays for people to keep their stuff lying about for a ship that does not turn up when she's expected. It's a bad lookout for him. He swears he will shut himself on board and starve to death in his cabin rather than sell her—even if he could find a buyer. And that's not likely in the least. Not even the Japs would give her insured value for her. It isn't like selling sailing-ships. Steamers *do* get out of date, besides getting old."

"He must have laid by a good bit of money though," observed Captain Whalley, quietly.

The Harbour-Master puffed out his purple cheeks to an amazing size.

"Not a stiver, Harry. Not—a—single sti-ver."

He waited; but as Captain Whalley, stroking his beard slowly, looked down on the ground without a word, he tapped him on the forearm, tiptoed, and said in a hoarse whisper—

"The Manila lottery has been eating him up."

He frowned a little, nodding in tiny affirmative jerks. They all were going in for it; a third of the wages paid to ships' officers ("in my port," he snorted) went to Manila. It was a mania. That fellow Massy had been bitten by it like the rest of them from the first; but after winning once he seemed to have persuaded himself he had only to try again to get another big prize. He had taken dozens and scores of tickets for every drawing since. What with this vice and his ignorance of affairs, ever since he had improvidently bought that steamer he had been more or less short of money.

This, in Captain Eliott's opinion, gave an opening for a sensible sailor-man with a few pounds to step in and save that fool from the consequences of his folly. It was his craze to quarrel with his captains. He had had some really good men, too, who would have been too glad to stay if he would only let them. But no. He seemed to think he was no owner unless he was kicking somebody out in the morning and having a row with the new man in the evening. What was wanted for him was a master with a couple of hundred or so to take an interest in the ship on proper conditions. You don't discharge a man for no fault, only because of the fun of telling him to pack up his traps and go ashore, when you know that in that case you are bound to buy back his share. On the other hand, a fellow with an interest in the ship is not likely to throw up his job in a huff about a trifle. He had told Massy that. He had said: " 'This won't do, Mr. Massy. We are getting very sick of you here in the Marine Office. What you must do now is to try whether you could get a sailor to join you as partner. That seems to be the only way.' And that was sound advice, Harry."

Captain Whalley, leaning on his stick, was perfectly still all over, and his hand, arrested in the act of stroking, grasped his whole beard. And what did the fellow say to that?

The fellow had the audacity to fly out at the Master-Attendant. He had received the advice in a most impudent manner. "I didn't come here to be laughed at," he had shrieked. "I appeal to you as an Englishman and a ship-owner brought to the verge of ruin by an illegal conspiracy of your beggarly sailors, and all you condescend to do for me is to tell me to go and get a partner!" . . . . The fellow had presumed to stamp with rage on the floor of the private office. Where was he going to get a partner? Was he being taken for a fool? Not a single one of that contemptible lot ashore at the "Home" had twopence in his pocket to bless himself with. The very native curs in the bazaar knew that much. . . . "And it's true enough, Harry," rumbled Captain Eliott, judicially. "They are much more likely one and all to owe money to the Chinamen in Denham Road for the clothes on their backs. 'Well,' said I, 'you make too much noise over it for my taste, Mr. Massy. Good morning.' He banged the door after him; he dared to bang my door, confound his cheek!"

The head of the Marine department was out of breath with indignation; then recollecting himself as it were, "I'll end by being late to dinner—yarning with you here . . . wife doesn't like it."

He clambered ponderously into the trap; leaned out side-ways, and only then wondered wheezily what on earth Captain Whalley could have been doing with himself of late. They had had no sight of each other for years and years till the other day when he had seen him unexpectedly in the office.

What on earth. . . .

Captain Whalley seemed to be smiling to himself in his white beard.

"The earth is big," he said, vaguely.

The other, as if to test the statement, stared all round from his driving-seat. The Esplanade was very quiet; only from afar, from very far, a long way from the sea-shore, across the stretches of grass, through the long ranges of trees, came faintly the toot—toot—toot of the cable car beginning to roll before the empty peristyle of the Public Library on its three-mile journey to the New Harbour Docks.

"Doesn't seem to be so much room on it," growled the Master-Attendant, "since these Germans came along shouldering us at every turn. It was not so in our time."

He fell into deep thought, breathing stertorously, as though he had been taking a nap open-eyed. Perhaps he, too, on his side, had detected in the silent pilgrim-like figure, standing there by the wheel, like an arrested wayfarer, the buried lineaments of the features belonging to the young captain of the *Condor*. Good fellow—Harry Whalley—never very talkative. You never knew what he was up to—a bit too off-hand with people of consequence, and apt to take a wrong view of a fellow's actions. Fact was he had a too good opinion of himself. He would have liked to tell him to get in and drive him home to dinner. But one never knew. Wife would not like it.

"And it's funny to think, Harry," he went on in a big subdued drone, "that of all the people on it there seems only you and I left to remember this part of the world as it used to be. . . ."

He was ready to indulge in the sweetness of a sentimental mood had it not struck him suddenly that Captain Whalley, unstirring and without a word, seemed to be awaiting something—perhaps expecting. . . . He gathered the reins at once and burst out in bluff hearty growls—

"Ha! My dear boy. The men we have known—the ships we've sailed—ay! and the things we've done. . . ."

The pony plunged—the syce skipped out of the way. Captain Whalley raised his arm.

"Good-bye."

CHAPTER 6

The sun had set. And when, after drilling a deep hole with his stick, he moved from that spot the night had massed its army of shadows under the trees. They filled the eastern ends of the avenue as if only waiting the signal for a general advance upon the open spaces of the world; they were gathering low between the deep stone-faced banks of the canal. The Malay prau, half concealed under the arch of the bridge, had not altered its position a quarter of an inch. For a long time Captain Whalley stared down over the parapet, till at last the floating immobility of that beshrouded thing seemed to grow upon him into something inexplicable and alarming. The twilight abandoned the zenith; its reflected gleams left the world below, and the water of the canal seemed to turn into pitch. Captain Whalley crossed it.

The turning to the right, which was his way to his hotel, was only a very few steps farther. He stopped again (all the houses of the sea-front were shut up, the quayside was deserted, but for one or two figures of natives walking in the distance) and began to reckon the amount of his bill. So many days in the hotel at so many dollars a day. To count the days he used his fingers: plunging one hand into his pocket, he jingled a few silver coins. All right for three days more; and then, unless something turned up, he must break into the five hundred—Ivy's money—invested in her father. It seemed to him that the first meal coming out of that reserve would choke him—for certain. Reason was of no use. It was a matter of feeling. His feelings had never played him false.

He did not turn to the right. He walked on, as if there still had been a ship in the roadstead to which he could get himself pulled off in the evening. Far away, beyond the houses, on the slope of an indigo promontory closing the view of the quays, the slim column of a factory-chimney smoked quietly straight up into the clear air. A Chinaman, curled down in the stern of one of the half-dozen sampans floating off the end of the jetty, caught sight of a beckoning hand. He jumped up, rolled his pigtail round his head swiftly, tucked in two rapid movements his wide dark trousers high up his yellow thighs, and by a single, noiseless, finlike stir of the oars, sheered the sampan alongside the steps with the ease and precision of a swimming fish.

"*Sofala,*" articulated Captain Whalley from above; and the Chinaman, a new emigrant probably, stared upwards with a tense attention as if waiting to see the queer word fall visibly from the white man's lips. "*Sofala,*" Captain Whalley repeated; and suddenly his heart failed him. He paused. The shores, the islets, the high ground, the low points, were dark: the horizon had grown sombre; and across the eastern sweep of the shore the white obelisk, marking the landing-place of the telegraph-cable, stood like a pale ghost on the beach before the dark spread of uneven roofs, intermingled with palms, of the native town. Captain Whalley began again:

"*Sofala.* Savee *So-fa-la,* John?"

This time the Chinaman made out that bizarre sound, and grunted his assent uncouthly, low down in his bare throat. With the first yellow twinkle of a star that appeared like the head of a pin stabbed deep into the smooth, pale, shimmering fabric of the sky, the edge of a keen chill seemed to cleave through the warm air of the earth. At the moment of stepping into the sampan to go and try for the command of the *Sofala* Captain Whalley shivered a little.

When on his return he landed on the quay again, Venus, like a choice jewel set low on the hem of the sky, cast a faint gold trail behind him upon the roadstead, as level as a floor made of one dark and polished stone. The lofty vaults of the avenues were black—all black overhead—and the porcelain globes on the lamp-posts resembled egg-shaped pearls, gigantic and luminous, displayed in a row whose farther end seemed to sink in the distance, down to the level of his knees. He put his hands behind his back. He would now consider calmly the discretion of it before saying the final word to-morrow. His feet scrunched the gravel loudly—the discretion of it. It would have been easier to appraise had there been a workable alternative. The honesty of it was indubitable: he meant well by the fellow; and periodically his shadow leaped up intense by his side on the trunks of the trees, to lengthen itself, oblique, and dim, far over the grass—repeating his stride.

The discretion of it. Was there a choice? He seemed already to have lost something of himself; to have given up to a hungry spectre something of his truth and dignity in order to live. But his life was necessary. Let poverty do its worst in exacting its toll of humiliation. It was certain that Ned Eliott had rendered him, without knowing it, a service for which it would have been impossible to ask. He hoped Ned would not think there had been something underhand in his action. He supposed that now when he heard of it he would understand—or perhaps he would only think Whalley an eccentric old fool. What would have been the good of telling him—any more than of blurting the whole tale to that man Massy? Five hundred pounds ready to invest. Let him make the best of that. Let him wonder. You want a captain—I want a ship. That's enough. B-r-r-r. What a disagreeable impression that empty, dark, echoing steamer had made upon him. . . .

A laid-up steamer was a dead thing and no mistake; a sailing-ship somehow seems always ready to spring into life with the breath of the incorruptible heaven; but a steamer, thought Captain Whalley, with her fires out, without the warm whiffs from below meeting you on her decks, without the hiss of steam, the clangs of iron in her breast—lies there as cold and still and pulseless as a corpse.

In the solitude of the avenue, all black above and lighted below, Captain Whalley, considering the discretion of his course, met, as it were incidentally, the thought of death. He pushed it aside with dislike and contempt. He almost laughed at it; and in the unquenchable vitality of his age only thought with a kind of exultation how little he needed to keep body and soul together. Not a bad investment for the poor woman this solid carcass of her father. And for the rest—in case of anything—the agreement should be clear: the whole five hundred to be paid back to her integrally within three months. Integrally. Every penny. He was not to lose any of her money whatever else had to go—a little dignity—some of his self-respect. He had never before allowed anybody to remain under any sort of false impression as to himself. Well, let that go—for her sake. After all, he had never *said* anything misleading—and Captain Whalley felt himself corrupt to the marrow of his bones. He laughed a little with the intimate scorn of his worldly prudence. Clearly, with a fellow of that sort, and in the peculiar relation they were to stand to each other, it would not have done to blurt out everything. He did not like the fellow. He did not like his spells of fawning loquacity and bursts of resentfulness. In the end—a poor devil. He would not have liked to stand in his shoes. Men were not evil, after all. He did not like his sleek hair, his queer way of standing at right angles, with his nose in the air, and glancing along his shoulder at you. No. On the whole, men were not bad—they were only silly or unhappy.

Captain Whalley had finished considering the discretion of that step—and there was the whole long night before him. In the full light his long beard would glisten like a silver breastplate covering his heart; in the spaces between the lamps his burly figure passed less distinct, loomed very big, wandering, and mysterious. No; there was not much real harm in men: and all the time a shadow marched with him, slanting on his left hand—which in the East is a presage of evil.

"Can you make out the clump of palms yet, Serang?" asked Captain Whalley from his chair on the bridge of the *Sofala* approaching the bar of Batu Beru.

"No, Tuan. By and by see." The old Malay, in a blue dungaree suit, planted on his bony dark feet under the bridge awning, put his hands behind his back and stared ahead out of the innumerable wrinkles at the corners of his eyes.

Captain Whalley sat still, without lifting his head to look for himself. Three years—thirty-six times. He had made these palms thirty-six times from the southward. They would come into view at the proper time. Thank God, the old ship made her courses and distances trip after trip, as correct as clockwork. At last he murmured again—

"In sight yet?"

"The sun makes a very great glare, Tuan."

"Watch well, Serang."

"Ya, Tuan."

A white man had ascended the ladder from the deck noiselessly, and had listened quietly to this short colloquy. Then he stepped out on the bridge and began to walk from end to end, holding up the long cherrywood stem of a pipe. His black hair lay plastered in long lanky wisps across the bald summit of his head; he had a furrowed brow, a yellow complexion, and a thick shapeless nose. A scanty growth of whisker did not conceal the contour of his jaw. His aspect was of brooding care; and sucking at a curved black mouthpiece, he presented such a heavy overhanging profile that even the Serang could not help reflecting sometimes upon the extreme unloveliness of some white men.

Captain Whalley seemed to brace himself up in his chair, but gave no recognition whatever to his presence. The other puffed jets of smoke; then suddenly—

"I could never understand that new mania of yours of having this Malay here for your shadow, partner."

Captain Whalley got up from the chair in all his imposing stature and walked across to the binnacle, holding such an unswerving course that the other had to back away hurriedly, and remained as if intimidated, with the pipe trembling in his hand. "Walk over me now," he muttered in a sort of astounded and discomfited whisper. Then slowly and distinctly he said—

"I—am—not—dirt." And then added defiantly, "As you seem to think."

The Serang jerked out—

"See the palms now, Tuan."

Captain Whalley strode forward to the rail; but his eyes, instead of going straight to the point, with the assured keen glance of a sailor, wandered irresolutely in space, as though he, the discoverer of new routes, had lost his way upon this narrow sea.

Another white man, the mate, came up on the bridge. He was tall, young, lean, with a moustache like a trooper, and something malicious in the eye. He took up a position beside the engineer. Captain Whalley with his back to them, inquired—

"What's on the log?"

"Eighty-five," answered the mate quickly, and nudged the engineer with his elbow.

Captain Whalley's muscular hands squeezed the iron rail with an extraordinary force; his eyes glared with an enormous effort; he knitted his eyebrows, the perspiration fell from under his hat—and in a faint voice he murmured, "Steady her, Serang—when she is on the proper bearing."

The silent Malay stepped back, waited a little, and lifted his arm warningly to the helmsman. The wheel revolved rapidly to meet the swing of the ship. Again the mate nudged the engineer. But Massy turned upon him.

"Mr. Sterne," he said, violently, "let me tell you—as a shipowner—that you are no better than a confounded fool."

CHAPTER 7

Sterne went down smirking and apparently not at all disconcerted, but the engineer Massy remained on the bridge, moving about with uneasy self-assertion. Everybody on board was his inferior—everyone without exception. He paid their wages and found them in their food. They ate more of his bread and pocketed more of his money than they were worth; and they had no care in the world, while he alone had to meet all the difficulties of shipowning. When he contemplated his position in all its menacing entirety, it seemed to him that he had been for years the prey of a band of parasites; and for years he had scowled at everybody connected with the *Sofala* except, perhaps, at the Chinese firemen who served to get her along. Their use was manifest: they were an indispensable part of the machinery of which he was the master.

When he passed along his decks he shouldered those he came across brutally; but the Malay deck hands had learned to dodge out of his way. He had to bring himself to tolerate them because of the necessary manual labour of the ship which must be done. He had to struggle and plan and scheme to keep the *Sofala* afloat—and what did he get for it? Not even enough respect. They could not have given him enough of that if all their thoughts and all their actions had been directed to that end. The vanity of possession, the vainglory of power, had passed away by this time, and there remained only the material embarrassments, the fear of losing that position which had turned out not worth having, and an anxiety of thought which no abject subservience of men could repay.

He walked up and down. The bridge was his own after all. He had paid for it; and with the stem of the pipe in his hand he would stop short at times as if to listen with a profound and concentrated attention to the deadened beat of the engines (his own engines) and the slight grinding of the steering chains upon the continuous low wash of water alongside. But for these sounds, the ship might have been lying as still as if moored to a bank, and as silent as if abandoned by every living soul; only the coast, the low coast of mud and mangroves with the three palms in a bunch at the back, grew slowly more distinct in its long straight line; without a single feature to arrest attention. The native passengers of the *Sofala* lay about on mats under the awnings; the smoke of her funnel seemed the only sign of her life and connected with her gliding motion in a mysterious manner.

Captain Whalley on his feet, with a pair of binoculars in his hand and the little Malay Serang at his elbow, like an old giant attended by a wizened pigmy, was taking her over the shallow water of the bar.

This submarine ridge of mud, scoured by the stream out of the soft bottom of the river and heaped up far out on the hard bottom of the sea, was difficult to get over. The alluvial coast having no distinguishing marks, the bearings of the crossing-place had to be taken from the shape of the mountains inland. The guidance of a form flattened and uneven at the top like a grinder tooth, and of another smooth, saddle-backed summit, had to be searched for within the great unclouded glare that seemed to shift and float like a dry fiery mist, filling the air, ascending from the water, shrouding the distances, scorching to the eye. In this veil of light the near edge of the shore alone stood out almost coal-black with an opaque and motionless solidity. Thirty miles away the serrated range of the interior stretched across the horizon, its outlines and shades of blue, faint and tremulous like a background painted on airy gossamer on the quivering fabric of an impalpable curtain let down to the plain of alluvial soil; and the openings of the estuary appeared, shining white, like bits of silver let into the square pieces snipped clean and sharp out of the body of the land bordered with mangroves.

On the forepart of the bridge the giant and the pigmy muttered to each other frequently in quiet tones. Behind them Massy stood sideways with an expression of disdain and suspense on his face. His globular eyes were perfectly motionless, and he seemed to have forgotten the long pipe he held in his hand.

On the fore-deck below the bridge, steeply roofed with the white slopes of the awnings, a young lascar seaman had clambered outside the rail. He adjusted quickly a broad band of sail canvas under his armpits, and throwing his chest against it, leaned out far over the water. The sleeve of his thin cotton shirt, cut off close to the shoulder, bared his brown arm of full rounded form and with a satiny skin like a woman's. He swung it rigidly with the rotary and menacing action of a slinger: the 14-lb. weight hurtled circling in the air, then suddenly flew ahead as far as the curve of the bow. The wet thin line swished like scratched silk running through the dark fingers of the man, and the plunge of the lead close to the ship's side made a vanishing silvery scar upon the golden glitter; then after an interval the voice of the young Malay uplifted and long-drawn declared the depth of the water in his own language.

"Tiga stengah," he cried after each splash and pause, gathering the line busily for another cast. "Tiga stengah," which means three fathom and a half. For a mile or so from seaward there was a uniform depth of water right up to the bar. "Half-three. Half-three. Half-three,"—and his modulated cry, returned leisurely and monotonous, like the repeated call of a bird, seemed to float away in sunshine and disappear in the spacious silence of the empty sea and of a lifeless shore lying open, north and south, east and west, without the stir of a single cloud-shadow or the whisper of any other voice.

The owner-engineer of the *Sofala* remained very still behind the two seamen of different race, creed, and colour; the European with the time-defying vigour of his old frame, the little Malay, old, too, but slight and shrunken like a withered brown leaf blown by a chance wind under the mighty shadow of the other. Very busy looking forward at the land, they had not a glance to spare; and Massy, glaring at them from behind, seemed to resent their attention to their duty like a personal slight upon himself.

This was unreasonable; but he had lived in his own world of unreasonable resentments for many years. At last, passing his moist palm over the rare lanky wisps of coarse hair on the top of his yellow head, he began to talk slowly.

"A leadsman, you want! I suppose that's your correct mail-boat style. Haven't you enough judgment to tell where you are by looking at the land? Why, before I had been a twelvemonth in the trade I was up to that trick—and I am only an engineer. I can point to you from here where the bar is, and I could tell you besides that you are likely as not to stick her in the mud in about five minutes from now; only you would call it interfering, I suppose. And there's that written agreement of ours, that says I mustn't interfere."

His voice stopped. Captain Whalley, without relaxing

the set severity of his features, moved his lips to ask in a quick mumble—

"How near, Serang?"

"Very near now, Tuan," the Malay muttered, rapidly.

"Dead slow," said the Captain aloud in a firm tone.

The Serang snatched at the handle of the telegraph. A gong clanged down below. Massy with a scornful snigger walked off and put his head down the engine-room skylight.

"You may expect some rare fooling with the engines, Jack," he bellowed. The space into which he stared was deep and full of gloom; and the gray gleams of steel down there seemed cool after the intense glare of the sea around the ship. The air, however, came up clammy and hot on his face. A short hoot on which it would have been impossible to put any sort of interpretation came from the bottom cavernously. This was the way in which the second engineer answered his chief.

He was a middle-aged man with an inattentive manner, and apparently wrapped up in such a taciturn concern for his engines that he seemed to have lost the use of speech. When addressed directly his only answer would be a grunt or a hoot, according to the distance. For all the years he had been in the *Sofala* he had never been known to exchange as much as a frank good-morning with any of his shipmates. He did not seem aware that men came and went in the world; he did not seem to see them at all. Indeed he never recognized his shipmates on shore. At table (the four white men of the *Sofala* messed together) he sat looking into his plate dispassionately, but at the end of the meal would jump up and bolt down below as if a sudden thought had impelled him to rush and see whether somebody had not stolen the engines while he dined. In port at the end of the trip he went ashore regularly, but no one knew where he spent his evenings or in what manner. The local coasting fleet had preserved a wild and incoherent tale of his infatuation for the wife of a sergeant in an Irish infantry regiment. The regiment, however, had done its turn of garrison duty there ages before, and was gone somewhere to the other side of the earth, out of men's knowledge. Twice or perhaps three times in the course of the year he would take too much to drink. On these occasions he would return on board at an earlier hour than usual; run across the deck balancing himself with his spread arms like a tight-rope walker; and locking the door of his cabin, he would converse and argue with himself the livelong night in an amazing variety of tones; storm, sneer, and whine with an inexhaustible persistence. Massy in his berth next door, raising himself on his elbow, would discover that his second remembered the name of every white man that had passed through the *Sofala* for years and years back. He remembered the names of men that had died, that had gone home, that had gone to America: he remembered in his cups the names of men whose connection with the ship had been so short that Massy had almost forgotten its circumstances and could barely recall their faces. The inebriated voice on the other side of the bulkhead commented upon them all with an extraordinary and ingenious venom of scandalous inventions. It seems they had all offended him in some way, and in return he had found them all out. He muttered darkly; he laughed sardonically; he crushed them one after another; but of his chief, Massy, he babbled with an envious and naïve admiration. Clever scoundrel! Don't meet the likes of him every day. Just look at him. Ha! Great! Ship of his own. Wouldn't catch *him* going wrong. No fear—the beast! And Massy, after listening with a gratified smile to these artless tributes to his greatness, would begin to shout, thumping at the bulkhead with both fists—

"Shut up, you lunatic! Won't you let me go to sleep, you fool!"

But a half smile of pride lingered on his lips; outside the solitary lascar told off for night duty in harbour, perhaps a youth fresh from a forest village, would stand motionless in the shadows of the deck listening to the endless drunken gabble. His heart would be thumping with breathless awe of white men: the arbitrary and obstinate men who pursue inflexibly their incomprehensible purposes—beings with weird intonations in the voice, moved by unaccountable feelings, actuated by inscrutable motives.

CHAPTER 8

For a while after his second's answering hoot Massy hung over the engine-room gloomily. Captain Whalley who, by the power of five hundred pounds, had kept his command for three years, might have been suspected of never having seen that coast before. He seemed unable to put down his glasses, as though they had been glued under his contracted eyebrows. This settled frown gave to his face an air of invincible and just severity; but his raised elbow trembled slightly, and the perspiration poured from under his hat as if a second sun had suddenly blazed up at the zenith by the side of the ardent still globe already there, in whose blinding white heat the earth whirled and shone like a mote of dust.

From time to time, still holding up his glasses, he raised his other hand to wipe his streaming face. The drops rolled down his cheeks, fell like rain upon the white hairs of his beard, and brusquely, as if guided by an uncontrollable and anxious impulse, his arm reached out to the stand of the engine-room telegraph.

The gong clanged down below. The balanced vibration of the dead-slow speed ceased together with every sound and tremor in the ship, as if the great stillness that reigned upon the coast had stolen in through her sides of iron and taken possession of her innermost recesses. The illusion of perfect immobility seemed to fall upon her from the luminous blue dome without a stain arching over a flat sea without a stir. The faint breeze she had made for herself expired, as if all at once the air had become too thick to budge; even the slight hiss of the water on her stem died out. The narrow, long hull, carrying its way without a ripple, seemed to approach the shoal water of the bar by stealth. The plunge of the lead with the mournful, mechanical cry of the lascar came at longer and longer intervals; and the men on her bridge seemed to hold their breath. The Malay at the helm looked fixedly at the compass card, the Captain and the Serang stared at the coast.

Massy had left the skylight, and, walking flat-footed, had returned softly to the very spot on the bridge he had occupied before. A slow, lingering grin exposed his set of big white teeth: they gleamed evenly in the shade of the awning like the keyboard of a piano in a dusky room.

At last, pretending to talk to himself in excessive astonishment, he said not very loud—

"Stop the engines now. What next, I wonder?"

He waited, stooping from the shoulders, his head bowed, his glance oblique. Then raising his voice a shade—

"If I dared make an absurd remark I would say that you haven't the stomach to. . . ."

But a yelling spirit of excitement, like some frantic soul wandering unsuspected in the vast stillness of the coast, had seized upon the body of the lascar at the lead. The languid monotony of his sing-song changed to a swift, sharp clamour. The weight flew after a single whirr, the line whistled, splash followed splash in haste. The water had shoaled, and the man, instead of the drowsy tale of fathoms, was calling out the soundings in feet.

"Fifteen feet. Fifteen, fifteen! Fourteen, fourteen. . . ."

Captain Whalley lowered the arm holding the glasses. It descended slowly as if by its own weight; no other part of his towering body stirred; and the swift cries with their eager warning note passed him by as though he had been deaf.

Massy, very still, and turning an attentive ear, had fastened his eyes upon the silvery, close-cropped back of the steady old head. The ship herself seemed to be arrested but for the gradual decrease of depth under her keel.

"Thirteen feet . . . Thirteen! Twelve!" cried the leadsman anxiously below the bridge. And suddenly the barefooted Serang stepped away noiselessly to steal a glance over the side.

Narrow of shoulder, in a suit of faded blue cotton, an old gray felt hat rammed down on his head, with a hollow in the nape of his dark neck, and with his slender limbs, he appeared from the back no bigger than a boy of fourteen. There was a childlike impulsiveness in the curiosity with which he watched the spread of the voluminous, yellowish convolutions rolling up from below to the surface of the blue water like massive clouds driving slowly upwards on the unfathomable sky. He was not startled at the sight in the least. It was not doubt, but the certitude that the keel of the *Sofala* must be stirring the mud now, which made him peep over the side.

His peering eyes, set aslant in a face of the Chinese type, a little old face, immovable, as if carved in old brown oak, had informed him long before that the ship was not headed at the bar properly. Paid off from the *Fair Maid*, together with the rest of the crew, after the completion of the sale, he had hung, in his faded blue suit and floppy gray hat, about the doors of the Harbour Office, till one day, seeing Captain Whalley coming along to get a crew for the *Sofala*, he had put himself quietly in the way, with his bare feet in the dust and an upward mute glance. The eyes of his old commander had fallen on him favourably—it must have been an auspicious day—and in less than half an hour the white men in the "Ofiss" had written his name on a document as Serang of the fire-ship *Sofala*. Since that time he had repeatedly looked at that estuary, upon that coast, from this bridge and from this side of the bar. The record of the visual world fell through his eyes upon his unspeculating mind as on a sensitized plate through the lens of a camera. His knowledge was absolute and precise; nevertheless, had he been asked his opinion, and especially if questioned in the downright, alarming manner of white men, he would have displayed the hesitation of ignorance. He was certain of his facts—but such a certitude counted for little against the doubt what answer would be pleasing. Fifty years ago, in a jungle village, and before he was a day old, his father (who died without ever seeing a white face) had had his nativity cast by a man of skill and wisdom in astrology, because in the arrangement of the stars may be read the last word of human destiny. His destiny had been to thrive by the favour of various white men on the sea. He had swept the decks of ships, had tended their helms, had minded their stores, had risen at last to be a Serang; and his placid mind had remained as incapable of penetrating the simplest motives of those he served as they themselves were incapable of detecting through the crust of the earth the secret nature of its heart, which may be fire or may be stone. But he had no doubt whatever that the *Sofala* was out of the proper track for crossing the bar at Batu Beru.

It was a slight error. The ship could not have been more than twice her own length too far to the northward; and a white man at a loss for a cause (since it was impossible to suspect Captain Whalley of blundering ignorance, of want of skill, or of neglect) would have been inclined to doubt the testimony of his senses. It was some such feeling that kept Massy motionless, with his teeth laid bare by an anxious grin. Not so the Serang. He was not troubled by any intellectual mistrust of his senses. If his captain chose to stir the mud it was well. He had known in his life white men indulge in outbreaks equally strange. He was only genuinely interested to see what would come of it. At last, apparently satisfied, he stepped back from the rail.

He had made no sound: Captain Whalley, however, seemed to have observed the movements of his Serang. Holding his head rigidly, he asked with a mere stir of his lips—

"Going ahead still, Serang?"

"Still going a little, Tuan," answered the Malay. Then added casually, "She is over."

The lead confirmed his words; the depth of water increased at every cast, and the soul of excitement departed suddenly from the lascar swung in the canvas belt over the *Sofala's* side. Captain Whalley ordered the lead in, set the engines ahead without haste, and averting his eyes from the coast directed the Serang to keep a course for the middle of the entrance.

Massy brought the palm of his hand with a loud smack against his thigh.

"You grazed on the bar. Just look astern and see if you didn't. Look at the track she left. You can see it plainly. Upon my soul, I thought you would! What made you do that? What on earth made you do that? I believe you are trying to scare me."

He talked slowly, as it were circumspectly, keeping his prominent black eyes on his captain. There was also a slight plaintive note in his rising choler, for, primarily, it was the clear sense of a wrong suffered undeservedly that made him hate the man who, for a beggarly five hundred pounds, claimed a sixth part of the profits under the three years' agreement. Whenever his resentment got the better of the awe the person of Captain Whalley inspired he would positively whimper with fury.

"You don't know what to invent to plague my life out of me. I would not have thought that a man of your sort would condescend. . . ."

He paused, half hopefully, half timidly, whenever Captain Whalley made the slightest movement in the deck-chair, as though expecting to be conciliated by a soft speech or else rushed upon and hunted off the bridge.

"I am puzzled," he went on again, with the watchful, unsmiling baring of his big teeth. "I don't know what to think. I do believe you are trying to frighten me. You very nearly planted her on the bar for at least twelve hours, besides getting the engines choked with mud. Ships can't afford to lose twelve hours on a trip nowadays—as you ought to know very well, and do know very well to be sure, only. . . ."

His slow volubility, the sideways cranings of his neck, the black glances out of the very corners of his eyes, left

Captain Whalley unmoved. He looked at the deck with a severe frown. Massy waited for some little time, then began to threaten plaintively.

"You think you've got me bound hand and foot in that agreement. You think you can torment me in any way you please. Ah! But remember it has another six weeks to run yet. There's time for me to dismiss you before the three years are out. You will do yet something that will give me the chance to dismiss you, and make you wait a twelve-month for your money before you can take yourself off and pull out your five hundred, and leave me without a penny to get the new boilers for her. You gloat over that idea—don't you? I do believe you sit here gloating. It's as if I had sold my soul for five hundred pounds to be everlastingly damned in the end. . . ."

He paused, without apparent exasperation, then continued evenly—

". . . With the boilers worn out and the survey hanging over my head, Captain Whalley—— Captain Whalley, I say, what do you do with your money? You must have stacks of money somewhere—a man like you must. It stands to reason. I am not a fool, you know, Captain Whalley—partner."

Again he paused, as though he had done for good. He passed his tongue over his lips, gave a backward glance at the Serang conning the ship with quiet whispers and slight signs of the hand. The wash of the propeller sent a swift ripple, crested with dark froth, upon a long flat spit of black slime. The *Sofala* had entered the river; the trail she had stirred up over the bar was a mile astern of her now, out of sight, had disappeared utterly; and the smooth, empty sea along the coast was left behind in the glittering desolation of sunshine. On each side of her, low down, the growth of sombre twisted mangroves covered the semi-liquid banks; and Massy continued in his old tone, with an abrupt start, as if his speech had been ground out of him, like the tune of a music-box, by turning a handle.

"Though if anybody ever got the best of me, it is you. I

don't mind saying this. I've said it—there! What more can you want? Isn't that enough for your pride, Captain Whalley? You got over me from the first. It's all of a piece, when I look back at it. You allowed me to insert that clause about intemperance without saying anything, only looking very sick when I made a point of it going in black on white. How could I tell what was wrong about you? There's generally something wrong somewhere. And, lo and behold! when you come on board it turns out that you've been in the habit of drinking nothing but water for years and years."

His dogmatic, reproachful whine stopped. He brooded profoundly, after the manner of crafty and unintelligent men. It seemed inconceivable that Captain Whalley should not laugh at the expression of disgust that overspread the heavy, yellow countenance. But Captain Whalley never raised his eyes—sitting in his arm-chair, outraged, dignified, and motionless.

"Much good it was to me," Massy remonstrated, monotonously, "to insert a clause of dismissal for intemperance against a man who drinks nothing but water. And you looked so upset, too, when I read my draft in the lawyer's office that morning, Captain Whalley—you looked so crestfallen, that I made sure I had gone home on your weak spot. A shipowner can't be too careful as to the sort of skipper he gets. You must have been laughing at me in your sleeve all the blessed time. . . . Eh? What were you going to say?"

Captain Whalley had only shuffled his feet slightly. A dull animosity became apparent in Massy's sideways stare.

"But recollect that there are other grounds of dismissal. There's habitual carelessness, amounting to incompetence —there's gross and persistent neglect of duty. I am not quite as big a fool as you try to make me out to be. You have been careless of late—leaving everything to that Serang. Why! I've seen you letting that old fool of a Malay take bearings for you, as if you were too big to attend to your work yourself. And what do you call that silly touch-

and-go manner in which you took the ship over the bar just now? You expect me to put up with that."

Leaning on his elbow against the ladder abaft the bridge, Sterne, the mate, tried to hear, blinking the while from the distance at the second engineer, who had come up for a moment, and stood in the engine-room companion. Wiping his hands on a bunch of cotton waste, he looked about with indifference to the right and left at the river banks slipping astern of the *Sofala* steadily.

Massy turned full at the chair. The character of his whine became again threatening.

"Take care. I may yet dismiss you and freeze to your money for a year. I may. . . ."

But before the silent, rigid immobility of the man whose money had come in the nick of time to save him from utter ruin, his voice died out in his throat.

"Not that I want you to go," he resumed after a silence, and in an absurdly insinuating tone. "I want nothing better than to be friends and renew the agreement, if you will consent to find another couple of hundred to help with the new boilers, Captain Whalley. I've told you before. She must have new boilers; you know it as well as I do. Have you thought this over?"

He waited. The slender stem of the pipe with its bulky lump of a bowl at the end hung down from his thick lips. It had gone out. Suddenly he took it from between his teeth and wrung his hands slightly.

"Don't you believe me?" He thrust the pipe bowl into the pocket of his shiny black jacket.

"It's like dealing with the devil," he said. "Why don't you speak? At first you were so high and mighty with me I hardly dared to creep about my own deck. Now I can't get a word from you. You don't seem to see me at all. What does it mean? Upon my soul, you terrify me with this deaf and dumb trick. What's going on in that head of yours? What are you plotting against me there so hard that you can't say a word? You will never make me believe that you—you—don't know where to lay your hands on a couple of hundred. You have made me curse the day I was born. . . ."

"Mr. Massy," said Captain Whalley, suddenly, without stirring.

The engineer started violently.

"If that is so I can only beg you to forgive me."

"Starboard," muttered the Serang to the helmsman and the *Sofala* began to swing round the bend into the second reach.

"Ough!" Massy shuddered. "You make my blood run cold. What made you come here? What made you come aboard that evening all of a sudden, with your high talk and your money—tempting me? I always wondered what was your motive. You fastened yourself on me to have easy times and grow fat on my life blood, I tell you. Was that it? I believe you are the greatest miser in the world, or else why. . . ."

"No. I am only poor," interrupted Captain Whalley, stonily.

"Steady," murmured the Serang. Massy turned away with his chin on his shoulder.

"I don't believe it," he said in his dogmatic tone. Captain Whalley made no movement. "There you sit like a gorged vulture—exactly like a vulture."

He embraced the middle of the reach and both the banks in one blank, unseeing, circular glance, and left the bridge slowly.

CHAPTER 9

On turning to descend Massy perceived the head of Sterne the mate loitering, with his sly, confident smile, his red moustaches and blinking eyes, at the foot of the ladder.

Sterne had been a junior in one of the larger shipping concerns before joining the *Sofala.* He had thrown up his berth, he said, "on general principles." The promotion in the employ was very slow, he complained, and he thought it was time for him to try and get on a bit in the world. It seemed as though nobody would ever die or leave the firm; they all stuck fast in their berths till they got mildewed; he was tired of waiting; and he feared that when a vacancy did occur the best servants were by no means sure of being treated fairly. Besides, the captain he had to serve under—Captain Provost—was an unaccountable sort of man and had taken a dislike to him for some reason or other. For doing rather more than his bare duty as likely as not. When he had done anything wrong he could take a talking-to, like a man; but he expected to be treated like a man, too, and not to be addressed invariably as though he were a dog. He had asked Captain Provost plump and plain to tell him where he was at fault, and Captain Provost, in a most scornful way, had told him that he was a perfect officer, and that if he disliked the way he was being spoken to there was the gangway—he could take himself off ashore at once. But everybody knew what sort of man Captain Provost was. It was no use appealing to the office. Captain Provost had too much influence in the employ. All the same, they had to give him a good character. He made bold to say there was nothing in the world against him, and, as he had happened to hear that the mate of the *Sofala* had been taken to the hospital that morning with a sunstroke, he thought there would be no harm in seeing whether he would not do. . . .

He had come to Captain Whalley freshly shaved, red-faced, thin-flanked, throwing out his lean chest; and had recited his little tale with an open and manly assurance. Now and then his eyelids quivered slightly, his hand would steal up to the end of the flaming moustache; his eyebrows were straight, furry, of a chestnut colour, and the directness of his gaze seemed to tremble on the verge of impudence. Captain Whalley had engaged him temporarily; then, the other man having been ordered home by the doctors, Sterne had remained for the next trip, and then the next. He had now attained permanency, and the performance of his duties was marked by an air of serious, single-minded application. Directly he was spoken to, he began to smile attentively, with a great deference expressed in his whole attitude; but there was in the rapid winking which went on all the time something quizzical, as though he had possessed the secret of some universal joke cheating all creation and impenetrable to other mortals.

Grave and smiling he watched Massy come down step by step; when the chief engineer had reached the deck he swung about, and they found themselves face to face. Matched as to height and utterly dissimilar, they confronted each other as if there had been something between them—something else than the bright strip of sunlight that, falling through the wide lacing of two awnings, cut crosswise the narrow planking of the deck and separated their feet as it were a stream; something profound and subtle and incalculable, like an unexpressed understanding, a secret mistrust, or some sort of fear.

At last Sterne, blinking his deep-set eyes and sticking forward his scraped, clean-cut chin, as crimson as the rest of his face, murmured—

"You've seen? He grazed! You've seen?"

Massy, contemptuous, and without raising his yellow, fleshy countenance, replied in the same pitch—

"Maybe. But if it had been you we would have been stuck fast in the mud."

"Pardon me, Mr. Massy. I beg to deny it. Of course a shipowner may say what he jolly well pleases on his own deck. That's all right; but I beg to. . . ."

"Get out of my way!"

The other had a slight start, the impulse of suppressed indignation perhaps, but held his ground. Massy's downward glance wandered right and left, as though the deck all round Sterne had been bestrewn with eggs that must not be broken, and he had looked irritably for places where he could set his feet in flight. In the end he, too, did not move, though there was plenty of room to pass on.

"I heard you say up there," went on the mate—"and a very just remark it was, too—that there's always something wrong. . . ."

"Eavesdropping is what's wrong with *you*, Mr. Sterne."

"Now, if you would only listen to me for a moment, Mr. Massy, sir, I could. . . ."

"You are a sneak," interrupted Massy in a great hurry, and even managed to get so far as to repeat, "a common sneak," before the mate had broken in argumentatively—

"Now, sir, what is it you want? You want. . . ."

"I want—I want," stammered Massy, infuriated and astonished—"I want? How do you know that I want anything? How dare you? . . . What do you mean? . . . What are you after—you. . . ."

"Promotion." Sterne silenced him with candid bravado. The engineer's round soft cheeks quivered still, but he said quietly enough—

"You are only worrying my head off," and Sterne met him with a confident little smile.

"A chap in business I know (well up in the world he is now) used to tell me that this was the proper way. 'Always push on to the front,' he would say. 'Keep yourself well before your boss. Interfere whenever you get a chance. Show him what you know. Worry him into seeing you.' That was his advice. Now I know no other boss than you here. You are the owner, and no one else counts for *that* much in my eyes. See, Mr. Massy? I want to get on. I make no secret of it that I am one of the sort that means to get on. These are the men to make use of, sir. You haven't arrived at the top of the tree, sir, without finding that out—I daresay."

"Worry your boss in order to get on," repeated Massy, as if awestruck by the irreverent originality of the idea. "I shouldn't wonder if this was just what the Blue Anchor people kicked you out of their employ for. Is that what you call getting on? You shall get on in the same way here if you aren't careful—I can promise you."

At this Sterne hung his head, thoughtful, perplexed, winking hard at the deck. All his attempts to enter into confidential relations with his owner had led of late to nothing better than these dark threats of dismissal; and a threat of dismissal would check him at once into a hesitating silence as though he were not sure that the proper time for defying it had come. On this occasion he seemed to have lost his tongue for a moment, and Massy, getting in motion, heavily passed him by with an abortive attempt at shouldering. Sterne defeated it by stepping aside. He turned then swiftly, opening his mouth very wide as if to shout something after the engineer, but seemed to think better of it.

Always—as he was ready to confess—on the lookout for an opening to get on, it had become an instinct with him to watch the conduct of his immediate superiors for something "that one could lay hold of." It was his belief that no skipper in the world would keep his command for a day if only the owners could be "made to know." This romantic and naïve theory had led him into trouble more than once, but he remained incorrigible; and his character was so instinctively disloyal that whenever he joined a ship the intention of ousting his commander out of the berth and taking his place was always present at the back of his head, as a matter of course. It filled the leisure of his waking hours with the reveries of careful plans and compromising discoveries—the dreams of his sleep with images of lucky turns and favourable accidents. Skippers had been known to sicken and die at sea, than which nothing could be better to give a smart mate a chance of showing what he's made of. They also would tumble overboard sometimes: he had heard of one or two such cases. Others again. . . . But, as it were constitutionally, he was faithful to the belief that the conduct of no single one of them would stand the test of careful watching by a man who "knew what's what" and who kept his eyes "skinned pretty well" all the time.

After he had gained a permanent footing on board the *Sofala* he allowed his perennial hope to rise high. To begin with, it was a great advantage to have an old man for captain: the sort of man besides who in the nature of things was likely to give up the job before long from one cause or another. Sterne was greatly chagrined, however, to notice that he did not seem anyway near being past his work yet. Still, these old men go to pieces all at once sometimes. Then there was the owner-engineer close at hand to be impressed by his zeal and steadiness. Sterne never for a moment doubted the obvious nature of his own merits (he was really an excellent officer); only, nowadays, professional merit alone does not take a man along fast enough. A chap must have some push in him, and must keep his wits at work, too, to help him forward. He made up his mind to inherit the charge of this steamer if it was to be done at all; not indeed estimating the command of the *Sofala* as a very great catch, but for the reason that, out East especially, to make a start is everything, and one command leads to another.

He began by promising himself to behave with great circumspection; Massy's sombre and fantastic humours intimidated him as being outside one's usual sea experience; but he was quite intelligent enough to realize almost from the first that he was there in the presence of an exceptional situation. His peculiar prying imagination penetrated it quickly; the feeling that there was in it an element which eluded his grasp exasperated his impatience to get on. And so one trip came to an end, then another, and he had begun his third before he saw an opening by which he could step in with any sort of effect. It had all been very queer and very obscure; something had been going on near him, as if separated by a chasm from the common life and the working routine of the ship, which was exactly like the life and the routine of any other coasting steamer of that class.

Then one day he made his discovery.

It came to him after all these weeks of watchful observation and puzzled surmises, suddenly, like the long-sought solution of a riddle that suggests itself to the mind in a flash. Not with the same authority, however. Great heavens! Could it be that? And after remaining thunderstruck for a few seconds he tried to shake it off with self-contumely, as though it had been the product of an unhealthy bias toward the Incredible, the Inexplicable, the Unheard-of—the Mad!

This—the illuminating moment—had occurred the trip before, in the return passage. They had just left a place of call on the mainland called Pangu; they were steaming straight out of a bay. To the east a massive headland closed the view, with the tilted edges of the rocky strata showing through its ragged clothing of rank bushes and thorny creepers. The wind had begun to sing in the rigging; the sea along the coast, green and as if swollen a little above the line of the horizon, seemed to pour itself over, time after time, with a slow and thundering fall, into the shadow of the leeward cape; and across the wide opening the nearest of a group of small islands stood enveloped in the hazy yellow light of a breezy sunrise; still farther out the hummocky tops of other islets peeped out motionless above the water of the channels between, scoured tumultuously by the breeze.

The usual track of the *Sofala* both going and returning on every trip led her for a few miles along this reef-infested region. She followed a broad lane of water, dropping astern, one after another, these crumbs of the earth's crust resembling a squadron of dismasted hulks run in disorder upon a foul ground of rocks and shoals. Some of these fragments of land appeared, indeed, no bigger than a stranded ship; others, quite flat, lay awash like anchored rafts, like ponderous, black rafts of stone; several, heavily timbered and round at the base, emerged in squat domes of deep green foliage that shuddered darkly all over to the flying touch of cloud shadows driven by the sudden gusts of the squally season. The thunderstorms of the coast broke frequently over that cluster; it turned then shadowy in its whole extent; it turned more dark, and as if more still in the play of fire; as if more impenetrably silent in the peals of thunder; its blurred shapes vanished—dissolving utterly at times in the thick rain—to reappear clear-cut and black in the stormy light against the gray sheet of the cloud—scattered on the slaty round table of the sea. Unscathed by storms, resisting the work of years, unfretted by the strife of the world, there it lay unchanged as on that day, four hundred years ago, when first beheld by Western eyes from the deck of a high-pooped caravel.

It was one of those secluded spots that may be found on the busy sea, as on land you come sometimes upon the clustered houses of a hamlet untouched by men's restlessness, untouched by their need, by their thought, and as if forgotten by time itself. The lives of uncounted generations had passed it by, and the multitudes of seafowl, urging their way from all the points of the horizon to sleep on the outer rocks of the group, unrolled the converging evolutions of their flight in long, sombre streamers upon the glow of the sky. The palpitating cloud of their wings soared and stooped over the pinnacles of the rocks, over the rocks slender like spires, squat like martello towers; over the pyramidal heaps like fallen ruins, over the lines of bald boulders showing like a wall of stones battered to pieces and scorched by lightning—with the sleepy, clear glimmer of water in every breach. The noise of their continuous and violent screaming filled the air.

This great noise would meet the *Sofala* coming up from Batu Beru; it would meet her on quiet evenings, at pitiless and savage clamour enfeebled by distance, the clamour of seabirds settling to rest, and struggling for a footing at the end of the day. No one noticed it especially on board; it was the voice of their ship's unerring landfall, ending the steady stretch of a hundred miles. She had made good her course, she had run her distance till the punctual islets began to emerge one by one, the points of rocks, the hummocks of earth . . . and the cloud of birds hovered—the restless cloud emitting a strident and cruel uproar, the sound of the familiar scene, the living part of the broken land beneath, of the outspread sea, and of the high sky without a flaw.

But when the *Sofala* happened to close with the land after sunset she would find everything very still there under the mantle of the night. All would be still, dumb, almost invisible—but for the blotting out of the low constellations occulted in turns behind the vague masses of the islets whose true outlines eluded the eye amongst the dark spaces of the heaven: and the ship's three lights, resembling three stars—the red and the green with the white above—her three lights, like three companion stars wandering on the earth, held their unswerving course for the passage at the southern end of the group. Sometimes there were human eyes open to watch them come nearer, travelling smoothly in the sombre void; the eyes of a naked fisherman in his canoe floating over a reef. He thought drowsily: "Ha! The fire-ship that once in every moon goes in and comes out of Pangu Bay." More he did not know of her. And just as he had detected the faint rhythm of the propeller beating the calm water a mile and a half away, the time would come for the *Sofala* to alter her course, the lights would swing off him their triple beam—and disappear.

A few miserable, half-naked families, a sort of outcast tribe of long-haired, lean, and wild-eyed people, strove for their living in this lonely wilderness of islets, lying like an abandoned outwork of the land at the gates of the bay. Within the knots and loops of the rocks the water rested more transparent than crystal under their crooked and leaky canoes, scooped out of the trunk of a tree: the forms of the bottom undulated slightly to the dip of a paddle; and the men seemed to hang in the air, they seemed to hang enclosed within the fibres of a dark, sodden log, fishing patiently in a strange, unsteady, pellucid, green air above the shoals.

Their bodies stalked brown and emaciated as if dried up in the sunshine; their lives ran out silently; the homes where they were born, went to rest, and died—flimsy sheds of rushes and coarse grass eked out with a few ragged mats—were hidden out of sight from the open sea. No glow of their houschold fires ever kindled for a seaman a red spark upon the blind night of the group: and the calms of the coast, the flaming long calms of the equator, the unbreathing, concentrated calms like the deep introspection of a passionate nature, brooded awfully for days and weeks together over the unchangeable inheritance of their children; till at last the stones, hot like live embers, scorched the naked sole, till the water clung warm, and sickly, and as if thickened about the legs of lean men with girded loins, wading thigh-deep in the pale blaze of the shallows. And it would happen now and then that the *Sofala,* through some delay in one of the ports of call, would heave in sight making for Pangu Bay as late as noonday.

Only a blurring cloud at first, the thin mist of her smoke would arise mysteriously from an empty point on the clear line of sea and sky. The taciturn fishermen within the reefs would extend their lean arms toward the offing; and the brown figures stooping on the tiny beaches, the brown figures of men, women, and children grubbing in the sand in search of turtles' eggs, would rise up, crooked elbow aloft and hand over the eyes, to watch this monthly apparition glide straight on, swerve off—and go by. Their ears caught the panting of that ship; their eyes followed her till she passed between the two capes of the mainland going at full speed as though she hoped to make her way unchecked into the very bosom of the earth.

On such days the luminous sea would give no sign of the dangers lurking on both sides of her path. Every thing remained still, crushed by the overwhelming power of the light; and the whole group, opaque in the sunshine,—the rocks resembling pinnacles, the rocks resembling spires, the rocks resembling ruins; the forms of islets resembling beehives, resembling mole-hills; the islets recalling the shapes of haystacks, the contours of ivy-clad towers—would stand reflected together upside down in the unwrinkled water, like carved toys of ebony disposed on the silvered plate-glass of a mirror.

The first touch of blowing weather would envelop the whole at once in the spume of the windward breakers, as if in a sudden cloudlike burst of steam; and the clear water seemed fairly to boil in all the passages. The provoked sea outlined exactly in a design of angry foam the wide base of the group; the submerged level of broken waste and refuse left over from the building of the coast near by, projecting its dangerous spurs, all awash, far into the channel, and bristling with wicked long spits often a mile long: with deadly spits made of froth and stones.

And even nothing more than a brisk breeze—as on that morning, the voyage before, when the *Sofala* left Pangu Bay early, and Mr. Sterne's discovery was to blossom out like a flower of incredible and evil aspect from the tiny seed of instinctive suspicion—even such a breeze had enough strength to tear the placid mask from the face of the sea. To Sterne, gazing with indifference, it had been like a revelation to behold for the first time the dangers marked by the hissing livid patches on the water as distinctly as on the engraved paper of a chart. It came into his mind that this was the sort of day most favourable for a stranger attempting the passage: a clear day, just windy enough for the sea to break on every ledge, buoying, as it were, the channel plainly to the sight; whereas during a calm you had nothing to depend on but the compass and the practised judgment of your eye. And yet the successive captains of the *Sofala* had had to take her through at night more than once. Nowadays you could not afford to throw away six or seven hours of a steamer's time. That you couldn't. But then use is everything, and with proper care. . . . The channel was broad and safe enough; the main point was to hit upon the entrance correctly in the dark—for if a man got himself involved in that stretch of broken water over yonder he would never get out with a whole ship—if he ever got out at all.

This was Sterne's last train of thought independent of the

great discovery. He had just seen to the securing of the anchor, and had remained forward idling away a moment or two. The captain was in charge on the bridge. With a slight yawn he had turned away from his survey of the sea and had leaned his shoulders against the fish davit.

These, properly speaking, were the very last moments of ease he was to know on board the *Sofala*. All the instants that came after were to be pregnant with purpose and intolerable with perplexity. No more idle, random thoughts; the discovery would put them on the rack, till sometimes he wished to goodness he had been fool enough not to make it at all. And yet, if his chance to get on rested on the discovery of "something wrong," he could not have hoped for a greater stroke of luck.

CHAPTER 10

The knowledge was too disturbing, really. There was "something wrong" with a vengeance, and the moral certitude of it was at first simply frightful to contemplate. Sterne had been looking aft in a mood so idle, that for once he was thinking no harm of any one. His captain on the bridge presented himself naturally to his sight. How insignificant, how casual was the thought that had started the train of discovery—like an accidental spark that suffices to ignite the charge of a tremendous mine!

Caught under by the breeze, the awnings of the foredeck bellied upwards and collapsed slowly, and above their heavy flapping the gray stuff of Captain Whalley's roomy coat fluttered incessantly around his arms and trunk. He faced the wind in full light with his great silvery beard blown forcibly against his chest; the eyebrows overhung heavily the shadows whence his glance appeared to be staring ahead piercingly. Sterne could just detect the twin gleam of the whites shifting under the shaggy arches of the brow. At short range these eyes, for all the man's affable manner, seemed to look you through and through. Sterne never could defend himself from that feeling when he had occasion to speak with his captain. He did not like it. What a big heavy man he appeared up there, with that little shrimp of a Serang in close attendance—as was usual in this extraordinary steamer! Confounded absurd custom that. He resented it. Surely the old fellow could have looked after his ship without that loafing native at his elbow. Sterne wriggled his shoulders with disgust. What was it? Indolence or what?

That old skipper must have been growing lazy for years. They all grew lazy out East here (Sterne was very conscious of his own unimpaired activity); they got slack all over. But he towered very erect on the bridge; and quite low by his side, as you see a small child looking over the edge of a table, the battered soft hat and the brown face of the Serang peeped over the white canvas screen of the rail.

No doubt the Malay was standing back, nearer to the wheel; but the great disparity of size in close association amused Sterne like the observation of a bizarre fact in nature. There were as queer fish out of the sea as any in it.

He saw Captain Whalley turn his head quickly to speak to his Serang; the wind whipped the whole white mass of the beard sideways. He would be directing the chap to look at the compass for him, or what not. Of course. Too much trouble to step over and see for himself. Sterne's scorn for that bodily indolence which overtakes white men in the East increased on reflection. Some of them would be utterly lost if they hadn't all these natives at their beck and call; they grew perfectly shameless about it, too. He was not of that sort, thank God! It wasn't in him to make himself dependent for his work on any shrivelled-up little Malay like that. As if one could ever trust a silly native for anything in the world! But that fine old man thought differently, it seems. There they were together, never far apart; a pair of them, recalling to the mind an old whale attended by a little pilot-fish.

The fancifulness of the comparison made him smile. A whale with an inseparable pilot-fish! That's what the old man looked like; for it could not be said he looked like a shark, though Mr. Massy had called him that very name. But Mr. Massy did not mind what he said in his savage fits. Sterne smiled to himself—and gradually the ideas evoked by the sound, by the imagined shape of the word pilot-fish, the ideas of aid, of guidance needed and received, came uppermost in his mind: the word pilot awakened the idea of trust, of dependence, the idea of the welcome, clear-eyed help brought to the seaman groping for the land in the dark: groping blindly in fogs: feeling his way in the thick weather of the gales that, filling the air with a salt mist blown up from the sea, contract the range of sight on all sides to a shrunken horizon that seems within reach of the hand.

A pilot sees better than a stranger, because his local knowledge, like a sharper vision, completes the shapes of things hurriedly glimpsed; penetrates the veils of mist spread over the land by the storms of the sea; defines with certitude the outlines of a coast lying under the pall of fog, the forms of landmarks half buried in a starless night as in a shallow grave. He recognizes because he already knows. It is not to his far-reaching eye but to his more extensive knowledge that the pilot looks for certitude; for this certitude of the ship's position on which may depend a man's good fame and the peace of his conscience, the justification of the trust deposited in his hands, with his own life, too, which is seldom wholly his to throw away, and the humble lives of others rooted in distant affections, perhaps, and made as weighty as the lives of kings by the burden of the awaiting mystery. The pilot's knowledge brings relief and certitude to the commander of a ship; the Serang, however, in his fanciful suggestion of a pilot-fish attending a whale, could not in any way be credited with a superior knowledge. Why should he have it? These two men had come on that run together—the white and the brown—on the same day: and of course a white man would learn more in a week than the best native would in a month. He was made to stick to the skipper as though he were of some use—as the pilot-fish, they say, is to the whale. But how—it was very marked—how? A pilot-fish—a pilot—a . . . But if not superior knowledge then. . . .

Sterne's discovery was made. It was repugnant to his imagination, shocking to his ideas of honesty, shocking to his conception of mankind. This enormity affected one's outlook on what was possible in this world: it was as if for instance the sun had turned blue, throwing a new and sinister light on men and nature. Really in the first moment he had felt sickish, as though he had got a blow below the belt: for a second the very colour of the sea seemed changed—appeared queer to his wandering eye; and he had a passing, unsteady sensation in all his limbs as though the earth had started turning the other way.

A very natural incredulity succeeding this sense of upheaval brought a measure of relief. He had gasped; it was over. But afterwards, during all that day, sudden paroxysms of wonder would come over him in the midst of his occupations. He would stop and shake his head. The revolt of his incredulity had passed away almost as quick as the first emotion of discovery, and for the next twenty-four hours he had no sleep. That would never do. At meal-times (he took the foot of the table set up for the white men on the bridge) he could not help losing himself in a fascinated contemplation of Captain Whalley opposite. He watched the deliberate upward movements of the arm; the old man put his food to his lips as though he never expected to find any taste in his daily bread, as though he did not know anything about it. He fed himself like a somnambulist. "It's an awful sight," thought Sterne; and he watched the long period of mournful, silent immobility, with a big brown hand lying loosely closed by the side of the plate, till he noticed the two engineers to the right and left looking at him in astonishment. He would close his mouth in a hurry then, and lowering his eyes, wink rapidly at his plate. It was awful to see the old chap sitting there: it was even awful to think that with three words he could blow him up sky-high. All he had to do was to raise his voice and pronounce a single short sentence, and yet that simple act seemed as impossible to attempt as moving the sun out of its place in the sky. The old chap could eat in his terrific mechanical way; but Sterne, from mental excitement, could not—not that evening, at any rate.

He had had ample time since to get accustomed to the strain of the meal-hours. He would never have believed it. But then use is everything; only the very potency of his success prevented anything resembling elation. He felt like a man who, in his legitimate search for a loaded gun to help him on his way through the world, chances to come upon a torpedo—upon a live torpedo with a shattering charge in its head and a pressure of many atmospheres in its tail. It is the sort of weapon to make its possessor careworn and nervous. He had no mind to be blown up himself; and he could not get rid of the notion that the explosion was bound to damage him, too, in some way.

This vague apprehension had restrained him at first. He was able now to eat and sleep with that fearful weapon by his side, with the conviction of its power always in his mind. It had not been arrived at by any reflective process; but once the idea had entered his head, the conviction had followed overwhelmingly in a multitude of observed little facts to which before he had given only a languid attention. The abrupt and faltering intonations of the deep voice; the taciturnity put on like an armour; the deliberate, as if guarded, movements; the long immobilities, as if the man he watched had been afraid to disturb the very air: every familiar gesture, every word uttered in his hearing, every sigh overheard, had acquired a special significance, a confirmatory import.

Every day that passed over the *Sofala* appeared to Sterne simply crammed full with proofs—with incontrovertible proofs. At night, when off duty, he would steal out of his cabin in pyjamas (for more proofs) and stand a full hour, perhaps, on his bare feet below the bridge, as absolutely motionless as the awning stanchion in its deck socket near by. On the stretches of easy navigation it is not usual for a coasting captain to remain on deck all the time of his watch. The Serang keeps it for him as a matter of custom; in open water, on a straight course, he is usually trusted to look after the ship by himself. But this old man seemed incapable of remaining quietly down below. No doubt he could not sleep. And no wonder. This was also a proof. Suddenly in the silence of the ship panting upon the still, dark sea, Sterne would hear a low voice above him exclaiming nervously—

"Serang!"

"Tuan!"

"You are watching the compass well?"

"Yes, I am watching, Tuan."

"The ship is making her course?"

"She is, Tuan. Very straight."

"It is well; and remember, Serang, that the order is, that you are to mind the helmsman and keep a lookout with care, the same as if I were not on deck."

Then, when the Serang had made his answer, the low tones on the bridge would cease, and everything round Sterne seemed to become more still and more profoundly silent. Slightly chilled and with his back aching a little from long immobility, he would steal away to his room on the port side of the deck. He had long since parted with the last vestige of incredulity; of the original emotions, set into a tumult by the discovery, some trace of the first awe alone remained. Not the awe of the man himself—he could blow him up sky-high with six words—rather it was an awestruck indignation at the reckless perversity of avarice (what else could it be?), at the mad and sombre resolution that for the sake of a few dollars more seemed to set at nought the common rule of conscience and pretended to struggle against the very decree of Providence.

You could not find another man like this one in the whole

round world—thank God. There was something devilishly dauntless in the character of such a deception which made you pause.

Other considerations occurring to his prudence had kept him tongue-tied from day to day. It seemed to him now that it would yet have been easier to speak out in the first hour of discovery. He almost regretted not having made a row at once. But then the very monstrosity of the disclosure . . . Why! he could hardly face it himself, let alone pointing it out to somebody else. Moreover, with a desperado of that sort one never knew. The object was not to get him out (that was as well as done already), but to step into his place. Bizarre as the thought seemed, he might have shown fight. A fellow up to working such a fraud would have enough cheek for anything; a fellow that, as it were, stood up against God Almighty Himself. He was a horrid marvel —that's what he was: he was perfectly capable of brazening out the affair scandalously till he got him (Sterne) kicked out of the ship and everlastingly damaged his prospects in this part of the East. Yet if you want to get on something must be risked. At times Sterne thought he had been unduly timid of taking action in the past; and what was worse, it had come to this, that in the present he did not seem to know what action to take.

Massy's savage moroseness was too disconcerting. It was an incalculable factor of the situation. You could not tell what there was behind that insulting ferocity. How could one trust such a temper? it did not put Sterne in bodily fear for himself, but it frightened him exceedingly as to his prospects.

Though of course inclined to credit himself with exceptional powers of observation, he had by now lived too long with his discovery. He had gone on looking at nothing else, till at last one day it occurred to him that the thing was so obvious that no one could miss seeing it. There were four white men in all on board the *Sofala*. Jack, the second engineer, was too dull to notice anything that took place out of his engine-room. Remained Massy—the owner—the interested person—nearly going mad with worry. Sterne had heard and seen more than enough on board to know what ailed him; but his exasperation seemed to make him deaf to cautious overtures. If he had only known it, there was the very thing he wanted. But how could you bargain with a man of that sort? It was like going into a tiger's den with a piece of raw meat in your hand. He was as likely as not to rend you for your pains. In fact, he was always threatening to do that very thing; and the urgency of the case, combined with the impossibility of handling it with safety, made Sterne in his watches below toss and mutter open-eyed in his bunk, for hours, as though he had been burning with fever.

Occurrences like the crossing of the bar just now were extremely alarming to his prospects. He did not want to be left behind by some swift catastrophe. Massy being on the bridge, the old man had to brace himself up, and make a show, he supposed. But it was getting very bad with him, very bad indeed, now. Even Massy had been emboldened to find fault this time; Sterne, listening at the foot of the ladder, had heard the other's whimpering and artless denunciations. Luckily the beast was very stupid and could not see the why of all this. However, small blame to him; it took a clever man to hit upon the cause. Nevertheless, it was high time to do something. The old man's game could not be kept up for many days more.

"I may yet lose my life at this fooling—let alone my chance," Sterne mumbled angrily to himself, after the stooping back of the chief engineer had disappeared round the corner of the skylight. Yes, no doubt—he thought; but to blurt out his knowledge would not advance his prospects. On the contrary, it would blast them as likely as not. He dreaded another failure. He had a vague consciousness of not being much liked by his fellows in this part of the world; inexplicably enough, for he had done nothing to them. Envy, he supposed. People were always down on a clever chap who made no bones about his determination to get on. To do your duty and count on the gratitude of that brute Massy would be sheer folly. He was a bad lot. Unmanly! A vicious man! Bad! Bad! A brute! A brute without a spark of anything human about him; without so much as simple curiosity even, or else surely he would have responded in some way to all these hints he had been given. . . . Such insensibility was almost mysterious. Massy's state of exasperation seemed to Sterne to have made him stupid beyond the ordinary silliness of shipowners.

Sterne, meditating on the embarrassments of that stupidity, forgot himself completely. His stony, unwinking stare was fixed on the planks of the deck.

The slight quiver agitating the whole fabric of the ship was more perceptible in the silent river, shaded and still like a forest path. The *Sofala*, gliding with an even motion, had passed beyond the coast-belt of mud and mangroves. The shores rose higher, in firm sloping banks, and the forest of big trees came down to the brink. Where the earth had been crumbled by the floods it showed a steep brown cut, denuding a mass of roots intertwined as if wrestling underground; and in the air, the interlaced boughs, bound and loaded with creepers, carried on the struggle for life, mingled their foliage in one solid wall of leaves, with here and there the shape of an enormous dark pillar soaring, or a ragged opening, as if torn by the flight of a cannon-ball, disclosing the impenetrable gloom within, the secular inviolable shade of the virgin forest. The thump of the engines reverberated regularly like the strokes of a metronome beating the measure of the vast silence, the shadow of the western wall had fallen across the river, and the smoke pouring backwards from the funnel eddied down behind the ship, spread a thin dusky veil over the sombre water, which, checked by the flood-tide, seemed to lie stagnant in the whole straight length of the reaches.

Sterne's body, as if rooted on the spot, trembled slightly from top to toe with the internal vibration of the ship; from under his feet came sometimes a sudden clang of iron, the noisy burst of a shout below; to the right the leaves of the tree-tops caught the rays of the low sun, and seemed to shine with a golden green light of their own shimmering around the highest boughs which stood out black against the smooth blue sky that seemed to droop over the bed of the river like the roof of a tent. The passengers for Batu Beru, kneeling on the planks, were engaged in rolling their bedding of mats busily; they tied up bundles, they snapped the locks of wooden chests. A pockmarked pedlar of small wares threw his head back to drain into his throat the last drops out of an earthenware bottle before putting it away in a roll of blankets. Knots of travelling traders standing about the deck conversed in low tones; the followers of a small Rajah from down the coast, broad-faced simple young fellows in white drawers and round white cotton caps with their coloured sarongs twisted across their bronze shoulders, squatted on their hams on the hatch, chewing betel with bright red mouths as if they had been tasting blood. Their spears, lying piled up together within the circle of their bare toes, resembled a casual bundle of dry bamboos; a thin, livid Chinaman, with a bulky package wrapped up in leaves already thrust under his arm, gazed ahead eagerly; a wandering Kling rubbed his teeth with a bit of wood, pouring over the side a bright stream of water out of his lips; the fat Rajah dozed in a shabby deck-chair—and at the turn of every bend the two walls of leaves reappeared running parallel along the banks, with their impenetrable solidity fading at the top to a vaporous mistiness of countless slender twigs growing free, of young delicate branches shooting from the topmost limbs of hoary trunks, of feathery heads of climbers like delicate silver sprays standing up without a quiver. There was not a sign of a clearing anywhere; not a trace of human habitation, except when in one place, on the bare end of a low point under an isolated group of slender tree-ferns, the jagged, tangled remnants of an old hut on piles appeared with that peculiar aspect of ruined bamboo walls that look as if smashed with a club. Farther on, half hidden under the drooping bushes, a canoe containing a man and a woman together with a dozen green cocoanuts in a heap, rocked helplessly after the *Sofala* had passed, like a navigating contrivance of venturesome insects, of travelling ants; while two glassy folds of water streaming away from each bow of the steamer across the whole width of the river ran with her upstream smoothly, fretting their outer ends into a brown whispering tumble of froth against the miry foot of each bank.

"I must," thought Sterne, "bring that brute Massy to his bearings. It's getting too absurd in the end. Here's the old man up there buried in his chair—he may just as well be in his grave for all the use he'll ever be in the world—and the Serang's in charge. Because that's what he is. In charge. In the place that's mine by rights. I must bring that savage brute to his bearings. I'll do it at once, too. . . ."

When the mate made an abrupt start, a little brown, half-naked boy, with large black eyes, and the string of a written charm round his neck, became panic-struck at once. He dropped the banana he had been munching, and ran to the knee of a grave dark Arab in flowing robes, sitting like a Biblical figure, incongruously, on a yellow tin trunk corded with a rope of twisted rattan. The father, unmoved, put out his hand to pat the little shaven poll protectingly.

CHAPTER 11

Sterne crossed the deck upon the track of the chief engineer. Jack, the second, retreating backwards down the engine-room ladder, and still wiping his hands, treated him to an incomprehensible grin of white teeth out of his grimy hard face; Massy was nowhere to be seen. Sterne scratched at the door softly, then, putting his lips to the rose of the ventilator, said—

"I must speak to you, Mr. Massy. Just give me a minute or two."

"I am busy. Go away from my door."

"But pray, Mr. Massy. . . ."

"You go away. D'you hear? Take yourself off altogether—to the other end of the ship—quite away. . . ." The voice inside dropped low. "To the devil."

Sterne paused: then very quietly—

"It's rather pressing. When do you think you will be at liberty, sir?"

The answer to this was an exasperated "Never"; and at once Sterne, with a very firm expression of face, turned the handle.

Mr. Massy's stateroom—a narrow, one-berth cabin—smelt strongly of soap, and presented to view a swept, dusted, unadorned neatness, not so much bare as barren, not so much severe as starved and lacking in humanity, like the ward of a public hospital, or rather (owing to the small size) like the clean retreat of a desperately poor but exemplary person. Not a single photograph frame ornamented the bulk-heads; not a single article of clothing, not as much as a spare cap, hung from the brass hooks. All the inside was painted in one plain tint of pale blue; two big sea-chests in sail-cloth covers and with iron padlocks fitted exactly in the space under the bunk. One glance was enough to embrace all the strip of scrubbed planks within the four unconcealed corners. The absence of the usual settee was striking; the teak-wood top of the washing-stand seemed hermetically closed, and so was the lid of the writing-desk, which protruded from the partition at the foot of the bed-place, containing a mattress as thin as a pancake under a threadbare blanket with a faded red stripe, and a folded mosquito-net against the nights spent in harbour. There was not a scrap of paper anywhere in sight, no boots on the floor, no litter of any sort, not a speck of dust anywhere; no traces of pipe-ash even, which, in a heavy smoker, was morally revolting, like a manifestation of extreme hypocrisy; and the bottom of the old wooden arm-chair (the only seat there), polished with much use, shone as if its shabbiness had been waxed. The screen of leaves on the bank, passing as if unrolled endlessly in the round opening of the port, sent a wavering network of light and shade into the place.

Sterne, holding the door open with one hand, had thrust in his head and shoulders. At this amazing intrusion Massy, who was doing absolutely nothing, jumped up speechless.

"Don't call names," murmured Sterne, hurriedly. "I won't be called names. I think of nothing but your good, Mr. Massy."

A pause as of extreme astonishment followed. They both seemed to have lost their tongues. Then the mate went on with discreet glibness:

"You simply couldn't conceive what's going on on board your ship. It wouldn't enter your head for a moment. You are too good—too—too upright, Mr. Massy, to suspect anybody of such a . . . It's enough to make your hair stand on end."

He watched for the effect: Massy seemed dazed, uncomprehending. He only passed the palm of his hand on the coal-black wisps plastered across the top of his head. In a tone suddenly changed to confidential audacity Sterne hastened on:

"Remember that there's only six weeks left to run. . . ." The other was looking at him stonily. . . "So anyhow you will require a captain for the ship before long."

Then only, as if that suggestion had scarified his flesh in the manner of red-hot iron, Massy gave a start and seemed ready to shriek. He contained himself by a great effort.

"Require—a—captain," he repeated with scathing slowness. "Who requires a captain? You dare tell me that I need any of you humbugging sailors to run my ship. You and your likes have been fattening on me for years. It would have hurt me less to throw my money overboard. Pam—pe—red us—e—less f-f-f-frauds. The old ship knows as much as the best of you." He snapped his teeth audibly and growled through them. "The silly law requires a captain."

Sterne had taken heart of grace meantime.

"And the silly insurance people, too, as well," he said,

lightly. "But never mind that. What I want to ask is: Why shouldn't *I* do, sir? I don't say but you could take a steamer about the world as well as any of us sailors. I don't pretend to tell *you* that it is a very great trick. . . ." He emitted a short, hollow guffaw, familiarly. . . . "I didn't make the law—but there it is; and I am an active young fellow; I quite hold with your ideas; I know your ways by this time, Mr. Massy. I wouldn't try to give myself airs like that—that—er—lazy specimen of an old man up there."

He put a marked emphasis on the last sentence, to lead Massy away from the track in case . . . but he did not doubt of now holding his success. The chief engineer seemed nonplussed, like a slow man invited to catch hold of a whirligig of some sort.

"What you want, sir, is a chap with no nonsense about him, who would be content to be your sailing-master. Quite right, too. Well, I am fit for the work as much as that Serang. Because that's what it amounts to. Do you know, sir, that a dam' Malay like a monkey is in charge of your ship—and no one else? Just listen to his feet pit-patting above us on the bridge—real officer in charge. He's taking her up the river while the great man is wallowing in the chair—perhaps asleep; and if he is, that would not make it much worse either—take my word for it."

He tried to thrust himself farther in. Massy, with lowered forehead, one hand grasping the back of the arm-chair, did not budge.

"You think, sir, that the man has got you tight in his agreement. . . ." Massy raised a heavy snarling face at this. . . . "Well, sir, one can't help hearing of it on board. It's no secret. And it has been the talk on shore for years; fellows have been making bets about it. No, sir! It's *you* who have got him at your mercy. You will say that you can't dismiss him for indolence. Difficult to prove in court, and so on. Why, yes. But if you say the word, sir, I can tell you something about his indolence that will give you the clear right to fire him out on the spot and put me in charge for the rest of this very trip—yes, sir, before we leave

Batu Beru—and make him pay a dollar a day for his keep till we get back, if you like. Now, what do you think of that? Come, sir. Say the word. It's really well worth your while, and I am quite ready to take your bare word. A definite statement from you would be as good as a bond."

His eyes began to shine. He insisted. A simple statement —and he thought to himself that he would manage somehow to stick in his berth as long as it suited him. He would make himself indispensable; the ship had a bad name in her port; it would be easy to scare the fellows off. Massy would have to keep him.

"A definite statement from me would be enough," Massy repeated, slowly.

"Yes, sir. It would." Sterne stuck out his chin cheerily and blinked at close quarters with that unconscious impudence which had the power to enrage Massy beyond anything.

The engineer spoke very distinctly:

"Listen well to me, then, Mr. Sterne: I wouldn't—d'ye hear?—I wouldn't promise you the value of two pence for anything *you* can tell me."

He struck Sterne's arm away with a smart blow, and catching hold of the handle pulled the door to. The terrific slam darkened the cabin instantaneously to his eyes as if after the flash of an explosion. At once he dropped into the chair. "Oh, no! You don't!" he whispered faintly.

The ship had in that place to shave the bank so close that the gigantic wall of leaves came gliding like a shutter against the port; the darkness of the primeval forest seemed to flow into that bare cabin with the odour of rotting leaves, of sodden soil—the strong muddy smell of the living earth steaming uncovered after the passing of a deluge. The bushes swished loudly alongside; above there was a series of crackling sounds, with a sharp rain of small broken branches falling on the bridge; a creeper with a great rustle snapped on the head of a boat davit, and a long, luxuriant green twig actually whipped in and out of the open port, leaving behind a few torn leaves that remained suddenly at rest on Mr. Massy's blanket. Then, the ship sheering out in the stream, the light began to return, but did not augment beyond a subdued clearness: for the sun was very low already, and the river, wending its sinuous course through a multitude of secular trees as if at the bottom of a precipitous gorge, had been already invaded by a deepening gloom —the swift precursor of the night.

"Oh, no, you don't!" murmured the engineer again. His lips trembled almost imperceptibly; his hands, too, a little: and to calm himself he opened the writing-desk, spread out a sheet of thin grayish paper covered with a mass of printed figures and began to scan them attentively for the twentieth time this trip at least.

With his elbows propped, his head between his hands, he seemed to lose himself in the study of an abstruse problem in mathematics. It was the list of the winning numbers from the last drawing of the great lottery which had been the one inspiring fact of so many years of his existence. The conception of a life deprived of that periodical sheet of paper had slipped away from him entirely, as another man, according to his nature, would not have been able to conceive a world without fresh air, without activity, or without affection. A great pile of flimsy sheets had been growing for years in his desk, while the *Sofala,* driven by the faithful Jack, wore out her boilers in tramping up and down the Straits, from cape to cape, from river to river, from bay to bay; accumulating by that hard labour of an overworked, starved ship the blackened mass of these documents. Massy kept them under lock and key like a treasure. There was in them, as in the experience of life, the fascination of hope, the excitement of a half-penetrated mystery, the longing of a half-satisfied desire.

For days together, on a trip, he would shut himself up in his berth with them: the thump of the toiling engines pulsated in his ear; and he would weary his brain poring over the rows of disconnected figures, bewildering by their senseless sequence, resembling the hazards of destiny itself. He nourished a conviction that there must be some logic lurking somewhere in the results of chance. He thought he had seen its very form. His head swam; his limbs ached; he puffed at his pipe mechanically; a contemplative stupor would soothe the fretfulness of his temper, like the passive bodily quietude procured by a drug, while the intellect remains tensely on the stretch. Nine, nine, nought, four, two. He made a note. The next winning number of the great prize was forty-seven thousand and five. These numbers of course would have to be avoided in the future when writing to Manila for the tickets. He mumbled, pencil in hand . . . "and five. Hm . . . hm." He wetted his finger: the papers rustled. Ha! But what's this? Three years ago, in the September drawing, it was number nine, nought, four, two that took the first prize. Most remarkable. There was a hint there of a definite rule! He was afraid of missing some recondite principle in the overwhelming wealth of his material. What could it be? and for half an hour he would remain dead still, bent low over the desk, without twitching a muscle. At his back the whole berth would be thick with a heavy body of smoke, as if a bomb had burst in there, unnoticed, unheard.

At last he would lock up the desk with the decision of unshaken confidence, jump up and go out. He would walk swiftly back and forth on that part of the foredeck which was kept clear of the lumber and of the bodies of the native passengers. They were a great nuisance, but they were also a source of profit that could not be disdained. He needed every penny of profit the *Sofala* could make. Little enough it was, in all conscience! The incertitude of chance gave him no concern, since he had somehow arrived at the conviction that, in the course of years, every number was bound to have its winning turn. It was simply a matter of time and of taking as many tickets as he could afford for every drawing. He generally took rather more; all the earnings of the ship went that way, and also the wages he allowed himself as chief engineer. It was the wages he paid to others that he begrudged with a reasoned and at the same time a passionate regret. He scowled at the lascars with their deck brooms, at the quartermasters rubbing the brass rails with greasy rags; he was eager to shake his fist and roar abuse in bad Malay at the poor carpenter—a timid, sickly, opium-fuddled Chinaman, in loose blue drawers for all costume, who invariably dropped his tools and fled below, with streaming tail and shaking all over, before the fury of that "devil." But it was when he raised up his eyes to the bridge where one of these sailor frauds was always planted by law in charge of his ship that he felt almost dizzy with rage. He abominated them all; it was an old feud, from the time he first went to sea, an unlicked cub with a great opinion of himself, in the engine-room. The slights that had been put upon him. The persecutions he had suffered at the hands of skippers—of absolute nobodies in a steamship after all. And now that he had risen to be a shipowner they were still a plague to him: he had absolutely to pay away precious money to the conceited useless loafers: —As if a fully qualified engineer—who was the owner as well—were not fit to be trusted with the whole charge of a ship. Well! he made it pretty warm for them; but it was a poor consolation. He had come in time to hate the ship, too, for the repairs she required, for the coal-bills he had to pay, for the poor beggarly freights she earned. He would clench his hand as he walked and hit the rail a sudden blow, viciously, as though she could be made to feel pain. And yet he could not do without her; he needed her; he must hang on to her tooth and nail to keep his head above water till the expected flood of fortune came sweeping up and landed him safely on the high shore of his ambition.

It was now to do nothing, nothing whatever, and have plenty of money to do it on. He had tasted of power, the highest form of it his limited experience was aware of—the power of shipowning. What a deception! Vanity of vanities! He wondered at his folly. He had thrown away the substance for the shadow. Of the gratification of wealth he did not know enough to excite his imagination with any visions of luxury. How could he—the child of a drunken boiler-maker—going straight from the workshop into the engine-room of a north-country collier! But the notion of the absolute idleness of wealth he could very well conceive. He revelled in it, to forget his present troubles; he imagined himself walking about the streets of Hull (he knew their gutters well as a boy) with his pockets full of sovereigns. He would buy himself a house; his married sisters, their husbands, his old workshop chums, would render him infinite homage. There would be nothing to think of. His word would be law. He had been out of work for a long time before he won his prize, and he remembered how Carlo Mariani (commonly known as Paunchy Charley), the Maltese hotel-keeper at the slummy end of Denham Street, had cringed joyfully before him in the evening, when the news had come. Poor Charley, though he made his living by ministering to various abject vices, gave credit for the food to many a piece of white wreckage. He was naïvely overjoyed at the idea of his old bills being paid, and he reckoned confidently on a spell of festivities in the cavernous grogshop downstairs. Massy remembered the curious, respectful looks of the "trashy" white men in the place. His heart had swelled within him. Massy had left Charley's infamous den directly he had realized the possibilities open to him, with his nose in the air. Afterwards the memory of these adulations was a great sadness.

This was the true power of money—and no trouble with it, nor any thinking required either. He thought with difficulty and felt vividly; to his blunt brain the problems offered by any ordered scheme of life seemed in their cruel toughness to have been put in his way by the obvious malevolence of men. As a shipowner everyone had conspired to make him a nobody. How could he have been such a fool as to purchase that accursed ship? He had been abominably swindled; there was no end to this swindling, and as the difficulties of his improvident ambition gathered thicker round him, he really came to hate everybody he had ever come in contact with. A temper naturally irritable and an amazing sensitiveness to the claims of his own personality had ended by making life for him a sort of inferno

—a place where his lost soul had been given up to the torment of savage brooding.

But he had never hated any one so much as that old man who turned up one evening to save him from an utter disaster,—from the conspiracy of the wretched sailors. He seemed to have fallen on board from the sky. His footsteps echoed on the empty steamer, and the strange deep-toned voice on deck repeating interrogatively the words, "Mr. Massy, Mr. Massy there?" had been startling like a wonder. And coming up from the depths of the cold engine-room, where he had been pottering dismally with a candle amongst the enormous shadows, thrown on all sides by the skeleton limbs of machinery, Massy had been struck dumb by astonishment in the presence of that imposing old man with a beard like a silver plate, towering in the dusk rendered lurid by the expiring flames of sunset.

"Want to see me on business? What business? I am doing no business. Can't you see that this ship is laid up?" Massy had turned at bay before the pursuing irony of his disaster. Afterwards he could not believe his ears. What was that old fellow getting at? Things don't happen that way. It was a dream. He would presently wake up and find the man vanished like a shape of mist. The gravity, the dignity, the firm and courteous tone of that athletic old stranger impressed Massy. He was almost afraid. But it was no dream. Five hundred pounds are no dream. At once he became suspicious. What did it mean? Of course it was an offer to catch hold of for dear life. But what could there be behind?

Before they had parted, after appointing a meeting in a solicitor's office early on the morrow, Massy was asking himself, What is his motive? He spent the night in hammering out the clauses of the agreement—a unique instrument of its sort whose tenor got bruited abroad somehow and became the talk and wonder of the port.

Massy's object had been to secure for himself as many ways as possible of getting rid of his partner without being called upon at once to pay back his share. Captain Whalley's efforts were directed to making the money secure. Was it not Ivy's money—a part of her fortune whose only other asset was the time-defying body of her old father? Sure of his forbearance in the strength of his love for her, he accepted, with stately serenity, Massy's stupidly cunning paragraphs against his incompetence, his dishonesty, his drunkenness, for the sake of other stringent stipulations. At the end of three years he was at liberty to withdraw from the partnership, taking his money with him. Provision was made for forming a fund to pay him off. But if he left the *Sofala* before the term, from whatever cause (barring death), Massy was to have a whole year for paying. "Illness?" the lawyer had suggested: a young man fresh from Europe and not overburdened with business, who was rather amused. Massy began to whine unctuously, "How could he be expected? . . ."

"Let that go," Captain Whalley had said with a superb confidence in his body. "Acts of God," he added. In the midst of life we are in death, but he trusted his Maker with a still greater fearlessness—his Maker who knew his thoughts, his human affections, and his motives. His Creator knew what use he was making of his health—how much he wanted it. . . . "I trust my first illness will be my last. I've never been ill that I can remember," he had remarked. "Let it go."

But at this early stage he had already awakened Massy's hostility by refusing to make it six hundred instead of five. "I cannot do that," was all he had said, simply, but with so much decision that Massy desisted at once from pressing the point, but had thought to himself, "Can't! Old curmudgeon. *Won't!* He must have lots of money, but he would like to get hold of a soft berth and the sixth part of my profits for nothing if he only could."

And during these years Massy's dislike grew under the restraint of something resembling fear. The simplicity of that man appeared dangerous. Of late he had changed, however, had appeared less formidable and with a lessened vigour of life, as though he had received a secret wound. But still he remained incomprehensible in his simplicity, fearlessness, and rectitude. And when Massy learned that he meant to leave him at the end of the time, to leave him confronted with the problem of the boilers, his dislike blazed up secretly into hate.

It had made him so clear-eyed that for a long time now Mr. Sterne could have told him nothing he did not know. He had much ado in trying to terrorize that mean sneak into silence; he wanted to deal alone with the situation; and —incredible as it might have appeared to Mr. Sterne—he had not yet given up the desire and the hope of inducing that hated old man to stay. Why! there was nothing else to do, unless he were to abandon his chances of fortune. But now, suddenly, since the crossing of the bar at Batu Beru things seemed to be coming rapidly to a point. It disquieted him so much that the study of the winning numbers failed to soothe his agitation: and the twilight in the cabin deepened, very sombre.

He put the list away, muttering once more, "Oh, no, my boy, you don't. Not if I know it." He did not mean the blinking, eavesdropping humbug to force his action. He took his head again into his hands; his immobility confined in the darkness of this shut-up little place seemed to make him a thing apart infinitely removed from the stir and the sounds of the deck.

He heard them: the passengers were beginning to jabber excitedly; somebody dragged a heavy box past his door. He heard Captain Whalley's voice above—

"Stations, Mr. Sterne." And the answer from somewhere on deck forward—

"Ay, ay, sir."

"We shall moor head upstream this time; the ebb has made."

"Head upstream, sir."

"You will see to it, Mr. Sterne."

The answer was covered by the autocratic clang of the engine-room gong. The propeller went on beating slowly: one, two, three; one, two, three—with pauses as if hesitating on the turn. The gong clanged time after time, and the water churned this way and that by the blades was making a great noisy commotion alongside. Mr. Massy did not move. A shore-light on the other bank, a quarter of a mile across the river, drifted, no bigger than a tiny star, passing slowly athwart the circle of the port. Voices from Mr. Van Wyk's jetty answered the hails from the ship; ropes were thrown and missed and thrown again; the swaying flame of a torch carried in a large sampan coming to fetch away in state the Rajah from down the coast cast a sudden ruddy glare into his cabin, over his very person. Mr. Massy did not move. After a few last ponderous turns the engines stopped, and the prolonged clanging of the gong signified that the captain had done with them. A great number of boats and canoes of all sizes boarded the off-side of the *Sofala*. Then after a time the tumult of splashing, of cries, of shuffling feet, of packages dropped with a thump, the noise of the native passengers going away, subsided slowly. On the shore, a voice, cultivated, slightly authoritative, spoke very close alongside—

"Brought any mail for me this time?"

"Yes, Mr. Van Wyk." This was from Sterne, answering over the rail in a tone of respectful cordiality. "Shall I bring it up to you?"

But the voice asked again—

"Where's the captain?"

"Still on the bridge, I believe. He hasn't left his chair. Shall I. . . ."

The voice interrupted negligently—

"I will come on board."

"Mr. Van Wyk," Sterne suddenly broke out with an eager effort, "will you do me the favour. . . ."

The mate walked away quickly towards the gangway. A silence fell. Mr. Massy in the dark did not move.

He did not move even when he heard slow shuffling footsteps pass his cabin lazily. He contented himself to bellow out through the closed door—

"You—Jack!"

The footsteps came back without haste; the door-handle

rattled, and the second engineer appeared in the opening, shadowy in the sheen of the skylight at his back, with his face apparently as black as the rest of his figure.

"We have been very long coming up this time," Mr. Massy growled, without changing his attitude.

"What do you expect with half the boiler tubes plugged up for leaks?" the second defended himself loquaciously.

"None of your lip," said Massy.

"None of your rotten boilers—I say," retorted his faithful subordinate without animation, huskily.

"Go down there and carry a head of steam on them yourself—if you dare. I don't."

"You aren't worth your salt then," Massy said. The other made a faint noise which resembled a laugh but might have been a snarl.

"Better go slow than stop the ship altogether," he admonished his admired superior. Mr. Massy moved at last. He turned in his chair, and grinding his teeth—

"Dam' you and the ship! I wish she were at the bottom of the sea. Then you would have to starve."

The trusty second engineer closed the door gently.

Massy listened. Instead of passing on to the bathroom where he should have gone to clean himself, the second entered his cabin, which was next door. Mr. Massy jumped up and waited. Suddenly he heard the lock snap in there. He rushed out and gave a violent kick to the door.

"I believe you are locking yourself up to get drunk," he shouted.

A muffled answer came after a while.

"My own time."

"If you take to boozing on the trip I'll fire you out," Massy cried.

An obstinate silence followed that threat. Massy moved away, perplexed. On the bank two figures appeared, approaching the gangway. He heard a voice tinged with contempt—

"I would rather doubt your word. But I shall certainly speak to him of this."

The other voice, Sterne's, said with a sort of regretful formality—

"Thanks. That's all I want. I must do my duty."

Mr. Massy was surprised. A short, dapper figure leaped lightly on the deck and nearly bounded into him where he stood beyond the circle of light from the gangway lamp. When it had passed towards the bridge, after exchanging a hurried "Good evening," Massy said surlily to Sterne, who followed with slow steps—

"What is it you're making up to Mr. Van Wyk for, now?"

"Far from it, Mr. Massy. I am not good enough for Mr. Van Wyk. Neither are you, sir, in his opinion, I am afraid. Captain Whalley is, it seems. He's gone to ask him to dine up at the house this evening."

Then he murmured to himself darkly—

"I hope he will like it."

CHAPTER 12

Mr. Van Wyk, the white man of Batu Beru, an ex-naval officer who, for reasons best known to himself, had thrown away the promise of a brilliant career to become the pioneer of tobacco-planting on that remote part of the coast, had learned to like Captain Whalley. The appearance of the new skipper had attracted his attention. Nothing more unlike all the diverse types he had seen succeeding each other on the bridge of the *Sofala* could be imagined.

At that time Batu Beru was not what it has become since: the centre of a prosperous tobacco-growing district, a tropically suburban-looking little settlement of bungalows in one long street shaded with two rows of trees, embowered by the flowering and trim luxuriance of the gardens, with a three-mile-long carriage-road for the afternoon drives and a first-class Resident with a fat, cheery wife to lead the society of married estate-managers and unmarried young fellows in the service of the big companies.

All this prosperity was not yet; and Mr. Van Wyk prospered alone on the left bank on his deep clearing carved out of the forest, which came down above and below to the water's edge. His lonely bungalow faced across the river the houses of the Sultan: a restless and melancholy old ruler who had done with love and war, for whom life no longer held any savour (except of evil forebodings) and time never had any value. He was afraid of death, and hoped he would die before the white men were ready to take his country from him. He crossed the river frequently (with never less than ten boats crammed full of people), in the wistful hope of extracting some information on the subject from his own white man. There was a certain chair on the verandah he always took: the dignitaries of the court squatted on the rugs and skins between the furniture: the inferior people remained below on the grass-plot between the house and the river in rows three or four deep all along the front. Not seldom the visit began at daybreak. Mr. Van Wyk tolerated these inroads. He would nod out of his bedroom window, toothbrush or razor in hand, or pass through the throng of courtiers in his bathing robe. He appeared and disappeared humming a tune, polished his nails with attention, rubbed his shaved face with eau-de-Cologne, drank his early tea, went out to see his coolies at work; returned, looked through some papers on his desk, read a page or two in a book or sat before his cottage piano leaning back on the stool, his arms extended, fingers on the keys, his body swaying slightly from side to side. When absolutely forced to speak he gave evasive, vaguely soothing answers out of pure compassion: the same feeling perhaps made him so lavishly hospitable with the aerated drinks that more than once he left himself without soda-water for a whole week. That old man had granted him as much land as he cared to have cleared: it was neither more nor less than a fortune.

Whether it was fortune or seclusion from his kind that Mr. Van Wyk sought, he could not have pitched upon a better place. Even the mail-boats of the subsidized company calling on the veriest clusters of palm-thatched hovels along the coast steamed past the mouth of Batu Beru river far away in the offing. The contract was old: perhaps in a few years' time, when it had expired, Batu Beru would be included in the service: meantime all Mr. Van Wyk's mail was addressed to Malacca, whence his agent sent it across once a month by the *Sofala*. It followed that whenever Massy had run short of money (through taking too many lottery tickets), or got into a difficulty about a skipper, Mr. Van Wyk was deprived of his letters and newspapers. In so far he had a personal interest in the fortunes of the *Sofala*. Though he considered himself a hermit (and for no passing whim evidently, since he had stood eight years of it already), he liked to know what went on in the world.

Handy on the verandah upon a walnut étagère (it had come last year by the *Sofala*—everything came by the *Sofala)* there lay, piled up under bronze weights, a pile of *The Times* weekly edition, the large sheets of the *Rotterdam Courant,* the *Graphic* in its world-wide green wrappers, an illustrated Dutch publication without a cover, the numbers of a German magazine with covers of the "Bismarck malade" colour. There were also parcels of new music—though the piano (it had come years ago by the *Sofala*) in the damp atmosphere of the forests was generally out of tune. It was vexing to be cut off from everything for sixty days at a stretch sometimes, without any means of knowing what was the matter. And when the *Sofala* reappeared Mr. Van Wyk would descend the steps of the verandah and stroll over the grass-plot in front of his house, down to the water-side, with a frown on his white brow.

"You've been laid up after an accident, I presume."

He addressed the bridge, but before anybody could answer Massy was sure to have already scrambled ashore over the rail and pushed in, squeezing the palms of his hands together, bowing his sleek head as if gummed all over the top with black threads and tapes. And he would be so enraged at the necessity of having to offer such an explanation that his moaning would be positively pitiful, while all the time he tried to compose his big lips into a smile.

"No, Mr. Van Wyk. You would not believe it. I couldn't get one of those wretches to take the ship out. Not a single one of the lazy beasts could be induced, and the law, you know, Mr. Van Wyk. . . ."

He moaned at great length apologetically; the words conspiracy, plot, envy, came out prominently, whined with greater energy. Mr. Van Wyk, examining with a faint grimace his polished fingernails, would say, "H'm. Very unfortunate," and turn his back on him.

Fastidious, clever, slightly sceptical, accustomed to the best society (he had held a much-envied shore appointment at the Ministry of Marine for a year preceding his retreat from his profession and from Europe), he possessed a latent warmth of feeling and a capacity for sympathy which were concealed by a sort of haughty, arbitrary indifference of manner arising from his early training; and by a something an enemy might have called foppish, in his aspect—like a distorted echo of past elegancies. He managed to keep an almost military discipline amongst the coolies of the estate he had dragged into the light of day out of the tangle and shadows of the jungle; and the white shirt he put on every evening with its stiff glossy front and high collar looked as if he had meant to preserve the decent ceremony of evening-dress, but had wound a thick crimson sash above his hips as a concession to the wilderness, once his adversary, now his vanquished companion. Moreover, it was a hygienic precaution. Worn wide open in front, a short jacket of some airy silken stuff floated from his shoulders. His fluffy, fair hair, thin at the top, curled slightly at the sides; a carefully arranged moustache, an ungarnished forehead, the gleam of low patent shoes peeping under the wide bottom of trousers cut straight from the same stuff as the gossamer coat, completed a figure recalling, with its sash, a pirate chief of romance, and at the same time the elegance of a slightly bald dandy indulging, in seclusion, a taste for unorthodox costume.

It was his evening get-up. The proper time for the *Sofala* to arrive at Batu Beru was an hour before sunset, and he looked picturesque, and somehow quite correct, too, walking at the water's edge on the background of grass slope crowned with a low, long bungalow with an immensely steep roof of palm thatch, and clad to the eaves in flowering creepers. While the *Sofala* was being made fast he strolled in the shade of the few trees left near the landing-place, waiting till he could go on board. Her white men were not of his kind. The old Sultan (though his wistful invasions were a nuisance) was really much more acceptable to his fastidious taste. But still they were white; the periodical visits of the ship made a break in the well-filled sameness of the days without disturbing his privacy. Moreover, they were necessary from a business point of view; and through a strain of preciseness in his nature he was irritated when she failed to appear at the appointed time.

The cause of the irregularity was too absurd, and Massy, in his opinion, was a contemptible idiot. The first time the *Sofala* reappeared under the new agreement swinging out of the bend below, after he had almost given up all hope of ever seeing her again, he felt so angry that he did not go down at once to the landing-place. His servants had come running to him with the news, and he had dragged a chair close against the front rail of the verandah, spread his elbows out, rested his chin on his hands, and went on glaring at her fixedly while she was being made fast opposite his house. He could make out easily all the white faces on board. Who on earth was that kind of patriarch they had got there on the bridge now?

At last he sprang up and walked down the gravel path. It was a fact that the very gravel for his paths had been imported by the *Sofala*. Exasperated out of his quiet superciliousness, without looking at any one right or left, he accosted Massy straightway in so determined a manner that the engineer, taken aback, began to stammer unintelligibly. Nothing could be heard but the words: "Mr. Van Wyk . . . Indeed, Mr. Van Wyk. . . . For the future, Mr. Van Wyk"—and by the suffusion of blood Massy's vast bilious face acquired an unnatural orange tint, out of which the disconcerted coal-black eyes shone in an extraordinary manner.

"Nonsense. I am tired of this. I wonder you have the impudence to come alongside my jetty as if I had it made for your convenience alone."

Massy tried to protest earnestly. Mr. Van Wyk was very angry. He had a good mind to ask that German firm—those people in Malacca—what was their name?—boats with green funnels. They would be only too glad of the opening to put one of their small steamers on the run. Yes; Schnitzler, Jacob Schnitzler, would in a moment. Yes. He had decided to write without delay.

In his agitation Massy caught up his falling pipe.

"You don't mean it, sir!" he shrieked.

"You shouldn't mismanage your business in this ridiculous manner."

Mr. Van Wyk turned on his heel. The other three whites on the bridge had not stirred during the scene. Massy walked hastily from side to side, puffed out his cheeks, suffocated.

"Stuck-up Dutchman!"

And he moaned out feverishly a long tale of griefs. The efforts he had made for all these years to please that man. This was the return you got for it, eh? Pretty. Write to Schnitzler—let in the green-funnel boats—get an old Hamburg Jew to ruin him. No, really he could laugh. . . . He laughed sobbingly. . . . Ha! ha! ha! And make him carry the letter in his own ship presumably.

He stumbled across a grating and swore. He would not hesitate to fling the Dutchman's correspondence overboard—the whole confounded bundle. He had never, never made any charge for that accommodation. But Captain Whalley, his new partner, would not let him probably; besides, it would be only putting off the evil day. For his own part he would make a hole in the water rather than look on tamely at the green funnels overrunning his trade.

He raved aloud. The China boys hung back with the dishes at the foot of the ladder. He yelled from the bridge down at the deck, "Aren't we going to have any chow this evening at all?" then turned violently to Captain Whalley, who waited, grave and patient, at the head of the table, smoothing his beard in silence now and then with a forbearing gesture.

"You don't seem to care what happens to me. Don't you see that this affects your interests as much as mine? It's no joking matter."

He took the foot of the table growling between his teeth.

"Unless you have a few thousands put away somewhere. I haven't."

Mr. Van Wyk dined in his thoroughly lit-up bungalow, putting a point of splendour in the night of his clearing above the dark bank of the river. Afterwards he sat down to his piano, and in a pause he became aware of slow footsteps passing on the path along the front. A plank or two creaked under a heavy tread; he swung half round on the music-stool, listening with his finger-tips at rest on the keyboard. His little terrier barked violently, backing in from the verandah. A deep voice apologized gravely for "this intrusion." He walked out quickly.

At the head of the steps the patriarchal figure, who was the new captain of the *Sofala* apparently (he had seen a round dozen of them, but not one of that sort), towered without advancing. The little dog barked unceasingly, till a flick of Mr. Van Wyk's handkerchief made him spring aside into silence. Captain Whalley, opening the matter, was met by a punctiliously polite but determined opposition.

They carried on their discussion standing where they had come face to face. Mr. Van Wyk observed his visitor with attention. Then at last, as if forced out of his reserve—

"I am surprised that you should intercede for such a confounded fool."

This outbreak was almost complimentary, as if its meaning had been, "That such a man as you should intercede!" Captain Whalley let it pass by without flinching. One would have thought he had heard nothing. He simply went on to state that he was personally interested in putting things straight between them. Personally. . . .

But Mr. Van Wyk, really carried away by his disgust with Massy, became very incisive—

"Indeed—if I am to be frank with you—his whole character does not seem to me particularly estimable or trustworthy. . . ."

Captain Whalley, always straight, seemed to grow an inch taller and broader, as if the girth of his chest had suddenly expanded under his beard.

"My dear sir, you don't think I came here to discuss a man with whom I am—I am—h'm—closely associated."

A sort of solemn silence lasted for a moment. He was not used to asking favours, but the importance he attached to this affair had made him willing to try. . . . Mr. Van Wyk, favourably impressed, and suddenly mollified by a desire to laugh, interrupted—

"That's all right if you make it a personal matter; but you can do no less than sit down and smoke a cigar with me."

A slight pause, then Captain Whalley stepped forward heavily. As to the regularity of the service, for the future he made himself responsible for it; and his name was Whalley—perhaps to a sailor (he was speaking to a sailor, was he not?) not altogether unfamiliar. There was a lighthouse now, on an island. Maybe Mr. Van Wyk himself. . . .

"Oh, yes. Oh, indeed." Mr. Van Wyk caught on at once. He indicated a chair. How very interesting. For his own part he had seen some service in the last Acheen War, but had never been so far East. Whalley Island? Of course. Now that was very interesting. What changes his guest must have seen since.

"I can look further back even—on a whole half-century."

Captain Whalley expanded a bit. The flavour of a good

cigar (it was a weakness) had gone straight to his heart, also the civility of that young man. There was something in that accidental contact of which he had been starved in his years of struggle.

The front wall retreating made a square recess furnished like a room. A lamp with a milky glass shade, suspended below the slope of the high roof at the end of a slender brass chain, threw a bright round of light upon a little table bearing an open book and an ivory paper-knife. And, in the translucent shadows beyond, other tables could be seen, a number of easy-chairs of various shapes, with a great profusion of skin rugs strewn on the teakwood planking all over the verandah. The flowering creepers scented the air. Their foliage clipped out between the uprights made as if several frames of thick, unstirring leaves reflecting the lamplight in a green glow. Through the opening at his elbow Captain Whalley could see the gangway lantern of the *Sofala* burning dim by the shore, the shadowy masses of the town beyond the open lustrous darkness of the river, and, as if hung along the straight edge of the projecting eaves, a narrow black strip of the night sky full of stars—resplendent. The famous cigar in hand he had a moment of complacency.

"A trifle. Somebody must lead the way. I just showed that the thing could be done; but you men brought up to the use of steam cannot conceive the vast importance of my bit of venturesomeness to the Eastern trade of the time. Why, that new route reduced the average time of a southern passage by eleven days for more than half the year. Eleven days! It's on record. But the remarkable thing—speaking to a sailor—I should say was. . . ."

He talked well, without egotism, professionally. The powerful voice, produced without effort, filled the bungalow even into the empty rooms with a deep and limpid resonance, seemed to make a stillness outside; and Mr. Van Wyk was surprised by the serene quality of its tone, like the perfection of manly gentleness. Nursing one small foot, in a silk sock and a patent leather shoe, on his knee, he was immensely entertained. It was as if nobody could talk like this now, and the over-shadowed eyes, the flowing white beard, the big frame, the serenity, the whole temper of the man, were an amazing survival from the prehistoric times of the world coming up to him out of the sea.

Captain Whalley had been also the pioneer of the early trade in the Gulf of Petchili. He even found occasion to mention that he had buried his "dear wife" there six-and-twenty years ago. Mr. Van Wyk, impassive, could not help speculating in his mind swiftly as to the sort of woman that would mate with such a man. Did they make an adventurous and well-matched pair? No. Very possibly she had been small, frail, no doubt very feminine—or most likely commonplace with domestic instincts, utterly insignificant. But Captain Whalley was no garrulous bore, and shaking his head as if to dissipate the momentary gloom that had settled on his handsome old face, he alluded conversationally to Mr. Van Wyk's solitude.

Mr. Van Wyk affirmed that sometimes he had more company than he wanted. He mentioned smilingly some of the peculiarities of his intercourse with "My Sultan." He made his visits in force. Those people damaged his grass-plot in front (it was not easy to obtain some approach to a lawn in the tropics), and the other day had broken down some rare bushes he had planted over there. And Captain Whalley remembered immediately that, in 'forty-seven, the then Sultan, "this man's grandfather," had been notorious as a great protector of the piratical fleets of praus from farther East. They had a safe refuge in the river at Batu Beru. He financed more especially a Balinini chief called Haji Daman. Captain Whalley, nodding significantly his bushy white eyebrows, had very good reason to know something of that. The world had progressed since that time.

Mr. Van Wyk demurred with unexpected acrimony. Progressed in what? he wanted to know.

Why, in knowledge of truth, in decency, in justice, in order—in honesty, too, since men harmed each other mostly from ignorance. It was, Captain Whalley concluded quaintly, more pleasant to live in.

Mr. Van Wyk whimsically would not admit that Mr. Massy, for instance, was more pleasant naturally than the Balinini pirates.

The river had not gained much by the change. They were in their way every bit as honest. Massy was less ferocious than Haji Daman no doubt, but. . . .

"And what about you, my good sir?" Captain Whalley laughed a deep soft laugh. "*You* are an improvement, surely."

He continued in a vein of pleasantry. A good cigar was better than a knock on the head—the sort of welcome he would have found on this river forty or fifty years ago. Then leaning forward slightly, he became earnestly serious. It seems as if, outside their own sea-gipsy tribes, these rovers had hated all mankind with an incomprehensible, bloodthirsty hatred. Meantime their depredations had been stopped, and what was the consequence? The new generation was orderly, peaceable, settled in prosperous villages. He could speak from personal knowledge. And even the few survivors of that time—old men now—had changed so much, that it would have been unkind to remember against them that they had ever slit a throat in their lives. He had one especially in his mind's eye: a dignified, venerable headman of a certain large coast village about sixty miles sou'west of Tampasuk. It did one's heart good to see him—to hear that man speak. He might have been a ferocious savage once. What men wanted was to be checked by superior intelligence, by superior knowledge, by superior force, too—yes, by force held in trust from God and sanctified by its use in accordance with His declared will. Captain Whalley believed a disposition for good existed in every man, even if the world were not a very happy place as a whole. In the wisdom of men he had not so much confidence.

The disposition had to be helped up pretty sharply sometimes, he admitted. They might be silly, wrongheaded, unhappy; but naturally evil—no. There was at bottom a complete harmlessness at least. . . .

"Is there?" Mr. Van Wyk snapped acrimoniously.

Captain Whalley laughed at the interjection, in the good humour of large, tolerating certitude. He could look back at half a century, he pointed out. The smoke oozed placidly through the white hairs hiding his kindly lips.

"At all events," he resumed after a pause, "I am glad that they've had no time to do you much harm as yet."

This allusion to his comparative youthfulness did not offend Mr. Van Wyk, who got up and wriggled his shoulders with an enigmatic half-smile. They walked out together amicably into the starry night towards the river-side. Their footsteps resounded unequally on the dark path. At the shore end of the gangway the lantern, hung low to the handrail, threw a vivid light on the white legs and the big black feet of Mr. Massy waiting about anxiously. From the waist upwards he remained shadowy, with a row of buttons gleaming up to the vague outline of his chin.

"You may thank Captain Whalley for this," Mr. Van Wyk said, curtly, to him before turning away.

The lamps on the verandah flung three long squares of light between the uprights far over the grass. A bat flitted before his face like a circling flake of velvety blackness. Along the jasmine hedge the night air seemed heavy with the fall of perfumed dew; flowerbeds bordered the path; the clipped bushes uprose in dark, rounded clumps here and there before the house; the dense foliage of creepers filtered the sheen of the lamplight within in a soft glow all along the front; and everything near and far stood still in a great immobility, in a great sweetness.

Mr. Van Wyk (a few years before he had had occasion to imagine himself treated more badly than anybody alive had ever been by a woman) felt for Captain Whalley's optimistic views the disdain of a man who had once been credulous himself. His disgust with the world (the woman for a time had filled it for him completely) had taken the form of activity in retirement, because, though capable of great depth of feeling, he was energetic and essentially practical. But there was in that uncommon old sailor, drifting on the outskirts of his busy solitude, something that fascinated his scepticism. His very simplicity (amusing enough) was like a delicate refinement of an upright character. The striking dignity of manner could be nothing else, in a man reduced to such a humble position, but the expression of something essentially noble in the character. With all his trust in mankind he was no fool; the serenity of his temper at the end of so many years, since it could not obviously have been appeased by success, wore an air of profound wisdom. Mr. Van Wyk was amused at it sometimes. Even the very physical traits of the old captain of the *Sofala,* his powerful frame, his reposeful mien, his intelligent, handsome face, the big limbs, the benign courtesy, the touch of rugged severity in the shaggy eyebrows, made up a seductive personality. Mr. Van Wyk disliked littleness of every kind, but there was nothing small about that man, and in the exemplary regularity of many trips an intimacy had grown up between them, a warm feeling at bottom under a kindly stateliness of forms agreeable to his fastidiousness.

They kept their respective opinions on all worldly matters. His other convictions Captain Whalley never intruded. The difference of their ages was like another bond between them. Once, when twitted with the uncharitableness of his youth, Mr. Van Wyk, running his eye over the vast proportions of his interlocutor, retorted in friendly banter—

"Oh. You'll come to my way of thinking yet. You'll have plenty of time. Don't call yourself old: you look good for a round hundred."

But he could not help his stinging incisiveness, and though moderating it by an almost affectionate smile, he added—

"And by then you will probably consent to die from sheer disgust."

Captain Whalley, smiling, too, shook his head. "God forbid!"

He thought that perhaps on the whole he deserved something better than to die in such sentiments. The time of course would have to come, and he trusted to his Maker to provide a manner of going out of which he need not be ashamed. For the rest he hoped he would live to a hundred if need be; other men had been known; it would be no miracle. He expected no miracles.

The pronounced, argumentative tone caused Mr. Van Wyk to raise his head and look at him steadily. Captain Whalley was gazing fixedly with a rapt expression, as though he had seen his Creator's favourable decree written in mysterious characters on the wall. He kept perfectly motionless for a few seconds, then got his vast bulk on to his feet so impetuously that Mr. Van Wyk was startled.

He struck first a heavy blow on his inflated chest: and, throwing out horizontally a big arm that remained steady, extended in the air like the limb of a tree on a windless day—

"Not a pain or an ache there. Can you see this shake in the least?"

His voice was low, in an awing, confident contrast with the headlong emphasis of his movements. He sat down abruptly.

"This isn't to boast of it, you know. I am nothing," he said in his effortless strong voice, that seemed to come out as naturally as a river flows. He picked up the stump of the cigar he had laid aside, and added peacefully, with a slight nod, "As it happens, my life is necessary; it isn't my own, it isn't—God knows."

He did not say much for the rest of the evening, but several times Mr. Van Wyk detected a faint smile of assurance flitting under the heavy moustache.

Later on Captain Whalley would now and then consent to dine "at the house." He could even be induced to drink a glass of wine. "Don't think I'm afraid of it, my good sir," he explained. "There was a very good reason why I should give it up."

On another occasion, leaning back at ease, he remarked,

"You have treated me most—most humanely, my dear Mr. Van Wyk, from the very first."

"You'll admit there was some merit," Mr. Van Wyk hinted, slily. "An associate of that excellent Massy. . . . Well, well, my dear captain, I won't say a word against him."

"It would be no use your saying anything against him," Captain Whalley affirmed a little moodily. "As I've told you before, my life—my work, is necessary, not for myself alone. I can't choose. . . ." He paused, turned the glass before him right round. . . . "I have an only child—a daughter."

The ample downward sweep of his arm over the table seemed to suggest a small girl at a vast distance. "I hope to see her once more before I die. Meantime it's enough to know that she has me sound and solid, thank God. You can't understand how one feels. Bone of my bone, flesh of my flesh; the very image of my poor wife. Well, she. . ."

Again he paused, then pronounced stoically the words, "She has a hard struggle."

And his head fell on his breast, his eyebrows remained knitted, as by an effort of meditation. But generally his mind seemed steeped in the serenity of boundless trust in a higher power. Mr. Van Wyk wondered sometimes how much of it was due to the splendid vitality of the man, to the bodily vigour which seems to impart something of its force to the soul. But he had learned to like him very much.

CHAPTER 13

This was the reason why Mr. Sterne's confidential communication, delivered hurriedly on the shore alongside the dark silent ship, had disturbed his equanimity. It was the most incomprehensible and unexpected thing that could happen; and the perturbation of his spirit was so great that, forgetting all about his letters, he ran rapidly up the bridge ladder.

The portable table was being put together for dinner to the left of the wheel by two pig-tailed "boys," who as usual snarled at each other over the job, while another, a doleful, burly, very yellow Chinaman, resembling Mr. Massy, waited apathetically with the cloth over his arm and a pile of thick dinner-plates against his chest. A common cabin lamp with its globe missing, brought up from below, had been hooked to the wooden framework of the awning; the side-screens had been lowered all round; Captain Whalley, filling the depths of the wicker-chair, seemed to sit benumbed in a canvas tent crudely lighted, and used for the storing of nautical objects; a shabby steering-wheel, a battered brass binnacle on a stout mahogany stand, two dingy life-buoys, an old cork fender lying in a corner, dilapidated deck-lockers with loops of tin rope instead of door-handles.

He shook off the appearance of numbness to return Mr. Van Wyk's unusually brisk greeting, but relapsed directly afterwards. To accept a pressing invitation to dinner "up at the house" cost him another very visible physical effort. Mr. Van Wyk, perplexed, folded his arms, and leaning back against the rail, with his little, black, shiny feet well out, examined him covertly.

"I've noticed of late that you are not quite yourself, old friend."

He put an affectionate gentleness into the last two words. The real intimacy of their intercourse had never been so vividly expressed before.

"Tut, tut, tut!"

The wicker-chair creaked heavily.

"Irritable," commented Mr. Van Wyk to himself; and aloud, "I'll expect to see you in half an hour, then," he said, negligently, moving off.

"In half an hour," Captain Whalley's rigid silvery head repeated behind him as if out of a trance.

Amidships, below, two voices, close against the engine-room, could be heard answering each other—one angry and slow, the other alert.

"I tell you the beast has locked himself in to get drunk."

"Can't help it now, Mr. Massy. After all, a man has a right to shut himself up in his cabin in his own time."

"Not to get drunk."

"I heard him swear that the worry with the boilers was enough to drive any man to drink," Sterne said, maliciously.

Massy hissed out something about bursting the door in. Mr. Van Wyk, to avoid them, crossed in the dark to the other side of the deserted deck. The planking of the little wharf rattled faintly under his hasty feet.

"Mr. Van Wyk! Mr. Van Wyk!"

He walked on: somebody was running on the path. "You've forgotten to get your mail."

Sterne, holding a bundle of papers in his hand, caught up with him.

"Oh, thanks."

But, as the other continued at his elbow, Mr. Van Wyk stopped short. The overhanging eaves, descending low upon the lighted front of the bungalow, threw their black straight-edged shadow into the great body of the night on that side. Everything was very still. A tinkle of cutlery and a slight jingle of glasses were heard. Mr. Van Wyk's servants were laying the table for two on the verandah.

"I am afraid you give me no credit whatever for my good intentions in the matter I've spoken to you about," said Sterne.

"I simply don't understand you."

"Captain Whalley is a very audacious man, but he will understand that his game is up. That's all that anybody need ever know of it from me. Believe me, I am very considerate in this, but duty is duty. I don't want to make a fuss. All I ask you, as his friend, is to tell him from me that the game's up. That will be sufficient."

Mr. Van Wyk felt a loathsome dismay at this queer privilege of friendship. He would not demean himself by asking for the slightest explanation; to drive the other away with contumely he did not think prudent—as yet, at any rate. So much assurance staggered him. Who could tell what there could be in it? he thought. His regard for Captain Whalley had the tenacity of a disinterested sentiment, and his practical instinct coming to his aid, he concealed his scorn.

"I gather, then, that this is something grave."

"Very grave," Sterne assented, solemnly, delighted at having produced an effect at last. He was ready to add some effusive protestations of regret at the "unavoidable necessity," but Mr. Van Wyk cut him short—very civilly, however.

Once on the verandah Mr. Van Wyk put his hands in his pockets, and, straddling his legs, stared down at a black panther skin lying on the floor before a rocking-chair. "It looks as if the fellow had not the pluck to play his own precious game openly," he thought.

This was true enough. In the face of Massy's last rebuff Sterne dared not declare his knowledge. His object was simply to get charge of the steamer and keep it for some time. Massy would never forgive him for forcing himself on; but if Captain Whalley left the ship of his own accord, the command would devolve upon him for the rest of the trip; so he hit upon the brilliant idea of scaring the old man away. A vague menace, a mere hint, would be enough in such a brazen case; and, with a strange admixture of compassion, he thought that Batu Beru was a very good place for throwing up the sponge. The skipper could go shore quietly, and stay with that Dutchman of his. Weren't these two as thick as thieves together? And on reflection he seemed to see that there was a way to work the whole thing through that great friend of the old man's. This was another brilliant idea. He had an inborn preference for circuitous methods. In this particular case he desired to remain in the background as much as possible, to avoid exasperating Massy needlessly. No fuss! Let it all happen naturally.

Mr. Van Wyk all through the dinner was conscious of a sense of isolation that invades sometimes the closeness of human intercourse. Captain Whalley failed lamentably and obviously in his attempts to eat something. He seemed overcome by a strange absent-mindedness. His hand would hover irresolutely, as if left without guidance by a preoccupied mind. Mr. Van Wyk had heard him coming up from a long way off in the profound stillness of the river-side, and had noticed the irresolute character of the footfalls. The toe of his boot had struck the bottom stair as though he had come along mooning with his head in the air right up to the steps of the verandah. Had the captain of the *Sofala* been another sort of man he would have suspected the work of age there. But one glance at him was enough. Time—after, indeed, marking him for its own—had given him up to his usefulness, in which his simple faith would see a proof of Divine mercy. "How could I contrive to warn him?" Mr. Van Wyk wondered, as if Captain Whalley had been miles and miles away, out of sight and earshot of all evil. He was sickened by an immense disgust of Sterne. Even to mention his threat to a man like Whalley would be positively indecent. There was something more vile and insulting in its hint than in a definite charge of crime—the debasing taint of blackmailing. "What could any one bring against him?" he asked himself. This was a limpid personality. "And for what object?" The Power that man trusted had thought fit to leave him nothing on earth that envy could lay hold of, except a bare crust of bread.

"Won't you try some of this?" he asked, pushing a dish slightly. Suddenly it occurred to Mr. Van Wyk that Sterne might possibly be coveting the command of the *Sofala*. His cynicism was quite startled by what looked like a proof that no man may count himself safe from his kind unless in the very abyss of misery. An intrigue of that sort was hardly worth troubling about, he judged; but still, with such a fool as Massy to deal with, Whalley ought to and must be warned.

At this moment Captain Whalley, bolt upright, the deep cavities of the eyes overhung by a bushy frown, and one large brown hand resting on each side of his empty plate, spoke across the table-cloth abruptly—

"Mr. Van Wyk, you've always treated me with the most humane consideration."

"My dear captain, you make too much of the simple fact that I am not a savage." Mr. Van Wyk, utterly revolted by the thought of Sterne's obscure attempt, raised his voice incisively, as if the mate had been hiding somewhere within earshot. "Any consideration I have been able to show was no more than the rightful due of a character I've learned to regard by this time with an esteem that nothing can shake."

A slight ring of glass made him lift his eyes from the slice of pineapple he was cutting into small pieces on his plate. In changing his position Captain Whalley had contrived to upset an empty tumbler.

Without looking that way, leaning sideways on his elbow, his other hand shading his brow, he groped shadily for it, then desisted. Van Wyk stared blankly, as if something momentous had happened all at once. He did not know why he should feel so startled; but he forgot Sterne utterly for the moment.

"Why, what's the matter?"

And Captain Whalley, half-averted, in a deadened, agitated voice, muttered—

"Esteem!"

"And I may add something more," Mr. Van Wyk, very steady-eyed, pronounced slowly.

"Hold! Enough!" Captain Whalley did not change his attitude or raise his voice. "Say no more! I can make you no return. I am too poor even for that now. Your esteem is worth having. You are not a man that would stoop to deceive the poorest sort of devil on earth, or make a ship unseaworthy every time he takes her to sea."

Mr. Van Wyk, leaning forward, his face gone pink all over, with the starched table-napkin over his knees, was inclined to mistrust his senses, his power of comprehension, the sanity of his guest.

"Where? Why? In the name of God!—what's this? What ship? I don't understand who. . . ."

"Then, in the name of God, it is I! A ship's unseaworthy when her captain can't see. I am going blind."

Mr. Van Wyk made a slight movement, and sat very still afterwards for a few seconds; then, with the thought of Sterne's "The game's up," he ducked under the table to pick up the napkin which had slipped off his knees. This was the game that was up. And at the same time the muffled voice of Captain Whalley passed over him—

"I've deceived them all. Nobody knows."

He emerged flushed to the eyes. Captain Whalley, motionless under the full blaze of the lamp, shaded his face with his hand.

"And you had that courage?"

"Call it by what name you like. But you are a humane man—a—a—gentleman, Mr. Van Wyk. You may have asked me what I had done with my conscience."

He seemed to muse, profoundly silent, very still in his mournful pose.

"I began to tamper with it in my pride. You begin to see a lot of things when you are going blind. I could not be frank with an old chum even. I was not frank with Massy—no, not altogether. I knew he took me for a wealthy sailor fool, and I let him. I wanted to keep up my importance—because there was poor Ivy away there—my daughter. What did I want to trade on his misery for? I did trade on it—for her. And now, what mercy could I expect from him? He would trade on mine if he knew it. He would hunt the old fraud out, and stick to the money for a year. Ivy's money. And I haven't kept a penny for myself. How am I going to live for a year. A year! In a year there will be no sun in the sky for her father."

His deep voice came out, awfully veiled, as though he

had been overwhelmed by the earth of a landslide and talking of the thoughts that haunt the dead in their graves. A cold shudder ran down Mr. Van Wyk's back.

"And how long is it since you have. . . ?" he began.

"It was a long time before I could bring myself to believe in this—this—visitation." Captain Whalley spoke with gloomy patience from under his hand.

He had not thought he had deserved it. He had begun by deceiving himself from day to day, from week to week. He had the Serang at hand there—an old servant. It came on gradually, and when he could no longer deceive himself. . . .

His voice died out almost.

"Rather than give her up I set myself to deceive you all."

"It's incredible," whispered Mr. Van Wyk. Captain Whalley's appalling murmur flowed on.

"Not even the sign of God's anger could make me forget her. How could I forsake my child, feeling my vigour all the time—the blood warm within me? Warm as yours. It seems to me that, like the blinded Samson, I would find the strength to shake down a temple upon my head. She's a struggling woman—my own child that we used to pray over together, my poor wife and I. Do you remember that day I as well as told you that I believed God would let me live to a hundred for her sake? What sin is there in loving your child? Do you see it? I was ready for her sake to live for ever. I half believed I would. I've been praying for death since. Ha! Presumptuous man—you wanted to live. . . ."

A tremendous, shuddering upheaval of that big frame, shaken by a gasping sob, set the glasses jingling all over the table, seemed to make the whole house tremble to the roof-tree. And Mr. Van Wyk, whose feeling of outraged love had been translated into a form of struggle with nature, understood very well that, for that man whose whole life had been conditioned by action, there could exist no other expression for all the emotions; that, voluntarily to cease venturing, doing, enduring, for his child's sake, would have been exactly like plucking his warm love for her out of his living heart. Something too monstrous, too impossible, even to conceive.

Captain Whalley had not changed his attitude, that seemed to express something of shame, sorrow, and defiance.

"I have even deceived you. If it had not been for that word 'esteem.' These are not the words for me. I would have lied to you. Haven't I lied to you? Weren't you going to trust your property on board this very trip?"

"I have a floating yearly policy," Mr. Van Wyk said almost unwittingly, and was amazed at the sudden cropping up of a commercial detail.

"The ship is unseaworthy, I tell you. The policy would be invalid if it were known. . . ."

"We shall share the guilt, then."

"Nothing could make mine less," said Captain Whalley.

He had not dared to consult a doctor; the man would have perhaps asked who he was, what he was doing; Massy might have heard something. He had lived on without any help, human or divine. The very prayers stuck in his throat. What was there to pray for? and death seemed as far as ever. Once he got into his cabin he dared not come out again; when he sat down he dared not get up; he dared not raise his eyes to anybody's face, he felt reluctant to look upon the sea or up to the sky. The world was fading before his great fear of giving himself away. The old ship was his last friend; he was not afraid of her; he knew every inch of her deck; but at her, too, he hardly dared to look, for fear of finding he could see less than the day before. A great incertitude enveloped him. The horizon was gone; the sky mingled darkly with the sea. Who was this figure standing over yonder? what was this thing lying down there? And a frightful doubt of the reality of what he could see made even the remnant of sight that remained to him an added torment, a pitfall always open for his miserable pretence. He was afraid to stumble inexcusably over something—to say a fatal Yes or No to a question. The hand of God was upon him, but it could not tear him away from his child. And, as if in a nightmare of humiliation, every featureless man seemed an enemy.

He let his hand fall heavily on the table. Mr. Van Wyk, arms down, chin on breast, with a gleam of white teeth pressing on the lower lip, meditated on Sterne's "The game's up."

"The Serang of course does not know."

"Nobody," said Captain Whalley, with assurance.

"Ah, yes. Nobody. Very well. Can you keep it up to the end of the trip? That is the last under the agreement with Massy."

Captain Whalley got up and stood erect, very stately, with the great white beard lying like a silver breastplate over the awful secret of his heart. Yes; that was the only hope there was for him of ever seeing her again, of securing the money, the last he could do for her, before he crept away somewhere—useless, a burden, a reproach to himself. His voice faltered.

"Think of it! Never see her any more: the only human being besides myself now on earth that can remember my wife. She's just like her mother. Lucky the poor woman is where there are no tears shed over those they loved on earth and that remain to pray not to be led into temptation—because, I suppose, the blessed know the secret of grace in God's dealings with His created children."

He swayed a little, said with austere dignity—

"I don't. I know only the child He has given me."

And he began to walk. Mr. Van Wyk, jumping up, saw the full meaning of the rigid head, the hesitating feet, the vaguely extended hand. His heart was beating fast; he moved a chair aside, and instinctively advanced as if to offer his arm. But Captain Whalley passed him by, making for the stairs quite straight.

"He could not see me at all out of his line," Van Wyk thought, with a sort of awe. Then going to the head of the stairs, he asked a little tremulously—

"What is it like—like a mist—like. . . ." Captain Whalley, half-way down, stopped, and turned round undismayed to answer:

"It is as if the light were ebbing out of the world. Have you ever watched the ebbing sea on an open stretch of sands withdrawing farther and farther away from you? It is like this—only there will be no flood to follow. Never. It is as if the sun were growing smaller, the stars going out one by one. There can't be many left that I can see by this. But I haven't had the courage to look of late. . . ." He must have been able to make out Mr. Van Wyk, because he checked him by an authoritative gesture and a stoical—

"I can get about alone yet."

It was as if he had taken his line, and would accept no help from men, after having been cast out, like a presumptuous Titan, from his heaven. Mr. Van Wyk, arrested, seemed to count the footsteps right out of earshot. He walked between the tables, tapping smartly with his heels, took up a paper-knife, dropped it after a vague glance along the blade; then happening upon the piano, struck a few chords, standing up before the keyboard with an attentive poise of the head like a piano-tuner; closing it, he pivoted on his heels brusquely, avoided the little terrier sleeping trustfully on crossed forepaws, came upon the stairs next, and, as though he had lost his balance on the top step, ran down headlong out of the house. His servants, beginning to clear the table, heard him mutter to himself (evil words no doubt) down there, and then after a pause go away with a strolling gait in the direction of the wharf.

The bulwarks of the *Sofala* lying alongside the bank made a low, black wall on the undulating contour of the shore. Two masts and a funnel uprose from behind it with a great rake, as if about to fall: a solid, square elevation in the middle bore the ghostly shapes of white boats, the curves of davits, lines of rail and stanchions, all confused and mingling darkly everywhere; but low down, amidships, a single lighted port stared out on the night, perfectly round, like a small, full moon, whose yellow beam caught a patch of wet mud, the edge of trodden grass, two turns of heavy cable wound round the foot of a thick wooden post in the ground.

Mr. Van Wyk, peering alongside, heard a muzzy boastful voice apparently jeering at a person called Prendergast. It mouthed abuse thickly, choked; then pronounced very distinctly the word "Murphy," and chuckled. Glass tinkled tremulously. All these sounds came from the lighted port. Mr. Van Wyk hesitated, stooped; it was impossible to look through unless he went down into the mud.

"Sterne," he said half aloud.

The drunken voice within said gladly:

"Sterne—of course. Look at him blink. Look at him! Sterne, Whalley, Massy. Massy, Whalley, Sterne. But Massy's the best. You can't come over him. He would just love to see you starve."

Mr. Van Wyk moved away, made out farther forward a shadowy head stuck out from under the awnings as if on the watch, and spoke quietly in Malay, "Is the mate asleep?"

"No. Here, at your service."

In a moment Sterne appeared, walking as noiselessly as a cat on the wharf.

"It's so jolly dark, and I had no idea you would be down to-night."

"What's this horrible raving?" asked Mr. Van Wyk, as if to explain the cause of a shudder that ran over him audibly.

"Jack's broken out on a drunk. That's our second. It's his way. He will be right enough by to-morrow afternoon, only Mr. Massy will keep on worrying up and down the deck. We had better get away."

He muttered suggestively of a talk "up at the house." He had long desired to effect an entrance there, but Mr. Van Wyk nonchalantly demurred: it would not, he feared, be quite prudent, perhaps; and the opaque black shadow under one of the two big trees left at the landing-place swallowed them up, impenetrably dense by the side of the wide river that seemed to spin into threads of glitter the light of a few big stars dropped here and there upon its outspread and flowing stillness.

"The situation is grave beyond doubt," Mr. Van Wyk said. Ghostlike in their white clothes they could not distinguish each other's features, and their feet made no sound on the soft earth. A sort of purring was heard. Mr. Sterne felt gratified by such a beginning.—

"I thought, Mr. Van Wyk, a gentleman of your sort would see at once how awkwardly I was situated."

"Yes, very. Obviously his health is bad. Perhaps he's breaking up. I see, and he himself is well aware—I assume I am speaking to a man of sense—he is well aware that his legs are giving out."

"His legs—ah!" Mr. Sterne was disconcerted, and then turned sulky. "You may call it his legs if you like; what I want to know is whether he intends to clear out quietly. That's a good one, too! His legs! Pooh!"

"Why, yes. Only look at the way he walks," Van Wyk took him up in a perfectly cool and undoubting tone. "The question, however, is whether your sense of duty does not carry you too far from your true interest. After all, I, too, could do something to serve you. You know who I am."

"Everybody along the Straits has heard of you, sir."

Mr. Van Wyk presumed that this meant something favourable. Sterne had a soft laugh at this pleasantry. He should think so! To the opening statement, that the partnership agreement was to expire at the end of this very trip, he gave an attentive assent. He was aware. One heard of nothing else on board all the blessed day long. As to Massy, it was no secret that he was in a jolly deep hole with these worn-out boilers. He would have to borrow somewhere a couple of hundred first of all to pay off the captain; and then he would have to raise money on mortgage upon the ship for the new boilers—that is, if he could find a lender at all. At best it meant loss of time, a break in the trade, short earnings for the year—and there was always the danger of having his connection filched away from him by the Germans. It was whispered about that he had already tried two firms. Neither would have anything to do with him. Ship too old, and the man too well known in the place. . . . Mr. Sterne's final rapid winking remained buried in the deep darkness sibilating with his whispers.

"Supposing, then, he got the loan," Mr. Van Wyk resumed in a deliberate undertone, "on your own showing he's more than likely to get a mortgagee's man thrust upon him as captain. For my part, I know that I would make that very stipulation myself if I had to find the money. And as a matter of fact I am thinking of doing so. It would be worth my while in many ways. Do you see how this would bear on the case under discussion?"

"Thank you, sir. I am sure you couldn't get anybody that would care more for your interests."

"Well, it suits my interest that Captain Whalley should finish his time. I shall probably take a passage with you down the Straits. If that can be done, I'll be on the spot when all these changes take place, and in a position to look after *your* interests."

"Mr. Van Wyk, I want nothing better. I am sure I am infinitely. . . ."

"I take it, then, that this may be done without any trouble."

"Well, sir, what risk there is can't be helped; but (speaking to you as my employer now) the thing is more safe than it looks. If anybody had told me of it I wouldn't have believed it, but I have been looking on myself. That old Serang has been trained up to the game. There's nothing the matter with his—his—limbs, sir. He's got used to do things on his own in a remarkable way. And let me tell you, sir, that Captain Whalley, poor man, is by no means useless. Fact. Let me explain to you, sir. He stiffens up that old monkey of a Malay, who knows well enough what to do. Why, he must have kept captain's watches in all sorts of country ships off and on for the last five-and-twenty years. These natives, sir, as long as they have a white man close at the back, will go on doing the right thing most surprisingly well—even if left quite to themselves. Only the white man must be of the sort to put starch into them, and the captain is just the one for that. Why, sir, he has drilled him so well that now he needs hardly speak at all. I have seen that little wrinkled ape made to take the ship out of Pangu Bay on a blowy morning and on all through the islands; take her out first-rate, sir, dodging under the old man's elbow, and in such quiet style that you could not have told for the life of you which of the two was doing the work up there. That's where our poor friend would be still of use to the ship even if—if—he could no longer lift a foot, sir. Providing the Serang does not know that there's anything wrong."

"He doesn't."

"Naturally not. Quite beyond his apprehension. They aren't capable of finding out anything about us, sir."

"You seem to be a shrewd man," said Mr. Van Wyk in a choked mutter, as though he were feeling sick.

"You'll find me a good enough servant, sir."

Mr. Sterne hoped now for a handshake at least, but unexpectedly with a "What's this? Better not to be seen together," Mr. Van Wyk's white shape wavered, and instantly seemed to melt away in the black air under the roof of boughs. The mate was startled. Yes. There was that faint thumping clatter.

He stole out silently from under the shade. The lighted port-hole shone from afar. His head swam with the intoxication of sudden success. What a thing it was to have a gentleman to deal with! He crept aboard, and there was something weird in the shadowy stretch of empty decks, echoing with shouts and blows proceeding from a darker part amidships. Mr. Massy was raging before the door of the berth: the drunken voice within flowed on undisturbed in the violent racket of kicks.

"Shut up! Put your light out and turn in, you confounded swilling pig—you! D'you hear me, you beast?"

The kicking stopped, and in the pause the muzzy oracular voice announced from within—

"Ah! Massy, now—that's another thing. Massy's deep."

"Who's that aft there? You, Sterne? He'll drink himself into a fit of horrors." The chief engineer appeared vague and big at the corner of the engine-room skylight.

"He will be good enough for duty to-morrow. I would let him be, Mr. Massy."

Sterne slipped away into his berth, and at once had to sit down. His head swam with exultation. He got into his bunk as if in a dream. A feeling of profound peace, of pacific joy, came over him. On deck all was quiet.

Mr. Massy, with his ear against the door of Jack's cabin, listened critically to a deep, stertorous breathing within. This was a dead-drunk sleep. The bout was over: tranquillized on that score, he, too, went in, and with slow wriggles got out of his old tweed jacket. It was a garment with many pockets, which he used to put on at odd times of the day, being subject to sudden chilly fits, and when he felt warmed he would take it off and hang it about anywhere all over the ship. It would be seen swinging on belaying-pins, thrown over the heads of winches, suspended on people's very door-handles for that matter. Was he not the owner? But his favourite place was a hook on a wooden awning stanchion on the bridge, almost against the binnacle. He had even in the early days more than one tussle on that point with Captain Whalley, who desired the bridge to be kept tidy. He had been overawed then. Of late, though, he had been able to defy his partner with impunity. Captain Whalley never seemed to notice anything now. As to the Malays, in their awe of that scowling man not one of the crew would dream of laying a hand on the thing, no matter where or what it swung from.

With an unexpectedness which made Mr. Massy jump and drop the coat at his feet, there came from the next berth the crash and thud of a headlong, jingling, clattering fall. The faithful Jack must have dropped to sleep suddenly as he sat at his revels, and now had gone over chair and all, breaking, as it seemed by the sound, every single glass and bottle in the place. After the terrific smash all was still for a time in there, as though he had killed himself on the spot. Mr. Massy held his breath. At last a sleepy, uneasy groaning sigh was exhaled slowly on the other side of the bulkhead.

"I hope to goodness he's too drunk to wake up now," muttered Mr. Massy.

The sound of a softly knowing laugh nearly drove him to despair. He swore violently under his breath. The fool would keep him awake all night now for certain. He cursed his luck. He wanted to forget his maddening troubles in sleep sometimes. He could detect no movements. Without apparently making the slightest attempt to get up, Jack went on sniggering to himself where he lay; then began to speak, where he had left off as it were—

"Massy! I love the dirty rascal. He would like to see his poor old Jack starve—but just you look where he has climbed to. . . ." He hiccoughed in a superior, leisurely manner. . . . "Shipowning it with the best. A lottery ticket you want. Ha! ha! I will give you lottery tickets, my boy. Let the old ship sink and the old chum starve—that's right. He don't go wrong—Massy don't. Not he. He's a genius—that man is. That's the way to win your money. Ship and chum must go."

"The silly fool has taken it to heart," muttered Massy to himself. And, listening with a softened expression of face for any slight sign of returning drowsiness, he was discouraged profoundly by a burst of laughter full of joyful irony.

"Would like to see her at the bottom of the sea! Oh, you clever, clever devil! Wish her sunk, eh? I should think you would, my boy; the damned old thing and all your troubles with her. Rake in the insurance money—turn your back on your old chum—all's well—gentleman again."

A grim stillness had come over Massy's face. Only his big black eyes rolled uneasily. The raving fool. And yet it was all true. Yes. Lottery tickets, too. All true. What? Beginning again? He wished he wouldn't. . . .

But it was even so. The imaginative drunkard on the other side of the bulkhead shook off the deathlike stillness that after his last words had fallen on the dark ship moored to a silent shore.

"Don't you dare to say anything against George Massy, Esquire. When he's tired of waiting he will do away with her. Look out! Down she goes—chum and all. He'll know how to. . . ."

The voice hesitated, weary, dreamy, lost, as if dying away in a vast open space.

". . . Find a trick that will work. He's up to it—never fear. . . ."

He must have been very drunk, for at last the heavy sleep gripped him with the suddenness of a magic spell, and the last word lengthened itself into an interminable noisy, indrawn snore. And then even the snoring stopped, and all was still.

But it seemed as though Mr. Massy had suddenly come to doubt the efficacy of sleep as against a man's troubles; or perhaps he had found the relief he needed in the stillness of a calm contemplation that may contain the vivid thoughts of wealth, of a stroke of luck, of long idleness, and may bring before you the imagined form of every desire; for, turning about and throwing his arms over the edge of his bunk, he stood there with his feet on his favourite old coat, looking out through the round port into the night over the river. Sometimes a breath of wind would enter and touch his face, a cool breath charged with the damp, fresh feel from a vast body of water. A glimmer here and there was all he could see of it; and once he might after all suppose he had dozed off, since there appeared before his vision, unexpectedly and connected with no dream, a row of flaming and gigantic figures—three nought seven one two—making up a number such as you may see on a lottery ticket. And then all at once the port was no longer black: it was pearly gray, framing a shore crowded with houses, thatched roof beyond thatched roof, walls of mats and bamboo, gables of carved teak timber. Rows of dwellings raised on a forest of piles lined the steely bank of the river, brimful and still, with the tide on the turn. This was Batu Beru—and the day had come.

Mr. Massy shook himself, put on the tweed coat, and, shivering nervously as if from some great shock, made a note of the number. A fortunate, rare hint that. Yes; but to pursue fortune one wanted money—ready cash.

Then he went out and prepared to descend into the engine-room. Several small jobs had to be seen to, and Jack was lying dead drunk on the floor of his cabin, with the door locked at that. His gorge rose at the thought of work. Ay! But if you wanted to do nothing you had to get first a good bit of money. A ship won't save you. True, all true. He was tired of waiting for some chance that would rid him at last of that ship that had turned out a curse on his life.

CHAPTER 14

The deep, interminable hoot of the steam-whistle had, in its grave, vibrating note, something intolerable, which sent a slight shudder down Mr. Van Wyk's back. It was the early afternoon; the *Sofala* was leaving Batu Beru for Pangu, the next place of call. She swung in the stream, scantily attended by a few canoes, and, gliding on the broad river, became lost to view from the Van Wyk bungalow.

Its owner had not gone this time to see her off. Generally he came down to the wharf, exchanged a few words with the bridge while she cast off, and waved his hand to Captain Whalley at the last moment. This day he did not even go as far as the balustrade of the verandah. "He couldn't see me if I did," he said to himself. "I wonder whether he can make out the house at all." And this thought somehow made him feel more alone than he had ever felt for all these years. What was it? six or seven? Seven. A long time.

He sat on the verandah with a closed book on his knee, and, as it were, looked out upon his solitude, as if the fact of Captain Whalley's blindness had opened his eyes to his own. There were many sorts of heartaches and troubles, and there was no place where they could not find a man out. And he felt ashamed, as though he had for six years behaved like a peevish boy.

His thought followed the *Sofala* on her way. On the spur of the moment he had acted impulsively, turning to the thing most pressing. And what else could he have done? Later on he should see. It seemed necessary that he should come out into the world, for a time at least. He had money—something could be arranged; he would grudge no time, no trouble, no loss of his solitude. It weighed on him now—and Captain Whalley appeared to him as he had sat shading his eyes, as if, being deceived in the trust of his faith, he were beyond all the good and evil that can be wrought by the hands of men.

Mr. Van Wyk's thoughts followed the *Sofala* down the river, winding about through the belt of the coast forest, between the buttressed shafts of the big trees, through the mangrove strip, and over the bar. The ship crossed it easily in broad daylight, piloted, as it happened, by Mr. Sterne, who took the watch from four to six, and then went below to hug himself with delight at the prospect of being virtually employed by a rich man—like Mr. Van Wyk. He could not see how any hitch could occur now. He did not seem able to get over the feeling of being "fixed up at last." From six to eight, in the course of duty, the Serang looked alone after the ship. She had a clear road before her now till about three in the morning, when she would close with the Pangu group. At eight Mr. Sterne came out cheerily to take charge again till midnight. At ten he was still chirruping and humming to himself on the bridge, and about that time Mr. Van Wyk's thought abandoned the *Sofala*. Mr. Van Wyk had fallen asleep at last.

Massy, blocking the engine-room companion, jerked himself into his tweed jacket surlily, while the second waited with a scowl.

"Oh. You came out! You sot! Well, what have you got to say for yourself?"

He had been in charge of the engines till then. A sombre fury darkened his mind: a hot anger against the ship, against the facts of life, against the men for their cheating, against himself, too—because of an inward tremor in his heart.

An incomprehensible growl answered him.

"What? Can't you open your mouth now? You yelp out your infernal rot loud enough when you are drunk. What do you mean by abusing people in that way?—you old useless boozer, you!"

"Can't help it. Don't remember anything about it. You shouldn't listen."

"You dare to tell me! What do you mean by going on a drunk like this?"

"Don't ask me. Sick of the dam' boilers—you would be. Sick of Life."

"I wish you were dead, then. You've made me sick of you. Don't you remember the uproar you made last night? You miserable old soaker!"

"No; I don't. Don't want to. Drink is drink."

"I wonder what prevents me from kicking you out. What do you want here?"

"Relieve you. You've been long enough down there, George."

"Don't you George me—you tippling old rascal, you! If I were to die to-morrow you would starve. Remember that. Say Mr. Massy."

"Mr. Massy," repeated the other, stolidly.

Deshevelled, with dull blood-shot eyes, a snuffy, grimy shirt, greasy trousers, naked feet thrust into ragged slippers, he bolted in head down directly Massy had made way for him.

The chief engineer looked around. The deck was empty as far as the taffrail. All the native passengers had left in Batu Beru this time, and no others had joined. The dial of the patent log tinkled periodically in the dark at the end of the ship. It was a dead calm, and, under the clouded sky, through the still air that seemed to cling warm, with a sea-weed smell, to her slim hull, on a sea of sombre gray and unwrinkled, the ship moved on an even keel, as if floating detached in empty space. But Mr. Massy slapped his forehead, tottered a little, and caught hold of a belaying-pin at the foot of the mast.

"I shall go mad," he muttered, walking across the deck unsteadily. A shovel was scraping loose coal down below—a fire-door clanged. Sterne on the bridge began whistling a new tune.

Captain Whalley, sitting on the couch, awake and fully dressed, heard the door of his cabin open. He did not move in the least, waiting to recognize the voice, with an appalling strain of prudence.

A bulkhead lamp blazed on the white paint, the crimson plush, the brown varnish of mahogany tops. The white wood packing-case under the bed-place had remained unopened for three years now, as though Captain Whalley had felt that, after the *Fair Maid* was gone, there could be no abiding-place on earth for his affections. His hands rested on his knees; his handsome head with big eyebrows presented a rigid profile to the doorway. The expected voice spoke out at last.

"Once more, then. What am I to call you?"

Ha! Massy. Again. The weariness of it crushed his heart—and the pain of shame was almost more than he could bear without crying out.

"Well. Is it to be 'partner' still?"

"You don't know what you ask."

"I know what I want. . . ."

Massy stepped in and closed the door.

". . . And I am going to have a try for it with you once more."

His whine was half persuasive, half menacing.

"For it's no manner of use to tell me that you are poor. You don't spend anything on yourself, that's true enough;

but there's another name for that. You think you are going to have what you want out of me for three years, and then cast me off without hearing what I think of you. You think I would have submitted to your airs if I had known you had only a beggarly five hundred pounds in the world? You ought to have told me."

"Perhaps," said Captain Whalley, bowing his head. "And yet it has saved you. . . ." Massy laughed scornfully. . . . "I have told you often enough since."

"And I don't believe you now. When I think how I let you lord it over my ship! Do you remember how you used to bullyrag me about my coat and *your* bridge? It was in his way. *His* bridge! 'And I won't be a party to this—and I couldn't think of doing that.' Honest man! And now it all comes out. 'I am poor, and I can't. I have only this five hundred in the world.' "

He contemplated the immobility of Captain Whalley, that seemed to present an inconquerable obstacle in his path. His face took a mournful cast.

"You are a hard man."

"Enough," said Captain Whalley, turning upon him. "You shall get nothing from me, because I have nothing of mine to give away now."

"Tell that to the marines!"

Mr. Massy, going out, looked back once; then the door closed, and Captain Whalley, alone, sat as still as before. He had nothing of his own—even his own past of honour, of truth, of just pride, was gone. All his spotless life had fallen into the abyss. He had said his last good-bye to it. But what belonged to *her,* that he meant to save. Only a little money. He would take it to her in his own hands—this last gift of a man that had lasted too long. And an immense and fierce impulse, the very passion of paternity, flamed up with all the unquenched vigour of his worthless life in a desire to see her face.

Just across the deck Massy had gone straight to his cabin, struck a light, and hunted up the note of the dreamed number whose figures had flamed up also with the fierceness of another passion. He must contrive somehow not to miss a drawing. That number meant something. But what expedient could he contrive to keep himself going?

"Wretched miser!" he mumbled.

If Mr. Sterne could at no time have told him anything new about his partner, he could have told Mr. Sterne that another use could be made of a man's affliction than just to kick him out, and thus defer the term of a difficult payment for a year. To keep the secret of the affliction and induce him to stay was a better move. If without means, he would be anxious to remain; and that settled the question of refunding him his share. He did not know exactly how much Captain Whalley was disabled; but if it so happened that he put the ship ashore somewhere for good and all, it was not the owner's fault—was it? He was not obliged to know that there was anything wrong. But probably nobody would raise such a point, and the ship was fully insured. He had had enough self-restraint to pay up the premiums. But this was not all. He could not believe Captain Whalley to be so confoundedly destitute as not to have some more money put away somewhere. If he, Massy, could get hold of it, that would pay for the boilers, and everything would go on as before. And if she got lost in the end, so much the better. He hated her: he loathed the troubles that took his mind off the chances of fortune. He wished her at the bottom of the sea, and the insurance money in his pocket. And as, baffled, he left Captain Whalley's cabin, he enveloped in the same hatred the ship with the worn-out boilers and the man with the dimmed eyes.

And our conduct after all is so much a matter of outside suggestion, that had it not been for his Jack's drunken gabble he would have there and then had it out with this miserable man, who would neither help, nor stay, nor yet lose the ship. The old fraud! He longed to kick him out. But he restrained himself. Time enough for that—when he liked. There was a fearful new thought put into his head. Wasn't he up to it after all? How that beast Jack had raved! "Find a safe trick to get rid of her." Well, Jack was not so far wrong. A very clever trick had occurred to him. Ay! But what of the risk?

A feeling of pride—the pride of superiority to common prejudices—crept into his breast, made his heart beat fast, his mouth turn dry. Not everybody would dare; but he was Massy, and he was up to it!

Six bells were struck on deck. Eleven! He drank a glass of water, and sat down for ten minutes or so to calm himself. Then he got out of his chest a small bull's-eye lantern of his own and lit it.

Almost opposite his berth, across the narrow passage under the bridge, there was, in the iron deck-structure covering the stokehold fiddle and the boiler-space, a storeroom with iron sides, iron roof, iron-plated floor, too, on account of the heat below. All sorts of rubbish was shot there: it had a mound of scrap-iron in a corner; rows of empty oil-cans; sacks of cotton-waste, with a heap of charcoal, a deck-forge, fragments of an old hen-coop, winch-covers all in rags, remnants of lamps, and a brown felt hat, discarded by a man dead now (of a fever on the Brazil coast), who had been once mate of the *Sofala,* had remained for years jammed forcibly behind a length of burst copper pipe, flung at some time or other out of the engine-room. A complete and impervious blackness pervaded that Capharnaum of forgotten things. A small shaft of light from Mr. Massy's bull's-eye fell slanting right through it.

His coat was unbuttoned; he shot the bolt of the door (there was no other opening), and, squatting before the scrap-heap, began to pack his pockets with pieces of iron. He packed them carefully, as if the rusty nuts, the broken bolts, the links of cargo chain, had been so much gold he had that one chance to carry away. He packed his side-pockets till they bulged, the breastpocket, the pockets inside. He turned over the pieces. Some he rejected. A small mist of powdered rust began to rise about his busy hands. Mr. Massy knew something of the scientific basis of his clever trick. If you want to deflect the magnetic needle of a ship's compass, soft iron is the best; likewise many small pieces in the pockets of a jacket would have more effect than a few large ones, because in that way you obtain a greater amount of surface for weight in your iron, and it's surface that tells.

He slipped out swiftly—two strides sufficed—and in his cabin he perceived that his hands were all red—red with rust. It disconcerted him, as though he had found them covered with blood: he looked himself over hastily. Why, his trousers, too! He had been rubbing his rusty palms on his legs.

He tore off the waistband button in his haste, brushed his coat, washed his hands. Then the air of guilt left him, and he sat down to wait.

He sat bolt upright and weighted with iron in his chair. He had a hard, lumpy bulk against each hip, felt the scrappy iron in his pockets touch his ribs at every breath, the downward drag of all these pounds hanging upon his shoulders. He looked very dull, too, sitting idle there, and his yellow face, with motionless black eyes, had something passive and sad in its quietness.

When he heard eight bells struck above his head, he rose and made ready to go out. His movements seemed aimless, his lower lip had dropped a little, his eyes roamed about the cabin, and the tremendous tension of his will had robbed them of every vestige of intelligence.

With the last stroke of the bell the Serang appeared noiselessly on the bridge to relieve the mate. Sterne overflowed with good nature, since he had nothing more to desire.

"Got your eyes well open yet, Serang? It's middling dark; I'll wait till you get your sight properly."

The old Malay murmured, looked up with his worn eyes, sidled away into the light of the binnacle, and, clasping his hands behind his back, fixed his eyes on the compass-card.

"You'll have to keep a good lookout ahead for land, about half-past three. It's fairly clear, though. You have looked in on the captain as you came along—eh? He knows the time? Well, then, I am off."

At the foot of the ladder he stood aside for the captain.

He watched him go up with an even, certain tread, and remained thoughtful for a moment. "It's funny," he said to himself, "but you can never tell whether that man has seen you or not. He might have heard me breathe this time."

He was a wonderful man when all was said and done. They said he had had a name in his day. Mr. Sterne could well believe it; and he concluded serenely that Captain Whalley must be able to see people more or less—as himself just now, for instance—but not being certain of anybody, had to keep up that unnoticing silence of manner for fear of giving himself away. Mr. Sterne was a shrewd guesser.

This necessity of every moment brought home to Captain Whalley's heart the humiliation of his falsehood. He had drifted into it from paternal love, from incredulity, from boundless trust in divine justice meted out to men's feelings on this earth. He would give his poor Ivy the benefit of another month's work; perhaps the affliction was only temporary. Surely God would not rob his child of his power to help, and cast him naked into a night without end. He had caught at every hope; and when the evidence of his misfortune was stronger than hope, he tried not to believe the manifest thing.

In vain. In the steadily darkening universe a sinister clearness fell upon his ideas. In the illuminating moments of suffering he saw life, men, all things, the whole earth with all her burden of created nature, as he had never seen them before.

Sometimes he was seized with a sudden vertigo and an overwhelming terror; and then the image of his daughter appeared. Her, too, he had never seen so clearly before. Was it possible that he should ever be unable to do anything whatever for her? Nothing. And not to see her any more? Never.

Why? The punishment was too great for a little presumption, for a little pride. And at last he came to cling to his deception with a fierce determination to carry it out to the end, to save her money intact, and behold her once more with his own eyes. Afterwards—what? The idea of suicide was revolting to the vigour of his manhood. He had prayed for death till the prayers had stuck in his throat. All the days of his life he had prayed, for daily bread, and not to be led into temptation, in a childlike humility of spirit. Did words mean anything? Whence did the gift of speech come? The violent beating of his heart reverberated in his head—seemed to shake his brain to pieces.

He sat down heavily in the deck-chair to keep the pretence of his watch. The night was dark. All the nights were dark now.

"Serang," he said, half aloud.

"Ada, Tuan. I am here."

"There are clouds on the sky?"

"There are, Tuan."

"Let her be steered straight. North."

"She is going north, Tuan."

The Serang stepped back. Captain Whalley recognized Massy's footfalls on the bridge.

The engineer walked over to port and returned, passing behind the chair several times. Captain Whalley detected an unusual character as of prudent care in this prowling. The near presence of that man brought with it always a recrudescence of moral suffering for Captain Whalley. It was not remorse. After all, he had done nothing but good to the poor devil. There was also a sense of danger—the necessity of a greater care.

Massy stopped and said—

"So you still say you must go?"

"I must indeed."

"And you couldn't at least leave the money for a term of years?"

"Impossible."

"Can't trust it with me without your care, eh?"

Captain Whalley remained silent. Massy sighed deeply over the back of the chair.

"It would just do to save me," he said in a tremulous voice.

"I've saved you once."

The chief engineer took off his coat with careful movements, and proceeded to feel for the brass hook screwed into the wooden stanchion. For this purpose he placed himself right in front of the binnacle, thus hiding completely the compass-card from the quartermaster at the wheel. "Tuan!" the lascar at last murmured softly, meaning to let the white man know that he could not see to steer.

Mr. Massy had accomplished his purpose. The coat was hanging from the nail, within six inches of the binnacle. And directly he had stepped aside the quartermaster, a middle-aged, pock-marked, Sumatra Malay, almost as dark as a Negro, perceived with amazement that in that short time, in this smooth water, with no wind at all, the ship had gone swinging far out of her course. He had never known her to get away like this before. With a slight grunt of astonishment he turned the wheel hastily to bring her head back north, which was the course. The grinding of the steering-chains, the chiding murmurs of the Serang, who had come over to the wheel, made a slight stir, which attracted Captain Whalley's anxious attention. He said, "Take better care." Then everything settled to the usual quiet on the bridge. Mr. Massy had disappeared.

But the iron in the pockets of the coat had done its work; and the *Sofala*, heading north by the compass made untrue by this simple device, was no longer making a safe course for Pangu Bay.

The hiss of water parted by her stem, the throb of her engines, all the sounds of her faithful and laborious life, went on uninterrupted in the great calm of the sea joining on all sides the motionless layer of cloud over the sky. A gentle stillness as vast as the world seemed to wait upon her path, enveloping her lovingly in a supreme caress. Mr. Massy thought there could be no better night for an arranged shipwreck.

Run up high and dry on one of the reefs east of Pangu—wait for daylight—hole in the bottom—out boats—Pangu Bay same evening. That's about it. As soon as she touched he would hasten on the bridge, get hold of the coat (nobody would notice in the dark), and shake it upside down over the side, or even fling it into the sea. A detail. Who could guess? Coat been seen hanging there from that hook hundreds of times. Nevertheless, when he sat down on the lower step of the bridge-ladder his knees knocked together a little. The waiting part was the worst of it. At times he would begin to pant quickly, as though he had been running, and then breathe largely, swelling with the intimate sense of a mastered fate. Now and then he would hear the shuffle of the Serang's bare feet up there: quiet, low voices would exchange a few words, and lapse almost at once into silence. . . .

"Tell me directly you see any land, Serang."

"Yes, Tuan. Not yet."

"No, not yet," Captain Whalley would agree.

The ship had been the best friend of his decline. He had sent all the money he had made by and in the *Sofala* to his daughter. His thought lingered on the name. How often he and his wife had talked over the cot of the child in the big stern-cabin of the *Condor;* she would grow up, she would marry, she would love them, they would live near her and look at her happiness—it would go on without end. Well, his wife was dead, to the child he had given all he had to give; he wished he could come near her, see her, see her face once, live in the sound of her voice, that could make the darkness of the living grave ready for him supportable. He had been starved of love too long. He imagined her tenderness.

The Serang had been peering forward, and now and then glancing at the chair. He fidgeted restlessly, and suddenly burst out close to Captain Whalley—

"Tuan, do you see anything of the land?"

The alarmed voice brought Captain Whalley to his feet at once. He! See! And at the question, the curse of his blindness seemed to fall on him with a hundredfold force.

"What's the time?" he cried.

"Half-past three, Tuan."

"We are close. You *must* see. Look, I say. Look."

Mr. Massy, awakened by the sudden sound of talking from a short doze on the lowest step, wondered why he was there. Ah! A faintness came over him. It is one thing to sow the seed of an accident and another to see the monstrous fruit hanging over your head ready to fall in the sound of agitated voices. "There's no danger," he muttered thickly to himself.

The horror of incertitude had seized upon Captain Whalley, the miserable mistrust of men, of things—of the very earth. He had steered that very course thirty-six times by the same compass—if anything was certain in this world it was its absolute, unerring correctness. Then what had happened? Did the Serang lie? Why lie? Why? Was he going blind, too?

"Is there a mist? Look low on the water. Low down, I say."

"Tuan, there's no mist. See for yourself."

Captain Whalley steadied the trembling of his limbs by an effort. Should he stop the engines at once and give himself away? A gust of irresolution swayed all sorts of bizarre notions in his mind. The unusual had come, and he was not fit to deal with it. In this passage of inexpressible anguish he saw her face—the face of a young girl—with an amazing strength of illusion. No, he must not give himself away after having gone so far for her sake. "You steered the course? You made it? Speak the truth."

"Ya, Tuan. On the course now. Look."

Captain Whalley strode to the binnacle, which to him made such a dim spot of light in an infinity of shapeless shadow. By bending his face right down to the glass he had been able before. . . .

Having to stoop so low, he put out, instinctively, his arm to where he knew there was a stanchion to steady himself against. His hand closed on something that was not wood but cloth. The slight pull adding to the weight, the loop broke, and Mr. Massy's coat falling, struck the deck heavily with a dull thump, accompanied by a lot of clicks.

"What's this?"

Captain Whalley fell on his knees, with groping hands extended in a frank gesture of blindness. They trembled, these hands feeling for the truth. He saw it. Iron near the compass. Wrong course. Wreck her! His ship. Oh, no. Not that.

"Jump and stop her!" he roared out in a voice not his own.

He ran himself—hands forward, a blind man, and while the clanging of the gong echoed still all over the ship, she seemed to butt full tilt into the side of a mountain.

It was low water along the north side of the strait. Mr. Massy had not reckoned on that. Instead of running aground for half her length, the *Sofala* butted the sheer ridge of a stone reef which would have been awash at high water. This made the shock absolutely terrific. Everybody in the ship that was standing was thrown down headlong: the shaken rigging made a great rattling to the very trucks. All the lights went out; several chain-guys, snapping, clattered against the funnel; there were crashes, pings of parted wire-rope, splintering sounds, loud cracks; the masthead lamp flew over the bows, and all the doors about the deck began to bang heavily. Then, after having hit, she rebounded, hit the second time the very same spot like a battering-ram. This completed the havoc: the funnel, with all the guys gone, fell over with a hollow sound of thunder, smashing the wheel to bits, crushing the frame of the awnings, breaking the lockers, filling the bridge with a mass of broken wood. Captain Whalley picked himself up and stood knee-deep in wreckage, torn, bleeding, knowing the nature of the danger he had escaped mostly by the sound, and holding Mr. Massy's coat in his arms.

By this time Sterne (he had been flung out of his bunk) had set the engines astern. They worked for a few turns, then a voice bawled out, "Get out of the damned engine-room, Jack!"—and they stopped; but the ship had gone clear of the reef and lay still, with a heavy cloud of steam issuing from the broken deck-pipes, and vanishing in wispy shapes into the night. Notwithstanding the suddenness of the disaster there was no shouting, as if the very violence of the shock had half-stunned the shadowy lot of people swaying here and there about her decks. The voice of the Serang pronounced distinctly above the confused murmurs—

"No bottom." He had heaved the lead.

Mr. Sterne cried out next in a strained pitch—

"Where the devil has she got to? Where are we?"

Captain Whalley replied in a calm bass—

"Amongst the reefs to the eastward."

"You know it, sir? Then she will never get out again."

"She will be gone in five minutes. Boats, Sterne. Even one will save you all in this calm."

The Chinaman stokers went in a disorderly rush for the port boats. Nobody tried to check them. The Malays, after a moment of confusion, became quiet, and Mr. Sterne showed a good countenance. Captain Whalley had not moved. His thoughts were darker than this night in which he had lost his first ship.

"He made me lose a ship."

Another tall figure standing before him amongst the litter of the smash on the bridge whispered insanely—

"Say nothing of it."

Massy stumbled closer. Captain Whalley heard the chattering of his teeth.

"I have the coat."

"Throw it down and come along," urged the chattering voice. "B-b-b-b-boat!"

"You will get five years for this."

Mr. Massy had lost his voice. His speech was a mere dry rustling in his throat.

"Have mercy!"

"Had you any when you made me lose my ship? Mr. Massy, you shall get five years for this!"

"I wanted money! Money! My own money! I will give you some money. Take half of it. You love money yourself."

"There's a justice. . . ."

Massy made an awful effort, and in a strange, half-choked utterance—

"You blind devil! It's you that drove me to it."

Captain Whalley, hugging the coat to his breast, made no sound. The light had ebbed for ever from the world—let everything go. But this man should not escape scot-free.

Sterne's voice commanded—

"Lower away!"

The blocks rattled.

"Now then," he cried, "over with you. This way. You, Jack, here. Mr. Massy! Mr. Massy! Captain! Quick, sir! Let's get—"

"I shall go to prison for trying to cheat the insurance, but you'll get exposed; you, honest man, who has been cheating me. You are poor. Aren't you? You've nothing but the five hundred pounds. Well, you have nothing at all now. The ship's lost, and the insurance won't be paid."

Captain Whalley did not move. True! Ivy's money! Gone in this wreck. Again he had a flash of insight. He was indeed at the end of his tether.

Urgent voices cried out together alongside. Massy did not seem able to tear himself away from the bridge. He chattered and hissed despairingly—

"Give it up to me! Give it up!"

"No," said Captain Whalley; "I could not give it up. You had better go. Don't wait, man, if you want to live. She's settling down by the head fast. No; I shall keep it, but I shall stay on board."

Massy did not seem to understand; but the love of life, awakened suddenly, drove him away from the bridge.

Captain Whalley laid the coat down, and stumbled amongst the heaps of wreckage to the side.

"Is Mr. Massy with you?" he called out into the night.

Sterne from the boat shouted—

"Yes; we've got him. Come along, sir. It's madness to stay longer." Captain Whalley felt along the rail carefully, and without a word, cast off the painter. They were expecting him still down there. They were waiting, till a voice suddenly exclaimed—

"We are adrift! Shove off!"

"Captain Whalley! Leap! . . . pull up a little . . . leap! You can swim."

In that old heart, in that vigorous body, there was, that nothing should be wanting, a horror of death that apparently could not be overcome by the horror of blindness. But after all, for Ivy he had carried his point, walking in his darkness to the very verge of a crime. God had not listened to his prayers. The light had finished ebbing out of the world; not a glimmer. It was a dark waste; but it was unseemly that a Whalley who had gone so far to carry a point should continue to live. He must pay the price.

"Leap as far as you can, sir; we will pick you up."

They did not hear him answer. But their shouting seemed to remind him of something. He groped his way back, and sought for Mr. Massy's coat. He could swim indeed; people sucked down by the whirlpool of a sinking ship do come up sometimes to the surface, and it was unseemly that a Whalley, who had made up his mind to die, should be beguiled by chance into a struggle. He would put all these pieces of iron into his own pockets.

They, looking from the boat, saw the *Sofala,* a black mass upon a black sea, lying still at an appalling cant. No sound came from her. Then, with a great bizarre shuffling noise, as if the boilers had broken through the bulkheads, and with a faint muffled detonation, where the ship had been there appeared for a moment something standing upright and narrow, like a rock out of the sea. Then that, too, disappeared.

When the *Sofala* failed to come back to Batu Beru at the proper time, Mr. Van Wyk understood at once that he would never see her any more. But he did not know what had happened till some weeks afterwards, when, in a native craft lent him by his Sultan, he had made his way to the *Sofala's* port of registry, where already her existence and the official inquiry into her loss were beginning to be forgotten.

It had not been a very remarkable or interesting case, except for the fact that the captain had gone down with his sinking ship. It was the only life lost; and Mr. Van Wyk would not have been able to learn any details had it not been for Sterne, whom he met one day on the quay near the bridge over the creek, almost on the very spot where Captain Whalley, to preserve his daughter's five hundred pounds intact, had turned to get a sampan which would take him on board the *Sofala*.

From afar Mr. Van Wyk saw Sterne blink straight at him and raise his hand to his hat. They drew into the shade of a building (it was a bank), and the mate related how the boats with the crew got into Pangu Bay about six hours after the accident, and how they had lived for a fortnight in a state of destitution before they found an opportunity to get away from that beastly place. The inquiry had exonerated everybody from all blame. The loss of the ship was put down to an unusual set of the current. Indeed, it could not have been anything else: there was no other way to account for the ship being set seven miles to the eastward of her position during the middle watch.

"A piece of bad luck for me, sir."

Sterne passed his tongue on his lips and glanced aside. "I lost the advantage of being employed by you, sir. I can never be sorry enough. But here it is: one man's poison, another man's meat. This could not have been handier for Mr. Massy if he had arranged that shipwreck himself. The most timely total loss I've ever heard of."

"What became of that Massy?" asked Mr. Van Wyk.

"He, sir? Ha! ha! He would keep on telling me that he meant to buy another ship; but as soon as he had the money in his pocket he cleared out for Manila by mail-boat early in the morning. I gave him chase right aboard, and he told me then he was going to make his fortune dead sure in

Manila. I could go to the devil for all he cared. And yet he as good as promised to give me the command if I didn't talk too much."

"You never said anything. . . ." Mr. Van Wyk began.

"Not I, sir. Why should I? I mean to get on, but the dead aren't in my way," said Sterne. His eyelids were beating rapidly, then drooped for an instant. "Besides, sir, it would have been an awkward business. You made me hold my tongue just a bit too long."

"Do you know how it was that Captain Whalley remained on board? Did he really refuse to leave? Come now! Or was it perhaps an accidental. . . . ?"

"Nothing!" Sterne interrupted with energy. "I tell you I yelled for him to leap overboard. He simply *must* have cast off the painter of the boat himself. We all yelled to him—that is, Jack and I. He wouldn't even answer us. The ship was as silent as a grave to the last. Then the boilers fetched away, and down she went. Accident! Not it! The game was up, sir, I tell you."

This was all that Sterne had to say.

Mr. Van Wyk had been of course made the guest of the club for a fortnight, and it was there that he met the lawyer in whose office had been signed the agreement between Massey and Captain Whalley.

"Extraordinary old man," he said. "He came into my office from nowhere in particular as you may say, with his five hundred pounds to invest, and that engineer fellow following him anxiously. And now he is gone out a little inexplicably, just as he came. I could never understand him quite. There was no mystery at all about that Massy, eh? I wonder whether Whalley refused to leave the ship. It would have been foolish. He was blameless, as the court found."

Mr. Van Wyk had known him well, he said, and he could not believe in suicide. Such an act would not have been in character with what he knew of the man.

"It is my opinion, too," the lawyer agreed. The general theory was that the captain had remained too long on board trying to save something of importance. Perhaps the chart which would clear him, or else something of value in his cabin. The painter of the boat had come adrift of itself, it was supposed. However, strange to say, some little time before that voyage poor Whalley had called in his office and had left with him a sealed envelope addressed to his daughter, to be forwarded to her in case of his death. Still it was nothing very unusual, especially in a man of his age. Mr. Van Wyk shook his head. Captain Whalley looked good for a hundred years.

"Perfectly true," assented the lawyer. "The old fellow looked as though he had come into the world full grown and with that long beard. I could never, somehow, imagine him either younger or older—don't you know. There was a sense of physical power about that man, too. And perhaps that was the secret of that something peculiar in his person which struck everybody who came in contact with him. He looked indestructible by any ordinary means that put an end to the rest of us. His deliberate, stately courtesy of manner was full of significance. It was as though he were certain of having plenty of time for everything. Yes, there was something indestructible about him; and the way he talked sometimes you might have thought he believed it himself. When he called on me last with that letter he wanted me to take charge of, he was not depressed at all. Perhaps a shade more deliberate in his talk and manner. Not depressed in the least. Had he a presentiment, I wonder? Perhaps! Still it seems a miserable end for such a striking figure."

"Oh, yes! It was a miserable end," Mr. Van Wyk said, with so much fervour that the lawyer looked up at him curiously; and afterwards, after parting with him, he remarked to an acqaintance—

"Queer person that Dutch tobacco-planter from Batu Beru. Know anything of him?"

"Heaps of money," answered the bank manager. "I hear he's going home by the next mail to form a company to take over his estates. Another tobacco district thrown open. He's wise, I think. These good times won't last for ever."

In the southern hemisphere Captain Whalley's daughter had no presentiment of evil when she opened the envelope addressed to her in the lawyer's handwriting. She had received it in the afternoon; all the boarders had gone out, her boys were at school, her husband sat upstairs in his big arm-chair with a book, thin-faced, wrapped up in rugs to the waist. The house was still, and the grayness of a cloudy day lay against the panes of the windows.

In a shabby dining-room, where a faint cold smell of dishes lingered all the year round, sitting at the end of a long table surrounded by many chairs pushed in with their backs close against the edge of the perpetually laid tablecloth, she read the opening sentences: "Most profound regret—painful duty—your father is no more—in accordance with his instructions—fatal casualty—consolation—no blame attached to his memory. . . ."

Her face was thin, her temples a little sunk under the smoother bands of black hair, her lips remained resolutely compressed, while her dark eyes grew larger, till at last, with a low cry, she stood up, and instantly stooped to pick up another envelope which had slipped off her knees on to the floor.

She tore it open, snatched out the enclosure. . . .

"My dearest child," it said, "I am writing this while I am able yet to write legibly. I am trying hard to save for you all the money that is left; I have only kept it to serve you better. It is yours. It shall not be lost; it shall not be touched. There's five hundred pounds. Of what I have earned I have kept nothing back till now. For the future, if I live, I must keep back some—a little—to bring me to you. I must come to you. I must see you once more.

"It is hard to believe that you will ever look on these lines. God seems to have forgotten me. I want to see you—and yet death would be a greater favour. If you ever read these words, I charge you to begin by thanking a God merciful at last, for I shall be dead then, and it will be well. My dear, I am at the end of my tether."

The next paragraph began with the words: "My sight is going. . . ."

She read no more that day. The hand holding up the paper to her eyes fell slowly, and her slender figure in a plain black dress walked rigidly to the window. Her eyes were dry: no cry of sorrow or whisper of thanks went up to heaven from her lips. Life had been too hard, for all the efforts of his love. It had silenced her emotions. But for the first time in all these years its sting had departed, the carking care of poverty, the meanness of a hard struggle for bread. Even the image of her husband and of her children seemed to glide away from her into the gray twilight; it was her father's face alone that she saw, as though he had come to see her, always quiet and big, as she had seen him last, but with something more august and tender in his aspect.

She slipped his folded letter between the two buttons of her plain black bodice, and leaning her forehead against a window-pane remained there till dusk, perfectly motionless, giving him all the time she could spare. Gone! Was it possible? My God, was it possible? The blow had come softened by the spaces of the earth, by the years of absence. There had been whole days when she had not thought of him at all—had no time. But she had loved him, she felt she had loved him after all.